Red Shadows at Saugatuck

by

Randy Overbeck

The Haunted Shores Mysteries

Cover Art by *Teddi Black*

The Wild Rose Press, Inc.
PO Box 708
Adams Basin, NY 14410-0708
Visit us at www.thewildrosepress.com

Publishing History
First Edition, 2025
Trade Paperback ISBN 978-1-5092-6209-0
Digital ISBN 978-1-5092-6210-6

The Haunted Shores Mysteries
Published in the United States of America

Acknowledgments

This is my sixth published novel—though a seventh completed manuscript is sitting on my agent's computer, waiting for an acquisition editor to discover it. The longer I've been at this, the more I realize no man is an island and no author succeeds alone. I want to thank those who contributed to making this writing as good as it can be, especially my beta readers and the Dayton Writers Critique Group, in particular, Kevin O'Brien and Archy Wiseman, who have been with me from the beginning. I'd also want to acknowledge and thank my skilled WPR editor, Ally Robertson. Of course, I couldn't indulge my newfound passion of writing without the support of my wife, Cathy and my family. I'd also like to take space here to recognize my mentor, the NY Times bestselling author, William Kent Kreuger, for his kind words of encouragement and support of my writing journey.

Equally important, I want to thank Liza Mize of the Saugatuck and Douglas Area Convention and Visitors Bureau for her advice and insight into the area and for helping to make sure I created an accurate portrayal of the wonderful community of Saugatuck, Michigan within these pages. Next, as readers will discover, this mystery deals with another area initially well outside my knowledge base and comfort zone. Although I completed extensive research into the issue of missing and murdered Indigenous women, I did not rely on paper and computer sources alone. I need and want to thank two elders in the Match-E-Be-Nash-She-Wash Band of the Pottawatomi Tribe, also known as the Gun Lake Tribe, James Day, Language and Culture Director and Franklin

Barker, Language Coordinator. They were gracious enough to take time to share understanding and knowledge of Native culture to help me, a white man and outsider, use my storytelling to represent the horrible reality of murdered and missing native women and girls.

I don't mind admitting I needed advice and assistance from all these to make the novel a reality and, I humbly submit, the story is all the more compelling as a result.

Thank you, one and all.

Praise for Dr. Overbeck's Fiction

Advance Praise for *Red Shadows at Saugatuck*
"*Red Shadows at Saugatuck* is a paranormal mystery that stole my soul and took my breath away… one of the finest books ever written. Dive into a world where spirits interact with humans and one man's gift saves many."-- 5++stars N N Light Bookheaven

"Overbeck's *Red Shadows at Saugatuck* is a gripping tale about finding justice for a missing Native American teenage girl…kept me turning pages well into the night."--John Dedakis, Former CNN Senior Editor and author of *Fake*.

Praise for "Lessons in Peril" *Cruel Lessons*
"A thrilling murder mystery…with an immersive plot, steady pace and stellar character development…one of the best mysteries of 2023." GOLD AWARD for Mystery of the Year, 2023 5 stars—ReaderViews,

"Brilliant from start to finish…Impressive storytelling left me with a racing heart and shivers. One of the best thrillers I've ever read." 5 stars —N.N. Light's Bookheaven.

"Masterfully written…Each new revelation adds to the suspense and keeps the reader on edge, eagerly anticipating what further secrets the story holds…a gripping crime thriller and amateur sleuth mystery." THE GOLD AWARD—Literary Titan

Cruel Lessons delivers an electrifying narrative from the opening pages…The narrative twists and turns, immersing readers in a maze of suspense, intricate characters and a vividly depicted era." 5 stars —Tom Dutta, Host, The Quiet Warrior Show

next book come out?""—Kings River Life Magazine

"Masterly spooky adventure…an accomplished work of mystery fiction fans won't want to miss out on. Highly recommended." 5 stars ReadersFavorite

"*Scarlet at Crystal River* pulled me in deeper and deeper and had me racing to the end to the final climax with this big twist…This twist left me with my jaw hanging open and in tears."—The Avid Reader

One of the things I love about the Haunted Shores Mysteries is how real the characters are, especially Darrell. He's not perfect and he's knows it."—Creative Deeds

Chapter 1

July 2007

"Daddy, when are we gonna get to the haunted house?"

Darrell glanced at the sparkling green eyes of his wife, Erin, on the seat next to him, watching a sly smile crease her beautiful face, wrinkling her freckles. Then his gaze went to the rearview mirror, eyeing his son strapped in the car seat. Leo had the same emerald irises as his mother, and they stared back wide-eyed, showing the impatience of a five-year-old.

"I thought you were sleeping," Darrell said, his gaze flicking from the boy to the road ahead.

"Da-a-ad?" his son started, but Darrell put up a hand to quiet him.

"Hold on." As the highway came out of a curve and the road straightened out, the setting sun dropped in the sky and Darrell flipped the shade down to keep the glare from blinding him. Signaling, he sped into the passing lane to get around a slower eighteen-wheeler and then returned to the middle lane. At least I-76 wasn't that busy in the early evening hours and driving the interstate didn't require *all* his attention. He had to reserve some for his offspring. Glancing back, he said, "After the big day at the amusement park, you said you were tuckered out and wanted to nap."

When in doubt, distract the five-year-old.

1

"It was great!" The boy grinned, a bright blue halo still encircling his mouth, even after his mother did her best to wipe it clean. Leo didn't seem to mind. "My favorite was climbin' the ropes and ridin' the swings. Whee!" He raised both hands to imitate the ride, which he'd been barely tall enough to qualify. "Except Mommy got a little sick." In an instant, the boy's expression morphed from joy to concern.

Erin said, "It was nothing. Mommy's fine."

"Mommy's fine, Daddy," young Leo echoed.

"Yeah, I'm glad." Darrell smiled at his son and brought his gaze back to the road. At the amusement park, he'd been concerned since Erin had always had an iron stomach. In the past nine years since relocating to the Eastern Shore of the Chesapeake Bay, he'd accompanied her on more sails than he could count. No matter how rough the waves—and how sick Darrell became, sometimes losing his lunch—none of it ever fazed her. So, he worried when she came off the swings and complained of being queasy. He was just glad it passed.

Erin half-turned, and the setting sun ignited her beautiful red hair. As she lifted one arm over the seat back, the top of her lime green blouse gapped a bit. Darrell shot a quick glance, smiling, and returned his eyes to the road. She saw him sneak a peek and grinned. She asked her son, "What was your favorite part?"

Leo didn't hesitate. "The swings…and the cotton candy." The boy had pleaded for blue cotton candy, his favorite color, a little bit of which still lingered around his mouth, and specks of it dotted his yellow shirt, partially obscuring the words, "I'm Mom's Favorite."

At the park, seeing the blue ring encircling the boy's

mouth had bothered Darrell, who wanted to take his son into the restroom and scrub his face. But after Leo looked in the mirror, he grinned and said, "Look at me - I'm blue!" Darrell's heart melted and he relented.

Leo asked, "What was your favorite, Mommy?"

"Hum, I need to think about that. That's a hard one for me."

Darrell glanced over to see Erin put her finger on her mouth, as if in deep thought, and winked at him. As his gaze returned to the road, he was grateful his wife was distracting their son—at least for a while.

She paused and then said, "Well, I think I liked the merry-go-round the best, with the beautiful painted horses.

"But they just go around in the circle…and they're slow. What about you, Dad? What was your favorite?"

Darrell didn't hesitate. "I loved the swings because I got to ride them with you." He smiled so his son could see it in the mirror.

The day at the family amusement park had been a delightful break for all three of them and watching Leo laugh so hard warmed Darrell's heart more than any championship or tournament win. The park, with its combination of kid-friendly rides and life-sized characters, entertained their son and amused his parents. The family had experienced only one hitch in the day. A brief, scary one.

In the middle of a hot afternoon, Darrell joined a long line to get some cool soft drinks, letting Erin and Leo sit under the shade of an umbrella in a cluster of tables. While he was gone, Leo, eyeing the men's restroom sign next door, decided he needed to go to the bathroom. When Erin got up to take him, he announced,

"Mom, I'm five years old now. I can go potty on my own."

Erin first insisted but, upon her son's pleading, gave in. "I'll be right here. Come right back."

Across from the restroom opening, Erin waited and watched but, when Darrell returned with three drinks a few minutes later, Leo had still not emerged. Darrell hurried into the restroom but found no sign of him. Frantic, he and Erin scattered, searching different avenues of the park. Three agonizing minutes later, Darrell found Leo, heading for another group of tables similar to where Erin had been sitting. The boy had simply followed a father and son who exited the bathroom through a different door and ended up going away from where he started. Their anxiety and uncertainty had lasted only one hundred eighty seconds but Darrell had never been more terrified in his life. Not even when they shot at his car in Florida. It all turned out to be much ado about nothing, but that's not what it felt like in the moment.

The inside of the Taurus was redolent with reminders of the amusement park, the odors of perspiration, popcorn and cotton candy still heavy in the car. They all needed to get to their hotel and shower to get the smells off them and then hopefully out of the car. He pressed down on the accelerator.

The drive was going fine but Darrell still felt a little guilty. The three of them were headed to the eightieth birthday party for his Aunt Gertrude at her mansion on Lake Michigan—the haunted house his son asked about—because they couldn't afford the airfare for the three of them. This past year, they'd bought their first house and their finances were stretched thin. He loved his job, teaching history and coaching, but it still irked him that he was so underpaid. Even with what Erin made as a nurse, they lived pretty much paycheck to paycheck. So, they were driving the 1500-mile round trip and, to make it more palatable, they'd decided on a few stops along the way. The first being the amusement park.

"But Dad, when *will* we get to the haunted house?"

A stubborn preschooler can only be forestalled so long. Darrell decided the best approach was straight on.

"We still have two more days before we'll get to Aunt Gertrude's place. And it is not a haunted house."

Leo was not to be put off so easily. "When I had my eyes closed, I heard you tell Mommy—"

"That was adults talking." Darrell glanced at his wife.

Erin raised her eyebrows and whispered, "He's your son."

They'd had this conversation before. He glanced in the rearview mirror and then concentrated on the road as he spoke. "What I told Mommy was when I was young, my brother Craig and some of my older cousins *told* me it was haunted. Older kids like to play tricks like that."

Leo said, "That doesn't mean it's *not* haunted."

Darrell sighed. "Well, I don't remember any signs it was haunted when I was there."

Erin asked, "When were you there last, at your Aunt Gertrude's?"

Darrell shook his head. He glanced from the road to Erin, then to Leo. "It's been a really long time, more than twenty years? I think I was about twelve. And it was Uncle Dave and Aunt Gertrude's place then."

"You haven't been back since?"

Darrell shrugged but kept his eyes on the road. As

they neared Pittsburgh, the traffic began to pick up, with more cars and trucks entering the highway and more drivers weaving between lanes. He slowed as a car cut in front of him. "Uncle Dave died a little later, I think. He was the friendly one and he and my mom were close. I don't think Aunt Gertrude was that interested in having us come around…I guess."

Leo interrupted, "But that's a really long time. There could be ghosts there now."

"How about we'll see when we get there?" Darrell looked again at the rearview mirror. "We're getting close to our hotel and need to stop. We have another big day tomorrow." He looked over at Erin who had a map spread across her lap. "Which exit do we want?"

Erin said, "We have about four more miles. When you're ready, I'd move to the inside lane."

Both Darrell and Erin knew exactly which exit they needed but they wanted to get their son off the "haunted" track.

For the past several years, Darrell had experienced little intrusion from the spirit world…and that was fine with him. After being stalked by the haunted bride in Cape May and then haunted by those poor children in Florida on their honeymoon, Darrell felt like his *gift* was fried. Since then, the ghosts had left him alone, mostly. In the years since, there had only been that one incident.

He and Erin had been out sailing and had stopped to fish in the shallows near Tilghman Island. Rods in hand, they'd drifted close to the shore when a man stepped into the boat. Startled, Darrell jumped and dropped his fishing rod, almost losing it in the water. Erin turned to see what was the matter and caught Darrell staring…at nothing. She couldn't see the apparition.

Eventually, Darrell was able to figure out what the ghost wanted—something about a dilapidated house on Tilghman Island—and was able to resolve the dilemma without threat to life or limb.

No mystery, no bullets, no murders.

But Darrell's concern wasn't about himself, nor was Erin's. Leo had apparently inherited more than a prominent nose from his father.

Fall, a year ago, Erin and Leo waited at the playground near the high school while Darrell finished practice one evening. She had come off a twelve-hour shift at the OB and hadn't gotten much sleep, so she told Leo to go ahead and play and she'd watch. The playground sat empty, the boy going from swings to monkey bars to the old-fashioned merry-go-round. As he played, he hooted and hollered, the occasional shouts of joy making Erin smile. Still, exhausted from being on her feet so long, she felt herself drifting but she heard Leo's voice carried by the fall breeze. He was talking, carrying on a conversation.

After a few minutes, he returned, with a wide smile and out of breath. "Mom, can we go over to the big slide?" Breath. "My friend Monica likes the big slide best and wants me to go with her."

Erin looked around. This late in the evening, with the autumn sun setting, the park was deserted, except for Leo and her. She glanced around and then stared at her son. "Who wants you to go on the big slide?"

Leo pointed to the air next to him. "My friend Monica. She says it's the most fun. I promise I'll be careful."

As she told Darrell later, she knew it was fairly normal for kids Leo's age to have imaginary friends. She smiled as she told her son to have fun on the slide. A few minutes later, Darrell came walking across the park, still in his coach's outfit, polo shirt with wide sweat marks under the arms and whistle around his neck. As he crossed the grass, he waved and Leo, atop the big slide, gave a huge wave back.

"Whee-e-e," the boy cried, speeding down the slide.

Darrell stooped down and gave Erin a peck. Glancing over to the boy, he said, "I see you let Leo go down the big slide."

She stared as Leo ran around to the ladder. He stopped there at the bottom as if he were waiting for someone to go ahead.

"It looks like he's having a great time." Darrell dropped onto the bench next to her. He reached his arm around Erin and felt her melt into him, her red hair nuzzling against the cotton of his shirt.

"I'm exhausted. Can we just order pizza tonight?" she asked.

"Fine with me." He chinned over towards Leo, who had made another trip down the slide. "It looks like our son has made a new friend. Who's the girl?"

Erin chuckled and didn't look up. "Oh, you mean his imaginary friend? He calls her Monica."

Darrell straightened, pointing toward the slide. "No, I mean her."

Erin's head jerked up. "What are you talking about? There's no one there." Her gaze went from Darrell to her son and back. In a few seconds, emotions washed across her face—confusion, then anxiety, then fear, as the reality set in. "Oh, God, you see her too?"

Darrell started, "You mean, you don't see—" Before he could get the rest out, Erin bolted from the bench and

Darrell jumped up. They both ran toward their son.

The next day, Darrell found the marker in a nearby cemetery. "Monica Boyle, 1969-1975. Here far too short. Gone far too early."

And Monica had not been Leo's last "imaginary friend."

Chapter 2

"What do you want to do first?" Darrell asked his son.

Leo scanned the woods and old buildings and stopped, pointing at a structure with a steeple. "Can we go see the old schoolhouse first?"

"Sure, let's check it out." He grabbed his son's hand and they headed across the grassy meadow, Erin a step behind.

Darrell glanced back at his wife, who looked stunning in a tube top with a rainbow across the front and pale blue shorts which showed off her nice legs. Of course, Darrell thought she pretty much always looked great, but today she seemed to beam. Her gaze went from their son and back to him, and she blessed Darrell with a wide smile crinkling her freckles, her emerald eyes shining.

He realized she was indulging him today, allowing him to get what she called "his history fix." When they were planning their cross country trip, he came across information on the Meadowcroft Rock Shelter and Historic Village, thirty miles outside Pittsburgh. He'd never heard of the place but with its exhibits of a prehistoric rock shelter, a recreated sixteenth-century Indian settlement and an eighteen-century village, it looked like a great opportunity to add to his history knowledge and maybe whet his son's appetite for the past as well.

In the 18th century schoolhouse, Leo slid into one of the old style desks, looking incongruous in his sleeveless blue tee and bright red Nike sneakers. But their timing was good as the docent delivered a short lesson from that time and Leo sat straight and listened. One of the volunteers even gave Leo the chance to pull the cord and ring the school bell, its bang echoing into the schoolroom.

Later, the boy stared wide-eyed at the old-time blacksmith, while the man with a worn leather apron used a forge to turn a piece of iron a hot orange. The space reeked with the smells of metal and fire and sweat. When the man lowered the hook he was making into water, releasing a loud hiss, Leo cowered behind his father's legs. When the blacksmith removed the long curved piece of iron from the water and showed it off, Leo stared, wide-eyed.

After lunch, they decided to check out the sixteenth-century exhibit, a recreated Monongahela Indian Village. They strolled among the wigwams and other structures, listening to the volunteers discuss what life was like for the inhabitants four hundred years earlier. Leo was intimidated at first with the unfamiliar surroundings and costumes but he brightened when he got to try out some of the toys native children played with, like a simple hoop game. He and Erin had the most fun learning how to throw an *atlatl*, a prehistoric spear used by the Monongahela people to hunt game—or at least, trying to throw the weapon. Working together, Mother and son made several valiant efforts but were never able to spear the deer model. Darrell hit the target on his first try.

Lips in a tiny pout, Erin called, "No fair. You've had all that practice throwing the football."

"Guilty as charged." Darrell glanced at his son and recognized weariness in his features. He figured the hustle of the past two days was catching up with him. "Mom, why don't you and Leo head over to the gift shop? I bet there's something there he might be interested in. Leo, I think they may have some of the Indian toys you were playing with."

The boy's eyes brightened. "Thanks, Dad." He tugged on his mom's arm.

Before Leo could drag her away, Erin asked, "What about you? You coming?"

Darrell said, "I want to check out one or two of the wigwams first. I'll meet you there in a few minutes."

He watched his son pulling his wife's arm, weaving between knots of people and making a beeline for the visitor's center. Darrell couldn't help but smile. The idea of snagging a souvenir toy had given Leo a second wind.

Darrell turned and followed a mother and two teens inside a nearby wigwam. After he stooped through the flap, he stood up. Except for himself and the other three visitors, the large circular structure stood empty with an unused fire pit in the center of the dirt floor and an opening above it. The sides were covered with animal skins stretched tight. At the ground level, the structure appeared to be a precise circle about fifteen feet in diameter and the walls were curved in such a way as to make a near-perfect half sphere. Its smooth curved lines and symmetry appealed to his compulsions. He inhaled and the air inside surprised him. It felt warm but not stifling, even on the hot summer afternoon. If this was a faithful reproduction, he marveled at the know-how of inhabitants some four hundred years ago.

With little to occupy them, the two boys grew restless, engaging in a shoving contest. The mom hustled her sons back through the opening, all three wiggling out the flap. A few seconds later, he followed and came out, the sun bright in his eyes. He blinked to adjust them and watched the trio head back in the direction of the other exhibits, the boys jostling with each other on the mulched trail. Darrell started to follow them—he realized he was pretty tired himself—but just then he heard some kind of chanting coming from across the clearing. At the other end of the grass sat another wigwam, a wisp of smoke rising through the opening. Intrigued, he headed across. At the wigwam, he opened the flap and peered in.

Inside, one man sat alone, chanting in a language Darrell couldn't understand. From what he'd read at the exhibits, he knew the language couldn't have been Monongahela. Their dialect had been lost to history long ago but the words sounded as if they were in some ancient native tongue. The man's voice rose and fell in a hypnotic cadence which drew Darrell in. He settled himself on the ground across the smoldering firepit from the chanter. After hesitating over what position to assume, he sat cross-legged, feeling the dirt and pebbles on his bare legs. He did his best to ignore them and focus on the old man.

Once inside the wigwam, his eyes adjusted and Darrell was able to make out the figure more clearly. The man's skin was amber-colored and he wore a headdress with white and black feathers sprouting from it. A deerskin tunic hung on his thin body, the top like a brown sash across his chest. Darrell realized the man looked exactly like the pictures of the Monongahela tribe he'd seen in the visitor's center when he'd paid for their tickets. Incredibly accurate re-enactor.

The Indian's face was drawn, creases of age lining the forehead and cheeks. His eyes, large brown orbs, appeared unfocused, looking across toward Darrell but seeming to stare at something in the distance. The chant continued for several more minutes, the man's tone rising and falling as the strange words tumbled out in a practiced rhythm. He thought the man must be authentic, his mastery of the language too complete to be acting or memorization.

At last, the old man finished his chanting and his eyes seemed to focus. He looked at Darrell sitting across from him. The Indian spoke again in a low voice. "I have prayed to the Great Spirit for help and he has answered my prayers. He has sent to us a real spirit talker. You, Darrell."

"What?" Darrell started, flitting from fascination to confusion to anxiety. He glanced down to see if they had printed his name on the ticket attached to his shirt. Only the date and a number. "How...how do you know my name?"

The man's old lips creased into a small smile. "The Great Spirit sent you to us. We know about your gift...and we need your help."

Darrell knew where this was going and wanted out. He started to get up. "I need to go meet my son and wife—"

The man reached across the small fire pit and grabbed Darrell's arm before he could even uncross his legs. The grip felt remarkably strong for an old man and Darrell stared at the weathered hand.

The Indian's voice became quieter and more earnest. "Your family is fine. *Please* hear me out. This will only take a few minutes and you will be on your way."

"O-kay." The wrinkled hand released him and Darrell settled back down.

The man spoke in a tone Darrell recognized as if he were teaching class. "As one who studies history, you know the ancient nations of this land are all connected, tribe to tribe. Even though we are different people, we are all one. Even when we have been at war with each other from time to time, we are still one people. The Great Spirit watches over us all."

Darrell managed, "I-I-I've read something about that."

"When the people of one nation suffer, all the nations feel their pain. Over the centuries our people have endured immense suffering. But, when it is the young ones who suffer, the pain is even greater. Their cries echo across the land, across borders, begging for help. The Great Spirit has told us *you* may be able to help these young ones."

"I don't understand."

"You are traveling to a land of the great water, a land our Ojibwe brothers call Mishigami."

"Michigan." Darrell nodded. "We're headed to Lake Michigan to visit family. Wait. How would you know that?"

The chanter went silent, not answering the question. He lifted a stick and stirred the fire. Sparks erupted from the pit, releasing the aroma of some pungent herb Darrell couldn't identify. When the man finished, he raised his gaze again. "Where you are headed are the lands of the

Pottawatomi nation, sometimes called the Gun Lake Tribe."

Darrell tried to figure out something to say to make sense of this strange exchange. "When I lived in Michigan, I'd heard of Gun Lake but haven't ever been there."

"Young Pottawatomi women, teenagers really, have gone missing. This is not a problem for only the Pottawatomi. They are not alone. A great many women and girls of other nations have suffered this tragedy as well." He stopped and then added. "But because you are going to Michigami, *you* can help the Pottawatomi girls. No one knows what happened to them. We fear they are lost to us but the Great Spirit says they have not yet taken the path of souls. No sign of their bodies have been found."

Darrell shook his head. "Look, I'm just going to Michigan for a family event. My Great Aunt is celebrating her eightieth birthday—"

The man grimaced and it halted Darrell mid-sentence. But when the man spoke, it was in a plaintive voice. "These young women have no one. The authorities do nothing. Now the Great Spirit has sent you to us."

Darrell shook his head again, but the man's pleading tone stopped him. "No one has seen these young ones and we fear the worst. If they are indeed gone, no one can bring them back. We fear they cannot be saved but you may be able to communicate with them. *You* can find justice for them. The Great Spirit says it is what you do. Then, they will be able to walk the path of souls."

Darrell stared at the old man across from him who simply looked back. What was he supposed to say? How could he tell this old one his earlier efforts "to find justice" almost got him killed. Almost got Erin killed, oh, God. And now he had a son, a precious five-year-old son. Before he could get any words out, the man stood, not without some difficulty.

"When the time comes, you will know what to do, *Darrell Henshaw*. The Great Spirit would not have sent you to us unless he knew that. He will guide you." He gave a short nod of his head, the ring of feathers doing a swaying dance in the gesture. "Now, go. Your family is waiting for you."

Darrell staggered to his feet, all the while staring at the lined face. Turning, he stooped through the opening and took two steps, almost colliding with a middle-aged woman, her brunette hair in a tight bun.

She asked, "Are you lost? That wigwam is off limits to visitors." She pointed to the one Darrell had just exited. "We reserve that for lectures when we host small groups here."

He recognized her, khaki pants and a maroon top with the Meadowcroft patch on her shoulder. She was one of the interpreters at the visitors center. Glancing at her shirt, he read her name tag. "Helen…you're with the National Park here, right?"

The woman's lips formed a tight line. "Yes, I'm the Assistant Director here. Why were you in that wigwam?"

"I heard some ancient chanting coming from the wigwam and went inside to check it out."

"Chanting? What do you mean chanting?" Her eyebrows climbed up her forehead.

Darrell's anxiety racketed up. "The chanting drew me in and when I went inside to investigate, I found this re-enactor portraying a Monongahela Indian native.

Good job, by the way. He looked and sounded like the real deal."

Helen's eyes narrowed. "We don't have anyone portraying a Native today."

"Well, a few minutes ago, this volunteer or whoever was doing a great job chanting some ancient Indian mantra in there." Darrell pointed to the wigwam.

He glanced over and noticed the wisp of fire no longer escaped through the hole in the top. And he hadn't seen the man come through the only opening. Had he exited while Darrell was talking with the woman? He shook his head. He would've seen him.

"I was just there and talked with some old Indian in full costume. He must still be in there." He took the three steps back to the wigwam.

The woman called, "You're not supposed to go in there."

Darrell pulled the flap back. He stuck his head in and glanced around.

Empty.

No sign of any fire in the pit.

No ancient Indian.

Darrell felt the prickle down his neck, a feeling he hadn't experienced in quite a while.

Damn. He needed to find Erin.

Chapter 3

They needed to talk. *He* needed to talk.

As soon as he caught up with Erin and Leo, Erin had sensed something was off with him. Her gaze told him so.

"Dad, look what Mom got me." Leo held out a miniature *atlatl*, a smaller version of the one he and his mom had tried to use to hit the target. "This way I can practice just like the Indians did. Maybe I can get even better than you."

Darrell rubbed his son's red locks. "That would be great. And I bet you can get really good at it." He smiled at his son, doing his best to ignore the prickle down his neck.

Erin asked, "You okay? What is it?"

"Nothing," Darrell started, then saw the look on Erin's face. She knew it was something. He shot a quick glance at their son, keeping the grin on his face. "Let's talk later."

It had to wait until they got to the motel. So, after they had Leo go to the bathroom, got him a glass of water and read him two books, one each by Mom and Dad, the boy yawned. They'd had a full day. Erin turned off the lights and Darrell closed the curtain, darkening the motel room as best they could.

Darrell kissed Leo on the forehead. "Mom and I have to have a little adult talk. We'll be right outside."

He pointed to the door to the motel room. "If you need us, all you have to do is call us. Got it?"

Leo nodded, yawning again, and Darrell yawned along with him. "Don't worry. Mom and I will be joining you quite soon. We're pretty tired too."

Leo yawned a third time. "Night, Dad. Night, Mom."

Both parents echoed, "Good night."

Once the boy closed his eyes, Darrell scanned the motel room. Two queen beds with a nightstand in the middle and a chair and small desk to one side. It was basic but clean with only a few dark stains on the worn carpet. It held a lingering antiseptic odor but it wasn't bad. He opened the door and he and Erin slid through, then he shut it quietly. He was glad they'd picked this plain motel with the car parked right outside the door to their room. Not only did it make it easy to unload the car, now they could sit in the two chairs out front *and* stay close to their son.

With the sun setting, the temperature had cooled, though thick humidity still hung in the air. Before they sat on the cheap plastic chairs, Darrell used a hotel towel to wipe off and clean each seat. Then, examining his, he placed a second towel on the seat of his chair. Once they were settled, Darrell glanced around. "I'd say you're not going to believe this, but we've been here before."

Then he started in, keeping his voice low. As best he could, he shared the strange exchange with the ancient Indian. It took a while and Erin had to lean close at times to hear it all as his words never got above a whisper. Twice, Darrell had to stop as a twenty-something woman passed them on her way to the vending area and then returned, filled ice bucket in hand, a minute later. Each time, Darrell smiled and nodded to her, pausing the retelling until she was back in her room and out of earshot. By the time Darrell finally finished, he was relieved to get it all out.

Years ago, he discovered he shouldn't keep things from Erin, a lesson he'd learned the hard way. In Florida, on their honeymoon, when two other ghosts—of children, no less—haunted him, asking for his help, he had tried to keep it from his new wife, with nearly disastrous consequences. He vowed he'd never do it again.

Erin was not a sensitive like him—and like their son. She might not be able to see ghosts but she understood and appreciated his gift, sometimes better than he. And more important, she had been there for him, every time he needed her.

When he got to the part about finding the wigwam empty after returning with the assistant director, she caught her breath.

She asked, "You think you could've dreamed it? The whole thing was some kind of vision?"

"I don't know. I can tell you one thing. That old man's hand on my arm felt real. His grip was incredibly strong." He shook his head. "But that wigwam was definitely empty when I went back inside and looked around. Maybe he had another way of getting out of the tent?"

"Could he have been a medium...I hate to say this...like Natalia?" She practically choked getting the name out. "Or maybe he was a ghost?"

Darrell scrunched his features. "A medium? I don't know. He didn't say anything about communicating with the dead." He shook his head. "A ghost, maybe. He seemed awfully definite about the missing girls."

"From Michigan? How would some old Indian in Pennsylvania, ghost or not, even know about missing girls in Michigan?"

"Under normal circumstances, I'd say he wouldn't." He glanced over at his wife. "But when we've gone down this rabbit hole before, you know not much is normal."

Erin stared at him. "Yeah and climbing out of those rabbit holes have been…treacherous. And now we have that beautiful boy in there sleeping like an angel." She nodded back toward the closed door. "You know I'm always behind you on this but I won't let anything happen to him."

Darrell met her gaze. "I couldn't agree more."

She got up and went over to the front passenger seat of the car. Opening the door, she reached inside and pulled out the map they'd been using. When she shut the door, she said over her shoulder, "We forgot to lock the car."

Darrell pulled the fob out and hit the button, the car locks responding with matching thunks.

Returning to the chair, Erin sat down again next to him. She pointed to the map. "You said your aunt's place is outside of Saugatuck?"

"Yeah. Saugatuck is on Lake Michigan and the Kalamazoo River, here." Darrell indicated a spot on the left side of the map. "My aunt's place is a few miles away, right on Lake Michigan." He slid his finger an inch to the shoreline.

Erin pointed to another spot almost directly east of Saugatuck. "It looks like we're going to drive past Gun Lake on our way there…looks like less than an hour from your aunt's place. Maybe we'll learn something when we get there."

Darrell sighed. "Let's keep our eyes and ears open and see what happens." He glanced back at the closed motel room door. "And we'll leave Leo out of it, for now."

Erin nodded. "I agree…but if these girls are dead, you know he's just as likely as you to see their ghosts. God only knows what happened to them." She shuddered. "Leo is too young to learn about the horror of what people do to each other."

"I agree. So far, his encounters with the spirit world have been pretty harmless. I'd like to keep it that way."

"So would I."

Darrell recalled the image of the haunted bride in Cape May, her white wedding gown drenched in blood. "If I end up getting sucked into seeking justice for any missing girls, I'm afraid what I encounter will be anything but harmless."

Chapter 4

"MISS-ING?" Leo pronounced, staring at the word printed in all caps across the top of a flyer. He glanced up at his dad for confirmation. "Is that right, Dad?"

Their son had been trying to read and every conquered word excited him. Erin and Darrell had read to him every day since he came home from the hospital and some of Darrell's most cherished moments involved sharing a favorite book with his son. And Leo seemed to love it as much as his dad.

But lately, he'd become even more excited about reading words himself. Besides reading along in the picture books, Leo figured out words from the back of cereal boxes, read words from signs they passed and even caught words he could make out on products in the grocery store.

The three of them had stopped at a gas station at Kalamazoo to grab some snacks, even though Aunt Gertrude—or rather her staff—would no doubt have plenty of food at the house. They'd each selected a few favorites from the store and they made their way together up to the cashier. The poster his son stood staring at had been affixed to the counter, the word in caps right at Leo's eye level. The flyer with MISSING across the top was taped to the edge of the counter and Darrell, juggling his and Leo's purchases, might have missed it. He set the bags of snacks on the counter, then stooped down to his son's level.

Darrell looked his son in the eyes and nodded. "That's right." He pointed to the paper the boy was staring at, his fingers tracing the words as he read them aloud for Leo. "Very good. MISSING. Have. You. Seen. Her." Below the headline was a color photo of a beautiful teenage girl, with flowing black hair and bewitching brown eyes, wearing a smile that looked like she was flirting. His gut clenched, realizing what his son had found. He started to rise.

His eyes still on the flyer, Leo asked, "Read me the rest?"

Darrell didn't want his son in the middle of this, whatever this was. He considered telling Leo they had to get going, then saw the plea on his son's features. He relented. As his fingertips slid down the sheet, he read the rest aloud while his son's gaze stayed fixed on the page. "Sheila Birdsong. Age 17. Height 5'4. Black hair, brown eyes. Member of the Gun Lake Tribe. Last seen on June 13, 2007. Please contact County Sheriff with any information."

Leo looked over at his dad. "Is that a long time? Has she been missing long?"

Darrell's glanced at the flyer and back at Leo. "A couple of weeks. That's why her family put up these flyers. To ask if anyone has seen her."

Leo didn't say anything at first, studying the photo. He looked so cute in his navy shorts, another novelty white tee and green eyes darkening with concern.

The boy asked, "So what do you think happened to her?"

His son expected him to have all the answers but today Darrell had none. "I don't think they know what happened to—" he glanced back at the poster. "What happened to Sheila."

"That comes to 8.77. Cash or charge?" the young female clerk announced, after scanning all the items they had deposited on the counter.

Two more people had queued up in line behind them and Darrell recognized impatience in their postures. He straightened up and paid. Taking the bag from the clerk, he handed it off to Erin. He grabbed his son's hand and led him around the counter, noticing Leo's eyes stayed fixed on the picture of the missing girl.

"Okay, next stop is Great Aunt Gertrude's mansion on the lake—and we'll see if it is haunted!" Darrell called in an excited voice, trying for some distraction. But, as he held the glass door open for Erin and Leo, hearing the bell tinkle again, he noticed more "Missing" flyers posted on the window next to the door. Two more missing Native girls, each with dark hair and shy smiles.

Once in the car, they let their son choose one of his treats to enjoy in the last leg of their trip. When Leo asked for cheese curls, Erin rolled her eyes and Darrell cringed. She said, "Well, I'll just have to clean him up before we meet everyone."

She got the plastic bag open and handed it back. Within a few minutes, their son was happily crunching in the back seat, the smell of artificial cheese filling the inside of the car. When she was satisfied he was occupied, Erin spoke, keeping her voice low. "You think Sheila is one of the 'young women' the Indian asked you to help?"

He reached inside his pocket and handed her a folded white paper. She opened the sheet and glanced at Darrell. "You took one of the flyers?" she whispered.

"There was a pile of them on the counter," he spoke as quietly as she. "I thought we might want it…for reference."

Erin studied the flyer. "Such a pretty girl. She looks so young. It says she's seventeen. And she's a member of the Gun Lake tribe. I wonder what happened to her?"

Darrell glanced at his son in the mirror and whispered, "The Indian said there were missing *girls*. What if Sheila," he pointed to the flyer Erin held, "is only one of them. I saw two other girls listed as missing on the posters around the door. Native girls."

Erin was silent for a minute, then she asked, "Didn't you tell me Saugatuck is a small town?"

"Yeah. I don't remember how big, but I think it's a pretty small town, maybe a thousand, not counting visitors. With other small towns like Douglass and Holland close by. Why?"

She said, "If their small towns are anything like ours on the Chesapeake Bay, then how do some girls go missing in the area without a trace? The date on the flyer was June something."

"Yeah, and the other two were May, I think."

Erin nodded. "I mean, if that happened in Wilshire or Oxford in the past few months, wouldn't tongues be wagging everywhere? Everybody is in everybody else's business."

"Good point. If some area teenagers went missing back home, it would be big time gossip. Maybe it is here too. We'll see if we learn anything when we get there."

"But we're not going to tell your family, right? About the missing girls and…um, the Indian?"

"Not if we can help it." Darrell thought for a bit, concentrating on the two lane road ahead. "I've never told them all about—"

"Your gift?" Erin offered. "But they knew about you losing your job in Wilshire? What did you tell them?"

He said, "I didn't tell them until I got the job back. Then I told them I had stumbled onto a conspiracy when I did my research."

"So they have no idea?"

"I think my mom suspects, but my dad is such a skeptic, I doubt he'd believe me even if a ghost sat on his lap."

"Still, I like your dad," Erin said. "He makes me laugh."

"I love my dad and he *loves* you. You've certainly charmed him."

"Speaking of family, do you think we should say anymore to…you know?" she said quietly, nodding toward the back seat. "I mean, do we tell him that 'missing' might mean…?" She didn't say the last word but Darrell understood. "You know, so he can understand in case he *sees* her and we're not there."

Darrrell glanced at the rearview mirror. His son was munching away, his hand and mouth now bright orange. The boy was going to need a wipe, maybe a whole box of wipes. Inside, Darrell winced again, then he reminded himself Leo was just a kid, an innocent kid.

He whispered, "Not yet. Once we get there and settled in, I'll take him on a walk and try to come up with something."

"How much longer, Mom?" Leo popped up from the backseat.

Erin turned and announced, "Not much longer. She glanced from the half empty bag to her orange-faced son. "I think you've had enough for now. Don't you?"

"They were yummy." He smacked two lips which looked almost golden.

"Let's get you cleaned up." She unbuckled her seatbelt. "No sudden moves, Dad." She reached down inside her monstrous bag and pulled out a box of wipes. Pulling two sheets out, she leaned back and went to work on Leo. Darrell took his eyes off the road for a few seconds and glanced at his wife, stretching over the bucket seat back. The light blue Jersey knit shorts tugged nicely on her legs and the lacey white blouse gapped slightly, making him want to stare more. His attention diverted, his hand slid on the steering wheel and the car swerved on the road. He pulled it back in the center, still peeking over at his wife's figure half draped over the seat back.

Erin glanced over at him. "Keep your eyes on the road, buster," she said, a mock scolding tone in her voice.

To Leo, she insisted, "Hold still and I'll get done faster." When Darrell glanced in the rearview mirror, he saw Leo cooperated and when Erin finished, she moved his chin back and forth. "Good as new. Let me see your hands." He did and she did one last swipe on each. "Okay."

Back in the front seat, she reached into the bag, grabbed a few cheese curls and started munching away.

Darrell glanced over, surprised. "I didn't think you liked those things."

"I'm really hungry. I don't know why. And these taste pretty good." She popped a few more into her mouth, then smacked her lips. "Don't know where that came from." She turned to the back seat. "Maybe I'm picking up your tastes, Leo."

Her son said, "I'll share, Mom."

Erin smiled. "Thanks, but I think that's enough for me." She closed the bag and stuffed it in the sack from the convenience store. "Now, I need to clean *me* up." She pulled a few more wipes out of her oversized purse and cleaned her hands and mouth, checking in the mirror from the visor.

When she put it all away, she turned in time to see a sign they were passing. She read it aloud, "Match-e-be-nash-she-wish Band of Pottawatomi Reservation," and then exchanged glances with Darrell.

In the back, Leo relaxed in his child seat, a contented smile on his now clean face. As only preschoolers can, he closed his eyes and in two minutes was napping quietly. Since they wanted to give their son a chance to rest before they arrived, both Darrell and Erin went silent. Just past the reservation sign, Darrell took the turnoff that led west to Lake Michigan and Saugatuck; the only sound in the car was the hum of tires on the blacktop.

In another forty-five minutes, Darrell pulled the car up to the stoplight and they recognized the large wooden billboard with SAUGATUCK in capital letters anchored with an artist's palette on one end. But, rather than heading straight into the small town, he turned left, following directions he'd received from his mom. The road narrowed but was well paved, weaving between towering elms and oaks and through groves of pine trees that blanketed both sides of the road like parallel curtains of deep green. At times, the trees reached so tall they blocked out the brilliant summer sun.

A few minutes into the tunnel of trees, Darrell saw the sign and slowed. The small white marker read simply PRIVATE DRIVE. He turned the car onto the lane which looked like it had been newly blacktopped. The tree cover here seemed even thicker with the pine trees closing in on both sides as if to crowd the lane. Peering into the green on either side, he could make out little except more and more densely populated trees. After another five minutes of driving, he rolled the car up to a black iron gate which stretched across the entire road. Atop the metal work, he read the words, "The Wentworth" in red letters.

Next to the driver's side stood a gray metal box with a number pad in the center and a black speaker to the right. He turned to Erin. "Didn't I give you the code my mom sent me? For the gate?"

Nodding, Erin reached into her cavernous bag, fumbled around, and came out with a small sheet of paper. "Here it is, 8367."

Rolling the window down, Darrell plugged in the numbers and waited. At first, nothing. Then, after a bit, the gate split in neat halves, each side opening slowly on silent hinges. As soon as he could, he accelerated through the gap, worried the gate might shut before they were through. He realized his anxiety was hardly rational, but he couldn't help it. Maybe he felt the woods were closing in on them.

Once on the other side of the gate, he saw no change in the road ahead, only more asphalt snaking through a channel of dark green. He kept driving. He caught no other signs, no indication of what lie ahead. Even if he were on the wrong road, there was no room to turn around, so he continued. With the window down, the smells of pine and decaying leaves floated in, followed by a breeze which carried a hint of the great lake beyond. At least, that's what he told himself.

Staring ahead, he thought he saw a brightening at the far end of his view. As the car drew closer, he could see the trees thinning out, the coverage not quite so thick. When the tree cover finally broke, he saw the expanse of the water beyond to the right, with the road rising up a hill. He slowed and both he and Erin leaned forward, straining to see the corner of a large structure that seemed to sprout out of the hill. His aunt's place?

He followed the road along the cleared forest floor and eventually up a slight incline. Once out of the woods, the black ribbon of asphalt ran up to the corner, revealing part of the rear and side of the large building. The drive then flowed down the side, running along the entire length of the structure—Darrell couldn't believe how large the mansion must be.

As he slowly navigated the lane, Erin's gaze took in the immensity of the mansion, her head craning to get a better view as he maneuvered around the massive house, pulling onto a circular driveway in front and stopped.

Her eyes wide, she whispered, "Oh my God!"

Chapter 5

Putting the car in park, Darrell got out and walked around the hood, then took three steps backward and turned, so he could take in the view of the imposing mansion. Erin, who had better parenting instincts, first released their son from bondage in the back seat and, his hand in hers, they joined Darrell, staring up at the monstrous house.

Erin shot a glance at her husband. "You told me it was a big place but from your description, I never dreamt...this." She pointed at the massive structure.

Darrell shook his head. "I remember it being really big, but I thought that was a creation of my young memory. Somehow, I don't remember all this."

The mansion was the largest "house" Darrell had ever seen, two stories easily covering 20,000 square feet, he'd guess. His gaze ran to the roof first, or rather roofs. This end of the building was topped with what looked like three rounded, cone-shaped roofs, each covered in pebbled gray-and-black shingles. Beyond the cones, four gabled roofs erupted, stiff and square, as if standing in attention behind the rounded versions. Five different chimneys sprouted from disparate points in the roofs, each one a tall construction of brick and mortar with a carved fieldstone cap.

On both floors, the rear and the side of the house were covered in white stucco broken up by tall window after window. He started counting them—four, eight, sixteen, twenty, and stopped. How come he hadn't noticed all the windows before?

At the rear or front—at least the part facing the water—the parade of windows was interrupted in the exact center of the second floor by a circular balcony edged with a curved, white-slotted railing. An American flag hung from the rail, flapping in the breeze off the water. He didn't recall the flag but he remembered tossing water balloons from that perch with his brother. Great fun, which got them in trouble with their aunt, of course.

Below the balcony, a set of stone steps led up to a pair of large wooden doors, each with an intricately carved circular design ending at a round stained-glass window. He stared. The doors alone looked like they cost more than his annual salary.

One step above ground level ran a wide, expansive porch which began fifty feet up the side and continued around the rear of the house. Stationed at strategic spots on the sweeping porch, round tables sat with red collapsible umbrellas, waiting to provide visitors with perfect, shaded views of the water.

"Dad, look at that!" Leo cried.

Darrell dragged his attention away from the mansion and glanced down at his son, who was looking away from the house, his gaze fixed on the water.

"It looks even bigger than the Ches'peake!" Leo yelled.

Behind the mansion, the lush green lawn sloped for about three hundred feet down to a rock-strewn shoreline with a patch of brown sand in the center and a set of white stairs along the one side. Beside the small beach, a white-painted wooded dock ran about a hundred feet out into the water. At the pier, two boats bobbed in the waves, a long, sleek sailboat with a double mast and speedboat with a huge motor at the rear. The rolling waves reminded Darrell of the first time he jumped into that water with Craig. They practically froze. Man, it had been cold.

Darrell crouched down so his face was level with his son's. He glanced from Leo to the wide expanse of water, glistening silver in the afternoon sun, dotted with small whitecaps. "That's Lake Michigan and it might look bigger than the Chesapeake Bay but it's not. In fact, the whole lake is only about half the size of Chesapeake Bay."

Leo protested, "But it looks so much bigger across than our Ches'peake." He pointed out at the water which seemed to go on forever.

Darrell placed his hand on his son's shoulder. "You're right there. The Chesapeake is much narrower. In some places, it's only about three miles across…" He pointed out to the water, "Lake Michigan is about *eighty miles* across. Almost three times as much. The Chesapeake is just a lot longer."

"Well, Master Darrell, I'd recognize you anywhere," a gruff voice called from behind. Darrell turned to find a man dressed in worn bib overalls, large sweat stains spreading through a white T-shirt. Atop his head he wore a tattered straw hat which blocked most of his features. He'd been so enthralled telling Leo about Lake Michigan, he hadn't even heard the man come up behind them.

"Mr. Salazar," Darrell said, closing the gap between them. Taking the outstretched hand, he shook, looking the man in the eye. The man looked much the same as Darrell remembered, though older of course.

Darrell said, "I'd think, in twenty years, I would've changed quite a bit."

The old man chortled, a laugh that sounded authentic as if he'd been caught at something and was trying to laugh off the misstep. "Aw, you caught me. We've read about your heroic exploits in Maryland. Even up here on the lake, we get the news from time to time, and some of those articles come with photos." He glanced down at Leo and grinned. "And who are your companions?"

Darrell turned. "I'd like you to meet my wife Erin and our son, Leo."

The man tilted his hat back and stared. A broad smile blossomed in the weathered, sunburned face, displaying more than a few broken or missing teeth. A pair of wire-rimmed glasses replaced the blocky plastic frames Darrell remembered and behind them, two chocolate irises looked back, one a little milky. Above the eyes, deep lines of age etched his forehead and below, a bulbous nose perched atop a pair of thin lips. He said, "I heard you found quite a looker." He winked at Erin. "Looks like you definitely married up."

Darrell said, "No argument there."

Erin said, "Very nice to meet you, Mr. Salazar," her voice the soothing tone Darrell had heard her use often with her patients. "I bet you have more than a few stories about my Darrell when he was young."

Salazar's eyes brightened. "Do I ever." He glanced around and whispered, "Let's talk later."

Erin laughed, a hearty laugh which lit up her whole face. Hearing it reminded Darrell how much he loved

36

that laugh.

She raised her eyebrows. "I can't wait."

Salazar nodded toward the boy. "And the little one takes after his mother, thank heaven." He chuckled. "How old are you, son?"

Leo beamed. "I'm five. I'll be six soon."

After a moment, Darrell said, "I'm a little amazed you're still here. How long has it been?"

"This August it'll be thirty-five years, if this old body holds up," Salazar said. "And I think you can call me Tom by now. You're not a little kid anymore."

"Okay, Tom." Darrell turned to Erin and Leo. "Mr. Salazar, er, Tom has been the gardener and all-around handyman for my aunt and uncle since—"

"Almost before you were born. Since seventy-two," the older guy finished, a hint of pride in his voice.

Just then, three figures emerged from the house, a young man in his early twenties and two teenage girls. The young man stepped forward. Full head of brown hair worn a little long and lightened from time in the sun, handsome in a Mediterranean way, swarthy skin, hard features, lots of teeth in the smile. "Sir?"

Salazar said. "Oh, Ilya." He turned to Darrell. "He handles the cars, parks them in the garage."

Darrell reached into his pocket and pulled out his keys. "Just let us get our bags."

"No need for that." Salazar spun around and spoke, voice transforming from warm greeting to icy directness. "Girls, you know the drill. Help our guests with their bags. They'll be staying in Guest Suite 2." The lines on his forehead deepened and his hand dismissed the two.

Both teens, dressed in distressed jean shorts and clean plain tees, kept their heads of long dark hair bowed.

They took quick steps to the rear of the Taurus and Darrell hurried to catch up with them and open the trunk. He went to reach for the bags.

Salazar said, his voice once again kindly, "Darrell, no need to assist. These girls are quite capable…and stronger than they look. We've trained them and Mrs. Embry pays them well for their service."

Darrell took a step back. "I guess we'll need them all." He gestured to the assorted luggage stuffed into the compartment.

He watched as the teens went to work, dislodging the bags and setting them, one by one, on the ground behind the car. They labored without talking, methodically, obviously having done this before. Their faces wore no expression until the one extracting Leo's bright blue suitcase with a smiley face. They both cracked a grin. But it fled as quickly as it appeared. Both girls had amber skin and long, straight hair, one a deep brown and the other black, which hung nearly to their waist. Both looked thin, almost emaciated, not from dieting, more from not having enough to eat, Darrell thought. When he caught their gazes, desolate eyes looked back, one pair dark brown and the other intense green.

The two thin teenagers snatched up bags, two each, and headed for the double doors. Darrell felt useless, watching two young girls struggling with the luggage and he reached down to grab the heaviest one to get it up the stone steps so they could roll it inside.

Salazar chided him. "Leave it. Rachel and Anna will get them. Your aunt is waiting. She's quite anxious to meet your family. Just give Ilya your keys, he'll take care of the car."

Aunt Gertrude was waiting.

Darrell sighed, tossed the young man the keys and reached for his son's hand. When he did, Leo tugged and Darrell stooped next to him. The boy's gaze stayed fixed on the two girls ahead, long dark hair flowing behind them and struggling to get the four suitcases up the steps and through the heavy doors. Leo's eyes never left the girls and he whispered, "They look a lot like…missing."

Chapter 6

"Darrell Everett Henshaw," called a shrill voice.

He'd recognize that voice anywhere, even though he hadn't heard it in twenty years. Remarkably, it still sounded the same as in his memory. Commanding, harsh, and insistent.

Darrell, Erin, and Leo followed the two girls through the large wooden doors. He agreed with his son. The two girls were definitely Native and most likely members of the nearby Gun Lake tribe. *And* they looked to be about the same age as Sheila Birdsong, the "missing" as Leo had said. He wanted to learn if they knew Sheila, knew anything about her disappearance. But, before his family got more than a few steps across the marble foyer, he heard his name called. Or rather commanded.

Darrell Everett Henshaw.

Those three words brought back memories of him playing with his brother, doing something a bit dangerous or risky, but fun. And those three words pronounced that way had meant he was going to be in trouble.

With the announcement of his name, the same old anxieties flooded back. He hesitated for a few seconds, then remembered he was a grown man with a beautiful wife and wonderful son. He took a long, slow breath and then tilted his head in the direction of the voice. "Let's go see Aunt Gertrude."

He steered his son into the great room, Erin right beside him. Like the house, the great room was massive. As he stepped across the polished planks of the hardwood floor, more memories struck him. He and his brother sliding across the gleaming brown floor on their stocking feet, racing to see who would get the gold medal. And Craig and he rolling spring-powered cars across the planks and running into the furniture, both of them giggling. Uncle Dave catching them, trying to scold but unable to keep from laughing himself. Then Aunt Gertrude scowling at the two of them and banishing them outside with a stern lecture on decorum.

Darrell scanned the large room.

A large stone hearth stood at the north end of the room, the fireplace overlaid with large brown tiles in a floral design. An antique black powder rifle rested on a rack above the mantel. Darrell wasn't sure how much of the décor was new, but he remembered the rifle. Both Uncle Dave and Aunt Gertrude were hunters. And western Michigan was certainly hunting country.

A tall lounge chair, upholstered in a brilliant red velvet, sat next to the quiet fireplace and a matching one flanked it on the other side of the hearth. Aunt Gertrude sat high in the first, while the second—no doubt Uncle Dave's—was empty. At her foot, a Persian rug with brilliant colors of red, blue and yellow swirls, covered the wood floor.

"So good to see you, Aunt Gertrude," Darrell said as he, Erin and Leo made their way across the space, their footfalls echoing in the vast room. When they stopped in front of her chair, Darrell got the impression of a makeshift throne. His aunt looked much the same as he remembered, though more shriveled with age. She had a slight frame with slightly stooped shoulders, but her figure eased back in the plush chair, the corners of her small mouth tugged slightly up. Her round face bore the marks of her years and summers in the sun, etching a river of lines across her wrinkled forehead and around a pair of deep-set eyes. Those eyes. Darrell remembered those eyes. Piercing blue-gray eyes that could turn to steel when angry. Today, they appeared soft, more blue than gray behind fashionable glasses.

"Aunt Gertrude, I'd like you to meet my wife Erin and our son, Leo." Darrell did the introductions.

Erin didn't hesitate and stepped forward. She took the old woman's small hand in hers and shook, offering her beautiful smile. Not to be outdone, Leo came up alongside his mom and said, "You have an awfully big house here."

Gertrude laughed, a laugh that shook her tiny body. She stared down at Leo. "You are right, young man." She squinted at the boy and read aloud the words on the front of his shirt. "I'm daddy's favorite!" and laughed. "I love it." She glanced up at Darrell. "I'm so glad you could all make it. It's been too long, Darrell."

"It's been quite a while," he agreed, deciding not to say any more. He almost said, you haven't invited family in years, but held his tongue. From talking with his parents, he learned his mother—Gertrude's sister-in-law—hadn't been welcomed in almost two decades. Instead, he said, "We're glad that we can be here to celebrate this momentous occasion with you."

Gertrude chuckled. "I'm not sure I'd call it momentous, but I have managed to slough through eighty years in this old shell." She glanced down at her body.

Erin spoke up. "You certainly have a beautiful place, here on the water."

"Thank you, dear." Gertrude managed a small smile. "From what I hear, you're quite the water person. An accomplished sailor."

Erin said, "My father started teaching me from the time I was tall enough to reach the helm. I've been sailing ever since."

Gertrude leaned forward in the chair. "What do you sail on the Bay?"

Erin's smile brightened. "Our family owns an Irwin Citation '34. My father restored it himself."

Gertrude said, "Nice boat."

"Thanks, but it's a poor cousin to your Mason I saw tied up at the dock. A 40 maybe."

Gertrude eased back in her chair, her gaze appraising Erin. "A 43 actually. Well, you certainly know your sailing crafts."

Erin grinned back, unfazed. "We were admiring her from the top of the hill. Hard to tell the difference from that far away."

"I used to love taking her out for a spin on the lake." Gertrude sighed. "I'm afraid these old bones can't handle it anymore. Can't manage the balance." She wobbled her head back and forth, then her face brightened. "You're welcome to give her a spin later, if you'd like."

Erin shot a quick glance at Darrell and then back at the host. "That's very generous, ma'am. I might just do that…if we have time and the conditions permit."

Gertrude glanced down at Leo again. "Do you go sailing too? Do you like the water?"

The boy flashed a wide smile. "I go with Mommy

and Daddy on *Second Wind*. That's our sailboat. But I have to wear a life jacket."

"That's probably a good idea." Gertrude gave a dismissive wave of her hand. "Now, you best skedaddle to your rooms and get settled. Darrell, your parents and brother should be here soon, and I've arranged for them to have the next two guest suites on your side of the house."

Darrell took his son's hand. "Thanks again for having us, Aunt Gertrude." He led Leo and Erin back into the hall, hurrying his steps. He hoped they could get to their rooms before the two Native girls had finished and left. Maybe ask them a few questions and learn something, anything, about the missing girl.

Chapter 7

The three of them paced down the hallway, which looked as fancy as the rest of the house. Tall ceilings, walls covered in dark cherrywood paneling, and pale, plush carpet under their feet greeted them as they made their way down the guest bedroom wing of the house.

When he got to the entry door, Darrell's gaze swept the suite, finding a separate sitting area with a comfortable loveseat on his left facing from a large, flat-screen TV in the center of a wall. Two open doors flanked the television. Directly across, he stared out two floor-to-ceiling windows. From what Salazar had told them, Darrell supposed the doors led to two separate bedrooms, one for him and Erin and a second for Leo. The entire sitting area was outfitted much like the great room with dark wood paneling on the walls, again polished so well it gleamed in the light streaming through the glass. The scent of lemon wood polish still hung in the air, faint but evident.

The suite was far nicer than any hotel he'd ever stayed in—or anything he could afford for his family. Darrell searched his mind but could not recall any memory of this space. Of course, in the decades since he'd been here, Uncle Dave or, more likely, Aunt Gertrude, could have completely renovated the mansion. Uncle Dave had certainly made enough money in his commercial construction and shipping business. Or maybe, as a child, the grandeur of the place hadn't registered.

Erin, who came in right behind Darrell, exclaimed, "My lord, take a look at that view."

When he glanced out the windows, he caught a sweeping view of Lake Michigan, small whitecaps visible on the waves.

Leo ran over to the second window, edged the curtain aside a few inches and put his face and hands on the glass. "Cool."

When Leo turned to face his dad, Darrell saw the imprints of the boy's fingers—still not completely clean despite Erin's best efforts—on the previously sparkling glass. He shrugged and smiled at his son. "It is pretty cool, isn't it?"

Hearing some mumbling coming from one of two bedrooms, Darrell crossed the space and peered in the doorway. The bedroom was appointed as luxuriously as the rest. In the center of the room sat a sprawling king size bed with an intricately carved headboard in a dark walnut. The bed was flanked on either side with matching nightstands in the same dark wood as the headboard. On each nightstand stood a fashionable lamp covered with what Darrell thought was a Tiffany lamp shade. Three floor-to-ceiling windows covered most of the left wall with a fancy armoire on the opposite wall.

In front of the bureau, the two dark-haired teens, heads close together, were conversing in a dialect he took to be Native but didn't understand. Each girl held an item of clothing in one hand and, as he watched, she placed the piece neatly on the shelf of the antique wardrobe. As he stepped into the bedroom, the two glanced his way, went silent, but continued their actions.

Erin came through the door next to him, went over to the girls and said in a soft voice, "Thank you so much for this but you didn't need to."

The one with the black hair, a few inches taller and probably the older of the pair, said, "We're glad to. This is our job. We are to make you feel at home."

"Anna, right?" Erin asked.

The black head nodded. "Yes, ma'am."

Erin examined the one shelf. "Nice job. I couldn't do better myself."

Anna beamed. "Thank you."

Leo had followed his mother into the bedroom and took one of his Hot Wheels cars out of his case. He rolled it along the floor next to the bed. With his son occupied for the moment, Darrell joined Erin by the two Native girls, who stood stiff at his approach, as if waiting for the other shoe to drop. Up close, he noticed the girls' clothes looked worn, rather than fashionable. Both T-shirts had stains on the sleeves.

Darrell asked, "Anna and Rachel, are you both from the Gun Lake Tribe?"

Neither said anything at first, exchanging quick glances, then Anna said, "Yes, we're both half-blood Pottawatomi." Nodding, Rachel took the last two items from the suitcases and placed them neatly on the shelf.

"How old are you?"

Anna said, "I'm sixteen and Rachel is my younger sister. She's fifteen."

Darrell asked, "Could I ask you a question? About another Pottawatomi girl?"

The two exchanged another glance, then Anna ventured, "I guess."

Darrell checked to make sure his son was still busy

and pulled the "Missing" flyer out of his pocket and unfolded it, extending it toward them. He whispered, "Did you…do you know her?"

Both girls stared at the flyer but neither made any move, both pairs of dark eyes going wide. Rachel shot a quick look at her sister.

When neither spoke, Darrell explained, "We saw this flyer at a store on our way here."

Anna whispered, "We're not allowed to talk about—"

"So, there you are. Aren't you done yet?" Salazar's sharp voice sliced into the room. He stood in the doorway, one hand on the polished wood frame. "What's taking you so long? Mr. and Mrs. Henshaw, Darrell's parents, just arrived and need your help with their bags. Chop, chop." He nodded down the hallway.

Anna shot a brief look at Darrell, then both girls started for the door, stepping quickly. Salazar never moved and the girls had to duck under his arm to get through the opening. In three seconds, they disappeared through the door, their hurried footfalls echoing down the corridor.

Still leaning against the doorframe, Salazar smirked. "Sorry, Darrell and Erin."

Darrell said, "Hey, don't blame the girls. We held them up, just asking them a question."

Salazar shook his head. "You don't know them like I do. They'd do anything to get out of a little work. Those two would dawdle all day if you let them. You have to stay on top of them. I know it's a cliché but it's just damn hard to get good people."

Chapter 8

His question had made the two Native teens nervous, but Darrell thought he saw recognition in their eyes. They might know something. He decided he'd wait until he could get a private moment with them, without anyone else eavesdropping. For now, he had other concerns. His parents had arrived and he—they—hadn't seen them in more than a year. He, Erin and Leo, still clutching his purple toy Mustang, followed Salazar down the long hallway.

As he walked through the fancy corridor, a mixture of emotions struck him—happiness and anxiety seeing his parents again, guilt for staying away from home so long, beaming pride at sharing his beautiful wife and growing son. Holding the front doors open for Erin then Leo, he caught sight of his mother. She had just stepped back out of the way of the teens unloading bags from the trunk of the white Volvo with the license plate of DR MOLR.

"Mom, you look great!" He hurried down the steps and wrapped his arms around her and lifted her up a few inches before setting her back down. She did too. A trim five-foot-six, the sunny, sleeveless top and cream-colored capri pants flattered her slender figure and reminded him she still had it...which wasn't always a good thing.

He loved his mother but had long ago come to terms

with the reality that she was far from perfect. As a teen, he'd stumbled upon her and another man, half-undressed and embracing in a parked car. Though he never confronted her about it—and didn't think she knew he'd discovered them—it had strained his relationship with her for years. Darrell wasn't sure how much his dad knew but was pretty sure his father had some idea. The *other* man had died in a car crash years ago and his parents had worked their way through it. They seemed content.

Once out in the world and confronted by some real evil and depravity, Darrell had learned to forgive and recognized that Susan Henshaw was human like everyone else.

"Whew. It's good to see you too." A smile with bright, white teeth lit up her soft face under a head of blonde curls. "It's been too long."

Darrell said, "I'm sorry about that. We've been talking on our way here and we decided we're going to find some way to get home more often."

"And we'd love to host you on the Shore," Erin said, coming next to Darrell.

"Erin, you look radiant," Susan Henshaw said. "Maybe, the invigorating Michigan air agrees with you." Darrell watched as his mother's brilliant blue eyes scanned his wife up and down. He wondered if his mom was appraising or complimenting.

"And who is this big guy?" a booming voice called from behind them. Darrell turned to see his father studying Leo. Charles Henshaw stood there with a mock question on his square face. At six-foot-one, he stood almost as tall as Darrell and still looked like the athlete he had been in college, even with the few midlife pounds he'd picked up. A pair of jeans and a navy polo shirt encased his tall frame as he leaned over the boy.

Leo placed both hands on his hips. "I'm Leo, your grandson."

Charles Henshaw shook his head. "Not possible. The last time I saw my grandson he was this small." He placed his hand below his knee. "How'd you get to be so big?"

"Simple. I grew," the boy explained.

The elder Henshaw gave a roaring laugh. "You certainly did but not so big I can't do this." He snatched up the boy and tossed him in the air before catching him.

One hand still clutching the toy car, Leo shrieked, "Whee! Again, again."

His grandpa obliged with two more throws and, when he set the boy on the ground, he huffed once. "Believe it or not, I used to do that to your dad."

"Hey, Dad," Darrell said, first reaching out a hand, then opening both arms. Charles Henshaw hugged back, squeezing for a few seconds and then releasing.

He and his dad were on good terms, even if emotions didn't come easy to his father. Now with a young son of his own, a wife to care for and a demanding career, Darrell began to understand the challenges that came with all that. That had increased his appreciation for his dad.

"Well, how is our teacher and crime fighter?" Charles asked, a hint of mischief in his green-brown eyes.

Darrell chuckled. "Thankfully, I haven't confronted any bad guys lately…unless you count opposing football teams." He placed a hand on Leo's shoulder. "This one has kept me pretty busy."

Erin stepped next to him. "Teaching, coaching, nursing and raising a little one have kept the Darrell Henshaw clan quite busy *and* happy."

Charles Henshaw's smile broadened and he gave Erin a kiss on the cheek. "You look even better than the last time I saw you." He turned his head, studying her. "I don't know, sunnier. How do you do it?"

Erin blushed, then recovered. "Oh, I don't know. Clean living and a man who loves me." Then she glanced down at Leo. "And the best little guy in the world."

Charles said, "I can't argue with the last part. Leo is my favorite grandson."

Leo released his dad's hand and went up to his grandpa, staring up. "I thought I was your only grandson."

Charles released another big laugh. "You're right and that's why you're my favorite." He picked the boy up, tossed him in the air again and caught him, Leo giggling the whole time.

The sound of another car rolling down the driveway interrupted their banter. Everyone stepped to the side. It pulled behind the Volvo, this one a modern red VW Beetle. The engine quieted and both doors opened. The driver struggled to disentangle himself from behind the wheel, working to free his legs, one at a time. When he stood, slightly slouched, Darrell knew why. It was Craig. His older brother came over to Darrell, limping slightly on the right side. He had a broad smile, stretching a brown moustache and goatee.

"Little brother!" Craig called as he grabbed Darrell, who was two inches taller, in a smothering bear hug. The years hadn't robbed much of his brother's strength and Darrell had a little trouble breathing. He pounded twice on Craig's back.

"Enough. I'm glad to see you too," Darrell managed between gasps.

A small woman got out of the passenger side of the Bug and came over to the two brothers, clasped together. "Okay, big guy, everyone knows you're the strong one." She placed a petite hand on Craig's arm. He released Darrell, stumbling before catching himself.

Seeing his brother's limp brought it all back.

The warning from the ghost Darrell didn't heed. His brother falling through the ice of the not-so-frozen lake. Craig suffering from frostbite and losing three toes. Even though it had been almost twenty years—Darrell had been only thirteen at the time—he still felt guilty every time he saw his brother limp. Darrell had never told Craig, or the rest of his family, about how the ghost had warned him not to go near the lake. Probably, Darrell felt most guilty because *he* hadn't gone sledding with his brother—he had hedged his bets—but he'd said nothing to Craig. He tried to tell himself, at least Craig was still here, which was more than the two other kids who had died in the same accident.

"Dianna, you look…" Erin stopped midsentence.

Her interruption dragged Darrell from his guilty memories. His wife was seldom at a loss for words. The two sisters-in-law stood facing each other, both hands clasped. Erin scanned the other woman up and down. Dianna wore cut-off jean shorts and a flowing, pink top that concealed her figure.

The two exchanged looks and Erin continued, "Are you…?"

"Pregnant?" Dianna finished for her. A smile lit up her small, heart-shaped face and she nodded twice. "Yep, almost four months now." She lifted the pink blouse a few inches to show a small but noticeable baby bump.

Craig limped over next to his wife and pointed to her abdomen. "I did that!" He smirked, showing a mouth of white teeth with a gap up front where he lost a tooth playing ice hockey on the same fateful lake. His wife playfully slapped his hand away. He continued, "We've been trying for a while and voila." He glanced over to Darrell. "Well, your wife is an OB nurse, so I guess you know how it works."

Darrell and Erin chuckled and Susan Henshaw joined the circle. "We're thrilled about getting another grandchild," she said, her rosy face beaming.

Charles Henshaw added, "It's about time. We're not getting any younger."

His wife said, "Just hush, Charlie."

Darrell looked from his sister-in-law to his mother. "Mom, you knew? Why didn't you tell me?"

Craig wrapped a protective arm around his wife. "We asked her not to. We told Mom and Dad a little more than a month ago but we knew we'd see you here and wanted to tell you ourselves."

Erin said, "I think it's incredible. Leo's going to get a cousin. Boy or girl, you know yet?"

Craig's face broke into another wide grin inside the Van Dyke combination he sported. His hand rested on his wife's belly. Husband and wife exchanged looks and he said, "We decided we wanted to be surprised. We don't know."

Erin took Dianna by the hand and wrestled her away from her husband's embrace. "Let's talk a little girl talk. A little mother talk, maybe even a little OB nurse talk." The two women walked down the sidewalk toward the water, the two chattering like hens.

Three sharp cracks on the tile stoop halted the homecoming conversations and everyone went quiet. As one, they turned toward the entrance. Aunt Gertrude stood in front of the elaborate double doors, a fancy carved wooden cane in her hand. At first, she simply stood there, her sharp blue-gray eyes examining each visitor, one at a time. Then she announced, "It looks like we're all here. Thank you for coming."

Darrell thought Aunt Gertrude appeared to be in vintage form. Her words sounded almost perfunctory, rather than originating from any actual gratitude. Of course, that could just be his take. Or it could be his Aunt Gertrude. At least, all his extended family was here. That was something.

The mistress, as Salazar called her, continued, "Let's adjourn to the veranda for drinks." Her glance gave the slightest indication of the extensive deck that ran along the west side of the mansion.

As she spoke, two men in servant uniforms moved down the length of the patio, going from table to table, cranking up the bright red umbrellas and brushing off the cushioned chairs. These two were young men, though not as young as the Indian girls, also early twenties, maybe. Their actions appeared deliberate, smooth and coordinated, as if they had performed this task many times before.

Gertrude continued, "We are supposed to have another spectacular sunset over Lake Michigan and the patio seating has the very best view in Saugatuck. Silvio tells me he has a special cocktail prepared for the occasion." Then Gertrude glanced at the slight form of Dianna, who seemed to shrink from the older woman's gaze. "And I've directed him to prepare a mocktail version for you because of your…um, condition."

Dianna squeaked, "Thank you."

Aunt Gertrude knew of Dianna's pregnancy before he and Erin, of course. She would demand nothing less.

Gertrude's gaze roamed over her guests' and settled on Craig. "Rachel and Anna will take all your luggage and get your belongings settled in your rooms."

His brother glanced back at his car. As if on cue, both Indian girls came through the front doors and approached the red Beetle. They pulled suitcases from the back seat and struggled with them up the steps, past Gertrude. "Thank you," he called loud enough for Aunt Gertrude and the servants to hear.

The matriarch flashed a knowing smile. "And, if you'll just leave your keys with your car, Ilya will see it gets settled in the garage."

The man with the brown hair, dark blue eyes and white smile appeared from around the side of the house, right on cue. It all looked perfectly choreographed but something about the young man seemed *off.*

Gertrude finished, "Okay, to the veranda and you can all bring me up-to-date on your lives."

She turned and walked around and down the deck, the cane making loud smacks as if announcing its path.

Chapter 9

"Is that Lake Michigan? It didn't look very far across." Leo pointed to the strip of water flowing in front of them.

Darrell squatted down next to his son. "No, that's the Kalamazoo River and *that* flows into Lake Michigan. And you're right. It's not that far across, only about three hundred feet, about the same length as my football field." He looked into Leo's eyes. "And guess what? We're going to cross it…on that."

They stared at the strange contraption floating toward them on the river.

During a lavish breakfast, complete with fine China, crystal and more food options than they could ever eat, Darrell had asked for tourist suggestions. He had researched some possibilities on the internet but wanted to see what his aunt recommended.

"You should take in the Saugatuck Chain Ferry," his aunt pronounced. "It's the only one of its kind in the country. As a historian, you'd appreciate it."

So, they were here.

The others in the family had visited Saugatuck before and done the tourist thing, so the Darrell Henshaw clan were on their own and had until lunch to do a little exploring. Aunt Gertrude had commanded them to arrive at The Butler Restaurant by 12:45 at the latest. A few major players in the town were throwing a birthday party for Aunt Gertrude at 1:00 and the family was all expected to be there.

Still, the omen about the "missing girls" hung over Darrell, even as he tried to shake it. He couldn't get the pretty face of the teen out of his mind and he knew, or at least sensed, Sheila Birdsong was dead. *And,* whether he wanted to or not, before long he would soon encounter her ghost. He could almost feel that chilling prickle on his neck. Almost. He'd been here before and had learned ignoring the ghost came with its own peril.

He thought the teens working at the mansion might know something but first they'd have to feel comfortable talking with him, though he wasn't sure how he was going to accomplish this. For now, he tried to put it out of his mind and have some simple tourist fun with his wife and son.

Cutting off the road from Aunt Gertrude's place onto County Highway A-2, he easily found his way to the small town. At the entrance, the fanciful wooden sign announcing the town's name, with a colorful artist palette, greeted them. The whole trip, getting from Gertrude's to the center of town, took only fifteen minutes, but exploring the small downtown took as long. As they drove down the tree-lined streets, he lowered the windows and both Darrell and Erin craned their necks left and right, checking out the quaint shops and inviting restaurants. At times, an enticing scent from one of the bistros they passed wafted in through the open windows.

Where Lake Street stopped at the water's edge, the square ahead held an explosion of color. Here, street and square were bordered by two rows of hydrangeas, bursting in the soothing colors of light blue and pink, the scent of honey-vanilla heavy in the air.

The day may have just started but the little town was bustling, and finding a place to park proved to be a challenge. Darrell was pleased to find a parking space on the far end of Water Street and slid the Taurus into the slot. They'd have to walk a bit but, checking his watch, Darrell figured they had enough time to ride the ferry and do some exploring.

A few minutes' stroll brought them to Wicks Park along the water. The scenic park had already drawn a good many visitors, from a group of middle-aged women in an outdoor yoga class—their bright orange mats a stunning contrast to the deep green grass—to a group of kids running and playing around the gazebo to elderly couples sitting on benches, gazing out at the lazy river traffic.

Darrell led his family across the park to the ferry entrance and the three of them stood under the wide sign proclaiming, "SAUGATUCK CHAIN FERRY EST 1857" in bold red letters. They weren't alone. A half a dozen other travelers, including a young family with a baby in a stroller, stood looking across the river. As they waited for the ferry to complete the short journey, Leo stared out at the approaching raft-like contraption, while Darrell checked out the river. It looked deep. A few hundred feet down river, a huge yacht pulled out of a slip and turned, its powerful engine releasing a rush of bubbles on the surface. The ripples in the water indicated the power of the current, likely not easy to manage. He'd had enough experience with being *in* the water to know they all needed to stay on top, in the safety of the ferry.

In another minute, the ferry pulled into the dock, butting against the wooden platform, the crewman having to step on land and drag one side of the boat so it would be level with the boarding deck. Excited, Leo was the first to board, Erin and Darrell right behind, passing beneath the boat's scalloped arch with the same red lettering against a white background edged with stars. It took little time for the passengers to load and pay the fare and, in five minutes, the crewman closed the gate and started cranking. The boat edged back into the water.

As the crewman turned the long metal handle, he called out in a booming voice, "Welcome aboard the Saugatuck Chain Ferry, the only one of its kind in the U.S. I'm your crewman and my name is Ron."

Darrell realized the lad must have uttered these opening words hundreds of times but the young man sounded as if he were really excited to have them aboard. He was taller, even taller than Darrell, with sun-bleached blond hair, a big nose and an even bigger smile. His face looked like it had seen a lot of summer. Darrell thought Ron was in his late teens and this was maybe a college summer job. Remembering his own summer jobs during college at a grocery store and burger joint, he figured this might be a pretty cool gig.

As the crewman cranked the wheel, his smile broadened. "Although this is a new boat and all, this ferry runs pretty much on the same system the first raft did in 1857. This ferry connects this side of Saugatuck to attractions like Oval Beach and Mt. Baldhead. As I turn this crank, it pulls the boat along the chain which runs under and across the river." He pointed into the dark water.

All the passengers looked over the side and watched the chain rise out of the water at one end of the ferry and then drop away at the other end. At the rail, Leo leaned over, staring into the river as the chain rose out of the water to connect with the boat. "That's cool," Leo exclaimed.

Darrell kept a firm grip on his son's shoulders. None of them were wearing life preservers and none were offered when they boarded the craft, so he figured it must not be that dangerous. Still, he was taking no chances.

Darrell asked, "The river doesn't look that wide, as rivers go. Couldn't the settlers wade or swim across or lead their horses across the shortest stretch?"

Ron beamed. "That's a great question. It's true it's not very far across but the river is deep, right here about nineteen feet. And the current here is really strong and the undercurrent can drag you under in a few seconds. Before the ferry, many settlers lost their lives trying to cross the river."

Darrell's grip on his son's shoulder tightened and he stared across. The other shoreline approached quickly. It looked like the ride would only take about five minutes. As they neared the Douglas side, the crewman leveled his gaze at Leo and smiled. "How'd you like to give it a few cranks?" He pointed to the handle.

Leo's eyes shot toward Darrell. "Can I?"

Darrell released the shoulder. "Give it a try."

Leo stepped over and the crewman helped him put both hands on the handle and turn. The rotation brought Leo to his tiptoes but he held on and moved the crank through rotation after rotation. His emerald eyes bright, he looked back over his shoulder and called, "Look Mom, Dad. I'm doing it. I'm moving the boat by myself."

Ron leaned down close to Leo. "And you are doing a great job but how about you let me take us into the dock? It can be a little tricky."

Leo nodded and the crewman took over again. The boy scurried back to his mom and dad. "I did it. I did it."

Erin smiled at her son. "Like a pro. I felt very safe with you at the crank."

The crewman announced, "We're approaching the west shore. From here, it's a short walk to Mt. Baldhead and Oval Beach. Thanks for riding the Saugatuck Chain Ferry."

The ferry butted against the wooden dock and settled. Ron set the crank and then, stepping to the front of the boat, opened the gate. Darrell let the couple with the baby in a stroller exit ahead of them. He said, "Okay, ready to explore Mt. Baldhead? I heard it's only three hundred steps to the top."

Leo glanced from his parents to the long black crank against the white box. "Could we ride again? I want to drive the ferry again." His eyes pleaded.

Darrell realized riding the ferry again would put them on the other side and they'd have to cross again to get to Mt. Baldhead. He glanced at his watch. A round trip would only take fifteen minutes and there would still be enough time to explore Mt. Baldhead. They were on vacation. Why couldn't he do what his son asked?

"You folks stayin or goin'?" Ron asked, his voice sympathetic.

Darrell guessed this was hardly the first-time passengers had to decide.

Leo spoke up to the crewman, "If we go back across, can I crank the handle again? Like I did before?'

Ron smiled. "Sure. It works the same way. We just turn the handle in the opposite direction."

That sealed it. Darrell paid another set of fares and Ron collected from another couple, a pair of acne-faced teens who held hands the whole ride. Within two minutes, he shoved off and the cranking resumed, the clanging of the chain echoing across the water. Once they were about a hundred feet out, Ron grinned at Leo. "Is my assistant ready to take over?"

Leo said, "You bet."

He walked over and the crewman again helped him position his small hands correctly. Within seconds, Leo was cranking away, feet planted on the deck stretching out of his tan shorts and tongue to one side of his mouth, a habit he'd inherited from his mother. When he was at the top of the rotation, his arms extended out of the sleeves of the bright red tee. Because the turning went in the opposite direction, Leo faced the Saugatuck shore, Darrell and Erin a few feet behind, looking that way as well. While he worked, Leo glanced back, beaming like he'd gotten a new toy.

For a minute, their son cranked away, the clang of the chain and the boy's huffing keeping time. Darrell glanced at the approaching shore and noticed a larger crowd had gathered at the dock, maybe fifteen people waiting for the ferry to come in. From his vantage point, they looked like elderly couples, two more young families with strollers and a gaggle of teenage girls.

Abruptly, the cranking halted. Darrell glanced at his son, who'd dropped the handle and stood, staring at the shore. The crewman, sensing something was wrong, stepped next to the box and started cranking again, rattling the chain and pulling the craft closer to the shore.

Leo let the crewman nudge him away from the handle. He stood still, focused on the shore. He raised one hand up and pointed. "Look, Dad. It's…MISSING."

Chapter 10

Missing?

Darrell stared at the small throng crowded around the dock entrance, examining figures, heads, faces. A group of teenagers dressed in swimming outfits stood off to the side, huddled in twos and threes and looking like they were in animated conversation. The half dozen or so girls sported a collection of hair colors from light blonde to brunette to coal black.

He stepped up next to his son, who glanced up at his dad. "See!" His small hand pointed urgently. "That's missing. Only, she must not be missing anymore." His voice held the hope of the innocent.

The handle cranked loudly and the chain rattled out and back into the water. The shore approached in what now looked like slow motion. Darrell strained his eyes, trying to study the crowd of people standing and waiting for the ferry. As he concentrated on the knot of adolescents, he noticed one girl near the back, skin a shade darker than the others, long black hair and brown eyes.

He crouched down next to his son. "You mean that girl, the one in the back?"

Leo nodded, his emerald eyes bright with expectation.

Darrell shook his head. "I don't think that girl is Sheila Birdsong, son." He looked into Leo's face. "She's just a girl who looks a little like her. Similar hair and eyes."

Leo dropped his arm and glanced at his dad. "But why couldn't it be her?"

The ferry crept closer to the shore, now less than fifty feet away. Darrell looked up again at the crowd, growing larger. The darker-skinned girl was still there, but she seemed to slide farther back in the group. As he stared, Darrell thought he saw her image shimmer, just a bit, like a picture on TV going slightly out of focus. He blinked his eyes closed and opened them again, staring at the people on the dock. She was still there, looking the same as the rest now. Most of the others were excited, talking and edging toward the entrance, anxious to board. But *she* stood still and alone at the rear of the group.

Then, Darrell felt the prickle on his neck.

He glanced down at his son whose gaze stayed fixed on the people waiting at the dock. Erin came up beside the two and asked, "Could it be Sheila?"

Darrell whispered, "Not the way you think."

"What?" Erin's gaze went from her son to the group waiting to board, to Darrell.

The crewman announced in a loud, formal voice, "Okay, looks like we got a large group ready to board for the next trip. If you want to ride back across the river, please keep to the right, that would be starboard on a ship." He chuckled. "Everyone exiting on the left, please."

Darrell spoke to his wife, keeping his voice low. "See the gaggle of girls on the right side of the dock." His gaze flicked to the group and back to her.

"Yeah." Her response was quiet and urgent.

"See the pair of girls with blonde hair, one with hot

pink highlights?"

She nodded.

"Now, see the teen behind them, darker skin, black hair?"

The ferry bumped as it struck the dock on one side and Ron jumped off to pull it in, grabbing the tow rope.

Erin stood on her tiptoes to look over the ones in front. She turned back to Darrell, a question in her eyes. "No."

Darrell rested a hand on his son's shoulder again. "Well, we do."

Leo looked up at his dad. "We can just wait till she gets on the ferry and then ask if she is okay. Explain her family is worried about her."

Darrell shook his head. "I don't think she's going to get on this ferry."

"But she's waiting there with everyone else." Leo shot another glance at the crowd milling around the ferry entrance. "Why won't she?" he pouted. "How do you know?"

Erin wrapped an arm around her son's shoulders. "Let's just get off and ask Sheila." Her voice sounded tight. The three of them queued up in line, waiting to exit the boat. As they stepped back on land, Leo's face stared up at the taller people they passed, waiting in line. His gaze kept darting to the right, where the teen girls had clustered. The adolescents passed them, walking in twos and threes. No single teen filed by.

After Darrell, Erin and Leo were able to step around the people pushing to enter the ferry, they came to the area where he and his son had seen the black-haired girl.

No one.

Leo's head pivoted left and right, left and right.

"Where'd she go?" Another sweep of his eyes. "She was just here. It's her, I know it is. She has to be here somewhere." His voice jumped an octave.

Before Darrell could stop him, the boy ran a few steps to the left, checking out the entrance to the ferry dock and the grassy area beyond. Then he scurried to the right, his eyes searching the people milling around the rest of Wicks Park.

Darrell knew what was happening, or he thought he did. Sheila—er, rather her ghost—was leaving breadcrumbs and he was supposed to follow them. He got that heavy feeling in his chest but shook it off. He followed his son's gaze and saw the kids playing on the gazebo. He watched as a long, sleek motorboat, painted white with a rainbow stripe down the side, glided silently down the Kalamazoo River, no doubt headed for Lake Michigan. To the left, a man and a woman headed toward a building painted in a scene reminiscent of Monet or Seurat. When they disappeared inside, he realized it was likely a set of restrooms.

"There she is!" Leo pointed at the restroom building.

Darrell looked in time to see the back of a girl with long black hair walk past the gaily painted building and disappear out of sight beyond the structure.

"Come on," Leo urged.

Before Darrell could stop him, Leo took off running in that direction. Darrell hustled after him, Erin's hurried footsteps right behind. When his son made it past the structure, he stopped, glancing around. Ahead of them, a young family sat together on a blanket, the mother holding up a baby and the father shaking a toy in front of the infant. A pair of teens were throwing a frisbee, one tossing it in long arcs across the green grass while a second ran to catch it, often in an acrobatic stunt. On the boardwalk along the water, an elderly couple sat together, still gazing out to the water, probably the same pair who'd been there when they boarded the ferry. A second wooden bench sat empty.

He brought his gaze back to his son, whose head looked like it was on a swivel. Then Leo turned and looked behind him, his eyes going wide. "It's a restroom. A girl's restroom." He'd seen the sign with the silhouetted figure in a dress and recognized it. "She must've gone in there." His gaze swung to his mom. "Can you go in and check?"

Confusion bloomed on Erin's features. Darrell realized she wouldn't want to let her son down but she knew she wouldn't be able to see Sheila's ghost. Why would Sheila even go inside the restroom building? Erin's gaze went from Darrell to her son. A small smile appeared on her face.

"Sure. I can go check." She patted her son's shoulder. "Probably a good idea to go to the bathroom anyway." She placed a soft hand on Leo's cheek. "Why don't you and Dad go do the same while I check this out?"

Darrell took his son's hand. "Sounds like a good idea. We'll meet you right back here in…five minutes?"

Erin glanced over at the restroom entrance as three women opened the door and went inside. "Better give me ten minutes." She looked down at her son. "If I find Sheila in there, it might be better to talk with her in private first."

"Got it. See you here in a few."

Darrell pulled Leo to the other door. He practically had to drag his son who wanted to keep his eyes focused on the door to the women's restroom. But, when they got inside the men's, Leo was dancing from foot to foot.

"You need to go one or two?"

Leo glanced up at him. "Both."

When they got inside, Darrell's gaze made a sweep of the small lavatory. A row of urinals and two stalls and he was relieved to find them both open. And they were alone, at least for the moment. Inside the first, he helped Leo get situated. "You want me to stay? You want my help?"

Leo looked up at his dad like he was crazy. "I'm a big guy. I can do this myself."

"Okay, okay. I'll be in right next door." Darrell backed out, closed the door, making sure it wouldn't lock. Then he sat down in the next stall.

Darrell tried to figure out how he was going to handle this. He'd planned to take Leo aside last night and talk about Sheila Birdsong or more precisely, her ghost. But he'd had too much to eat and drink, celebrating with his brother and parents. He'd simply forgotten and Erin took Leo to bed while he toasted another round with Craig, the two of them sitting in the deck chairs, recalling the antics of their youth. Now, he had little choice. He was going to have to tell his young five-year-old son about the ugly side of life, at least some of it.

The sound of a flush interrupted his train of thought and recrimination. It was close.

"Leo? You done?"

His words were drowned out by the loud splash of water gushing from a faucet.

"Leo? You there?"

Another flush released a loud rush of water drowning out his son's words.

"What? Leo, you okay?"

"I'm fine, Dad," his son answered.

Darrell started, "Okay, stay there—" but his words were swallowed by the deafening sound of air rushing out of the dryer.

Darrell tried yelling over the cacophony. "Leo, just stay there and I'll be right there."

The blast of air covered most of what his son said. He thought he heard "outside" through the air noise. Darrell hurried his efforts, pulling his pants up, flushing the toilet and exited the stall. His gaze darted around. No Leo. He called, "Leo!" and listened. No answer.

God, he needed to get out there, check on Leo. He looked at his hands and the faucet. He had to wash them, had to. Turning the spigot, he splashed soap on his fingers and ran his hands under the running water. He leaned over and turned off both handles with his elbows. He stepped over to the now finally silent air dryer. He couldn't take time for that and wiped his hands on his tan shorts as he hurried out the door, gaze darting around. No Leo. He looked at the women's door.

"Leo!" he screamed.

His head swiveled like it was on a pivot, right, left, right, left. Same family on a blanket and the young dad's gaze met his. Two teens still tossing frisbee. The elderly couple hadn't moved. The speedboat had disappeared. He glanced back toward Water Street and saw a few tourists drifting in and out of shops across the street. Three cars rolled past without stopping.

Oh, God. No bright red T-shirt.

Chapter 11

He heard Erin chuckling and whirled. Maybe Leo went into the girls' restroom to look for Sheila himself. He'd insisted he was too big to go potty with the girls but still. He'd been so anxious to find Sheila.

"That sounds like fun. Thanks for the advice," Erin said to another woman exiting with her. "We'll need to check it out. I think our son would love it."

Seeing no sign of his son with Erin, Darrell yelled, "Leo!"

Erin hurried over to Darrell then looked past him and around. "What's happened? Where's Leo? He's not with you?"

Darrell managed, "I-I-I don't know. He just came out here." His gaze went on a swivel again. The words came tumbling out. "Leo finished before me and before I could get off, zip up and get out, he'd gone out the door." He shot a glance at the women's restroom then back at his wife. "When I didn't see him right out here, I thought he might've gone into the girls' to check for himself. You didn't see him?"

"Take a breath," she commanded, staring into his face. He did and she continued, "Now Leo exited out of the restroom before you. How much before?"

"Not long." He shook his head. "Less than a minute. Half a minute…I don't know."

"Okay, then he has to be around here. The park isn't

that big. He couldn't have wandered very far. We'll find him."

His wife's words carried a steely calm but he could hear the contained panic in the syllables. She must have seen him stare out at the calm water of the river, a hundred feet away. She added, "Leo has a good head on his shoulders and knows to be careful around water. And remember he's a great swimmer."

He nodded.

Erin continued, "I'll go back in and check just to be sure he didn't duck into a stall when I came out." She glanced around. "Why don't you ask that couple?" She pointed toward the young family on the blanket. "Maybe they saw him."

"Good idea." Darrell nodded. She turned and disappeared through the restroom door. The pit in his stomach hit him. He felt like he was going to vomit. He swallowed hard and walked over to family on the blanket. "Have you seen a little boy in a bright red tee with short auburn hair?"

The father stopped making cooing sounds with the baby and both young mother and father looked up at Darrell, who leaned over. "My son slipped out of the bathroom ahead of me and—" He gulped. "And by the time I got out here, he seemed to have wandered off somewhere. He's five and oh, he has on tan shorts."

The two looked at each other and the father started. "I'm sorry. I was concentrating on Alexis here and—"

The wife cut in. "Red shirt, little guy. Yeah, I saw him just a minute ago." She pointed toward the painted structure. "He was standing there, looking at the door to the women's. I figured he was waiting for his mom." She looked over at her husband. "Then Alexis here started crying and I turned my attention to her." The baby cooed, as if on cue. "When I looked back up, he was gone."

Darrell choked out, "Did you see where he went? Which direction? Anything?"

"I'm sorry, no," the young mother said and sounded like she meant it. "I just figured he went into the restroom. I'm sorry I can't be more help."

"Thank you anyway," Darrell managed to say, fighting the tears that were forcing their way out. He stood straight and looked around, scanning the whole park, searching for a flash of red.

Erin stepped next to him. "No luck in the restroom. Anything from the couple?"

Darrell repeated what the mom had told him.

"Okay, Okay." Erin was nodding up and down. "In these few minutes, Leo couldn't have gone very far." Darrell wasn't sure if these words were trying to persuade him or her. "I'll head south and check that side of the park. Ask around." She pointed toward the gazebo. "You check the north side." She looked past the park at the boats sitting in the slips. "Maybe he wandered out of the park over by the boats. Maybe got interested in the sailboats."

"Okay. Okay," Darrell repeated, his gaze jerking around the north side of the park.

She reached her hand to his. "Don't worry. We'll find him." She met his eyes and held them until he nodded his assent. "If you find him, yell. I'll do the same. I'll meet you back here in—" She glanced at her watch. "Five minutes."

"Five minutes. Got it."

Erin released his hand and hurried off. He watched her for a few seconds, then turned and headed toward the boys throwing the frisbee.

He should've moved faster getting out of the restroom.

He should've skipped washing his hands, damn it. A few germs weren't going to kill him, but his son—. He couldn't think like that.

He ran toward the two guys. All the while, he kept sweeping his gaze, hoping, praying for a sight of that fire engine red shirt. At least, he was glad they'd had him wear that shirt today. By the time he made it to the two boys, he was huffing

One teen grabbed the thrown disc and turned to face Darrell. His buddy took a few quick steps to join them. The second teen, tall, wiry with a thatch of blond hair, asked, "Somethin' wrong?"

Darrell tried to catch his breath. "We're looking for our son. He wandered off a minute ago. He's five and about this tall, short auburn hair." Darrell held his hand up to his waist. "Oh, and he's wearing a bright red shirt."

The teens looked at each other. The taller one said, "I didn't notice anyone like that. Did you, Jamie?"

The second boy shook his head. "Naw, I was too busy trying to catch your lousy throws."

Darrell thanked them then hustled toward the gazebo. He saw another family having lunch on a picnic table closer to the river. A mom, a dad and two pre-teen girls, all four with brown hair and dark eyes. He repeated the story, getting the same response.

His thoughts spiraled out of control. If something happened to his son, he'd go crazy. He loved that boy more than life itself. He knew this all had to do with the missing girls, with Sheila Birdsong. Dead Sheila Birdsong. Right that moment, he wanted to strangle the old Indian in Pennsylvania. He wanted to curse his "gift."

Pulling his flip phone from his pocket, he opened it and stared. Who could he call? His brother? His Dad? Certainly not Aunt Gertrude. 911? How long had it been, five minutes? Less? He shook his head and tried to stamp down his panic. It was too soon for calls. If they didn't find him in the next few minutes, he'd get on the phone.

He fought to control his nerves and think. Like Erin said, Leo was not a silly boy. He would not simply wander off. Whichever direction he went, he was heading there *on purpose*. He went there looking for Shiela. And Leo had no idea how dangerous that could be.

Darrell noticed an older couple on the bench north on the boardwalk facing the river. He doubted they could've seen anything since they had their backs to the park area but still. He was desperate. After a similar exchange, he came away with the same response.

How could a little boy walk right past these people and nobody notice? Darrell breathed in and out, slowly. He tried to calm himself, thinking if someone had tried to grab Leo, the boy would have screamed bloody murder. Erin and he had drilled him about "stranger danger." And they had even made him memorize their secret safe word. *Hasty Hullabaloo*. Leo knew enough to not go with someone who didn't know the safe word.

So, Leo went somewhere on his own.

Darrell moved onto a parking lot which edged the north end of the park, his gaze constantly searching for a splash of red. He saw every other color but not that bright red tee Leo loved. Just beyond the edge of the park and parking lot, white pier after white pier extended from the asphalt, boats bobbing at the docks. Most were small, sleek powerboats and he turned to see a long sailboat, its single mast tall and lonely, putter past down the still Kalamazoo River, powered by an electric motor.

Glancing back towards the boats, he caught a glimpse of something, someone on the foot of the third pier, two arms raised, waving. Three teenagers, two boys and a girl, walked in front of him, jostling each other and laughing. They blocked his view for a few seconds. As soon as they passed, he stared again toward the slips. It wasn't red which caught his eye. It was *her.* Long black hair, deep brown eyes, long slim arms.

He shook his head and stared again. Right then, he didn't care about any damn ghost. He only wanted to find his son. Then, he realized Leo would have followed Sheila, er, Sheila's ghost. He took off in a run toward the peer. He dodged another group of two couples, cutting across his path heading for the boardwalk. He covered the last fifty feet in a few seconds.

He pulled up at the foot of the third white slip. No Sheila. At least, no ghost that he could see. But this *was* where he'd seen her. Panic welled up in his chest again, and his breathing got tight. He tried to take a deep breath but could only cough. This was killing him.

He stood next to a large, sleek boat, gleaming black with a white stripe down the side at the water level. He stared up and saw it rise high above the water. He thought it must be a damn yacht.

What was he doing here? Why would the ghost lure him here? If that was what she did.

He checked the length of the slip and saw no one, nothing. He turned back toward the park, certain he'd missed something, some clue. Glancing at his watch, he realized he'd have to meet Erin at the restroom building in another minute. And tell her he'd failed. Maybe she'd have better news. Maybe she'd be there with Leo, all smiles. He needed to get going. He didn't want her worrying about him, too.

He took one step from the dock onto the blacktop and heard, "Have you seen Sheila? A pretty Indian girl?"

The question came from the yacht behind him.

Chapter 12

Darrell spun around, his breath catching in his throat. He stared in the direction the words came from. Up. He'd know that voice anywhere.

His gaze raked the sailboat. He didn't see Leo, but he was sure his son's voice had come from the direction of the craft. The way the boat was berthed, only the stern deck was visible from the park area. That appeared to be empty.

"She must've come this way. You sure you didn't see her?" Leo asked. "She has this long black hair."

Then a man's voice. "Son, I don't know what you're talking about. We pulled in a few minutes ago." A pause. "Where are your parents? Do they know you're here?"

The voices were definitely coming from the yacht. Darrell hurried down the length of the slip and the aft deck came into view, just beyond the end of the pier. The sight he saw almost made him weep. Leo's head was barely visible above the railing.

"They do now," Darrell called loud enough to be heard on board.

Leo walked over to the rail and looked down. "Hey, Dad," he called, not a care in the world.

"Hey, son," Darrell managed, fighting to keep the pent-up fear out of his voice. Then, remembering their plan to meet at the restroom, he hollered back toward the park at the top of his lungs, "Erin, I found him."

The two couples he'd run past turned and stared at him. He ignored them.

"We're over here on the dock," he yelled toward the park.

After a beat, he heard, "I got it. Headed that way."

Darrell turned back. He climbed the three wooden stairs that brought him to the deck and stepped on board. Weak-kneed, he walked over to Leo and wrapped him in his arms. He managed, "Hey," and fought back tears.

A scent caught his attention, something out of place. Leo in hand, he walked over to where an older man sat, smoking a cigar, a tumbler half full of a golden liquid on the table in front of him. The strong aroma of the smoldering ash floated across the deck.

Darrell said, "I apologize if my son was bothering you."

The man laughed nervously. "No bother. Just figured he was lost."

Leo protested, "I wadn't lost. I saw Sheila come—"

Darrell cut him off. "Leo, Come on. Let's go meet your mom. She was worried about you."

The captain pointed the cigar at Leo. "No problem. You have quite an articulate young man."

Leo turned back to the man and Darrell followed his son's gaze. He looked to be in his mid-fifties, with a few fringes of gray hiding within a head of black hair beneath the white captain's hat. Even though he was sitting, Darrell judged him to be maybe six feet, his long legs extending beyond the chair. He had a few wrinkles across his forehead and around blue-gray eyes. The man grinned and Darrell noticed perfect white teeth and a straight aquiline nose, both of which looked too good to be natural.

Darrell uttered a nervous laugh. "You mean my prodigal son." He roughed the boy's hair. "Thank you for entertaining him, at least till I could find him." Then remembering his manners, he said, "I'm Darrell Henshaw and this is my wandering son, Leo."

The man's eyes brightened, turning more blue than gray. "Darrell Henshaw. Gertrude Embry's nephew?"

Darrell shrugged. "Guilty as charged."

"There you are. Ahoy," Erin called from the blacktopped parking lot, almost out of breath. She hurried across to the slip and up the stairs to the deck. "Permission to come aboard?" she directed the last to the captain.

The man gave a hearty laugh. "Of course."

Darrell realized, in his worry about Leo, he'd completely forgotten about shipboard protocol. He said, "And this is Erin, my wife and Leo's mom."

Erin scurried past Darrell and hugged her son. Then she straightened up. "I see you found another sailboat, son."

Leo smiled at his mom. "Yeah and it's even bigger than ours."

The man stood up and reached out a hand. "I'm Dwight Newsom." He shook Darrell's hand first, then Erin's. Leo stepped up and extended a hand and Newsom shook it as well, chuckling.

"Did I hear voices? Do we have visitors, Dwight?" a high-pitched voice called. A woman came through the door of the cabin. She looked to be younger than her husband by at least a decade. She had a halo of blonde hair, large plump lips and sapphire eyes accented with blue eye shadow. A white knit beach dress showed off a still shapely figure.

"Cynthia, this is Darrell Henshaw, Gertrude's nephew from Maryland. And this is his family, Erin and little Leo."

"Small world. I'm Cynthia Newsom, his better half," she laughed as if it were an old joke.

Dwight Newsom explained, "Darrell, your uncle was a mentor of mine. Helped me get started in shipping. I wouldn't be where I am today without his help." He looked down and continued, "He died so young, but we've stayed in touch with Gertrude over the years."

Cynthia squeaked, "That's why we're here. For Gertrude's eightieth birthday bash. Such a wonderful woman." Her eyes got large. "Are you guys here for the same reason?"

Before Darrell could figure out how to respond, Erin answered, "We wouldn't miss it. We drove across the country to get here."

Dwight Newsom nodded, "That's right. Gertrude told us you were this super football coach in Maryland. Had amassed this incredible record."

Darrell was again surprised his aunt knew about his coaching *and* that she had bragged to her friends. "Football coach, yes. Not sure about the super."

Erin placed a hand on Darrell's shoulder. "Don't let him fool you. He really is quite the coach. Forty-eight and six in the last five seasons. Taken his team to the regionals four years in a row."

"Impressive," Newsom added.

Leo tugged on Darrell's pant leg and he leaned down to his son. "You okay?"

"I have to go to the bathroom," Leo whispered.

"Again?"

Leo nodded. Darrell checked his watch. It had been

less than ten minutes since he left the restroom. A five-year-old's bladder. He straightened up. "Okay. Looks like we need to go. My son needs to use the facilities. Thanks again for keeping him safe."

"Nonsense," Cynthia blurted. "We have a perfectly good head right here on the ship. Come on, I'll show him."

Leo looked at his mom and dad, a question on his face. Darrell fought down a surge of panic and glanced at his wife. Erin peered through the open door to the interior, then met his gaze. She shrugged as if to say it'll be all right, a mom smile on her face. "Go ahead. We'll wait right here for you."

Cynthia and Leo disappeared through the cabin door. Darrell and Erin watched them go then she turned to Newsom. "You have a beautiful boat here. A boat this size, I'd guess a Mercedes Benz engine, doing what, seventy-five horsepower?"

Newsom straightened. "You know your crafts. It's a Hickney 55-footer. You pilot?"

Erin chuckled. "Nothing this grand. My family has an Irwin Citation 34 back on the Chesapeake."

Darrell said, "She's too modest. Erin is quite the sailor."

Newsom appeared to eye her up and down, his mouth breaking into a grin. "And what do you do, Erin, when you're not navigating the Chesapeake?"

Erin's gaze went back to the cabin door and she smiled. "I'm an OB nurse in Maryland."

Right then, Leo burst through the door onto the deck, his eyes wide. "Dad, I saw her! I just saw her. Sheila's here, right here on the boat!"

Chapter 13

Darrell glanced from his son to Dwight Newson, whose facial expressions morphed. He watched different emotions race across the stranger's features—confusion, worry, suspicion? Unsure, he figured he better explain. "Sorry. When we stopped at Kalamazoo on our drive here, we saw some posters about missing teens. You know the ones they put up at gas stations? Well, Leo read about this one girl, Sheila, and ever since he read about her, he *really* wants to find her. He thinks he sees her sometimes."

Even as the words tumbled out of his mouth, he heard his own hypocrisy. *He* thought he had seen the missing girl—or, rather her ghost—right before he stumbled into the right spot to hear his son's voice.

The cabin door opened and Cynthia slipped out, followed by a girl in an adapted steward uniform, white blouse and short navy skirt.

"See, Dad?" Leo whispered, pointing.

The steward looked young, maybe mid-teens. This girl had the amber skin of the Natives, deep brown eyes and long, straight dark hair, though Darrell realized it was more dark brown than coal black like the teen pictured on the flyer. Darrell thought he saw a resemblance but didn't know if the two girls were related or he simply couldn't distinguish the subtle differences in Native Indians.

"Oh, I get it." A broad smile crossed Newsom's face. "Leo must've seen Sarah and thought she was someone else."

In a tentative movement, the girl raised her hand and glanced toward Newson. When she did, Darrell noticed she wore a multi-colored bracelet. Not fancy, like it was hand woven with colors of blue, purple and white. The young woman asked in a quiet voice, "Is there anything else I can get for you before I go ashore, Mr. Newsom?"

Newsom said, his voice with a slight edge. "Sarah, don't be rude. Say hi to Darrell, Erin and little Leo…who mistook you for someone else."

"Hi, glad to meet you," the girl servant said, barely above a breath, then turned back to Newsom.

He waved her away. "No, we're fine. We simply need to change and head over to The Butler for Gertrude's birthday party." Newsom turned to Darrell. "I guess we'll see you there."

"I guess you will. I think that's our cue to leave." Darrell looked at his watch. "See you in about an hour." He took his son's hand and headed for the steps.

Erin joined him but called back, "Thanks for the save. I mean, with Leo."

The man grinned broadly under his captain's hat. "Any time…for a fellow sailor."

Cynthia piped up, "Your little Leo was no trouble at all. He reminds us of our grandson, Bradley, our daughter's boy. They're over in Vermont and we don't see them that much. Bradley was about Leo's age last time we saw him."

"Thanks again," Erin acknowledged them with a wave.

They went down the three steps, traveled the length

of the slip and headed back across the asphalt and into the park. Darrell felt eyes on his back but fought the urge to glance over his shoulder to see if the Newsoms were watching. Looking across, he noticed Erin kept her face forward as well. When they were back onto the grass of the park and far enough away he was certain his voice wouldn't carry back to the boat, he stopped and pulled Leo in close to him. Erin closed the huddle and they stood there for a moment, none of them talking.

Smothered between his mom and dad, Leo squeaked out, "Am I in trouble?"

Darrell struggled to answer because he needed to brush tears out of his eyes. "You gave us a real scare," he finally managed when he trusted his voice enough to speak.

Leo picked up on his dad's anxiety and started to tear up. "I didn't mean to. When I came out of the restroom, I was planning to wait for you, I was." He looked up, his face determined even through the tears on his cheeks. "But then, I saw her, Sheila. and I went over to talk with her. Then, then—"

Darrell said, "Hold up a minute." He looked around and spotted an empty picnic table sitting in the shade of an ancient tree. "Let's go over there and sit down so we can all talk."

Without waiting, he led his son and wife to the wooden table. Erin sat next to Leo and Darrell sat on the opposite side, leaning across so their faces would be close together. As they settled in, his gaze took in the surrounding park. It was around noon and most of the tourists must've headed to restaurants for lunch. There were a few kids still playing around the gazebo, one doing a frantic air guitar. This would have to do.

This was not how he expected to have the conversation with his son. How could he convey to a five-year-old the depravity of some people, without traumatizing him? Yet somehow, Darrell had to explain the gift he and his son had, seeing ghosts, often comes with strings attached. And those strings can get them entangled in serious danger. He believed Leo had seen Sheila's ghost—just as Darrell had—and followed her to the yacht, though right now he had no idea why. How could he share all this? How much could a five-year-old comprehend? He wished he'd paid better attention in those Child Development classes he'd taken in college.

He decided he'd let Leo start and follow his lead.

He glanced across the picnic table and saw Erin wrap her arm around Leo's shoulders and give them a gentle squeeze. Darrell said, "Why don't you just tell us what happened…from the beginning."

Leo nodded twice, up and down, and started in. "Well, after we saw Sheila from the ferry and then couldn't find her when we got off, I felt bad. I really want to help her, Dad. So, after I went to the bathroom and washed my hands, I went outside to wait for you." His glance wandered over to the restroom building painted with the image of a child and his mom holding an umbrella. Then he looked at his parents, first Erin and then Darrell. "While I was waiting for you, I saw her again, over there." He pointed back to a spot on the blacktopped space off the park. "I know you told me to wait but I was afraid I was going to miss her again, so I walked over there."

He stopped and stared at his dad. "I didn't want you to worry so I glanced back to tell you where I was. You know when you came out of the bathroom. Only you weren't out yet. I didn't know what to do. I'm sorry." Leo's words sounded desperate.

Erin put her hand atop his and gave him that heart-warming smile of hers. "Don't worry. We're not mad at you. Go ahead and tell us what happened next, okay?"

Leo nodded again. "I'll try…but I'm not sure." His eyes went from one parent to the other. "When I turned back around from checking on you and looked at where Sheila had been, she wasn't there. It was like she…disappeared. Again, just like at the ferry dock. I looked everywhere, back toward the bathroom and then across the park. I couldn't find her anywhere."

His little head did an imitation of the swivel he was describing. If Darrell hadn't been so tense about the entire situation, he might've found it funny.

"Then I saw her over on the third slip and she waved at me. You know, like hello?" He raised his arm and did a wiggle with his hand to demonstrate. "So I ran over to the slip but—" He stopped.

"But what?" Erin coaxed, her voice gentle.

"But when I got there, I couldn't find her again. Then I saw the man up on the boat and thought he might've seen her, so I went up and asked him." The tears welled back up and Leo muttered, "I guess I messed up. I'm sorry." He started crying full now.

Erin squeezed his shoulders. "You are one brave guy!" She kissed him on the cheek. That seemed to help and he sniffed his tears back, staring up at his mom and dad.

Then she glanced up at Darrell as if to say, "You're on!"

Chapter 14

Darrell swallowed hard again. Over the years, parents had told him they could never face a classroom full of teenagers and try to motivate them to learn. While he didn't disagree, that task was easy compared to this. God, where could he start?

He took a slow breath. "Son, you know Mom and I call you a big guy?"

Leo squared his tiny shoulders. "I am a big guy."

"That is true and you proved it today." He met his son's eyes. "When you're big, when you're older, you have to deal with things little kids don't have to worry about."

"Like what?"

Darrell couldn't think of a simple way to answer, so he tried another approach. "Remember when we explained about Monica?"

"You mean my friend at the playground others can't see?"

Darrell nodded. "Do you remember we explained Monica had died in a car accident? And since she didn't get to play that much on the playground when she was alive, she came back to play with you?"

Leo nodded hard. "She's a ghost and that's why the other kids can't see her." He stuck his chest out. "But you and I can see ghosts." He looked up at his mom and dad. "That's why I was excited to see if Great Aunt

Gertrude's house was haunted. I thought maybe I'd see some ghosts there."

In spite of everything, Darrell found himself chuckling at his son's enthusiasm. "We haven't seen any yet. We'll have to see if we find any ghosts in that old mansion. I wouldn't be surprised, though." He shifted his head so his eyes were directly across from his son's. "But here's the thing. I—and you—can't see ghosts unless they want us to see them. And when they do, they usually have a reason."

"You mean like Monica wanting to play with me?"

"Kind of." Darrell glanced at Erin and sighed. He looked back at his son. "Sometimes when ghosts show themselves to us, it can get us in trouble. It can become...dangerous."

Leo frowned, the question evident in his eyes. "You mean some ghosts are trouble? Like they're bad?"

"Yes," Darrell answered, a little too quickly. Then he added, "No, no, not exactly. They might be good but can still get us, you and me, in trouble."

"How?"

This was not going the way Darrell hoped. Leo was an intelligent and inquisitive child but he was only five. He might be a grown-up five, but he was still *five*. The concepts of life and death, good and evil were too much for him to grasp.

Darrell glanced around the park. All the others went about their own business. The young family still lounged on the blanket. The two teens returned to their acrobatics with the frisbee. No one seemed to pay them any attention. At least that was good. Darrell studied his son's face and decided he needed to try something else.

"Son, I hate to say this but, when families put up

flyers saying their child is missing…" He stopped and took a quick breath. "They often find out the kid died or had been killed. Not always, but it occurs far too often."

He wasn't sure if Leo understood but he was in this far. He needed to keep going. "I'm afraid that's what *may* have happened to Sheila." He stopped and waited to see how Leo would react.

The boy shook his head hard, red hair flipping with the motion. "But we just saw her, standing there with all the other people waiting for the ferry."

Erin placed a hand on his arm. "When you and Dad could see Sheila among the crowd, I…I couldn't see her. I don't think anyone else could either."

Leo's gaze flicked from his dad to his mom. "You mean, Sheila's a, a, a…ghost?" The word caught in his throat.

Darrell said, "I think so, yes."

"So, when I saw her when I came out of the restroom, I was seeing a ghost?"

"Yes, probably."

Leo went silent and dropped his gaze to the tabletop. He stuck the edge of his tongue out of the corner of his mouth and Darrell knew the boy was trying to think. Darrell didn't say anymore, waiting for his son to process, as much as his five-year-old brain could. After a moment, Leo's eyes came up and he looked at his dad, tongue back in place.

"You said ghosts don't let us see them unless they want us to?"

Darrell nodded again. "Pretty much. Yeah."

Leo was nodding now. "Well, that means Sheila wants us to see her. Why? You said she has a reason."

Darrell was amazed at his little boy. Leo was getting

to it.

He heaved another slow breath. "I'm afraid something's happened to Sheila, something bad, and she wants us to find out what."

Leo glanced over to the slip where he'd no doubt seen Sheila's image—and where Darrell saw her too. He brought his gaze back to his dad. "Then, we need to help her."

Darrell let out a laugh. "It's not that simple…and we have to be careful."

Erin pulled her son in close. "We want you to know we're proud of you. You have a special gift, just like your dad." She said these words to his hair as he cuddled against her. "But you can't run off like you did. You scared us."

Leo dropped his head. "Okay."

"And we don't want you to tell anyone else about this. This is our family secret. Anytime you see something, a ghost, you need to tell your dad or me. We'll know what to do. How to protect you."

Leo looked from his mom to his dad, a worried look on his face. "Protect me?"

Darrell reached across the wooden table and took his son's hand. "If something happened to Sheila, something bad, then most likely, some bad people did something to her." He looked to see if his son's face registered understanding.

"That's terrible."

"It *is* terrible. And if someone did something bad to her, they won't like us asking questions. So, we have to be careful."

Leo nodded, looking serious beyond his age. "I still think we need to help Sheila."

Erin took her son's face in her hands. "I'm proud of you for wanting to help. It shows you are a good person and we love you for that."

Darrell said, "I want to help Sheila too, though I'm not sure how we're going to do that right now." Darrell glanced at his watch. "That will have to keep till later. We need to make our way over to Aunt Gertrude's party."

As they walked down Water Street, Leo holding the hands of both Mom and Dad, Darrell's tension eased, at least about Leo. Still, he couldn't help it. His brain was reeling, jumping to the next questions.

Why had Sheila appeared at Wicks Park? Did something happen here?

Was there a reason she led Leo over to the slip?

He glanced down at his son, skipping across the sidewalk. How was he going to protect Leo if the ghost dragged him into the whole thing?

Chapter 15

"Interesting history, isn't it?" a familiar voice called from behind.

Darrell turned to see his brother Craig limp up next to him, a grin above the goatee. His wife Dianna hurried over to Erin and Leo. The pregnant woman leaned down and hugged their son, who stared at the small baby bump.

Arriving a few minutes ahead of their required time, Darrell, Erin and Leo had stopped at the small park outside the restaurant, first to enjoy the fragrant aroma of shimmering pink and blue hydrangeas. Then Darrell had noticed the display with the historical photos and descriptions. He was about halfway through the information when Craig grabbed his attention.

Leo whispered to his mom, though loud enough for all four adults to hear. "Is she fat?" He pointed to Dianna's belly.

Erin giggled. "Leo, it's not polite to say things like that, but no. Aunt Dianna and Uncle Craig are having a baby."

The boy's eyes got big. "A baby! A boy like me?"

"They don't know," Erin said. "We'll just have to wait and see."

"I see you're checking out the history of the old place." Craig pointed to the display. "Do you ever take off your historian hat?"

Darrell tapped the sign. "Well, did you know this

building dates back to 1890?"

Craig's eyebrows rose. "I wonder if Aunt Gertrude was at the groundbreaking?"

Darrell couldn't keep the smile off his face. "We are here to celebrate her birthday. Maybe we can ask her."

Craig smirked. "You first."

Darrell said, "Well, then did you know this restaurant used to be a gristmill, then a three-story hotel?"

Craig wrapped an arm around his wife. "As a matter of fact, I did. In fact, Di and I spent a romantic weekend here a couple years ago in one of the great B & B's. Can't remember the name."

Dianna popped up, "The Rosemont Inn." She smiled up at Craig. "Beautiful place with a great view of Lake Michigan. Your brother did good on that one."

Craig gave his wife's shoulders a gentle squeeze. "Yeah, we did the touristy thing then. Took the tour on the Star of Saugatuck and even rode the chain ferry."

Leo said, "We rode the ferry today. It was fun. They let me crank the chain!"

"Way to go, little man." Craig held his hand up in a high five position. Leo hesitated at first, then slapped his palm to Craig's. Both laughed.

Dianna said, "Make sure you make time for the Saugatuck Dune Ride. It's great fun and Leo is going to love it." She glanced down at the boy. "Unless he gets scared easy."

Leo squared his small shoulders. "Nope. Mom and Dad say I'm a big guy."

Dianna chuckled. "I'm sure you are."

Erin glanced at her watch. "I hate to break this up but I think we better get in there." She pointed to the restaurant. "I suspect Aunt Gertrude will have your hides if we're late."

The man at the podium cleared his voice. "Gertrude Embry may be celebrating her eightieth birthday, but I think we can all admit she has aged well, like fine wine. In her time with us, this remarkable woman has made a real difference, in our town, in our area and in our lives. When her husband Dave died years ago, we were all devastated. But after his death, Gertrude Embry picked up the pieces and moved on."

Darrell kept his face forward and eyes toward the stage but he tuned out the speaker. He couldn't help it. This was the fourth, or fifth local—he'd lost track—to pay tribute to his aunt.

This one had been introduced as Roger Herrold, president of Capstone Shipping, another obese, older man with a bald head, and heavily tanned hands and face as if he spent a lot of time in the sun. He claimed to have Dave Embry to thank for getting him into shipping as well, and making him a fortune. Dressed as if he were ready for a two-day sail, blue blazer over blue and white striped shirt and white slacks, he recalled an anecdote when a younger Gertrude and Dave had partied with him on his yacht. The audience roared in laughter and Darrell heard his aunt call, "You better watch it, Roger, or I'll start telling stories on you." This brought another round of raucous laughter.

Darrell didn't know any of the speakers, except for Dwight Newsom, the man they'd met on the yacht earlier this morning. He'd been the second to honor his aunt. A few more declarations and he thought this group might put her up for sainthood.

The praise and accolades coming from the podium

simply didn't jive with his distant memories of his aunt. His memories of her—taciturn, stern, always right—were one-hundred-eighty degrees from the warm and funny tributes coming from the microphone. Of course, he had to admit his memories were twenty years old and then seen through the eyes of a mischievous youth. Still, his mom had asked them to be here for the big day—though it was more like a big week—and he was glad to be able to give Erin and Leo a glimpse of *his* Michigan. And Saugatuck looked to be quite an interesting town.

Of course, he couldn't yet figure how the town and missing girls intersected but sensed more was coming.

Needing some distraction, he glanced around the room. His aunt had commandeered much of the famous restaurant for the event. Dark, wood-paneled walls and subdued lighting created a serious, sophisticated ambiance, even in the summer midafternoon. From the vintage maps to the wooden helm, the restaurant carried out the nautical theme well.

White-coated waiters moved about the space, silently clearing dishes and refilling drinks from the extensive bar. Wanting to keep his wits about him, Darrell had stayed with only two beers, though he eyed the cocktails being delivered with envy. And even he had to admit the clam chowder and fried Lake perch had been excellent. The restaurant had even prepared chicken fingers for his son. In fact, the food had gone down far more easily than the tributes.

Leo highjacked his distracted train of thoughts. In the middle of the latest speech, his son tugged on his dad's shirt sleeve and Darrell leaned close. "I got to go to the…you know, the bathroom," the boy whispered.

"Again? Now?" Darrell whispered back.

Leo lowered a hand to his crotch. "Yeah, now."

Fortunately, Erin had had the foresight to snag a table on the side of the room, so any unplanned exit would be less noticeable. After a quiet word to his wife, he took his son's hand and led him down the left side past a long, polished bar, where the chairs sat silent, nudged against the edge. Behind the bar, sparkling bottles of liquor stood perfectly aligned on three stacked shelves, their blue, brown and silver colors beckoning under the spotlights. He and Leo turned right and headed toward the door with the universal men's room stick symbol.

At the door, Leo looked up at his dad. "I can do this myself."

Darrell shook his head. "Oh, no. If I let you out of my sight, your mom will kill me." He held the door open and followed his son in. They both did their thing—Leo proud to be able to use the urinal and pee, though he had to stand on his tiptoes to do it. They washed their hands and headed out the way they'd come. Darrell was hoping to get back before their absence was noticed.

When he turned to head back toward the newest speaker, Leo stopped him with another tug, on his shorts this time. Darrell met his son's eyes, whose gaze had slid to the rear. Leo said, in an urgent half-whisper, "It's them. The girls who look like missing." He pointed back toward the darkened entryway.

Darrell didn't see them at first. The two girls—he struggled to recall their names and then remembered, Anna and Rachel—stood huddled together in the near darkness, their amber skin and dark hair making them almost invisible in the half-light. What figures and complexions he could make out gave them an appearance even more similar to the photo of Sheila Birdsong, the missing girl from the poster. The two teens leaned against the wall in a relaxed posture.

Darrell glanced back toward the lunch celebration. He could pick up bits and pieces of another litany of his aunt's good deeds, this time from the president of the local Rotary Club. Darrell figured if they were gone a few more minutes, they wouldn't be missed. He looked down at his son and saw the enthusiasm in the bright young face. He said, "Let's go talk with them."

Taking Leo's hand, the two of them walked across the foyer and came up to the Indian girls. Seeing Darrell approach, both girls straightened, standing stiff, almost at attention, as if they were worried they'd get caught lounging.

Darrell tried for nonchalance. "Hey, Anna, Rachel."

"Sir," both girls responded but didn't ease their stance. The dark eyes exchanged some silent agreement.

Leo looked up at the girls. "I like your hair," he said, his head turning from one teen to the other. "Did it take a long time to grow that long?"

Both teens released a small grin and the younger one—Rachel?—said, "Pretty long. A few years, at least."

Leo eyed the heads of both girls. "I'd be worried it would get too tangled. I hate it when my mom has to comb out the knots in my hair. It makes me cry sometimes." He patted the top of his head. "And my hair isn't near as long as yours."

"We like it like this. It's the way our mothers and grandmothers have worn their hair." Rachel ran a hand down the back of her head. "It's one of the few traditions we've been able to keep." She smiled down at Leo. "But yeah, it can get pretty tangled up, especially when we're working."

Darrell shot a quick glance toward the interior and brought it back to the teens. "Girls, could we ask you a few questions?"

The two Indians exchanged nervous looks. After a bit, Anna said, "I guess."

He pulled the flyer from his pocket, opened it up and handed it to the older girl. He placed a hand on Leo's shoulder. "We saw this flyer about this missing girl at a store in Kalamazoo."

Leo pointed a small index finger at himself. "I'm the one who saw it."

Darrell thought he saw the girls' expressions soften. He said, "Well, since she is from the Gun Lake Tribe, the same as you, we wondered if you know her."

Neither girl spoke and they both shifted from one foot to the other. Their glances traveled to the interior of the restaurant. Darrell looked back. No change. The audience chuckled at the speaker's comment and then went silent again. He turned back to the girls.

Anna nodded once. "Yeah, we knew her. Know her."

He caught the slip. "Did you know her from the tribe? From school? Were you friends?"

The teens exchanged another furtive glance. After a beat, Anna spoke. "We knew her from school and from around."

Darrell studied her face, then the face of Rachel. He read anxiety, he thought, and fear, maybe. He pushed, "Do you know what happened to her? Where she went?"

Anna started shaking her head before Darrell finished. Then Rachel stared at her sister, a question in her eyes. Anna stared back then looked at Darrell. Her face in a scowl, she asked, "Why are you asking questions about Sheila? Why would you care about her?"

Before Darrell could answer, Leo chimed in, "We're worried about her. Dad said she's been missing for a few weeks." He pointed to the flyer Anna still held in her hand. "Dad said she could be in trouble and we want to help her. If we can."

The teens exchanged looks again and Rachel muttered something in a language Darrell couldn't understand but he couldn't miss the plea in the younger girl's eyes.

After another pause—with some polite applause floating in from the gathering—Anna whispered, "We don't know what happened to her." Her gaze swept toward the crowd and back to Darrell again. "She used to work for Mrs. Embry."

"What?" The word came out of his mouth before he realized it, and it came out too loud.

Anna shot another glance toward the gathered crowd and brought her eyes back. "Yeah, she had the job we're doing now. She and another girl, Shanea, worked for Mr. Salazar and Mrs. Embry before us."

Darrell was pretty certain that was the name on another MISSING poster in Kalamazoo. He thought of several more questions to ask, like what did this Shanea look like and how old was she, but realized he had little time. Instead he asked, "What happened? They get fired? Quit?"

"Shanea was gone first. Mr. Salazar said she quit, but Sheila told us Shanea wouldn't have quit. She needed the money. A few weeks later, Sheila supposedly quit."

Darrell shook his head, trying to process all this. The

people at the birthday celebration seemed to be stirring and he realized he had little time left. Then, the crowd erupted in major applause and he saw people standing up. He knew they'd have company any minute and asked, "When did all this happen?"

Anna shook her head and had to speak up because of the noise of the crowd. She leaned closer. "I don't know when Shanea left, but I know when Sheila left because Salazar came to the tribal elders and asked for new workers. That's how we got the job." She looked over at Rachel.

Two couples passed the four of them, smiling at Leo. Darrell smiled back and said, "Restroom." Grinning, the couples nodded and passed out the door. He knew he was out of time. To the teens, he asked, "When was that? When did you start the job?"

More people kept exiting past their group and he could see the rising panic in both teens' features. Still, Anna leaned in even closer. In a level barely above a whisper, she said, "Two weeks before Sheila went missing."

Darrell glanced back into the restaurant and saw Salazar shaking hands, then heading their way. He looked back at both Indian teens and whispered, "Do you know what happened to Sheila?"

Both girls had followed his gaze and no doubt recognized Salazar approaching them and Darrell watched apprehension reignite on their faces. "Anna?" he pressed. "Rachel?"

The two brought their gaze back to Darrell and then exchanged a look. He said, "Please."

Anna started walking toward her approaching boss and Rachel followed behind, looking worried. While still within earshot, without turning around, Anna said, "Well, she didn't run away."

Chapter 16

"How much longer?" Leo whined. "I can't wait to ride in one of the big dune buggies." He pointed at the three converted "cars," sitting in the bays next to the walkway.

"I think we'll be in the next group," Darrell said, trying to placate his son.

Last night, after he'd confided in Erin what the girls shared, she counseled patience and argued for a little family fun. Hesitant at first, he agreed to take them all on the Saugatuck Dune Ride Erin had heard about and Dianna had mentioned. After breakfast, the three of them made their way to the attraction, a little out of town. As they stood there waiting in line, questions about the fate of the missing girls hounded Darrell.

The missing Indian girls worked for his Aunt Gertrude? At least two of them?

Both girls went missing not very long after leaving her employ?

How the hell could he even raise these questions with his aunt?

He probably would have lost himself in the darkness of the questions had it not been for his son. As they stood waiting on the porch, Leo kept jumping from one foot to the other on the wooden boards.

Erin asked, "You need to go potty?"

Leo scowled at her. "Mom, it's the bathroom. No,

Dad had me go before we left Great Aunt Gertrude's. I just can't wait to ride." Leo's gaze went to the huge dune buggy and came back to his dad. "How much longer?" he repeated.

"Not much longer, son." Then he had an idea. "Start counting. I bet we'll be called before you reach fifty."

Darrell and Erin had been helping their son learn his numbers and he'd recently bragged about being able to count to a hundred. Leo started, his voice, soft, "One, two, three, four, five—"

While his son counted, Darrell stared out at the dune buggies though the name hardly did them justice. Each vehicle was more the size of a huge 4 x 4 truck mounted on monster wheels, with the top sheared off. The "buggy" had been converted to accommodate five rows of seats which held twenty passengers, four to a row.

"Those holding tickets for ten o'clock, you're up," piped up the receptionist. "Ten o'clock can board now." She pointed to the third buggy.

"That's us," Erin said, holding up the tickets.

Leo stopped counting. He'd reached thirty-seven. He hollered, "Whoopee," and charged toward the waiting vehicles. Erin and Darrell hustled behind their son. After the three of them and the other passengers climbed in, their driver, who said his name was Jeff, introduced himself and went over the warnings and instructions. Then he called, "Y'all hold on now. It's goin' to be a great ride." The man's face and arms looked leathery and from his appearance and speech, Darrell figured he'd been an outsider, maybe from the UP.

They were off. As they rode up and down the hills, swaying together as the buggy maneuvered through the course, it felt almost magical. The open-air vehicle practically sailed through the enormous mounds of sand, navigating a twisty route.

Of course, Erin was right and the distraction worked. As he was bouncing down the dunes at a breakneck speed, the questions, which had haunted him, slid back into his subconscious. Erin sat close by in the back seat of the adapted car with their son snug between them. Every rise they crested, every hill they barreled down, every curve they swung around—Leo gave out a yelp of sheer joy and Darrell's anxiety eased, at least for a while.

Ahead, the path of golden sand snaked between green hillsides covered with grass and trees. Coming over the next rise, Darrell stared ahead and could see the ruts the overinflated tires hugged as they went around bends and up and down rises. By staying in the channels, the vehicle could race up and down, around and over the dunes, but could always keep the wheels anchored in the ruts. It was like a roller coaster ride through woods, grassy slopes and golden mounds of sand with incredible vistas around every corner. But rather than a sixty- or ninety-second ride, theirs went on for close to fifteen minutes, before they stopped.

When the vehicle finally halted, they had crested a tall hill and sat on what looked like a huge, flat expanse of sand with a few scrub bushes and three tall trees visible. For what looked like miles, hills and mounds of sands flowed in every direction, like granular waves. The mineral smell of the sand was strong with only a hint of the lake in the air.

Jeff, the driver, turned in his seat. "This here is a great place to check out the terrain, stretch your legs and snap a few photos. I'll even take the pitchers if you'd like. A little later, I'll give ya a history lesson or two, maybe tell ya something ya didn't know about our land by the lake."

A pair of binoculars dangling from his neck, he hopped down from his front seat and guided a few of his passengers onto the step and then onto the sandy ground. He watched Leo, sliding across the large seat ready to step down. "The step's a pretty big one. Ya want a little help?" He held his hand out.

Leo didn't take it but instead concentrated on putting one foot onto the metal step and reaching his other leg to the ground. It was a stretch but he made it. Once on terra firma, Leo pronounced, "See. I did it. I'm a big guy. Ask Mom and Dad."

"You certainly are." Jeff grinned at the boy, then winked at Erin.

Darrell took his son's hand and scanned the area. The visitors from two other vehicles must've arrived earlier as some were already mulling around and one group was gathered together, listening to another driver.

He studied the others. The tourists were largely white, several families with a few kids, an older couple about his parents' age, as well as two blond-haired guys, obviously traveling together. The only exceptions were a pair of blacks—an older fellow with a head of white hair and likely his grandson—and a young Hispanic couple who clung so tight to each other Darrell guessed they were on their honeymoon. Among the twenty or so from the three cars, he saw no one with reddish-brown skin and dark hair. He turned and surveyed his own group. No Native Americans.

Jeff, the driver, called loud enough for all his riders, who were mulling around, to hear. "Why don't I give ya a little background on the area, so you'll know what to look fer when you're wandering around up here." He pointed to a tall, straggling elm, growing out of the sandy soil. "Let's head over to that tree there."

Darrell, Erin and Leo followed the driver and, after a bit, the rest of the riders joined them.

"Behold the power of nature," Jeff began, sweeping his arm across the vista. The driver wasn't tall, maybe five foot eight with a lanky build and had a scraggly mop of brown hair under a battered Chicago Cubs cap. "Believe it or not, when this land was settled in the early 1800's, there were forests of trees as far as the eye could see, all around us and all the way to the water." He pointed east where the sun had moved up a notch. "If you look past them dunes there, you can see the blue of Lake Michigan." He moved his hand toward the northeast. "If you look there, you can see where the Kalamazoo River meets the lake. In fact, Saugatuck is an Indian word which means 'mouth of river.' Anyway, in 1830, a family named Butler traveled from Connecticut and settled a village which would become the town of Saugatuck right at the mouth of the Kalamazoo River there."

The tourists followed the driver's gestures and scanned the area. The rolling dunes filled the view from left to right and all the way to the water. A few small batches of trees struggled to gain hold in the sand but otherwise the sand covered everything, golden tan in the bright sun.

Leo asked, "What happened to all the trees?"

Jeff looked down at their son. "Great question." He glanced at Darrell and Erin. "You have one bright boy here." He rested a hand on Leo's shoulder. "In fact, when

107

this land was settled, the wood was quite valuable. They needed wood to build the towns and the cities around. So, they set up a town called Singapore right about there." He pointed to a spot in the center of the horizon ahead. "If you look carefully, ya can see it."

He crouched down next to Leo. "Can you see the town?" Leo shook his head. "Why don't you try with these?" He handed the boy the pair of binoculars from around his neck.

Leo took the binoculars, large in his small hands, and brought them to his eyes. He peered through the lenses in the direction the driver indicated and then said, "I still don't see any town." Using both hands, he handed the glasses back to Jeff.

The driver accepted them, straightened up and addressed the small group. "The town of Singapore was settled in 1837. It became a thriving lumber and shipbuilding town with four lumber mills and about two hundred people. For the next thirty years or so, the small town supplied lumber to build the other towns and villages around."

Darrell was intrigued. He'd grown up in Michigan, only a few hours from here across the peninsula and he'd never heard the name of Singapore, at least not Singapore, Michigan. He asked, "What happened to the town?"

Jeff chuckled. "You could say it was a victim of its own success. Through much of the nineteenth century, the lumber mills hummed and they kept shipping wood down the river and across the lake. But you may remember reading a great fire struck Chicago in 1871, burning down much of the city. They desperately needed lumber to rebuild so they turned to Singapore." The driver shook his head. "But by now, the only woods left were the ones surrounding the town. They had stripped the rest of the land of trees. So they had little choice but to cut down the remainin' trees and ship the lumber to Chicago. With the last trees gone, the workers drifted away, one by one, family by family, and they deserted the town. A few buildings were moved, but they simply left most structures—houses, stores, a church. There are three of these Singapore buildings still preserved in Saugatuck, by the way. Anyway, without the trees to protect it, over the years the winds off the lake brought sand and now the village of Singapore is buried under those three large mounds." He brought the binoculars up, scanned, then pointed. "Right there."

Jeff offered the field glasses and several members of the group took turns staring out at the dunes of sand. Darrell and Erin lowered themselves next to Leo, one on each side, and together they looked across at the dunes against the watery expanse. Leo asked, "Did the people get buried in the sand?"

Before Darrell could answer, the driver chuckled. "No worries there. The people left long before the sand reclaimed the land."

Darrell stood back up and asked the driver, "You said Singapore and Saugatuck were settled in the 1830's. Weren't there Indians living around here then?"

Jeff shrugged. "Yes and no. The Indians were here long before the settlers, mainly the Ottawa and Chippewa tribes. But in a treaty in 1836, the U.S. government basically swindled those and other tribes out of sixteen million acres of land in the Upper and Lower Peninsula of Michigan."

Confused, Leo asked, "That was a long time ago.

What happened to those Indians? The ones who lived here?"

Chapter 17

The driver, Jeff, who had leaned over to look at Leo, straightened and tried to smile but looked embarrassed for the first time. "Well, that was way before my time but I think many Indians moved onto reservations while a few probably stayed in the area." He shook his head without losing the smile. "But, on the bright side, if the U.S. hadn't done that treaty, Singapore would never have existed…and we wouldn't have Saugatuck today." He glanced at the rest of the group. "Anyone have any other questions?"

The tourists looked first at Darrell and Leo and then at Jeff, but no one said anything. When no more questions came, Jeff finished, "Well, feel free to roam about and check out the area. You can take any of the paths. Be careful climbing on the dunes. The sand can shift easily and then we'd have to dig you out. I hope we remembered to bring a shovel this time." He laughed out loud and checked his watch. "I'll meet you back in the buggy in, let's say ten minutes, 10:30. If you want to know anything else, I'll hang around here for a while."

Leo pointed to the other side of the flat area. "Can we take that trail?"

Darrell nodded at Erin who said, "We don't have much time but let's give it a try." She and Darrell each took a hand and Leo hopped between them. They went past the dune buggy and down the way their son had indicated. When the three of them made their way about halfway down the sandy path, a rabbit hopped across the trail ahead, scuttling down the sand.

"Look, Dad!" Leo shouted and rushed ahead. Darrell and Erin hurried after their son. When the boy got to the spot where the bunny had crossed the track, he stopped and peered around. "Where'd he go?"

Darrell pointed at a cluster of bushes, tall grasses and two towering trees. "He probably dodged into cover over there. Rabbits have to be very good at hiding to stay alive."

Leo stared at the greenery, his gaze sweeping back and forth. "I don't see any rabbit."

Darrell chuckled. "Then I'd say he hid pretty well, wouldn't you?"

Leo said, "I guess so." Resigned, he stared farther down the path which dipped along the incline of the hill. His eyes lit up. "Hey, Dad, did you see her?" He pointed straight ahead. "Another Indian girl."

Darrell looked where his son pointed and saw someone stride around a boulder…or thought he did. Lithe figure, amber skin. Long black hair flowed down the back as she disappeared around the bend. Looked like a girl. He only caught sight of her for a few seconds before she vanished around the turn. Vanished?

He turned to Erin, "Did you see her?"

Erin said, "I didn't notice anyone down there." She glanced around the clearing, her gaze settling on a few of the tourists who had come with them. "It was probably one of our riders. I only count four here with us."

"I want to see if I can catch up to her." Leo ran down the sandy slope.

Before Leo took two steps, Darrell was in motion,

hustling after his son, and caught up. The two ran together then, their feet making soft plodding sounds on the sandy ground. The path continued down the incline then veered to the left around a huge boulder where the girl had disappeared. They followed it around the bend. When they got past the giant rock, they saw the sandy path led down another slope and then back up. More tall grasses and small, stunted trees erupted from the sides of the hill bordering the path, though the path was all sand with the parallel runts for the tires clearly visible. But they didn't see any person, Indian or otherwise.

Leo glanced around. "Where *she'd* go? She was right ahead of us, another Indian girl, like Anna and Rachel." He looked up at his dad. "You saw her, didn't you?"

Erin walked up next to the two of them. Darrell looked at her then at his son. "Yeah, I thought I saw…someone." His gaze did a one-eighty, searching the ground ahead of them. "I don't see anyone now."

Leo looked up at Erin. "Mom, you saw her, didn't you?"

Erin shook her head slowly. "No, I didn't, but I didn't look as quickly as you and Dad."

"Or," Darrell whispered to his wife, "maybe *you* couldn't see her."

Erin glanced from husband to son, then shrugged. "So, what else is new?"

Darrell squeezed his wife's shoulder. His gaze swept the area. He saw no one ahead of them and only heard the chatter of the other riders back up the hill. As his eyes made the sweep, he sensed… *something*. He felt the slightest prickle down his neck but didn't say anything to Erin or Leo, at first. He kept staring, thinking there was someone, something he was supposed to notice.

The sensation slowly swelled and the questions returned, swirling around his brain as he stared. What was going on here? If Sheila's ghost was trying to communicate with him, with them, what *was* the message? Up here on top of this massive dune, what were they supposed to see? What was he supposed to do?

"Three minutes!" their driver called from back up the hill. "We're bugging out in three minutes."

Erin, ever practical, said, "We better get going. It's going to take us almost that long to get back to the buggy." She looked at her son. "Sorry, this might have to remain a mystery. Your dad can tell you he's had plenty of those in the past."

"True enough," Darrell said and reached for his son's hand.

Instead of taking it, Leo pointed back past his dad at the boulder they'd cut around. When Darrell turned, he saw what Leo was pointing at. On a concave shelf on the side of the boulder sat a small, colored object. Erin turned at the same time, her eyes widening. Hurrying over, she got there first and picked it up. Both Leo and Darrell crowded around as she held it out in the palm of her hand.

She said, almost in a whisper, "It looks like a friendship bracelet."

Darrell studied the object. It was a chain of beads in the brilliant, alternating colors of deep purple, sky blue, and white braided into repeating arrow shapes. It looked to be fairly new. At least, it hadn't been in that crevice very long. He picked it up from her hand and examined it. It felt hot in his palm, he thought, maybe from the heat of sun-warmed rock. No name or identifying words. Maybe another tourist left it here, from an earlier group? Could've been anyone's, but still. The prickle resurged down his neck, escalating this time.

Erin asked, "I wonder who left it here?"

Darrell turned the bracelet over in his hand. It seemed to radiate heat...and the braided band looked familiar. He'd seen it before, or one like it. Where? Why was it important?

"Two minutes!" screamed Jeff from the top of the rise.

Darrell stuffed the bracelet in his pocket, feeling the heat radiating through the cotton fabric. He snatched his son's hand. "We gotta go. Let's see how fast you can run." The three of them took off, climbing the incline, crossing the flat expanse of sand, and arrived at the buggy in time, a bit out of breath.

As they climbed aboard, Darrell felt the bracelet in his pocket...radiating heat. What did that mean?

Chapter 18

The driver called, "Hold on. This part of the ride could get a little bumpy."

Jeff punched it and the fat tires of the dune buggy spun in the sand, then caught and plunged forward, throwing the passengers back against their seats. Without slowing, the driver hurtled through more sets of curls between huge mounds of sand as grasses, shrubs and trees passed by in a blur. Then he drove the vehicle down a sharp incline and onto a well-worn path as they entered a dense forest, with pines and maples and elms towering around them. The tall trees cut off the sun, darkening the whole area, and the air cooled some. Jeff slowed the vehicle and set it to idle.

He turned to face the riders. "If you keep your eyes peeled, you might see some wildlife down here. Sometimes we come across rabbits, a red fox and even a deer or two." He pointed around. "The forest floor has more vegetation for them to eat. I'll take it easy to give us a chance to spot some."

He turned back, put the car in gear and rolled slowly forward, the big engine purring. All the riders, including Darrell, Erin and Leo, rotated their heads, searching between the dense trees and tall grasses for some sign of wildlife. Erin spoke up first, though she kept her words to a whisper. Leaning down next to Leo, she pointed off to the right at maybe two o'clock. "Look, there's a deer.

A doe, I think, though I don't see her baby yet."

Darrell followed her outstretched arm and saw the deer, her tan and white body barely visible behind a thatch of small elms. The animal's head came up and two black eyes stared back. There was quiet muttering among the other passengers, then Leo blurted out, "Oh, I see it." His arm shot out.

At Leo's raised voice, the deer's head jerked back and forth. It turned and bounded deeper into the forest, the rustle of branches announcing its departure. Two seconds later, a small tan-and-white form followed, the splash of colors only visible for a moment.

Their son turned and asked, "Did you see the smaller one? Is that her baby?"

Erin nodded, keeping her gaze where the two deer had disappeared. "I think it is." She looked at Leo. "The younger one is called a fawn."

"That's right," Jeff announced, turning toward his passengers. "I've seen them both before but not very often. We got pretty lucky. I guess you got the full fifty-cent tour this time." He chuckled. "But we probably charged you a little more than that." He turned back and put the car in gear. "We're about finished and I hope you enjoyed it."

The riders broke out in spontaneous applause and Darrell joined them, though not as spirited as the others. He found the return ride as interesting as the first half but he had trouble staying in the moment. Throughout the whole return trip, the bracelet burned in his pocket. That was the only way he could describe it. Not enough to hurt him but hot enough to distract him and remind him it was there.

When they disembarked from the large dune buggy,

Darrell thanked the driver, tipping him well, and the three of them headed to their car, Leo babbling on about how much he loved it and wanted to do it again.

Erin laughed. "We'll see. We're not going to be here very long and we have more fun ahead."

As soon as they were inside the Taurus and had rolled the windows down to cool off the interior, Leo blurted out, "That was the most fun ever!" He held his hands up in the air mimicking a rider on a rollercoaster show they'd watched together.

Darrell and Erin laughed. She darted a hand to her son's underarms and tickled. "More fun than this?"

Leo giggled over and over again. "Okay, Mom, okay." He laughed again and caught his breath. "That's fun too."

Darrell looked across at Erin, whose eyes narrowed and lips pursed. He knew that look. "You okay?"

She nodded. "Just a little queasy." She put a hand on her abdomen. "Probably the crazy ride. Jeff really whirled us through those last few curves. Give me a bit to let my stomach settle."

Darrell checked and saw Leo looked distracted, preoccupied again with his toy car. He pulled the bracelet out of his pocket and slipped it to Erin. "I need you to keep this safe in that monster purse of yours. I've no idea how but I think it may be important. And it's too hot to stay in my pocket."

Erin took the bracelet and, glancing back at Leo, whispered, "It's pretty and it doesn't look like it's been there very long. Not sun-bleached." Turning it over in her hand, she said, "You know I think I've seen it before…or maybe one like it." She held the colored band between them. "You recognize it?"

Darrell turned and stared at the interwoven colors. "I thought the same thing. Maybe, we saw it in a store we visited?"

"Doesn't feel right. Somewhere else." She paused, shaking her head. "You think the ghost, Sheila, left it. That's why you and Leo could see her and I couldn't." She rubbed the multi-colored bracelet between two fingers. "It feels hot."

"Yeah." He glanced again at his son and whispered, "We'll talk more later." He belted his son into his car seat, the urge to keep Leo safe suddenly weighing on him. Staring into his son's face, Darrell injected extra enthusiasm into his question. "You ready for the next adventure?"

"What's next?" Leo sounded leery.

Hovering over his son, Darrell turned his head sideways. "I don't know if you can do this next one. They say only big guys can manage it."

Leo pouted, "Hey, I'm a big guy."

Darrell stared at his son, his tone mock serious. "You think you can make it to the top of Mt. Baldhead? They say you have to climb three hundred steps."

Leo giggled. "It's really called Mt. Baldhead. What does it have, a bald head?" He laughed again.

Chuckling, Darrell said, "I guess we'll have to climb to the top to find out."

Chapter 19

It took them only a few minutes to make the short drive to the other side of Saugatuck where Mt. Baldhead rose out of the sand dunes. Darrell turned the car into one of the few remaining parking spots in the small gravel lot.

After they all got out of the car, Erin sighed, her palm on her stomach. "I think we all need a drink. I do." She reached into the back seat and pulled water bottles from the cooler Gertrude's staff had packed for them. She handed out a bottle to each, the plastic glistening with condensation. As they drank, they gazed at the rippling water running past in the river below. A sleek powerboat slid by slowly, its keel white and teak deck shining in the sun. A tall man in a blue blazer and captain's hat stood at the helm and gave a one-finger wave. Darrell waved back.

He sauntered over to read the historical plaques while Leo wandered across the parking lot to the foot of the stairs. Hands on hips, Leo stared up the long flight and declared, "I can't even see where it ends."

Erin came up alongside him and looked up the long ascent. She moved her hand around on her stomach. "I'm a little queasy. I think I'll let my two big guys tackle Mt. Baldhead."

Joining them, Darrell searched her face. "You okay? Not like you to give up on a challenge."

Erin smiled. "I'll be fine. Just don't feel like it today. That dune buggy ride was fun but maybe a bit much for me. It's cool down here under the trees. I'll wait in the car while you guys conquer the mountain and tell me about it."

When she insisted, Darrell walked her back to the car. Handing her his water, he kissed her and joined his son at the foot of the stairs. Leo took his gaze off the wooden steps and glanced back toward the car. "Is Mom okay? Is she sick?"

Darrell took his son's water bottle. "Here, let me hold on to this. Your mom will be fine. I think her stomach's bothering her a little bit." He shrugged. "Or it could be female stuff. Things you and I wouldn't understand." He leaned close and whispered, "Maybe the climb to Mt. Baldhead *is* only for big guys."

Leo laughed as they started climbing. "I still think it's a crazy name."

Holding hands, they took the stairs together, while Darrell's other hand held the water bottle to share. The steps, railings and frames were all made of treated wood and Darrell wondered how long the wood would last, especially with the harsh winters next to the lake. He stared up the long set of wooden steps which stretched as far as he could see. As they raised one foot after the other to the next step, Darrell tried to count them but soon lost track. Leo's head swiveled from side to side and his gaze roamed the slopes on both sides of the stairs, taking in the trees, bushes and grasses sprouting out of the steep grounds.

About every fifty steps, the designers had built in a wooden platform and bench for tiring climbers to rest. Darrell and Leo passed the first and second platform without pausing. But, as they approached the third, Darrell examined his son—face flush, breathing labored and arms swinging—and decided he needed a break. He realized the steps seemed even steeper than normal steps and maybe he could use a rest as well.

"How about we stop and sit for a bit?" Darrell asked and Leo nodded.

When they settled on the bench, Darrell handed his son the bottle of water and Leo drank. He gave it back and Darrell did the same. While they sat, they watched a few people climb past them, a teenage couple and a sixty-something man and wife, hand in hand. Darrell noticed none of the four appeared to be even breathing hard. He took a slow, deep breath. He needed to get himself in better shape.

Leo's gaze followed the others and, when they passed, he asked, his voice low, "So the missing girl we saw, Sheila, is a ghost, right?"

"Yeah, I'm pretty sure."

"Well, she looked like her picture. Can I see the paper again?"

Pulling the flyer from his pocket, Darrell handed it to him, the sheet now dog-eared around the edges. Leo studied it for a minute then returned it. "If Sheila wants our help, why did she walk away from us? Why didn't she tell us something, something that would help?"

"I don't know." Darrell shook his head. "Even though I've been through this a few times, it's always hard to figure out what to do and exactly what the ghosts want."

Leo's voice got serious. "What do *you* think happened to her?"

Darrell shook his head slowly. "I don't know." He

wasn't sure how much he wanted to tell his son, but he'd promised not to lie to him. "But I'm afraid something bad."

Leo's features scrunched together. "Well, if she's already *dead*," he whispered the word, his gaze shooting around, "how are we supposed to help her?"

"I don't know that either." Darrell struggled with how he could explain this to his son without traumatizing him. "Maybe she wants us to find out what happened to her…and maybe find out why she was killed."

Eyes wide, Leo stared at his dad. "If something bad did happen, if someone killed her, why doesn't she just tell us?"

"It doesn't work like that…or maybe she doesn't know what happened. We'll have to keep asking questions and see what we learn. Okay?"

Leo nodded and Darrell placed a hand on his shoulder, "A few deep breaths like mom taught us?" Another nod and they took some long breaths together. "You ready to get moving again?"

Leo nodded and they resumed their climb, one foot after another. Watching his young son extend his short leg to the next step, Darrell realized the steps were both wide and high, especially for a little one. Leo used his free hand to hold onto the rail, his gaze roaming the steep slopes. He said, "I don't see any animals. Not even rabbits."

"I don't know. Maybe it's too steep for them as well or maybe not enough food for them on the hillside."

As they climbed higher, Darrell could feel his heart beat rising, right along with the altitude. He took a few extra breaths. They passed the next landing and kept going.

Darrell said, "More than halfway now."

Leo beamed and kept stepping without pausing for the next twenty steps. As they approached the next landing, the sound of a few tired voices floated down to them.

"Uncle Jim, I'm not sure I can make it all the way to the top," a young boy pleaded.

Another voice, older, male, said, "I know it's a long climb but I think you can make it. Besides we're almost to the top. How about I hold your hand and I'll help you get there?"

When Darrell and Leo came up to the landing, they saw a young boy, close to the same age as Leo, Darrell guessed, and a tall, middle-aged man. The boy wore a blue-and-white striped shirt and blue shorts and had a thatch of blond hair. The man, whose hair could've been a match to the boy's, crouched next to him, his face even with the child's. He wore some kind of black uniform, its creases sharp, and polished black shoes, a few blond grains of sands dotting the ebony sheen. When he stood straight, holding the boy's hand, Darrell realized he was quite tall, well over six feet, and recognized the "Douglas Police" patch on his shirt.

Leo stared at the boy and Darrell gave a nod to the cop as they continued up the final flight of stairs. When they crested the top one and stepped onto the platform, they found an L-shaped, wooden walkway and a steep trail curling down the back side of the huge mountain. Leo looked past his dad and pointed. "What's that?"

Darrell turned and saw the large, white sphere suspended in the air atop a tower. He walked over to read the plaque with the historical description. After scanning the paragraph, he explained, "That's a radar installation used to track enemy signals. It's been out of use for years but they've kept it the way it was."

Darrell walked over to one side of the walkway and looked through the trees. "Hey, come over here and catch this scene."

Leo walked over and stared where his dad indicated. "I can't see anything but more trees."

"I can fix that." Darrell picked up his son and raised him up to his level, the boy resting his legs on the railing. Once Leo was settled and Darrell held him, he pointed, "That is the Kalamazoo River and this side is Saugatuck where we took the chain ferry and that's the Saugatuck marina." He indicated the water inlet where half a dozen boats were nestled in their docks.

As a few footsteps on the stairs sounded, they turned to watch the man and boy reach the summit, stop and look around, exactly as Darrell and Leo had. The man said, triumph evident in his voice, "We made it. You made it, Gary."

Darrell let Leo down, who walked over to say hi to the boy. The man joined Darrell at the rail and said, "This view gets me every time."

Darrell said, "I know what you mean." He reached out his hand. "Darrell Henshaw and this is my son, Leo. Our first time."

The man shook. "I'm Jim Thatcher and this young guy who just conquered Mt. Baldhead is my nephew, Gary." He pointed to the police patch and added, "His first time but not mine."

Darrell explained about his family and their reason for visiting Saugatuck.

"You're part of Gertrude Embry's family? I heard the clan was gathering for her big birthday celebration. I haven't seen Gertrude for a while. How is she?" The officer's face lit up with a broad smile.

Unsure how to answer, Darrell said, "You know my Aunt Gertrude. Feisty as ever."

Jim chortled. "I'm sure she is."

While they exchanged greetings, Leo and his new friend started talking. After a bit, Leo walked over to his dad. "Gary said his uncle is a policeman. Maybe he can help?"

The cop looked down at Leo, his blue eyes soft. "Help with what?"

Under the officer's stare, Leo looked embarrassed but managed in a small voice, "We're trying to find Sheila Birdsong. She's missing."

Darrell, intent on the experience of the climb, hadn't wanted to go there. Not now. But his fearless son jumped in.

Officer Thatcher switched his stare to Darrell, a question in his eyes. Darrell pulled out the wrinkled flyer and handed it to him. Then he explained how they'd come upon the missing poster and Leo's interest in finding the girl. He added, "It's not only Leo. I'm a high school teacher, work with kids like her." He pointed to the flyer. "We're both concerned."

Officer Thatcher relaxed his posture and gave Leo a knowing smile. "I think that's very noble of you, son, but I wouldn't waste too much time worrying about a missing Indian girl. Don't let it spoil your vacation. Most of them work the fields in Allegan County, those interested in working. We don't see many Gun Lake kids over here in Douglas or Saugatuck."

"Sheila worked for Great Aunt Gertrude but she quit," Leo piped up.

"She did, huh?" the officer said, shaking his head. "Well, I wouldn't spend too much energy on this." He handed the flyer back to Darrell. "It says she's seventeen. My guess is she probably took off, to the big city of Chicago or someplace. I've heard a lot of Indian teens do that, take off and nobody hears from them for a while. Then, a few years later. they show back up…sometimes with a new papoose." He patted Leo on the shoulder. "I think it's nice you're concerned, but I wouldn't worry too much about her. I have a feeling she'll come sauntering back home when she's ready."

Chapter 20

After leaving Thatcher and his nephew on the walkway at the top, Darrell and Leo found the trip down a good bit easier than going up. The steps passed quickly and they approached the last rest station, the one closest to the bottom. Leo pointed to the bench and Darrell said, "Sure."

After they settled onto the wooden seat, Leo glanced back up the stairs. No one, including the officer or Gary, was evident. He whispered, "You think the policeman could be right? Sheila just…ran away?"

Like his son, Darrell stared up the stairs and, relieved to see no figures coming down yet, he turned back. "Maybe…but I don't think so. If she ran away, I don't think we'd be seeing her, or rather her ghost."

"Then why would the policeman say she probably ran away?"

"That's a very good question." Darrell looked again up the stairs and then at his son. "Sometimes, when people don't have an answer, they choose an explanation which seems…innocent." Still, Darrell thought Officer Thatcher's explanation might not be so innocent but he wasn't ready to burden his son with that.

A clatter on the steps above caused both to glance up the staircase. Darrell said, "Let's get a move on. We can't let them beat us to the bottom." They jumped up and hustled down the last fifty steps, both breathless by the time they crossed the parking lot.

When they got to the car, Erin popped out of the front seat. "Hail the conquering heroes!" She hugged both and kissed Darrell.

Darrell asked, "You okay? Still queasy?"

Erin said, "I'm fine. Even got a quick cat nap while you two accomplished the great stair climb." She glanced at her watch. "But we better get back to Wentworth. Remember we're supposed to participate in the family outdoor games before dinner."

"I completely forgot." He turned to Leo. "Okay, get in, big guy."

The officer's words burning in his ear, Darrell would've preferred to talk with Erin right then. He wanted her take on what Thatcher said about Sheila as well as the vision and the bracelet. The bracelet. He knew he'd seen it before—or one a lot like it—but couldn't remember where or when. Maybe she'd come up with something. And he wanted to let her in on his discussion with Leo about seeing Sheila's ghost.

He turned in his seat and took another look at his son, face flushed from the climb and both hands holding the bottle as he drank. He decided he'd wait. Fun and games at Aunt Gertrude's called. The trip back to the mansion wouldn't take long and besides, he decided he didn't want to worry about young ears. Any discussion would have to wait until he and Erin could get a few quiet moments in their room tonight.

When they arrived, they were barely out of the car when Ilya had his hand out for the Taurus keys. The swarthy-skinned man, face hard like granite, didn't utter a word. He climbed in, closed the door and drove the car away like he owned it. The young man's moves were efficient and economical and his posture and bearing carried a certain arrogance. Darrell stared, watching the car disappear around the building. Something about the whole thing bothered him but he couldn't put his finger on it.

Before he had time to ponder, Craig pulled him aside, insisting Darrell and Erin join him and Dianna for a new sack toss game. This game, which consisted of two slanted boards on supports with a single wide hole in the center, had been set up on the carefully trimmed lawn twenty feet down from the wide circular driveway.

When his brother dragged him over to the game, he leaned in close. Craig whispered, a little too loudly, "You know what they call this?" He pointed to one of the red, white and blue painted boards. "Corn Hole!" His eyebrows did a little dance and he indicated the large hole cut into the wood. "Get it. Corn hole." He laughed and slapped Darrell on the back.

The two teen girls hurried through the front doors. One after another, they hefted three fancy patio chairs through the doorway and placed them onto the flat asphalt driveway, a pair for Darrell's mom and dad and a grander one for Aunt Gertrude. Brandishing the carved wooden cane, Aunt Gertrude paraded through the wide doors, held open by Rachel and Anna. The whole family, except Leo, stopped what they were doing and watched. And, with all the pomp she could muster, she maneuvered down the three steps, finally collapsing into her reserved seat.

Once freed from the car, Leo thrilled at the chance to have the run of the lawn and play his imaginary games, not needing another soul. Darrell watched him. He drew back the toy *atlatl* and threw the pretend spear across the green grass at some imaginary deer, sometimes hitting his target and celebrating. Other times, he'd miss and shrug in imagined disappointment.

Like Darrell and Erin, the other family members gathered in the yard were dressed in light summer outfits, simple T-shirts and shorts, though Aunt Gertrude wore a long, bright yellow sundress and a large, floppy beach hat.

When she was seated, Salazar and Ilya appeared and stationed themselves on each end of the grouping, arms crossed, heads up, like two unmatched sentries. The Indian girls delivered the spectators drinks, ice clinking in tall colorful tumblers. Looking over the whole scene from under the wide brim of her hat, Gertrude sipped and smiled. Replacing the glass in its holder, she clapped her hands together and pronounced, "Let the games begin."

For the game of cornhole, the two couples paired up, Darrell and Craig on one end and Erin and Dianna on the other. Darrell tried to forget about the ghost, at least for the moment, and enjoy the game which turned out to be harder than it looked. It required concentration and coordination. After several practice tries, he developed a toss with a smooth arch and drop, which worked fairly well. Hundreds of practices arching a basketball through the hoop with his students no doubt helped. When he landed his second bag through the opening to Craig's one, he acknowledged his brother's limp might be affecting his throwing motion—and the guilt about Craig's accident resurfaced. Dianna fared better than her husband but Erin played her close and Darrell and Erin managed to win the first round.

For the second game, his mom and dad replaced Craig and Dianna, who took the seats vacated by the parents. Within a minute, Rachel and Anna had frosty glasses filled with today's special cocktail delivered to his brother, though Dianna settled for a Coke. Through broad teeth, Craig smirked through his goatee at Darrell and toasted the icy glass toward him, making Darrell wonder if the two hadn't lost the game on purpose. Gertrude sat in her special chair, a little higher than the others as if some metaphor for her station—or at least what she thought it was.

The game was fun, Silvio's drink for the day delicious and Darrell did his best to get into the family activity, but his mind kept wandering. The recurring questions about the missing girl taunted him. While his dad and mom did a few practice throws, he glanced up at the imposing mansion. Trying his best to keep a smile on, Darrell's gaze swept over the group, Gertrude presiding in her seat, Ilya and Salazar at their positions.

Was there some connection between Sheila going missing and his family? Aunt Gertrude? Some connection to this place? He knew Sheila Birdsong worked here. Did that mean anything? When his dad stepped over to retrieve his tumbler, Darrell noticed Salazar lean over and say something to Aunt Gertrude.

He decided he needed to speak with the man, to ask a few questions. But what excuse could he use for "interrogating" him? He glanced over and watched Leo a few feet away playing with the Indian toy they'd bought him in Pennsylvania. Maybe, just maybe, he could use his son's insatiable curiosity.

Chapter 21

So, when the games ran their course and his family were on their third round of drinks—Darrell was still nursing his first—he asked Salazar if they could talk for a few minutes. The caretaker nodded. "Of course."

Darrell led the way down the hill, taking the long flight of stairs, and they came out onto the dock which stretched into the lake like a white gloved finger. Darrell eyed the sleek sailboats and sporty powerboats dotting the surface of the lake. At the pier, a long, sleek sailboat sat next to the dock, the waves rocking it gently against the red dock fenders. As they crossed the white planks, their feet making slapping sounds on the wood, Darrell took in the yacht he'd only seen from the top of the hill.

The elongated hull was painted a deep blue, a shade somewhere between the gray blue of the water and bright azure of the sky. At the waterline, two narrow stripes ran down the side and around the boat, first a white line and beneath it, a green. The sail was down of course, rolled up tarp-like and held in place with the standard rigging next to the tall central mast. It was far bigger and more impressive than Erin's family's sailboat, *Second Wind*.

As Darrell slowed, admiring the vessel, he heard Salazar come up beside him and he walked down to the end of the pier.

It was another warm July day in Michigan, temperatures in high eighties. While he'd been toiling in

133

the cornhole competition, Darrell had sweated, his light blue T-shirt now sporting dark circles under his arms. As he stepped down the hill, rivulets of sweat dripped down his back and under his armpits. The accumulated perspiration annoyed him and, when he noticed the stains on his shirt expanding, he felt the compulsion to change, get into something fresh. He fought it and diverted his attention upward.

The sun blazed so bright in the west, it seemed to bleach out the almost cloudless sky, turning it to a pale blue. But, when he'd stepped away from the land and onto the white planks, a strong breeze from the water blew over him, sending delightful coolness. The wind drove ripples across the water, propelling quiet wavelets onto the small sandy beach beside the dock. Darrell inhaled, feeling relieved.

When Darrell looked over at the older man, Salazar's face was turned toward the sky, his eyes closed. He spoke without opening his eyes. "Young Darrell, these are the days that make it all worthwhile. As your aunt would say, summer days on the shore of Lake Michigan are absolutely glorious." He turned to face Darrell, gray eyes bright and a wide smile stretching the creases of his face, revealing the missing and cracked teeth. "What can I do for you?"

Darrell decided to jump in. "You know having a son, having Leo, I think is the best part of my life."

Salazar raised one black eyebrow. "Perhaps you should not let your lovely wife hear that." Then he grinned.

"No, it's not that. Erin is my rock, my partner, my love and my life would not be the same without her. But having a son, it's...it's not like anything else. I watch him grow and learn and become this great kid and…all I can do is wonder." Darrell glanced over at the man and thought about what he was saying. "I'm sorry. I don't even know if you have a family, a son."

Salazar shook his head slowly. "Sadly, no." Then he gave a wink of one gray eye. "Not that I know of."

Darrell chuckled and the caretaker went on. "No, I'm afraid not. Never met the right woman, I guess. I've devoted my life to serving your uncle and later your aunt." He raised a hand. "Don't get me wrong. It's been a good life and I've been able to see things and accomplish things I would never've dreamed." He shook his head again. "But I've never had the privilege of being a father." His eyes met Darrell's. "It looks to me like you're doing quite a good job with master Leo."

Darrell shrugged. "Leo is a great kid but probably Erin should get most of the credit. He continually amazes me. Leo has this insatiable curiosity. He asks me about *everything.*" Darrell gave his head a quick shake. "Know what I mean?"

Salazar laughed. "That I do. Yesterday, when we were walking through the great room, young Leo looked up and asked why we put windows in the ceiling."

Darrell giggled. "That's Leo." He reached into his pocket and pulled out the folded flyer, its edges curling. Using both hands, he smoothed the paper and handed it to Salazar. "On our way here, we stopped at a store for a snack and that flyer was attached to the front of the counter. Leo came up to it and started to read it. He's getting pretty good with words."

Darrell flapped his hand as if shooing a fly. "Anyway, he saw that and asked me about it and I tried to explain the situation, the 'missing' part and all."

Salazar looked serious. "Difficult stuff for a kid."

"Yeah, but Leo is also a kid who cares...about everything and everybody. He gets upset when we have to kill bugs in the house." He chuckled. "When he learned about the missing girl, he decided he, we needed to do something. To see if we could help find her."

Salazar handed the flyer back to Darrell. "That's nice of Leo but you know these native girls take off all the time. Bad family life, alcoholism, drugs, or simply being rebellious teenagers. They get tired of living here or on the reservation and they take off for the big city. They just run away. That's probably hard for a kid like Leo, great home and all, to understand."

Nodding, Darrell refolded the paper, trying to smooth down the curled edges. "I tried to explain that to Leo but, you know, he has the innocence of a kid. When I told him, he said 'Isn't there something we can do?'" Darrell did another wave of the hand holding the flyer. "Anyway, yesterday at the birthday party at Butlers, he talked with Rachel and Anna and asked them about Sheila."

Darrell stopped and waited, seeing if this drew any reaction from Salazar, but the creased old face remained unchanged, though he thought the gray eyes got harder. He went on, "The girls said Sheila used to work here, for Aunt Gertrude. Is that right?"

Darrell felt guilty using his son as an excuse to question Salazar but thought it might help break down the caretaker's defenses. Staring at the stony face and slight scowl of the old man, he now questioned his plan. For several seconds, neither man spoke and Darrell wanted to say something to fill the void, to smooth things over, but he waited. Like in his classroom, he figured if he held off, the caretaker would say something to fill the silence.

Salazar slouched his posture and the frown morphed into what looked like an embarrassed grin. The caretaker shrugged. "The girls are right. Sheila did work for us, for a while. She was not very dependable and I called her on being late and giving your aunt and me a lot of attitude. She didn't take it well. One day, she simply stopped showing up."

He glanced back up toward the house and Darrell followed his gaze. Up top, the two Indian girls hurried to deliver another round of drinks. "That's when I hired Rachel and Anna. I wish they hadn't said anything. I don't want Mrs. Embry dragged into any Indian mess."

Darrell caught the irritation in the man's voice and worried he'd gotten the two girls in trouble. He pushed on, unfolded the flyer and studied it for a second. "Would that have been around the time Sheila went missing? June 13?"

"Hell, Darrell, I can hardly keep track of what day it is." He shrugged. "It was probably a few weeks before then. Like I said, these Native teens are not dependable and sometimes just take off. I hear about it all the time." He raised one leathery hand. "I'm not blaming them with the bad homes they come from."

Darrell tried to size up Salazar, to assess how honest he was being, but the old man's face remained inscrutable, his eyes like granite. Then, the sun escaped from one of the few clouds and shone right at Darrell, the rays momentarily blinding him. He raised a hand to block it. When he did, the old caretaker turned and strode back across the dock headed for the shore. Over his shoulder, the man called, "I better get back to see if

Gertrude needs anything."

Darrell turned and watched Salazar cross the white planks and march up the hill toward the house, his shoulders square and his posture erect. Darrell studied the man and questioned himself. He was sure the caretaker knew more than he admitted but what could Darrell do about it? Who else might have more information about Sheila? His aunt?

The idea of trying to question her made him squirm.

Chapter 22

"How did Salazar react? When you asked him about Sheila?" Erin whispered, once Leo was asleep in the adjoining room and the door closed.

They sat cross-legged atop the luxurious bedspread, ready for bed but neither interested in sleep or lovemaking, at least not yet. Before, Darrell had checked to make sure the bed covers were laid out precisely in the center, not drawn too short or stretched too long. They were perfect. In fact, everything about the room was set symmetrically and the whole place was spotless.

Darrell shook his head. "Like a statue. Nothing." Then he shared what Salazar had told him, keeping his voice low. "I definitely got the impression there was more to the story. Since then, I've been trying to decide if he was being cagey or protecting Aunt Gertrude…or something else. I'm thinking I need to talk with Aunt Gertrude about Sheila. Not something I'm looking forward to."

Erin said, "Can't imagine your aunt permitting anything to tarnish her big celebration."

"That's not all. Leo and I had an interesting encounter atop the stairs to Mt. Baldhead. We met a Douglas Police Office and his young nephew there. And your son asked this cop if he could help us find Sheila." Then he relayed Officer Thatcher's take on the missing girl.

Erin said, "That sounds pretty much like what Salazar told you." She scrunched her eyebrows together. "If they both said the same thing, you think it could be true?"

Darrell stared into his wife's beautiful emerald eyes. "Leo asked me the same question. After we made it most of the way down the steps."

"What'd you tell him?"

Darrell shook his head. "I told him maybe but I doubted it. That if she ran away, then why would her ghost be haunting us?"

"He handle that okay?"

"I think so. You know Leo. Five going on twenty-five. I'm sure he'll have more questions tomorrow."

Erin tilted her head. "Well. It didn't seem to bother him after Mt. Baldhead. He had a great time playing with his toys in the grass."

"I think we won the lottery with that kid." Then he asked, "Hey, do you have the bracelet we found?"

"Sure." She reached over the side of the bed and dragged up her mom purse. Setting the large bag on the covers, she rifled around, came out with the multi-colored bracelet and laid it on the maroon comforter. For a minute, they stared at the beads woven into the arrow pattern of purple, blue, and white, neither one speaking.

Finally, Darrell said in a quiet voice, "I'm pretty sure I've seen it somewhere. Or one like it." He pointed at it. "But I can't remember where. How about you?"

He looked at his wife but she kept staring at the bracelet. "I know what you mean. I *have* seen it before, but where?" She sighed and shook her head. "Maybe if we sleep on it, it'll come to us." Scooping it up, she returned it to her bag and lowered the bag to the floor.

Climbing off the bed, she pulled the bedspread and cover sheet down.

Darrell matched her actions and both slid into bed. When she leaned in to kiss him goodnight, Darrell whispered in her ear. "Maybe if we, you know, it might reinvigorate my memory."

She patted the pajama fabric covering his groin. "I don't think *that* is connected to your memory. Nice try, big boy, but I'm still a little queasy. Raincheck, I promise."

Darrell kissed her again. "Of course. You can't knock a guy for trying." He flipped off the lights.

He lay flat on his back, watching the Caribbean fan turning slowly in the darkened room.

Without moving, he said, "I feel bad for Sheila but I don't have any idea how to help the girl. The last thing I want to do is disappoint Leo but still. Besides asking Aunt Gertrude about it—God, won't that be fun?—I have no idea what to do."

Erin stretched an arm across his chest. "Maybe something will come up, you'll get some clue. That's happened before."

"Yeah, maybe."

"Goodnight. Hey, maybe you'll dream about it." She yawned and repeated, "Goodnight, my love."

Within a few minutes, Darrell heard the quiet breathing of his wife which told him she'd drifted off. But for him, sleep would not come. Between the dune buggy ride and the climb up Mt. Baldhead, he was exhausted but his mind could not settle down. He glanced again at Erin's face, beautiful and composed in the dim light. Moving slowly—he didn't want to wake her—he slid out of the bed and stepped across the room.

First, he opened the adjoining door to check on Leo. The boy's body curled into a ball, his son slept, dead to the world. Darrell backed out, shutting the door quietly.

He stepped out of their suite and eased down the hallway, passing the closed mahogany doors of his parents' suite and Craig and Dianna's room. As he moved through the house, with no lights on and only the dim light of the stars and moon streaming in, the whole house gave off a dark, almost creepy vibe.

Darrell stifled a yawn. Maybe he'd get something to eat in the kitchen and head back to bed. He turned into the great room, his bare feet making swishes on the wooden floor. In the middle of the vast room, he stared up through the skylights at the tiny stars and listened, but the only sounds he heard were the quiet whoosh of the summer wind in the trees and the faraway roll of the waves against the shore.

He caught some movement in the rear of the room and turned. He whirled and called in a hoarse whisper, "Hello?"

No answer.

He peered back toward the fireplace, focusing his eyes, trying to adjust to the dark. His heart beat hard inside his chest. As he stood there, staring, he caught another movement, a smooth gliding or walking at the other end of the room. It couldn't be his aunt. He tried to whisper but found his voice hoarse. He tried, "Mr. Salazar? Tom?"

The figure moved behind the tall chairs and past the fireplace, heading for the far right door toward where, he'd learned, the servants' quarters existed. He first thought it was Rachel or Anna and either didn't want it known there were out "prowling" at night or doing what he was doing, raiding the kitchen. The figure looked taller so it had to be Rachel. He relaxed and called, his voice soft, "Rachel?" The figure didn't respond and Darrell didn't want to raise his voice so he hurried his steps, trying to close the gap.

An idea struck him. Maybe, with everyone else asleep, he might be able to talk more with the Native teen and learn something, anything more about Sheila. He called "Rachel" again, this time a little louder, his voice carrying in the great room. He was afraid he might wake someone. As he approached, the figure stopped in the open door, back to him. Her silhouette was outlined in the half moonlight and starlight slicing through the windows.

The figure then turned to face him and Darrell's heart jumped. He stopped where he was and stood, frozen to his spot. He whispered, "Sheila?" the word carrying across the space and hanging in the air. She lowered her head as if she were squinting. Her dark eyes narrowed and stared back at Darrell but she said nothing. He hesitated and then took a tentative step toward the figure, glancing around. He expected any minute he'd hear the grating voice of Salazar or a demanding shout from his aunt. Instead, everything was still.

Or he thought Erin would roll over and bump him and wake him from another dream. But that didn't happen.

He stood there and Sheila, or Sheila's ghost, stayed put, though the image seemed to shimmer around the edges. He struggled to find the right words, to even know what to ask. He managed, "What can I do?"

No response.

"I don't know where to start."

The ghost stared across the space and her eyes never left his. The image of her body appeared to weaken as if the light was being slowly bleached out. Only the face remained clear. The lips never moved but Darrell heard, "Shelbyville"—or at least, thought he did.

He stood there staring intently at the ghost and watched as her image grew fainter and fainter, until the doorframe held only a sliver of moonlight. Darrell rubbed his eyes, then closed and opened them. Nothing, or at least no ghost. Only the shadows cast by the moonlight through the vertical windows.

"Shelbyville?" he repeated under his breath.

Chapter 23

The next morning, Darrell told Erin about the late-night visitor almost before her eyes opened. She grinned at him. "Well, Leo was right."

"Huh?"

"Remember, Leo was so excited to find out if the mansion was haunted. Well, you just confirmed it for him." The grin widened. "I can't wait to see his face when you tell him. He'll want to go exploring at midnight."

Darrell chuckled. "I think I'll hold off on the haunted mansion flash...at least for now." He met his wife's gaze. "Any idea about her message, Shelbyville?"

Erin scrunched her eyes together. "You ask a lot of a girl before she's even out of bed." She nodded toward the bathroom door. "I think I need to head in there first."

With that, she slid off the bed and padded into the bathroom, closing the door softly. Darrell watched his wife move and stared. She had gained some pounds when Leo was born and had fought to lose them in the next few years. He thought she looked beautiful with or without the pounds, but she'd been self-conscious about it. He loved the way she moved, the easy curves of her body. Once again, he thanked God he'd gotten so lucky. Salazar was right. He'd definitely married up.

"Oh-h-ohm," came from the bathroom.

Darrell came over and stood next to the closed door.

"Erin, everything okay in there?"

He heard a flush and then her voice, "I'm okay but the steak Miguel fixed last night didn't sit so well. My queasy stomach just made a revolt. I'll be out in a minute."

He remembered her complaining about some stomach issues lately. He hoped she hadn't caught some bug. When the door opened, he immediately searched her face. She didn't look pale and she flashed a tired smile. She went back to the bed and snatched up her mammoth purse. Sitting cross-legged again, she pulled items from the cavernous bag, setting one after another on the bed—bottles of sunscreen, half-used packs of gum, small candies Leo loved, movie ticket stubs torn in half, handkerchiefs, a cylinder of bright red lipstick, a large wallet, its leather colored a steel-gray and finally, three maps. Tossing everything else back in the bag, she sorted through the three maps, separating the one for Michigan.

Darrell climbed up on the bed next to her and she said, "When I was in there throwing up," she nodded to the closed bathroom door, "I thought I remembered seeing the name on some of the signs we passed. She folded the map to the southwest corner of the state and laid it flat between them. They bent over the paper. She dotted a point on the map about an inch east of Saugatuck. "Here it is, Shelbyville." Leaning over the folded map, she studied the small lettering. "Looks like it's near the Potawatomi Reservation. Maybe there's some connection."

She handed it to Darrell so he could examine it more closely. He said, "Looks like Shelbyville's about an hour from here. A trip there and back is going to take a couple of hours and who knows how long it would take me to ask around." He shook his head. "My absence is going to be noticed."

Erin put a finger to her lips. "Maybe that's where she's from, where she lived before she worked for your aunt. I'm guessing someone there will be able to help."

"Yeah, but how do I find them?" He snapped his fingers. "I can ask Rachel or Anna. If I can get them aside."

"Not right away." Darrell frowned and Erin continued, "Did you forget today is our big foray to Oval Beach. Aunt Gertrude said we're all going for a little time in the sun right after breakfast, in her words, 'before it gets ungodly hot.' I'm sure the girls will be running in circles getting everything together. Maybe you can get them alone after."

****

Ninety minutes later, Darrell, Erin and Leo walked down the three steps from the wide front doors to their waiting Taurus. Ilya had brought all four cars out of the garage and had parked them, one behind the other, on the circular driveway. The Taurus was last in the little parade so they had to wait. Darrell looked around to thank Ilya and found him leaning against the front stone of the house, right of the front doors. Darrell pointed to the cars and said, "Thanks."

Ilya nodded, his face blank but his grey-blue eyes sharp and staring.

Darrell's gang was followed close behind by Craig and Dianna, with Craig fussing over his wife. He held her one hand as she descended. "Okay, one more step."

Dianna slapped his hand away. "I'm pregnant, not an invalid."

Craig leaned over next to his brother. "She had a fainting spell yesterday."

As she climbed inside the bright red VW Bug, Dianna said, "It was nothing. I got a little lightheaded. That's all."

Craig closed her door and limped over to his side. "Can't be too careful." He climbed inside.

Half a minute later, Darrell's mom came up beside him, dressed in a sheer white cover up, bright primary colors swirling beneath. She called back over her head, "Charles, get a move on it." A few seconds later, Darrell's dad appeared at the door, clad in navy board shorts and a Saugatuck T-shirt.

Darrell extended a hand and his mom said, "Thanks, son." She and his dad climbed into the waiting white Volvo, started it up and were off, the quiet engine purring.

Next, Rachel and Anna stepped through the doors and each held one open. The crack, crack, crack announced the arrival of his aunt and she appeared in the doorway. She stood there for a bit, her head raised to the sky, a pale blue cover up hanging on her frail body. Without looking at either teen, she asked, "Is my chair ready?"

In unison, the girls answered, "Yes, ma'am. All packed."

"Good," Gertrude grumped.

Before she went down one step, Salazar appeared beside her, holding her one arm. He opened the door to the large Lincoln Navigator, its black paint gleaming. He helped her into the passenger seat, shut her door quietly and walked around to the driver's side. Salazar hollered over to Darrell, "You'll follow us, okay? Not very far.

Maybe fifteen minutes."

"We'll be right behind you," Darrell said. He, Erin and Leo hustled into their shining blue Taurus. While he buckled up and turned the ignition, Erin got Leo settled in his car seat and got herself belted in.

The parade of cars arrived at Oval Beach fourteen minutes later, according to the clock on the dash, and each paid the parking fee. Craig must've known where to go because he headed for the north end of the parking lot. Each car pulled into an empty slot, leaving the last handicapped space for Gertrude's car. A thought flitted across Darrell's mind: had his Aunt Gertrude arranged to have these spots reserved? He didn't see how, even as he realized they'd gotten the last remaining slots at this end of the parking lot.

He, Erin and Leo exited and they stood beside the car. Before they even walked on the sand, Erin had them slathered with sunblock. She took care of Leo first, even making sure his tender ears were covered. Then she slipped off her cover up and applied the SP-50 to her skin. When she handed the bottle to Darrell for his next round, he glanced up and stared wide-eyed. Erin set one foot on the bottom frame of the car and applied the white cream over her exposed limbs. And exposed was the right word, Darrell decided. She wore the same sunny yellow two-piece she had donned years ago in Cape May, the bikini and top displaying her beautiful curves and flat tummy. "I haven't seen you in that since Cape May," he said, his eyes wide.

Erin chuckled. "It has taken me a few years to shed the flab I picked up with Leo."

Darrell smiled. "You look as ravishing as you did on that bed at the Inn of Cape May."

"Easy, boy. We have company." Erin gestured to Leo whose gaze switched between his mom and dad.

Darrell laughed. "What do you think, son? Doesn't your mom look great?"

Leo flashed a broad smile. "I think mom always looks great."

Darrell clapped his son on the shoulder. "I think you are exactly right."

They made their way from the parking lot to the sand and stared at the long smooth beach in front of them. The sand, more tan than bleached white like in Cape May, seemed to stretch for half a mile north, with the beach widest where they stood at the entrance, maybe a hundred fifty feet deep back from the water. Darrell stared north and saw the sand narrowed as it wound around the lake. Everywhere he looked, tall, wild grasses edged the sand, the tops waving slightly in the breeze off the water.

Darrell checked his watch. 11:15. It was early but the beach was starting to fill up with bathers, their towels dropped like colorful markers on the tan sand. The teen Indians hurried past them, scurried down the beach a hundred yards or so and placed bright yellow flags— markers, Darrell guessed—in the sand about fifty feet back from the water's edge. He noticed, though bright beach towels dotted the surface of most of the sand, the wide expanse the two teens had staked out was empty of any towels or umbrellas.

His aunt had a reserved spot on a public beach?

As soon as they finished, the two youths disappeared back up the dunes, no doubt heading back to the car. He and Leo ran ahead to a spot well behind the flags and together they laid out three bright beach towels, his and

Erin's striped red-white-and-blue and Leo's, a bright blue with a horse across the front. He and Leo walked around all three, inspecting them to make sure the fabric was pulled tight and the corners were flat.

"Nice job," Erin started and was interrupted.

"Careful!" They heard his aunt scream from the top of the dune. "Not that way. Over to the left. Okay, now straighten it out."

In a few seconds Aunt Gertrude appeared on the ramp, rising over the opening in the dune. Behind her, the teens pushed a large red wheelchair, the kind with fat tires for the sand. Gertrude sat up in the thing, looking like some queen being transported by her servants.

How appropriate, Darrell thought.

Chapter 24

"In the center, girls. I want to be able to watch everything. At my age, it's all I get to do," Gertrude demanded.

Rachel and Anna worked to guide the oversized wheelchair into the center of the flagged off area, having to back up and readjust the chair several times, its fat tires dragging in the sand. When Aunt Gertrude nodded, the girls hustled back to the car and, within seconds, returned carrying two large bags, overflowing with beach equipment. Out of one, Rachel pulled a tall umbrella, opened it and positioned it over Gertrude's head.

"A little to the left, I think," Gertrude called behind her. "When the sun gets a little higher, it's going to come right over my shoulder."

The teens edged the bright red-and-white umbrella a few inches to the side and worked the post into the sand. From the second bag, Anna placed a small cooler on the sand next to the chair and Rachel opened a small collapsible table and set it above the cooler. Then Anna retrieved a pitcher and a glass and set them on the table. She filled the tumbler with lemonade. Then they came around in front of Aunt Gertrude.

"Go ahead, have fun." She dismissed them with a wave of her hand. She eased back in her chair and looked out from underneath another floppy beach hat, this one yellow, white and lilac. "But not too far, in case I need you," she called.

The Native teens strolled past where Darrell, Erin and Leo stood, watching the whole scenario unfold. As they neared, Leo flashed a smile and held his hand up, palm out for slapping. Anna grinned back at him and gave his small hand a tap. "See you in the water."

"Let's go, Dad," Leo called, his eyes following the Indian girls as they waded into the waves. Darrell and Erin grabbed a hand and they headed for the slate blue lake.

Watching the teens splash into the water ahead of them, Darrell scanned the shoreline and saw mostly young, tanned white faces and bodies mixed in with quite a few small families, all white. Off to one side, he spotted a few blacks and a Latino couple but no Indians. Other than Anna and Rachel.

Aunt Gertrude had chosen the perfect day. It dawned warm and the temperature hovered now in the high seventies, predicted to climb another ten degrees. But the constant breeze off Lake Michigan brought soothing relief from the high temps and humidity. The sun shone so bright—not quite overhead yet—it washed some of the color from the sky, turning the wide blue expanse fainter. No sliver or puff of a cloud marred the blue expanse.

It was as if his aunt had even ordered up the perfect weather for the day as well. The waves, which rolled in, were smooth and constant, not enough to overwhelm swimmers. Holding Leo between them, Darrell and Erin ventured farther out into the water, raising his small body up to meet the rolling waves. Leo laughed at each wave he conquered and his laughter helped Darrell forget his other concerns and enjoy the moment with his beautiful wife and delightful son.

In the middle of their fun, Craig and Dianna came over and joined them. His brother sliced his hand across the water and, before he knew it, Darrell and Erin were in a fierce water-splashing fight with Craig and his wife. They backed up and when Leo was able to stand on the sand, he joined in, slicing the water toward his uncle.

In mock surrender, Craig held up both hands and called, "You win. We give up. You have a special weapon. Leo."

Leo laughed even harder then, so hard, he swallowed a bit of lake water. Erin was at his side in a second until he coughed twice and the fit passed. After they floated for a while in the fresh water, riding the small whitecapped swells, Darrell, Erin and Leo let the waves push them back to the shore, Craig and Dianna a few waves behind. Their butts in the sand, their legs stretched into the cool water, the five of them sat there, letting small wave after wave roll over them.

After a few minutes, Leo turned to his dad. "Can we build a sandcastle? Will this sand work as well as the sand on the beach on the Ches'peake?"

Darrell scooped up the sand at their feet and patted it into a small mound. It held together nicely before a bigger wave came in and washed furrows in the little hill. "Looks like it works great but we'll have to move it away from the waterline…if we want it to last a while."

He stood up in the shallow wavelets, letting the water drip down his legs and Leo followed his example.

Erin rose to her feet next to them then lowered her face to Leo's level. "I think I'll let you and your dad take care of this." She eyed their towels farther up the sand.

"I hear a towel calling my name."

Darrell looked over the top of his son. "You okay?"

She smiled, though he thought the smile wasn't as bright as usual. "I'm pretty tired...and still a little queasy."

Dianna came over, pushing water from her one-piece, blue-gray suit, which she'd confided had room for her growing abdomen. "I'm bushed too." She patted her stomach. "This little one could use some time in the horizontal position. Care if I join you?"

Darrell said, "That sounds like a great idea. It'll give you ladies, mothers, a chance to catch up. Feel free to use my towel. Miguel lent us more. They're in the car."

Craig came over to his nephew. "Is this sandcastle thing only for you and your dad or can an uncle join in the fun?"

Leo said, "Sure, Uncle Craig. Mom always says the more the merrier."

The three males paced around the beach, looking for the right space for the sand construction, far enough away from the water but not too far from their towels. After a little back and forth, Leo announced, "*This* is perfect."

Leo, Darrell and Craig commenced excavating sand for "Sir Leo's castle." Craig and Darrell took turns hauling moist sand to the spot and Leo worked at creating walls that would stand up. Soon, thanks to their combined efforts, they had plenty of sand to play with and all three worked at building up the fortress.

Fifteen minutes later, two shadows fell over the construction and Darrell looked up to see the teens standing above them, blocking the sun. Anna and Rachel smiled down at Leo and Rachel said, "You're doing pretty good, but I think you could use a few tools."

The Natives exchanged a glance and Rachel ran over to where Aunt Gertrude sat in her chair, now dozing under her beach hat. Grabbing a few things from one of the bags, she hurried back to the sandcastle and handed two plastic toys to Leo. "This one," she pointed to a yellow plastic cylinder opened at one end with notches in the other end, "you use to make the turrets of the castle." She then handed him a bright red plastic bucket with a similar mold in the bottom. "And this one is really good for making towers."

Leo looked over at the Indian teen. "Thanks, Rachel." He glanced at his dad, a question in his eyes. "How about if Anna and Rachel join us? We can make it even bigger."

"A fine idea," Darrell turned to both girls. "Would you be so kind to contribute to the construction of Sir Leo's castle?"

Both girls giggled—delighted, little girls' giggles—and Darrell realized it was the first time he'd heard an innocent, joyful sound from either of the two. He edged back and let the teens close to the castle. They were young and enthusiastic and soon the castle was twice its size with turrets and towers sprouting along the sides.

He watched the girls work with the sand as one wall collapsed. Leo laughed again and the teens followed, the three of them reinforcing the sand wall, while Craig worked on the opposite side. Darrell let his gaze wander the shoreline, taking in the couples holding hands, the families splashing in the waves and another family building its own sandcastle. Not near as grand as Sir Leo's castle, he thought.

He saw a few singles here and there, lying on beach

towels taking in the sun. Seeing Leo and the two girls working on the sandcastle together, with Craig now supervising, the memory of another sandcastle seven years before flashed in his mind. The two immigrant kids about the same age as Leo playing in the sand as the waves washed away their castle. No, the ghosts of two immigrant children, he corrected himself.

Darrell stared up and down the beach but saw no sign of Sheila, or rather her ghost. He wondered if he dreamt her visit last night and then remembered her word, Shelbyville. Maybe this would be a good time to pull one of the teens aside, probably Rachel. He could ask her about Shelbyville, see if she could shed any light on the clue. If that was what it was.

"Girls, I need some more lemonade," Aunt Gertrude called loudly, her head swiveling, making the colors of the beach hat dance.

On impulse, both girls stopped mid-action and began to rise. Rachel whispered to Anna, "Stay. I got this." In two seconds, she rose and hurried over to where Gertrude sat. Darrell watched as Anna's shoulders relaxed and then he glanced over to see Rachel pull ice cubes from the cooler and drop them into the plastic tumbler. She refilled the lemonade and leaned close to say something to Gertrude. His aunt nodded and Rachel hurried back across the sand. She resettled herself next to the others.

Darrell wondered why Salazar wasn't by his aunt's side, tending to her needs, and realized he hadn't come down to the beach with everyone else. Darrell let his gaze wander across the beach and then back up to the parking lot. There, he saw the caretaker in his old straw hat, standing behind one of the smaller dunes, staring down on the beach. For a moment, their eyes met and Salazar gave a slight nod.

Darrell rejoined the huddle around the emerging castle. It was impressive, four long walls with two inner chambers. Using the smaller plastic form, Leo scooped up another mound of wet sand to form yet another turret.

"I never knew my grandson was also a gifted architect," a soft voice cooed. "That's quite a commanding sandcastle."

Leo beamed up at his grandma. "It's called Sir Leo's castle." He pointed to the rest of his team. "I've had some expert help. Anna and Rachel brought these." He held up the plastic forms.

Susan Henshaw smiled at her grandson and gave a wink to the others. "Even a gifted architect needs a great team." She glanced down the beach and back. "I do think yours is definitely the finest sandcastle on the whole shore."

"Yeah, until the water washes it away." Leo chuckled.

"Sir Leo," Susan continued, "do you think I could steal one of your workers for a few minutes?" She placed a hand on Darrell's shoulder.

"Sure, we're almost done anyway."

"Great." Then to Darrell, "can we talk for a bit?" She took a few steps away.

Darrell stood up and brushed the sand off the back of his shorts. "Okay, big guy. I'll be back in a few to inspect the final construction." He stepped across the sand to join his mother. When he pulled up even with her, she began to stroll down the beach away from the sandcastle crew and other throngs of people. It was obvious she wanted a private chat and that made Darrell nervous.

His relationship with his mom was…complicated. He loved her but— After catching her in a compromising position as a teen, he'd looked at his mother through a different lens and the strained relationship hung over him like one of his OCD obsessions.

When they were far enough away from any eavesdroppers, his mom stopped and turned to face him. Even in her fifties, Susan Henshaw carried herself well. She had no trouble showing off her figure in a brief two piece, not quite a bikini like Erin's but not that far off. He'd been more comfortable if she wore a discreet, colorful one piece like most other women her age, but Susan Henshaw was not like most older women.

Without preamble, she started in, "I talked with Tom Salazar last night. He told me about your conversation after the lawn games."

Darrell didn't like where this was going. "I simply asked him about a girl that's gone missing."

His mom huffed, "Why would you care about some strange girl? One you never met?"

Darrell blew out a breath and shook his head. "I'm not sure you'd understand."

Susan Henshaw shielded her eyes with one hand and put the other on her hip. "Try me."

Darrell realized this was not a request, so he gave it his best shot. "Our last stop before we got here was Kalamazoo. At this gas station we saw this flyer for this pretty, teenage Native girl who has gone missing. Leo was barely able to read the words on this flyer and her predicament got to him. To be honest, it got to me too. This girl is the same age as the kids in my classes. She's been missing weeks and nobody knows what happened to her."

"We get flyers like that every week in Ann Arbor," his mother announced, as if that explained it all. "Girls like her go missing all the time."

Darrell turned his head and stared at her. "What's that supposed to mean?" The words came out sharper than he intended and he saw his mother wilt.

"I know you, Darrell. I know you have a caring heart. It's one of the things that makes you such a good teacher and coach. And your dad and I love you for it." She stopped and stared down, her pink painted toenails making small lines in the fine sand. "When you get wrapped up in something, like with the poor young woman in Cape May, you go off the deep end."

Darrell hadn't told his parents about the haunted bride in Cape May and realized they—or at least his mom—had paid more attention to the coverage of his heroics than he thought.

"You have a wife and small son to think about," his mom said.

Darrell glanced at the sandcastle crew and, farther on, to the towels where Erin lay next to Dianna. "They're the best part of my life."

His mom nodded. "That's as it should be. But don't forget you have more family. Your father and I seldom get to have time with you and we're so happy you made the trip." She looked into Darrell's eyes. "And remember why we're here, to celebrate with your aunt. We're grateful we got this invitation…and I don't want to upset her."

"Grateful?" Darrell snapped, a little too loud. He paused, looking to see if his word carried across the sand but no one paid them any attention. "Our aunt has this huge mansion on the shore and we haven't been invited for what...twenty years? Since Uncle David died."

"Well, we're here now. Let's make the most of it." She shook her head once. "I don't want you to upset Aunt Gertrude or her staff with questions about some...squaw." She flipped her hand, the pink fingernails flying in front of his face. The way she pronounced the final word made Sheila sound dirty. He started to give some retort but she wasn't done.

She took his hand. "Let the law officials take care of it. That's what they're paid for." She gave her head another shake, her dirty blonde hair flipping in the motion. "I don't want to see you jaunting off on some wild goose chase about some teen you've never even met and maybe getting yourself in danger. I love you and I don't want anything to happen to you."

Chapter 25

"I don't want to see anything happen to you." His mom's words echoed as Darrell made his way back to the sandcastle. What did she mean by that?

After completing the grandest castle on the sand and two more jaunts into the warm lake, his family decided they were famished and needed "immediate sustenance"—Erin's words. And this was despite devouring the snacks Miquel had packed them. They pulled up their towels and admired Sir Leo's Castle one last time, taking a few photos to commemorate. Together, they headed across the sand.

In front of them, Rachel and Anna maneuvered the oversized wheelchair across the beach and up the ramp, and Darrell learned to stifle his instincts to help. He stood aside. Once on the parking lot, Aunt Gertrude announced, "If you want to check out the town, you're welcome to, but if you want to come back to Wentworth, Miguel will fix you whatever you'd like."

Even before Gertrude's invitation, Erin and Darrell had conferred as they crossed the beach and decided they needed a little time away from family. Darrell knew he needed time away from his mom. Based on a tip Erin had gotten from Dianna, they decided on Coral Gables, a charming restaurant nestled on Water Street with tables facing the Kalamazoo River. Because it was well past the lunch hour, they had little trouble snagging a table on the outside terrace with a delightful view of the water, where they wouldn't feel out of place in their swim shirts and coverups.

Walking behind the hostess to their table, Darrell picked up bits of conversations as they passed other late diners. One snippet caught his attention.

"Relax. They're not from here and Gertrude said they'll be gone in a week."

Darrell tried to look, without looking, and saw two older couples dressed in fancy nautical clothes, and recognized the one pair. The Newsoms, whom they met when Leo wandered onto their yacht following Sheila. And, even though he only got a brief glimpse, the other man looked familiar. When the hostess stopped and indicated their table, he, Erin and Leo slid into chairs facing the river. When he turned to glance back where the two couples sat, the name came to him. Roger Herrold, president of Capstone Shipping and one of the men saluting his aunt at the celebration at The Butler. He'd learned it never hurt to remember names.

As they sat together under a bright red umbrella, large pleasure boats and sleek sailboats slid by at a leisurely pace, heading down the river on their way to the open waters of Lake Michigan. The sun high in the sky now, the day had warmed considerably and the breeze off the water added a touch of coolness to their dining experience. Smiling at his wife and son, Darrell relaxed.

The waiter arrived, a tall young man stood with a tight smile on his rectangular face, longish black hair held up in a pony tail. He handed Erin and Darrell menus. His smile broadened at Leo and he said, "I suppose you want a menu as well."

Leo looked up at the tall man. "Of course. I can

read…some."

The waiter's smile never wavered. "I'm sure you can." He handed Leo a printed paper with sea creatures outlined on it as well as three crayons. "I bet you can color too." He turned toward Darrell. "Can I get you any drinks while you check out the menu?"

Darrell looked up into almond-shaped brown eyes. "Thanks." He pointed to Erin. "We'll have iced tea and Leo will have lemonade."

The waiter disappeared and all three buried their noses in the menus.

"So, we meet again," a man's voice asked, pulling Darrell's attention from the food choices. He looked up to find four people standing next to their table. The visitors stood with the high sun over their shoulders and Darrell used a hand to block the glare.

"I apologize. I'm not sure if you remember us. We're the Newsoms, Dwight and Cynthia," the woman added in a high voice. Darrell could make out a nest of blonde hair atop her head and the man wore a captain's cap. She continued quickly, "We met a few days ago, the day of your aunt's birthday bash. We were so charmed by your son." She turned to the boy. "Leo, if I remember correctly."

Remembering his manners, Darrell rose. "Yes, of course, when our son wandered onto your boat." He nodded. "Darrell and Erin."

Erin shook Cynthia's extended hand.

The older woman glanced over at her husband and then at Leo. "Leo won our hearts when he wandered onto our boat. He so reminded us of our Bradley, we called our grandson that evening, didn't we, Dwight?"

Dwight Newsom nodded, then gestured behind him.

"And these are the Herrolds, Roger and Jane." The other man reached past Newsom, extending his hand.

Darrell shook a fleshy hand. "I remember, from Aunt Gertrude's birthday bash at the Butler. Capstone Shipping, right?"

Standing, the man looked to be the opposite of Newsom. Short, with a bald head and bushy brown eyebrows laced with gray and a massive belly. Jane Herrold looked to be petite, black-haired with an oversized, round face.

"Very good," the man bellowed and laughed, the sound coming from deep inside.

Dwight Newsom asked, "So how goes your search?"

"Our search?" Darrell offered.

"When your son climbed onto our boat, he said he was searching for some girl," Newsom said.

Leo looked up from his menu. "Sheila. Sheila Birdsong." He returned his attention to coloring the mermaid's tail blue.

Erin reached into her massive bag and, after fishing around, she came out with the dog-eared flyer and handed it to Darrell, who held it up. "Leo and I saw this missing poster at a gas station in Kalamazoo and we've been asking around."

Dwight Newson tapped the paper with one finger. "Kalamazoo is quite a ways from here."

"I guess," Darrell said.

After a bit of silence, Roger Herrold asked in a raspy voice, "Any luck finding her?"

Darrell flashed a look at his son and said quickly, "Nothing so far."

Erin looked again at the Newsoms. "We apologize

for Leo coming on to your boat uninvited and disturbing you."

Cynthia clucked. "Nonsense. Your son was a delight and a perfect gentleman."

Her husband added, "And now I understand he simply mistook our Sarah for this Sheila…"

"Sheila Birdsong," Leo finished without looking up from his creation.

Cynthia patted Leo on the arm. "I think it's nice you're looking for this girl but I wouldn't get your hopes up, young man. These Native youths often simply take off. Looking for a better life. At least, that's what I've heard."

Another few awkward seconds of silence later, Roger Herrold said, "It was good to meet you in person." He nodded at Darrell and Erin. Leo didn't look up from his coloring.

Dwight Newsom added, "Well, I hope you have some success finding this poor girl."

Roger Herrold said, "I hope you enjoy your lunch on this gorgeous day." He gestured to the river flowing by. "The view kinda makes it, doesn't it?" With Dwight Newsom leading, the two couples turned and threaded their way through the tables and disappeared into the interior of the restaurant.

Erin caught Darrell's eye and said, "That felt a little strange."

Before Darrell had a chance to respond, the waiter returned with their drinks. After placing them on the table, he stood, hands behind his back, and smiled. "Have you decided?"

On the waiter's recommendation, Erin and Darrell ordered the lake perch and Leo stuck with chicken nuggets. After the server took orders and collected the menus, he disappeared.

Seeing the flyer still on the table, Darrell slid it to Erin who returned it to her mom purse. Darrell glanced from his son to his wife and then toward the interior of the restaurant. Eyebrows raised, he whispered, "Later."

In a few minutes, the server brought their food, managing to balance all the plates on one tray. They all dug in and all conversation gave way to crunches and sighs of delight. Their hunger took over and, in a few minutes, they devoured the fish and chicken as well as the cole slaw and fries.

As soon as the last bite was consumed, the uniformed waiter reappeared at their table, as if he'd been watching them. "I hope you enjoyed your meal, sir," he said and his brown eyes held Darrell's longer than normal.

Darrell looked up at the almond-shaped eyes which gave away nothing. "The perch sandwich was one of the best I've had."

Erin added, "It was all delicious. Even Leo finished his."

The boy held up a plate with only a few crumbs. "See?"

The waiter chuckled, relaxing his sharp features. "I do."

He glanced at Darrell and then seemed to notice Darrell's wallet, lying atop the table. Darrell caught the server eyeing his wallet, so he pulled out a credit card and extended it to the waiter.

The waiter snatched the charge card. "Is there anything else I can get any of you?"

Erin shook her head and Darrell said, "I could use a

bit more iced tea."

"I'll be right back with a refill." The server nodded and stepped away.

Thirty seconds later, the tall waiter was back. "Here you go, sir."

The waiter placed another tall glass of tea in front of Darrell, beads of condensation dotting the glass. As the young man stood over him, Darrell studied his features and swarthy complexion. He decided he had to be Native.

The server smiled and set a small silver tray with a pen weighting down a few small papers. "Whenever you're ready. Feel free to stay as long as you want and enjoy this beautiful day." His rust-colored arm indicated the river and sky. His brown eyes narrowed at Darrell. "Please review the bill to make sure I got it right. The two top sheets are for our records and the pages at the bottom are for you to keep. I'll be back to pick it up whenever you're ready."

Darrell downed some of the sweet tea, its iciness feeling good in his throat still parched from the time on the beach. He reached for the tray. Picking up the pen, he used it to flip through the sheets, the itemized bill and the credit card slip needing his signature, followed by his copy. He signed the receipt and reached to pull his copy, the third paper, free from the clip. When he did, he noticed a fourth paper below, small and looking like it had been ripped from a larger piece, one edge torn irregularly. Pulling it out, he saw some handwriting on the slip.

Darrell examined it, then glanced around for the waiter. No one seemed to take notice and he didn't see their server anywhere around. Making sure no one was watching, Darrell slid the last paper beneath the table edge and read the words.

We've heard you have taken a special interest in the missing Gun Lake girls. If you want to know more about what happened to them, be at Carlos' Diner 10:00 a.m. tomorrow.

Chapter 26

"Are you okay in there?" Darrell called through the bathroom door.

"Keep your pants on...or off. I'll be out in a minute."

Darrell had waited for hours to get Erin alone to share the note he'd been passed at lunch. First, on the ride back to Wentworth, he decided he didn't want to get his son involved and chose to hold off. Then when they got to the mansion, Erin fussed with Leo, putting him down for an afternoon nap, something he didn't often do but he really needed today.

Then, his dad had stopped him, saying he wanted some time to talk with him. "Looking into people's mouths all day might pay pretty well, but can get downright boring." His father pulled him aside and continued, "Not near as interesting as wrestling with teenagers every day. How about you share a few war stories with your father?"

So, Darrell and Charles Henshaw sat on the veranda, downed a few beers and talked. Of course, Darrell didn't tell him about the ghosts. But, between the football and basketball teams and trying to teach high schoolers why government was important, he had plenty of tales. Not to mention all the high school pranks the kids pulled. He rambled and his dad listened, asking questions and laughing at Darrell's jokes. It was the first time in years he could remember having any time like this with his dad. It felt great.

Still, even while he and his dad talked, he felt the note in his pocket and wanted to show it to Erin, get her take. The few times he looked for her, he saw her huddled with Dianna and figured the two were having great mommy talks. He didn't want to interrupt but, with each hour, he grew more anxious.

Then, they had another family dinner, an old-style barbeque with ribs, chicken and corn on the cob, enjoyed on the side porch under the red umbrellas. Like every meal prepared by Aunt Gertrude's staff, it too was delicious.

Through it all, Sheila's probable fate taunted him and he figured the note might actually lead him somewhere. His one good fortune for the evening had occurred by accident. In between drinks and dinner, he needed the restroom and didn't want to use the one in their suite as it was right next to Leo's room. His son was a notoriously light sleeper when napping. So, he headed for the other side of the house and ran into Rachel, alone, in the hallway. Glancing to make sure no one else was around, he pulled out the note and showed it to her.

When she read the scribbled words, her eyes got wide and then she handed it back to him as if the paper contained germs.

"Are you going to go?" Rachel whispered.

Darrell nodded his head hard. "Yeah, if I can figure out a way not to let everyone in this house know."

"I won't say anything," the Indian teen said.

"Thanks. The only problem is I don't know where Carlos' Diner is...and I didn't want to ask Salazar or Gertrude. For obvious reasons."

Rachel stared at him, her brown eyes looking much older than her sixteen years. "Carlos' Diner is a dive in Shelbyville, right off the highway I think." Right then, the single word whispered by Sheila's ghost came back to him. "Shelbyville."

So, at ten thirty at night, he and Erin had finally gotten some alone time and *she* had scooted into the bathroom before he could even say anything. She had looked different, her face flush and her smile crooked.

He'd said, "I missed you today." Before she disappeared inside, he'd given her a long passionate kiss which she returned in kind. Then, she placed a hand on his chest, grinned at him and gave a gentle shove.

"I'll only be a minute."

That had been five—no, seven minutes ago. Darrell paced a straight pattern on the plush rug in front of the bathroom door. Across the small space twenty-seven times. With each minute, it became harder to wait. This was the first real lead to finding what happened to Sheila, or at least he thought it was. Twice, he stopped mid-pacing and started to say something, to try to hurry Erin along, but then he remembered she'd been queasy lately. Maybe she was still feeling iffy. He could wait. Erin had always been worth waiting for.

Being separated the way they had been this afternoon and evening reminded Darrell how much he needed her, how much she was a part of him. Just as his patience was wearing thin and he was set to knock on the door, it opened. Erin stood there, her beautiful figure silhouetted under her new rose nightgown, which was so sheer it did little to conceal her delicious curves and the two points up high. She stood there in the doorway, framed in the light from the bathroom which gave her whole body a glow. Her face wore a wide, almost embarrassed smile.

And she held a small, pink and white plastic tube in her one hand.

Her smile became even more crooked and she asked, "How'd you like to have another kid?"

Chapter 27

Darrell stood there dumbfounded and stared at his wife. "W-w-what?"

Her eyes dropped to the floor. "You know, how I've been queasy lately and how I threw up yesterday morning?"

Darrell had trouble finding his voice so he merely nodded.

"And I've tired more easily and needed to take a break, like when you and Leo climbed Mt. Baldhead yesterday?"

Finally, Darrell said, "Yeah, I was worried you might be coming down with something."

"Well, I was sharing how I felt with Dianna—whom I really love, by the way—and she said my symptoms sounded a lot like hers in her first few months." She brought her free hand up and laid it on his bare chest. "I thought she was silly. After all, I've been on the pill for years. But the pill isn't a hundred percent effective. Anyway, she had one of those home pregnancy tests. She said she'd picked it up for one of the gals at work and had forgotten to give it to her. Anyway, she gave it to me."

Her other hand held the tube and she brought it up to eye level and Darrell stared at the indicator. Two lines. Right next to the key which indicated "pregnant." His gaze shifted to Erin's beautiful emerald eyes, now moist.

"What do you think?" she asked, her voice barely above a whisper.

Darrell broke out in a huge smile and grabbed his wife around the waist. He lifted her off her feet, twirled her around, set her down gently and kissed her. "I think it's fantastic. We're going to have another Leo!"

Erin eyes twinkled. "Or maybe a Lily?"

Darrell laughed too loudly, then caught himself and whispered, "That would be just as grand."

"We hadn't planned it. I mean you're taking classes for your masters and with my work in OB—"

He cut her off with a kiss. "We'll make it work. We'll find a way." He looked down his wife's lithe figure. "You don't look…how far along are you?"

Erin shook her head. "Not far. Six or maybe seven weeks. I simply thought I was late with everything we have going on."

Darrell said, "My parents are going to have two more grandkids this year. My dad will be over the moon. You know he and I had a great talk today."

Erin pursed her lips. "I don't think we should tell them. Not yet. It's awfully early and anything could go wrong. The test could even be a false positive."

Darrell gave a slow nod of his head. "Yeah, of course. But Dianna?"

"I can tell her. I mean, the first question she's going to ask when we're alone tomorrow will be about the test. She already said she wouldn't say anything till I'm ready." Then she continued, "I don't think we can tell Leo, not just yet. Not till we're sure."

Darrell agreed. "I love that guy but there's no way he'd keep it to himself. He'd be telling mom and dad and anyone who listened."

Erin said, "I want to wait till we get home, get it confirmed then tell Leo."

"Sounds good. How about you? How are you feeling now?" Darrell asked, concern in his voice.

"Right now? I feel fine."

He smiled. "Great! I think this calls for a physical celebration." He grabbed Erin around the waist again and carried her over to the bed. He used one hand to pull down the covers and the other to set her down. He undid the tie on his pajama pants and let them drop to the floor. He didn't even bother to fold them. Naked, he crawled onto the king size bed.

Erin eyed him up and down, her grin wide. "Be careful what you ask for, tiger. You might just get it."

Later, when they were delightfully spent and tired, they lay back on the bed, their sweating skin against the sheet, the covers scrawled on the floor. Only one hand touching, they stared at the ceiling fan making its slow rotation in the dim room.

After a few moments, Erin whispered, "When we first got up here, you said you needed to talk with me about something."

Hearing her quiet, whispery voice, Darrell realized they hadn't exactly been quiet...before. He hadn't cared then but decided he better keep his voice down. "And I thought *I* had something important to share."

He rose, slid off the bed and went to where he had piled up the clothes he'd worn today, while he'd been waiting for Erin to exit the bathroom. Finding his navy shorts, he went through the pockets until he found the torn slip of paper. He brought it over, knelt on the bed and handed it to Erin, who sat up against the headboard, still completely naked and obviously comfortable that way.

Her eyes ran over the words and then came up to meet his. "When did you get this?"

"It was attached to our lunch bill from Coral Gables this afternoon. Remember our server, he looked Native and he said 'Please check to make sure everything is correct' or something like that. Anyway, I've had this since then and I've been dying to talk to you about it."

Still holding the note in one hand, she used her other to pat his chest and then lower. "You poor baby."

He squirmed out of her reach. He needed to talk this out with her, didn't he? He looked over at her, two feet away, and saw her beautiful curves shimmer with perspiration. No, he needed her take on this.

"Anyway, I was lucky to catch Rachel in the hallway and asked her where this Carlos' Diner was and guess what she told me."

He saw the light flash on in his wife's green eyes. "Shelbyville," she said without hesitation.

He nodded. "The one and same as Sheila told me in the vision. I took another look at the map—while you were doing your thing in the bathroom—and figured it's almost an hour away."

She pointed to the paper. "Ten o'clock tomorrow. You planning on going? You're going to need some cover."

He nodded again. "I had an idea on that." He stared into her emerald eyes. "How about I tell everyone I'm heading to the history museum. You know, to get my history fix. I'll do a quick tour and then head over to Carlos' Diner."

Erin yawned, jaws opening wide. "With the driving,

it'll be tight but it might work." Her eyes fluttered closed, then opened wide. "Hey, I can do some grumbling about not wanting to go on another history fieldtrip, but I don't want to just hang around the mansion all morning." The two emerald irises shone. "Maybe, Leo and I will take a short sail on Aunt Gertrude's Mason."

"That sounds like a plan. We work pretty well together. Have I ever told you that?" Darrell leaned in and kissed her again, feeling his passion surge back.

Erin kissed him back but put a hand on his bare chest. "Easy, big boy. Enough for tonight. I'm exhausted and we're going to need our sleep." She punctuated her words with another wide yawn. "Good night."

He echoed, "Good night," then added, "I know you can handle pretty much any sailboat, but that's Lake Michigan out there, not the Chesapeake." He nodded toward the window. "Be careful, for all three of your sakes. Okay?"

"Same to you," she mumbled as she pulled the covers up and snuggled under them. "Based on your past experience with your ghosts, you have no idea what you may be walking into." She yawned a third time.

Darrell stared at his wife's face, barely visible in the dull light coming through the large windows. Beautiful heart-shaped face. Two full pink lips, slightly pouted in slumber. Tresses of red hair falling across her face. Even the few freckles which shown as tiny, darkened spots on her cheeks. He loved this woman so much it hurt at times.

He watched as her breathing smoothed out, her chest moving up and down slightly. She could sleep in a hurricane. He'd do anything to protect her...and Leo and now, another one. She was right. He needed to watch himself tomorrow.

Chapter 28

Up early, Darrell showered, shaved and dressed quietly as Erin slumbered on. Mid-process, the contented smile on her face almost drew him back to bed but he had things to do. He leaned over and kissed her. He grabbed breakfast, settling for some homemade croissants, and explained to his mom and dad and the staff he had an early appointment at the history museum. Luckily, Aunt Gertrude hadn't risen yet. She would've asked a hundred questions. As it was, his dad said, "Those who are ignorant of the past are doomed to repeat it. Right, son?"

Between bites of the buttery confection, Darrell mumbled, "Right."

Walking down the hardwood floor in the long hallway, he realized he'd need to go get his car. He hadn't been back to the large garage behind the house. When he stepped through the expansive front doors and down the steps, Darrell pulled up short. There, on the circular asphalt driveway sat his Taurus, its blue color gleaming in the morning sun.

Ilya stood beside the front door to the car, keys in hand. He wore a small smile but it didn't reach his eyes, their blue-gray color hard. Darrell stepped up and accepted the keys, eyeing the servant more closely. He looked to be in his mid-twenties, with a darker complexion, which could be from his ancestors or maybe simply days in the Midwest sun. Looking at him now, Darrell couldn't decide if his features were Mediterranean or Latin, or somewhere in between. He wore the jeans and T-shirt Darrell had seen him in before. When he took the keys, Darrell noticed, for the first time, Ilya's hands were smooth, with few callouses and his fingernails were neat and trimmed.

"Thanks," Darrell said, though he suspected the question must have shown on his face.

Ilya chuckled, though the laugh seemed forced. "Rachel heard you were heading out and told me. I knew you'd be needing your car, so I wanted to have it ready. Miss Gertrude likes for us to anticipate our guests' needs." He opened the driver's door.

Darrell nodded and slid inside.

Before Ilya shut the door, he asked, "You need directions to the museum?"

Taken aback by the question, Darrell managed, "It's in Douglas on the main drag?"

Ilya said, "Yeah, it's in an old schoolhouse on Center and Washington. You can't miss it." The frozen smile stayed as he shut the door with a thud.

Darrell started the car and the twenty-something waved. As Darrell drove around and past the mansion, the five red umbrellas on the veranda sliding by, he thought, every move we make, someone is watching, listening.

It took him only ten minutes to make the trip to Douglas and when Darrell walked up to the front door of the old schoolhouse, a man was turning a key in the lock. The man was middle age, with short black hair and dull brown eyes behind wire-rimmed glasses. He wore navy shorts and a yellow polo with the logo for the museum over the pocket. As they entered together, Darrell introduced himself.

"Nate Wenstrup," the man said, "I'm the museum director."

Darrell glanced around, pleased they were alone in the small museum. "I only have a few minutes and would like to learn a little about the Natives who first settled in the area."

The director nodded and Darrell noticed a thinning spot atop his head, which he didn't try to hide. Wenstrup pushed the frames up the bridge of his nose and said, "Everyone's in a hurry today. How about I give you the shortened version?"

It took him only a few minutes to cover the basics. He explained how the Natives had lived here for centuries but were forced, through treaties which were never really honored, to give up much of the area of Western Michigan to encroaching settlers. The Pottawatomi, or Gun Lake Tribe as they've come to be called, were later inhabitants, or remnants of the original Natives, who frequented the area in the early 1800's to hunt and fish.

Darrell was amazed how much the director could recite without notes or prompts. When he finished, Wenstrup said, "We have copies of several original documents including the 1805 Treaty of Detroit and the 1819 Treaty of Saginaw, if you'd like to take a deeper look."

Darrell's gaze took in the small museum, two small rooms of the converted one-room schoolhouse. "Copies of the original treaties, I'm impressed. I'm a history teacher and I'm always talking to my students about the importance of primary sources."

The director beamed. "Another of the faithful."

Darrell glanced at his watch. 8:45. "I'd love to take time to look at them but that will have to wait for another day. I've another appointment to keep."

He shook the director's hand. "Thanks, I'll be back when I have more time."

Darrell hurried out the schoolhouse door and slid into his car, starting it up and pulling away from the curb. As he came around the corner onto Washington Street, he glanced back at the museum, thinking maybe the director would be watching him. He saw no one in the museum window. He *was* getting paranoid.

In between their lovemaking last night, he and Erin had reviewed the map, hovering over the large multi-colored paper spread open on the bed, perspiration from their naked bodies dripping onto the map. Erin had marked the route he needed to take since it was mostly through back country roads. Now, he had the map open on the seat next to him, folded and creased to the precise corner of the state he needed. Stopped at the light coming out of town, he studied the route. Noting one slight discoloration when their sweat had dotted the paper, he grinned. When he remembered what their earlier lovemaking had led to, his grin broadened. Another little one. He couldn't wait.

The driver behind him honked his horn, jerking Darrell back to the present. He drove through the intersection and turned onto the Blue Star Highway. Last night, they'd guessed the trip would take a little less than an hour and Darrell wanted to be there on time.

A few miles down the highway, he turned onto 63rd Street and, when the road opened up before him, he accelerated, the powerful V-6 responding with a throaty growl. As he drove, he glanced from side to side. A tall gray silo wearing a silver metal cap flew by on the left, accompanied by two long red barns set at right angles. Beyond them, long fields with perfectly straight rows lined both sides of the asphalt. Crossing the country roads, a funny thought occurred to him. Out here in this very rural landscape, why had they decided to name the roads like downtown Manhattan or Boston? Here he was barreling down 63rd Street and, according to the direction Erin had marked, he was about to turn onto 123rd Street.

The road ahead of him was nearly empty, with only an old, red pickup and a shiny yellow Corvette convertible coming the other way and passing him. From time to time, he glanced in the rearview mirror, seeing even less traffic. For a while, another pickup trailed behind and then turned into the driveway of a quaint two-story farmhouse he passed, complete with chickens in the side yard. The only other car he saw behind him was a dark colored SUV and Darrell only caught sight of it about a half mile behind him when the road straightened out again.

The panorama around him exploded with rural beauty, rows of light green cornstalks waving in the summer wind mixed between gatherings of trees, their full leaves shimmering almost emerald in the sunlight. Seeing the occasional copse of trees, he pondered what the land may have looked like when the Indians hunted and fished around here, before white settlers like his family pushed into these lands. And cut down all the trees. Must have been quite a different vision.

Then he remembered where he was headed and why, and stopped daydreaming.

Glancing down at the instrument panel, he noticed

the needle wavered close to E. He shot a glance at his watch. Damn. He had to stop to fill up or run the risk of running out, alone on a back road. Then he'd have to call his family and ask for help. *And* he'd have to explain what he was doing out here in the middle of nowhere.

Glancing up at the road ahead, he read a small green sign with "Hamilton" printed in crisp white letters along another sign posting a lowered speed limit sign. A little way beyond both signs, he saw something that caused him to release a breath. About a quarter mile ahead, the bright sign of a gas station and convenient store shone above the trees.

Slowing, he put on his blinker and checked his rearview mirror. The lone car behind him, a shiny black SUV, closed the distance when he braked. A large one with tinted windows. He shot a glance ahead at the gas station and then back at the car now close behind him. Unconsciously, he recognized the shape and remembered the commercial he'd seen for it. A Cadillac SRX.

He almost missed the driveway and turned sharply into the gas station, jerking to a stop next to the pump. Hustling, he plugged his credit card into the machine, pressed the button, set the nozzle in place and started the gas flowing. He used the automatic trigger and, for a minute, waited, watching the numbers sliding by. Then he noticed his mouth felt dry and decided to get himself some water. He shot another quick glance at the pump and, figuring he had enough time, trotted inside. Grabbing a bottle and paying the teenager behind the counter took less than a minute but it was enough time for his gaze to linger on a few more flyers for missing children, including another for Sheila Birdsong. Those flyers reminded him why he was here, doing this.

Returning to the car, he set the water bottle on top of the car roof, unhooked the spout—making sure he did not spill a drop of the gasoline on the car or the concrete—and reinserted the hose into the pump. As he grabbed the water off the roof, he glanced across and noticed the SUV had pulled into a bay four slots down from him. He studied it, definitely a Cadillac. The car sat there idling, smoke from the exhaust feathering up from the rear past the tinted windows. No one moved to the gas pumps. The driver's window was part way down but the car sat in the shadows and Darrell could see little. He could make out only a thatch of brown hair as the driver held a cell phone to his ear.

Darrell shrugged and decided he *was* getting paranoid. Sliding into his seat, he started the engine. As soon as he was back on 123rd Street, he accelerated, speeding as much as he dared. He checked his watch again. He could still make it. Just. He glanced back, hoping no state troopers were lurking, ready to pull him over.

When none of the black and white cruisers appeared in his rearview, he relaxed. Then he looked again. Farther back, maybe a quarter mile, the large, black SUV rolled behind him. Glancing from the road ahead to the rearview mirror, he studied the front grill of the car. In the center of the grill, he could just make out the silver, gold and red Cadillac shield and above it, a windshield too dark to see through.

He mashed the accelerator.

Chapter 29

It looked to be a perfect day for sailing.

That was the first thought Erin had, glancing around. She and Leo climbed the ladder and stepped onto the deck of the beautiful Mason sailboat. Taking a deep inhale, she studied the sky and then the horizon below. Perfect azure above and steel blue beneath. A few white puffs scuttled across the sky and small whitecaps on the water tried to match their motion. The wind blew steady from the northwest, refreshingly cool on her face.

Leo's hand in hers, they walked the length of the yacht. They strode down the port side around the long white cabin—with five windows, she counted them as they passed—and back the starboard side. Aft again, she stared into the interior of the cabin. She admired the highly polished bright work and comfortable cushions, which perfectly matched the blue painted hull. She'd never had the chance to pilot such a grand sailing craft before. Gertrude had said it was a Mason 43, forty-three feet in length, and it looked every bit.

Leo's wide eyes took in the boat as they explored. "This is even bigger than grandpa's boat."

Erin smiled at him. "Yes, it certainly is." Pulling out a child lifejacket, she secured it around his small body. She indicated the wooden bench next to the helm. "This is your seat." Patting his shoulder, she smiled at him. "I need to get everything ready."

Now, she undid the dock lines and secured them on the deck, then returned to the helm. She took a few minutes to study the electronic screen. Gauges and electronic equipment icons dotted the monitor. At her fingertips, she had readings of wind speed and direction, water depth, even sonar for showing schools of fish. From this small screen, she could even control the engine, sails and anchor. Next to the monitor, she patted the ship radio, grateful it was there if she needed it.

With a touch, she started the electric engine. She eased the yacht away from the pier. The engine throttled quietly as the boat slid out of the harbor and toward the lake. Once in the open water, she hustled around the deck, untying the halyards and releasing the sails. Returning to the readout, she found the right icon and pressed. Another electric motor whirred. The giant sail opened, followed by the jib.

As soon as the wind filled the sails, the boat surged, rising briefly in the water. Leo called, "Whee!" and held both hands up.

She copied her son's actions, though kept one hand on the metal ring of the helm. "You're right. Awrighta!" She clicked off the electric motor. As the breeze blew past her, she lifted her face toward the sky. It had been too long. *This* was where she loved to be. Like this, out on the water, wind rushing past, standing on the deck of a sailboat. Between her duties as a mother—which she loved—and her hours at the hospital, she had far less time on the Bay back home.

Erin shot a glance at Leo, who sat mesmerized at the water and sky surrounding them. *He* was totally worth it. She nodded. But that didn't mean she didn't miss being out here on the water. And now, they were going to have a second one. She smiled at the thought. Then she recalled her waking hours and grimaced.

When she rose out of bed this morning, she felt that now-too-familiar nausea come on. That led to time next to the porcelain throne. Wiping her mouth at the sink after, she considered returning to bed. But the queasiness passed and she decided she could do this. Now, wind at her back, hands on the steering wheel, she was thrilled she'd chosen to sail.

With the electronic controls, she found the large sailboat easy to manage, the helm responsive to her slightest touch. The handling was so easy, she began to feel jealous of such luxury. It was almost as if the boat could sail itself.

Then she realized her dad's boat was more of a real sailboat. Unlike the *Fantasea,* it required actual skill and training to navigate the craft over the waters. But that didn't mean she couldn't enjoy *this* luxury…at least for a while.

The wind was perfect this morning, a stiff breeze— but not too stiff—across the water. She inhaled the scent. She noted down here, close to the water, the lake smelled fresh, not like the brackish odor of the Bay. Invigorating.

Aunt Gertrude had been almost solicitous when Erin inquired about taking the boat out. Darrell's aunt had extended an offer for her to sail on their first day here. At the time, Erin thought that might've been merely faux courtesy. But, when Erin made the request over breakfast, the woman seemed excited.

"With Darrell off gallivanting on some history quest, I think that's a great idea. It looks like you'll have a nice wind and good weather, at least till tonight." She pointed a toast corner across the table at Erin. "It's been too long since *Fantasea* has been out on the water. I'm too old and Salazar's been too busy." Then she finished, "Salazar has the keys and can get you started. He'll answer any questions you might have."

After breakfast, the caretaker had given her a quick primer on the yacht. When they finished, he even suggested a possible destination or two within easy sailing distance. Erin had decided on Pirate Isle, a sixty-to-ninety minute sail, depending on the wind. She checked the gauge on the screen to judge their speed. If this wind kept up, they'd be there within the hour.

She turned to check on Leo, whose gaze stayed fixed on the water ahead. He said, "Look, another sailboat."

Off the port side, Erin could make out the silhouette of a large sailboat, skimming across the water towards them. Then she corrected herself. A sailing yacht. Using the screen controls, she reefed the sails partway, allowing the *Fantasea* to slow. The other sailboat was crossing, heading to the northwest. She wanted to give it room.

As the boat neared, she recognized it. The yacht was the *Wanderlust,* the boat Leo had stumbled upon looking for Sheila's ghost. Its white and gold sail unfurled, the black hull beneath shined. As it closed the distance, she could make out Dwight Newsom. He wore the same captain's hat and stood at the helm.

"Ahoy, again," she hollered when the craft was close enough for her to be heard. She waved.

Newsom looked up and stared. He waved and reached down next to the helm. Her radio crackled and she heard, "Ahoy to you. I see Gertrude let you take out *Fantasea*. What do you think?"

Erin ignored the radio and yelled, "Wicked boat. I

love it."

As she watched, the Indian servant girl came out of the cabin, tray in hand, balancing a tall drink. Newsom took the glass and, tilting it toward Erin, took a long sip and winked.

The girl—Erin struggled to recall her name and then it came to her, Sarah—gave a tiny wave back—as if she didn't want Dwight to notice. In the tiny wave, Erin recognized the flash of color on her wrist. Blue and white and purple. The bracelet they'd seen her wearing when they met her before. And exactly like the bracelet they found at the dune buggy ride—

"Mom," Leo said, with some urgency.

Erin glanced over at her son. He leaned forward and stared at the other yacht. She asked, "Is something wrong? Are you all right?"

Leo looked at his mom then back at the other boat. He said a hoarse whisper, "Sheila is on that boat."

Erin shook her head and glanced back at the sailboat. "That isn't Sheila, son. That's Sarah. We met her the other day, remember?"

"Not her." Leo pointed at the yacht as it crossed in front of them. "Next to Sarah. I see *two* Indian girls on that boat. The other one is Sheila." His voice dropped to a quiet whisper. "Or I guess, Sheila's ghost."

"Great day for sailing!" Newsom called, as he opened his sails and the boat picked up speed, skidding across the water in front of them.

Before the *Wanderlust* passed, Erin stared hard. All she saw was a single girl casting another feeble wave with her hand.

Chapter 30

At least Carlos' Diner turned out to be easy to find. It sat right on the main drag.

When Darrell pulled into the gravel parking lot marked with crater-sized potholes, he stopped and stared at the restaurant through his windshield. The small building looked like it had been condemned...or should be. Paint peeled off the stucco, a piece of plywood covered what had been a large glass window and the two steps up to the door were crumbling. The logo was lit up but several bulbs had burned out, so it blinked "CAR O INER." He got out of his car and glanced around. This had to be the place. With the condition of the building, he was surprised to find six, no seven cars parked in the small lot. Which raised another concern he hadn't considered until now. If there were several patrons inside, how would he decide whom to approach? He didn't think the person would wear some kind of Indian headdress and he could hardly walk up to each one and ask them if they sent him a secret note.

He glanced at his watch. 9:54. He'd made it in time. He shot a look over his shoulder at the passing traffic on the road, sporadic with only one or two cars driving by on the main drag. No black SUV. He'd watched the Cadillac hang behind him most of the trip into Shelbyville on 128th, always about a quarter mile back. Not close, but never out of sight. Shortly before he entered the town limits and the scenery had gone from farmhouses and barns to streets lined with vintage houses snug next to each other, the SUV must have turned and disappeared. Even though Darrell had shot repeated looks in the rearview mirror, trying to keep an eye on the car, he had missed his pursuit—if that's what it was—turning off the main road. Maybe he was simply being paranoid. Still, he released a breath when he didn't see the Cadillac SUV anywhere around the diner.

He strode across the lot, careful to avoid the numerous potholes, and climbed the cracked steps. Grabbing the door, which had another board covering the fissured glass, he pulled it open and heard the tinkling of a small bell announce his arrival. He stepped inside and looked around. A small counter with five stools ran across the center of the space in front of him and three tables with four chairs were arranged right and left of the counter. The tops of all surfaces, counter and tables, were dark red, looking very old-fashioned. The floor was covered with a gray linoleum, splotched with stains and riddled with small cracks.

The counter stools sat empty. Five men were scattered among the six tables and no head turned toward him. His gaze took in the five and noticed they all looked old, heads of mostly gray hair and hands which raised the coffee cups covered in wrinkled skin. Two men sat together at one of the tables on the left, talking quietly. Each of the remaining three sat alone.

"Oh, hi there," called a high female voice.

Darrell turned to see an older waitress coming through a door behind the counter. She wore a traditional waitress outfit, white blouse and skirt, sleeves and neck edged in brown and a small, pocketed apron in front, also in brown. A nest of red hair sat atop her head with the ends of two pencils sticking out.

"I didn't hear ya come in." She pointed behind Darrell at the door. "Ya can't hear that darn bell when you're in the kitchen." She came around the counter and stood in front of Darrell, wearing a tired smile. "You wanna sit at the counter or ya can take any open table?" She gestured right and left. "We're pretty easy goin' 'round here."

Darrell stuttered, "I-I-I'm not sure." His gaze swept around the room, searching the five figures perched at the tables. No one made any movement. "I only came here to—"

"Gladys, you can seat him with me." The man sitting alone at the table on the right pronounced these words without moving his head, his voice a deep bass. "And bring us both a cup of coffee."

"Got it, chief." The waitress disappeared into the kitchen as quickly as she appeared.

Sensing every eye on him, though no face turned, Darrell walked over to the table and pulled out a chair. The metal legs sliding on the cracked linoleum made a loud scratching sound in the quiet diner, which reminded him of chalk screeching across an old blackboard. He shot one more glance around the small restaurant and settled himself into the uncomfortable straight-backed chair. He extended a hand across the red Formica top. "Darrell Henshaw."

They shook, the other man's hand callous and his grip firm. "I know," was all the older man said.

Darrell stared at the figure across from him. The man had a head of long hair and it hung to his shoulders. Rather than merely gray, the strands were coal black interspersed with a profusion of gray. He had a high forehead, pronounced with long furrows, and the square face of a Native, his skin the color of tanned leather. The skin beside his eyes was etched with prominent crow's feet, so noticeable they looked like faded war paint. He stared at Darrell with hard, gray eyes, a stare which did not look kind.

Darrell tried to figure where to start, how to start. He stammered, "Ch-ch-chief? Is that what I should call you?"

"Here you go," Gladys announced as she set two steaming cups of coffee down. She turned to Darrell, pulled a pencil out of her hair and held it over a small pad. "Now, what can I get ya?"

The old man's face tilted slightly toward the waitress. "Perhaps in a minute, Gladys." He turned his gaze back and Darrell saw his nose had a patrician look, straight and long above thin lips.

"Okey then. I'll give ya a little time." She turned and walked around the counter, the red hair and brown and white uniform disappearing through the swinging aluminum door.

The old Indian's eyebrows raised, which Darrell noticed were coal black, not a gray hair in them. "Well, Darrell Henshaw, why have you come?"

Darrell peered across at the man. "I-I-I thought you knew. Are you the one who sent me this note?" He pulled the slip of paper from his pocket and slid it across the table.

The Indian glanced at the paper and then back at Darrell. "No."

Darrell glanced around the small diner, checking out the other four patrons. They paid him no attention. "Is there someone else I should talk with?" he asked, his voice raspy.

"No. I did not send you the note but I had a friend do so." He peered at the note then at Darrell. "Why are *you* here?"

Darrell wilted under the stare of the hard gray eyes. The man must be more than twice Darrell's age but he radiated a fearsome strength. Darrell tried, "I-I thought you knew. If you had the note sent, you know."

"I want to hear it from your own lips."

"Um. Okay." Darrell cast another glance at the other men in the diner but they hardly moved. They looked like they were merely part of the scenery, taking an occasional slow bite, sipping coffee, holding the fork in mid-air.

He reached into his other jeans pocket and pulled out the folded and dog-eared flyer about Sheila Birdsong going missing. He opened the paper and spread it out on the red Formica, smoothing out the creases as best he could, before sliding it to the older man. "A few days ago, when we were returning to Michigan, we saw this poster at a convenience store. In Kalamazoo." He took a quick breath. "Actually, Leo—he's our five-year-old son—he saw it on the counter when we were checking out and asked me to explain what it meant. So I did and Leo asked if we could help find her while we were here."

Darrell realized he was rambling but couldn't help himself. The man across from him simply stared, expressionless, and the look alone intimidated Darrell.

"You see, we're really from Maryland and we're here for a week or so to celebrate my aunt's eightieth birthday. Anyway, we've asked around if anyone has seen Sheila, but we've not had much luck." He stopped, suddenly out of breath.

"You have not found Sheila Birdsong?" It was a question but didn't sound like one.

Before, in his rambling, Darrell had dropped his eyes and couldn't meet the harsh gaze. Now, he straightened and forced himself to meet the old man's stare. "No. We found out a few things about her but not much."

The old Indian's gaze stayed fixed on Darrell. "You are not being truthful with me, Darrell Henshaw. You already know you will not find Sheila. Not the way your son had hoped."

"What?" Darrell managed.

"You know the girl is dead."

Chapter 31

It was as if someone had sucked all the air out of the room. The old Indian's accusation stunned Darrell and he had trouble finding his breath or his voice. Finally, he managed, "You *know* Sheila is dead, not just missing."

"I did not say that." The old Indian's gaze finally flinched. He looked down at the steaming coffee in front of him and then back up at Darrell, the black bushy eyebrows raising. "I said *you* know the young Sheila is dead."

"I-I don't understand." Darrell shook his head.

"We know of your gift." He released an audible sigh. "We have members who also can communicate with the dead, like you."

"I wouldn't call it *communication.* I—"

The old Indian cut him off. "You have seen Sheila's spirit. Her ghost, you would say."

"Yes, um, we think so."

"We?" The man spoke the single word sharply.

Darrell caught himself. Did he want to divulge his son was a sensitive? Expose Leo to…this?

"We?" The old Indian repeated. "You and someone else saw her spirit?"

Darrell figured he was in this far…and he somehow thought the man would know if he were lying. "My son, Leo, is also a sensitive. And he saw Sheila's—" he caught himself. "Sheila's spirit along with me."

"Where did you see this spirit?"

"In Saugatuck. At the dock for the Saugatuck Chain Ferry. And then she seemed to lead us to a sailboat. Er, rather Leo said he saw her on the yacht. I didn't."

"A yacht? What boat?"

Darrell tried to remember. Boat owners chose particular names sometimes, like Mr. Caveny's *Second Wind.* He tried to picture the boat. Long, sleek black hull with a stripe of white showing above the water line. Polished brown wooden deck. Long cabin, he remembered walking past six windows to find Leo in the aft compartment. Fancy sitting area near the cockpit. After they climbed off the boat he turned and looked back and read the name across the back. *Wanderlust.*

He said, "I think the boat was named *Wanderlust.* Why? Does that mean something?"

The man shook his head. "I do not know yet."

Darrell realized this man had asked quite a few questions. And had told Darrell…nothing. He glanced at the torn note still lying on the Formica and read it again, this time upside down. "We've heard you have taken a special interest in the missing Gun Lake girls. If you want to know more about what happened to them, meet me tomorrow at 10:00 a.m. at Carlos' Diner."

He pointed to the ripped piece of paper. "The note told me to come if I want to know more about the missing teens. Well, I'm here and I want to know more." When the words were out of his mouth, Darrell realized they sounded demanding.

Any "demand" didn't seem to affect the old Indian. He maintained his stare and asked, "Why do you want to know…about our missing girls?"

Darrell shook his head. This wasn't going the way

he hoped. He was worried about how he would explain his long absence to his family. And he was concerned about the trailing SUV, paranoid or not. "Look, you don't know me but I'm a high school teacher. I teach kids like Sheila and the other missing girls. So, when I saw the posters, my heart went out to them and their families. And my son, Leo—he's five—got excited about helping to find them."

"This Leo, the same one with the gift?"

Darrell nodded. "I explained to Leo it was a long shot. Sometimes teenagers merely run away."

The Indian stiffened. "Sheila did not run away."

Darrell nodded again. "Yes, when we saw her ghost, I mean spirit, I realized she probably didn't just run away."

The old man insisted, "Sheila would not run away."

Darrell eased back in his chair. "How do *you* know that? The note says you can tell me more about what happened to her. So far, you've told me very little."

The man took a deep breath and started to open his mouth when the waitress returned, pencil in hand. Gladys merely said, "Well?"

Darrell glanced from the man to the waitress. It looked like this might take a while and he *was* hungry. All he'd had was that croissant. He said, "How about a couple of eggs, scrambled and a little bacon?"

"Okey," she said, scribbling a few notes on the pad. She left.

Darrell returned his gaze to his table partner who watched the woman disappear into the kitchen before speaking. "I have much to share. But first, I must ask why would Darrell Henshaw of Maryland care about a few Native teenagers in Michigan?"

Darrell shrugged. "I can't explain it. Yeah, I'm a white guy and these are Native teenagers whom I never knew. I'm a teacher. I care about kids. It's in my DNA. Black, brown, red, white—it doesn't matter. So, I've asked around." He shook his head. "And whenever I ask about Sheila, I get the same answer. 'You know teenage Indian girls. They get it into their heads and they take off.' Something about people's answers seemed off."

"Sheila Birdsong did not run away," the man repeated.

"Okay, when I saw her spirit, I figured something bad had happened to her but I have no idea what. This is not my first rodeo. I'm hoping you can help me, point me in some direction. That's why I'm here and not back with my family at Saugatuck."

The man nodded, seemingly satisfied. "Okay, I will tell you what I know. Perhaps, it will help you." The old Native let his gaze roam around the diner, as if noticing the other patrons for the first time. His glance returned to Darrell. "This is not simply about Sheila Birdsong. We have lost far too many girls and women."

Darrell said, "I saw four or five missing flyers, all posted at the gas station in Kalamazoo. And they all looked like Native girls."

The old Indian nodded again. "We have lost far too many Potawatomi women. Too many. And our tribe is hardly alone." He leaned forward. "Native females— women and girls—are going missing or murdered all across this country. And across Canada."

"Lots of women and girls?" Darrell asked, his mind jumping to what he'd learned about human trafficking in New Jersey. The hard way.

"No one knows. Hundreds. Probably thousands."

Thousands? Darrell had never heard of this, even when he did his research on human trafficking some eight years ago. He asked, "How long? How long has this been going on?"

The old Indian shook his head. "No one knows. Decades."

Decades, Darrell repeated to himself. He said, "I don't live around here anymore but I've never heard of any of this." He didn't want to sound skeptical but thousands? Decades?

The Chief stared hard at Darrell. "Those who have studied this have uncovered Native women have disappeared at a rate ten times that of white women. Across the tribes, hundreds, probably thousands of girls and women disappearing. Some are found later, raped and murdered, but most are never seen or heard from again." His voice had taken on a brittle edge.

"Hundreds of missing girls?" Darrell mumbled.

"Or more likely, thousands. And no one does anything."

"What about the authorities? The police?"

The old Indian barked a laugh and shot a glance at another diner. As if he could feel the old man's stare, this other man, also a Native with black hair and glasses, met the gaze and rose. He pulled a few bills out and left them on the table. He put on his hat and Darrell saw the dark blue uniform, realizing he was police, tribal police. The local cop stomped past their table and out the door, the little bell announcing his exit.

Before either could say anymore, Gladys returned with a plate of bright yellow eggs, two slices of brown bacon and two triangles of buttered toast, their odors tempting. She set them in front of Darrell along with silverware. "Anything else I can get ya?"

Darrell said, "Thank you, no."

With that, Gladys made herself scarce again. Darrell held up a fork. "Do you mind?"

"Please eat them while they are hot." The man looked toward the door. "The police. Sometimes they look into it but do nothing."

Between bites, Darrell got out, "And this has been going on decades?"

"Yes."

"Decades? I've never heard anything about this. This should be major news. How could all those women and girls go missing and no one notices?" Darrell grabbed a piece of bacon and crunched on it.

"I did not say no one notices." Before Darrell could interrupt with a question, he continued, "Some notice. Some disappearances are investigated, but not much is ever done. They put names into files. No one cares because these are Indian girls."

Darrell ate the second piece of bacon and let the man explain.

"To whites, they are disposable, second-class individuals. To Natives, these girls are loose and get what they deserve. And it continues to happen."

Darrell pointed an empty fork at the man. "Still?"

"And yes, some, a few girls do run away. They wish to leave an abusive boyfriend or husband, but not many. And not Sheila."

Darrell stopped with a forkful of eggs between the plate and his mouth, setting it back down. "You keep saying that. No offense, but why are you so sure about Sheila?" He put the eggs in his mouth.

"Because I know Sheila. I knew Sheila. Her mother

is my cousin. She would not run away."

Darrell nodded and finished the last of the eggs. They were quite good. "You seem very sure. Why?"

"Sheila had a good job and was saving to go to college next year. She was planning to go to Western Michigan. She wanted to become a nurse."

Darrell could hear the pride in his voice and guessed this was more than mere tribal loyalty. He said, "She was working for my Aunt Gertrude, Gertrude Embry and then left that job."

"Gertrude Embry is your aunt?" The Indian seemed almost animated.

"Yeah, she's the aunt who's celebrating her eightieth birthday. That's what brought us to Michigan."

"What did the family say about Sheila's disappearance?"

Darrell said, "I asked and not much. She left the job there for another, better job she said. They claimed to not know more than that. When I pressed the caretaker—he was her boss—he said the same as everyone else. He figured she ran away."

Neither spoke for a bit then Darrell asked, "Do you know anything about this new job she took?"

The Indian shook his head. "Not much. Her mother said she was excited about it. The girl said the new job would pay for much of her first year of college."

Both fell silent again. The old man seemed to gather himself in his chair before he spoke. "Darrell Henshaw, I tell you about the missing and murdered women not because I expect you can do anything about them. As I said, hundreds, more likely thousands have been lost." He stopped and gave the hard stare to Darrell again. "But I believe you can do something about one girl, Sheila

Birdsong. I believe the Great Spirit sent you to us to help her."

"But I'm pretty sure she's dead." Darrell cringed as he said the words.

"That may be true. But, if you can find some justice for Sheila Birdsong, you may save other Native teens from the same fate."

Chapter 32

As soon as she'd been sure they were out of earshot of the *Wanderlust,* she asked Leo to tell her again what he saw.

He said, "Mom, you told me if I saw Sheila's ghost, or any ghost, to let you or Dad know."

"That's right and I'm glad you did." She'd looped the rope over the helm, keeping the sailboat on course. "You're certain you saw two Indian girls on the deck?"

Leo nodded hard and pointed toward the boat, which was becoming a shrinking spot in the distance. "Yeah, Sarah was standing there holding a tray with one glass and next to her, I saw Sheila." He waited a second and then asked, "You didn't see them both?"

Erin shook her head. "No, I only saw Sarah and saw her wave to me...or maybe to you. I didn't see anyone else, other than Mr. Newsom."

"That's because Sheila's a ghost, just like Dad said," Leo announced with assurance.

A gust of wind filled both sails and the helm bucked against the rope. Erin stepped back to the steering wheel and adjusted the line. She turned back to Leo. "Okay, I'm proud of you for telling me. How about we'll talk about this with Dad when we get back and for now, just have fun sailing?"

"Okay, sure," Leo agreed.

After that, neither mentioned the word ghost. Erin

figured his five-year-old brain was simply glad to jump to something else. For the next thirty minutes, mother and son talked about everything else—Aunt Dianna's coming baby, Leo's favorite toy, what Dad was doing.

In between their conversations, Leo explored the boat, most fascinated with the cabin. She heard him bouncing on the cushions below. After a few minutes inside, he came back to the helm, his face flush.

"Mom, they have two beds in there! And big ones. And a large toilet, not like the tiny one on Grandpa's boat," he said in one breath. "There's a kitchen with a refrigerator, packed with drinks. Can I have one?"

Erin chuckled again. "Okay, let's remember this boat isn't ours. How about you can take a bottle of water? No pop."

"Gee, Mom."

So, if Leo did see Sheila's ghost on the Newsom yacht—for the second time—what did that mean? And what did it mean if Sarah had a bracelet which appeared to match the one they found on the dune buggy ride? The one Darrell thought was haunted. She needed to talk with him. And maybe he'd learn something at Shelbyville that would help.

Looking ahead, she said, "I think *that* could be our destination. Pirate Isle. See the tall cliff on the back side."

Leo leaned forward in his seat and peered where his mother pointed. "That place with the tall green hill? That's Pirate Isle?"

Erin nodded and turned to the helm. "Based on the description Mr. Salazar gave me, I think so." She shielded her eyes and looked in that direction. Ahead of them and to the right, a mass of green and tan rose out of the blue waters. She could barely make out some tall trees which edged the sloping hill on one side. Below the cliff, a sheer rock face met the water. The waves broke against the sharp crevices. According to the caretaker, a small, quiet harbor lay on the other side.

Leo squinted his eyes, staring into the sun. "Are there pirates on the island?"

Erin chuckled. "I don't think so. It's simply a name. Maybe there was a rumor about pirates there a long time ago." She looked back at her son. "Do you know what is on this island?"

"Ghosts?"

Erin laughed. "I don't think it's inhabited by people or ghosts. No one lives there. But according to Mr. Salazar, there's a beautiful little waterfall on the back side of the island. We'll have to anchor in the cove on the other side." She pointed to the left side of the isle. The natural harbor was coming into view.

Leo beamed. "Good thing we wore our swimming suits. I've never seen a real waterfall. Only on TV."

"If the waterfall is like Mr. Salazar described, you're in for a fun time."

Erin touched the screen to adjust the jib, causing the boat to turn slightly starboard. She eased the helm right and the *Fantasea* slid into the cove. She glanced at her watch. A quick trip.

Erin guided the sailboat around to the right side, again marveling how easy it was to control. She said, "Mr. Salazar explained there's no dock or pier. We have to guide the boat into the cove and tie her up."

As she rode past the front of the isle, she caught sight of the rocky side, the water crashing against the sharp rocks. That could be dangerous. With a slight movement of the helm, the yacht made the turn past the rocky face. A little farther on, the open harbor came into full view. Touching the icons on the screen, she lowered the sails and started the diesel engine. The sailboat glided into the calm waters and, when they were close enough, Erin turned off the engine.

Everything went quiet. She could hear the wind rustle the leaves in the trees and the soft gurgle of the waves lapping the shore. She did a three-sixty. Nothing beyond the island but open blue water. No pleasure boats, no freighters, no sailboats. She walked across the deck and peered over the side. The cove appeared to be deep enough so the keel of the yacht didn't touch and the boat swayed in the waves. Clicking the icon to lower the anchor, she listened to the chain uncoiling on the short trip to the bottom. On shore, she saw a strong tree full of leaves with a sturdy trunk. That should work.

"You stay put a minute while I tie up the boat," she told Leo.

"Can I help? I'm pretty good at tying up dock lines."

Erin patted her son on the shoulder. "That you are but we don't have a dock here." She pointed to the shore and he got out of his seat to look. "I need to tie the boat to the tall tree there which means I have to swim across the cove. You stay here a minute while I take care of this."

With that, she went down the ladder over the side of the boat. The rope in one hand, she swam a few yards until the bottom came up to meet her feet. She walked up the sand and pebbles over to the tree. A bowline knot would work. She pulled it tight around a branch which stuck out into the water. But, in pulling the knot tight, she heard the wood snap. The limb broke but still hung attached though loose. She examined the tree again and decided to use the sturdy trunk. She looped the rope around it and pulled taut. The bowline knot was tight. Satisfied the boat was secure, she made her way back to the yacht. Leo leaned over the edge, watching her come up the ladder.

She climbed onto the deck, feeling the water sluice down her legs. "You ready for a little adventure?"

Leo nodded, then looked down at his life vest. "Do I need this?"

"Well, I don't know what the pool will be like by the waterfall so I think we better keep it with us. How about you keep it on until you swim to the shore and then you can take it off? We'll carry it from there."

He nodded, heading for the ladder. In three seconds, he was over the side. Erin heard his splashes as he paddled toward the shore. She glanced around, making sure everything was turned off and she wasn't forgetting anything.

"Come on, Mom," Leo called, already standing on the sand. "I can't wait to see a waterfall for real."

Reaching into the hold, she grabbed the picnic basket Silvio had packed for them. One final glance across the deck. "Okay *Fantasea*, don't go anywhere and be here when we get back."

Chapter 33

"Mrs. Birdsong?" Darrell asked through the screen door. "My name is Darrell Henshaw and your cousin Edgar sent me over. I'm looking for your daughter and trying to find out what happened to her."

"You're a little late," the woman muttered.

Darrell found it strange those were the first words the woman spoke. The face he could make out in the dimness through the screen looked to be somewhere between thirty and fifty. She had a broad forehead above a long nose and thin lips.

"If Edgar sent you, I guess it's okay." She unlocked the screen door and stepped aside so Darrell could enter. Two large, circular silver earrings dangled from protruding lobes and they swayed in her movement.

Before Darrell finished his conversation at the diner, Edgar—the old Indian had only confided his name when he told Darrell to use it—had advised Darrell to talk with Hannah Birdsong, Sheila's mother. Actually, Edgar had offered the suggestion but from him, it came out more like a command. He'd indicated she might know more than she had told him.

After Darrell left the diner and climbed inside the car, he debated whether he could take time for another stop, regardless of the Indian's "suggestion." Glancing at his watch, he realized his long absence would definitely be noticed. He did some quick calculations. If he headed back now, his "history obsession," as his aunt had called it, would have taken more than three hours. Then, the old Indian's words came back to him. "Hundreds, probably thousands have been lost." Thousands of missing girls and women! It was hard to comprehend.

He glanced at the sky and saw the dark, threatening clouds. He would need to hurry or he'd get caught in the rain. In the end, he decided Sheila's mother was here in Shelbyville and he would not likely get another chance to talk with her. Checking again for his tail and not recognizing any of the few cars on 128th, he followed Edgar's directions to the small bungalow, on a side street only five minutes from the diner.

Once inside, he gave Hannah Birdsong basic information about himself as a teacher and coach. "When I saw the flyer about your daughter going missing, my heart went out for her," he explained.

She led him into some kind of small parlor or family room with a loveseat and a recliner squeezed into the space. Both showed signs of considerable wear and looked like they had been rescued from the dump. But the two and everything else in the room was spotless and the whole place appealed to Darrell's obsession for cleanliness.

Hannah invited him to take the sofa while she sat in the chair. "Are you a teacher from around here? I don't remember my daughter ever mentioning you." Even with the courtesy, the woman's skepticism came through the question.

Darrell shook his head. "No, ma'am. I live with my wife and son in Maryland. And I teach there. We're in the area visiting family. My aunt is Gertrude Embry."

He saw something flash in the woman's grey eyes—

worry, distrust, resentment?

She said, "Sheila worked for Gertrude Embry...before she went missing." Her tone shifted to anger. "I told her I didn't want her to make the trip to Saugatuck to work. I wanted her to work in the fields like the other kids." She shook her head. "But Sheila was headstrong, exactly like her father. She worked for Mrs. Embry for weeks. Said she didn't much like the job but Mrs. Embry paid her well."

Hannah Birdsong got up and walked over to the mantel. Darrell turned and saw, at the end of the mantel, two small trophies with a silver figure holding a basketball. Both trophies had "Sheila Birdsong" engraved on a gold plate on the wooden block. Below her name, the first one had the words "Most Improved Player 2006" inscribed, and the second had "MVP 2007."

Hanna moved past Darrell and reached for two framed pictures and handed both to him. The first held a torso shot of Sheila, gleaming black hair, deep brown eyes shining, broad smile at the camera. He decided it was likely the one they'd used for the missing posters. The second held an informal pose of mother and daughter dressed smartly, probably out for some event. Sheila stood a few inches taller than her mother and the teen had an arm around the older woman. Both wore wide, relaxed smiles.

"Your daughter is certainly a beautiful young woman." Darrell handed the photos back to Hannah.

Mrs. Birdsong accepted the frames and mumbled, "*Was* a beautiful young woman."

Her response puzzled Darrell, so he said, "Edgar was very insistent. Sheila wasn't some flighty teenager who up and decided one day to run away."

"My daughter wouldn't run away. She never met a challenge she couldn't handle."

Darrell said, "When I spoke with the caretaker at my aunt's place—Tom Salazar, he was her boss—he said Sheila quit working for my aunt because she got a better job. He didn't know where. What did she tell you about the new job?'

Both pictures gripped in her hands, Hannah Birdsong's head made tiny shakes. "She didn't say much. I tried to ask but you know how teenagers can be." Her gaze went to Darrell's, seeking conspiracy.

"Boy, do I ever. You should try dealing with a whole classroom full of them."

She said, "No thanks. One was enough."

There it was again, past tense. Darrell pressed, "Mrs. Birdsong, did Sheila tell you anything about the new job? Where it was? Who she'd be working for?"

"Mr. Henshaw, I tried to get her to tell me."

He interrupted her. "Darrell's fine. You can call me Darrell."

She nodded. "Okay, then just call me Hannah."

"Hannah, did Sheila say *anything* about the new job?"

The mother's fingers touched her lips which bore no lipstick. "She told me the job was only for six weeks and paid a lot better than working for Gertrude Embry. She claimed she'd be able to make enough to cover her first year at college." She clutched the picture of the teen to her chest. "She was going to Western Michigan next year. Going to be a nurse."

Darrell thought about Sheila's claim. He didn't know what colleges cost in Michigan now—he attended almost ten years ago—but he talked with his seniors in Maryland about college all the time. He knew, even with in-state tuition, the cost of an entire year of college carried a hefty price tag.

"Sheila told you she'd make enough money in a few weeks to pay for a year of college?" He swallowed. "I hate to raise this but that's an awful lot of money. Is there a chance in this new job she would be doing something…illegal? Like maybe drugs?"

Hannah rose and set the two photo frames down with a thud. "Never. Sheila hated drugs. She didn't even drink. She had a friend in high school who OD'ed on heroine and died. She wouldn't." She stood over Darrell. "And she swore to me she wasn't doing anything illegal or dangerous." She shook her head as if the movement would shake the idea from her brain. Then she collapsed back into the chair. "Now that she's gone, I guess it doesn't matter anyway."

"She's gone?" This time Darrell didn't let it pass. "Hannah, do you know something about what happened to your daughter?"

"No, not really," she groaned and the tears fell full, wetting both cheeks. "I just know she's gone."

Darrell sat up on the couch. "You do. How? How do you know she's gone?" Knowing what he knew, seeing Sheila's ghost, he realized the hypocrisy of his question, but he wanted to hear Hannah's response.

She sniffed. "So many girls just disappear. My Sheila will become one more number."

Darrell persisted, "Hannah, if you know something, please tell me. I want to help your daughter however I can."

Hannah stared at him through teary eyes. "She's

beyond help now." Then, after a bit, she added, "Besides, you wouldn't understand. You're not Potawatomi."

Darrell nodded. "You're right. I'm not Native." He folded both arms over his chest. "But you would be surprised what I might understand."

Hannah Birdsong stared at him and Darrell thought she was trying to decide if he was worthy of her truth. She dropped her gaze to the floor. "I've dreamt of my daughter many nights, dreamt of water. And that's where I saw my Sheila, in the water."

"In the water?" Darrell had no idea what she meant.

The mother raised her head up to meet his gaze. "I know my daughter is now lost to me. I see her in my dreams. She's a mermaid now."

Chapter 34

"One more time, please, Mom?" Leo's eyes pleaded. His auburn hair dripped water onto his shoulders.

Erin stood in the pool and glanced up at the tall waterfall they had just come down. She checked her Seiko Sports watch. The time had flown by. She tried to calculate how long it would take to get back to the boat and sail to Wentworth. She remembered the warning about a storm tonight.

"Ple-e-e-ease!"

"Okay, one more but then we have to pack up to go."

She took her son's hand and together they climbed the makeshift steps of rocks alongside the waterfall. She'd lost count how many times they made this trip.

After arriving on the island and tying the boat up, they had to find the waterfall. They followed the beaten path quite a while, until they heard the sound. The sunlight slashed through the leaves. At times, she could see large swaths of blue sky above. Other times, the canopy of trees would close in and she would see only a ceiling of green. The path looked worn, like many had traveled here before them.

On the yacht, they hadn't noticed the temperature. On board, the rush of the wind kept them cool. But once they stepped on land, the sun bore down on them, the summer heat oppressive. After their circuitous trip through clusters of trees, they rounded a bend and an incredible sight greeted them. Nestled among the trees, the waterfall dropped a short amount—she judged it to be about ten feet but discovered it was closer to fifteen— into a sparkling pool of almost clear, blue water. They waded into the pool and found it two to ten feet deep, depending on how far out they went. Leo put on the life jacket again.

Later, playing in the water, they'd noticed the rock steps along the side of the waterfall. Erin checked them out first. It required some grabbing and pulling but she made it to the top easily. Once there, she stood in the rushing stream and waved. Leo jumped up and down in the pool below. Waving and laughing herself, she lost her balance, slipped and went over the waterfall.

She plopped feet first into the pool of water at the bottom and popped back up. Her fright and anxiety turned to delight. After a second try and planned descent, Erin figured it was safe enough. Leo joined her in the climb and slide down the fall.

That had been hours ago.

They had stopped only long enough to enjoy the sumptuous lunch Silvio had packed for them. Inside the basket, they found cold chicken, fresh fruit and carrots with dip, all nestled in a cooler compartment. Then, they went back to climbing, sliding and swimming.

After the final trip down, Erin grabbed her son's hand and they waded to the rocky shore. His face beaming, Leo said, "We have to tell Dad about this place. He'd love it."

Erin's gaze roamed the quiet oasis. She was surprised no one else joined them the entire day. "I'm sure we had more fun than he did. He's definitely going to be jealous." She laughed.

They walked over to the spot they had cleared of small rocks. Erin re-folded the blanket she'd found in the basket and returned it there. She glanced around to make sure they hadn't left anything. Satisfied, she took her son's hand and they started back the way they came.

This day's adventure had been nearly perfect. She'd had so much fun with her son, she forgot all her troubles. She had put out of her mind the stress of dealing with Darrell's family, especially his eccentric aunt. And for a while, she hadn't even thought about Darrell's quest for yet another poor ghost victim.

Maybe she needed to re-assess her view of Darrell's aunt. The *Fantasea* was an incredible boat—yacht, she mentally corrected—and no doubt, quite expensive. Gertrude had proved to be very generous with her willingness, no, her insistence on lending it to Erin and Leo. Gertrude knew Erin was a more than competent sailor, but still. Erin remembered the accolades lavished on Gertrude at the luncheon. She began to appreciate them in a different light.

And Tom Salazar. He'd hit a home run with the suggestion of Pirate Isle and its waterfall. Maybe her original judgment of him had been premature as well. He'd made it easy for Erin to master the controls of the sailboat and told her how to find the island. And his instructions were spot on, including finding the quiet harbor to anchor the *Fantasea* and tie her up.

The return trip through the island seemed longer. As they walked, Erin began to feel the first edges of water fatigue. She'd had it before, the tiredness the body experiences from a day playing in the water. She'd have thought, after all her time in and around the water on the

Chesapeake Bay, she'd be immune. That didn't appear to be the case. Or maybe, it was because she was returning to all the cares which were dragging her down. Performing for Darrell's family, helping Darrell deal with another ghost haunting and the thought of the missing girls. Or, it could be her condition. Although she'd felt fine after the nausea episode this morning, she knew pregnancy, even early on, could sap her strength.

Her arms and legs weary, she looked over at Leo. He was trudging along as well, his young shoulders sagging as he walked. Partway through the path carved between the tangle of trees, she spied a flat rock.

"I think we're due for a break. Let's rest here a bit."

Leo sighed. "Thanks mom. How did you know I needed a rest?"

She smiled at him. "Moms just know."

Leo climbed up on the rock and tried to lay down but the bulky life vest wouldn't let him.

"Here, I think I can take that now," she said.

She unbuckled it and he slid out of it. While he lay on the rock, Erin stretched, first her back, then her legs. She watched Leo's eyes close. She longed to do the same. Simply lay on the rock next to him and take a long siesta. But the rock wasn't big enough, so she squatted on the edge. She'd let Leo lay there for a few minutes. But, when she felt her own eyes drooping, she decided it was time.

"Okay, big guy, you can sleep on the trip back to Aunt Gertrude's. I'll do my best to make it a smooth sail." She extended her hand and Leo took it. She pulled him off the rock and they headed down the trail.

Why does the return trip always seem to take longer?

She tried to remember how long they'd walked down the trail on their trip from the boat to the pool and waterfall. They had been excited and full of energy and she hadn't kept track. She glanced at her watch again. It couldn't be that much farther. They came around another bend and the sky opened up again over their heads. She scanned it, looking for any darkening clouds, but found only an azure canopy marked by a few white puffs.

Salazar had said a storm was predicted for later, sometime this evening and warned her. "It may only be a little rain, but the forecast is not clear. I don't know what the storms are like on the Chesapeake but on Lake Michigan, you can never be too careful. If you can help it, you don't want to be out there in a storm."

She studied the sky, as much as she could see. Satisfied, she kept following the path, Leo's hand in hers. She sensed rather than remembered the clearing was not that far ahead. She and Leo climbed the path up a small incline and then it turned to the right. The sand and pebble-strewn beach came into view first. She released a long breath. They had to duck under the limbs of some trees and she saw the tall trunk of the tree she had knotted the dock tie to. Only the rope wasn't there.

Her stomach tightened. She released Leo's hand and hurried ahead along the shoreline. She pulled up short. Her gaze swept left and right. It was not possible.

The *Fantasea* was nowhere to be seen.

Chapter 35

"A mermaid?" Darrell said aloud, once back inside the safety of the Taurus. Replaying the entire conversation in his head, he put the car in gear and pulled out onto the small street. When the lane met 128th, he scanned the road both ways and saw only an older sedan pass, heading west and a dented black pickup traveling east. No black SUV. He pulled out and hit the accelerator.

"She dreamt Sheila was in water?" He'd read many Native peoples put great faith in dreams and was not surprised the Potawatomi did as well. Hannah had explained in their culture, women were responsible for water and men responsible for fire. She'd said, "Now Sheila's spirit will guard the waters forever."

What did that mean? Guard the waters? A mermaid? They were practically surrounded by water. Lake Michigan and the Kalamazoo River. He'd like to have gone back to Edgar and ask if a mermaid held any special meaning for their culture.

Glancing up, he saw a line of darkening clouds to the west, precisely where he was heading. He needed to get a move on. The rain would no doubt slow him down. He glanced at his watch. Yikes. He sped up.

He couldn't wait to share what he learned with Erin. Maybe she'd see something he didn't. She often had an insight or idea that never occurred to him. Then he realized he could call her. He saw the flip phone on the seat beside him. He hadn't had the cellphone very long and still hadn't gotten use to the idea he could call from anywhere. He looked out the side window and watched rows and rows of cornstalks pass. Well, almost anywhere. Besides, he didn't know if she and Leo would be back after their short sail. If she wasn't, he'd only get someone else at Wentworth and tell them what?

As he drove, he thought back. So far, when he caught glimpses of Sheila's ghost, or spirit as the Natives would say, he'd seen no hint of water. No dripping, no wet hair, just her image. When he got back to Wentworth, he'd ask Leo, since he'd seen her more and find out if his son saw anything which would suggest water.

The inside of the car exploded with light, bright and pulsing. Darrell jerked his glance to the rearview. Damn. A police cruiser rolled behind him perfectly matching his speed. He shot a look at the speedometer. He was going a little over the posted sixty-five but not that much. Taking a deep breath, he slowed and pulled onto the narrow shoulder. His heart thudded. Just what he needed, a speeding ticket. How would he explain this, if Gertrude heard of it? She seemed to know everyone around.

A tall figure clad in dark blue appeared in his side window. Darrell buzzed it down and turned off the ignition.

"License and registration," the man barked.

Darrell reached into the glove compartment. This time his OCD had served him well. The compartment was organized, the contents neatly arranged. He knew precisely where the required paper was and retrieved it. He reached into his wallet, extracting his Maryland license and handed them out the window.

The officer took them and said nothing. As Darrell watched out his side mirror and then in his rearview, the cop went back to his cruiser. Its strobe lights still flashing, the car sat only a few feet behind Darrell's rear bumper, so he couldn't even make out what jurisdiction the officer worked for.

Darrell tensed.

It was only a few miles over the limit. How bad could it be? His gaze glued now to the rearview, he watched as the man extracted his long body from the car and walked up to Darrell's door.

"Step out of the car," the officer demanded.

Darrell noted there was none of the formal courtesy he had heard from other cops when they had stopped him. Opening the door, he slid out, careful to keep his hands up. "I-I-I apologize, Officer—" he squinted, searching for the cop's name tag—"Officer Firestone. I didn't realize I was speeding. I was thinking about something else."

Darrell glanced up at the man's face and realized he'd seen him before. At the diner. This officer had exchanged a dark look with Edgar before stomping out the door. Darrell straightened and studied the man, balancing his feet on the sloping shoulder of the road.

Like he noted before, the officer looked old, though perhaps not as old as he'd first thought. Late fifties maybe. Lines of gray threaded through black hair, parted on one side and dull gray eyes peered through black-framed glasses. His lips were a drawn slash when he asked, "You are from Maryland. What brings you to Michigan?" He held up the license, his gaze flicking from the card to Darrell's face.

"Visiting family. Up here for my aunt's eightieth birthday. Gertrude Embry."

"You're related to Gertrude Embry?"

Darrell could tell from the tone this was not a compliment. "Yeah, she's my aunt." When the cop made no response, he added, "Her husband was my mom's brother. He passed several years ago."

"Know you were going over the speed limit?" the cop snapped.

"I-I-I'm sorry. Like I-I said I was thinking about something else," Darrell stuttered.

"Like the missing Birdsong girl?" Firestone snapped.

Darrell wasn't sure how to respond. He tried to read the man's face. He now realized the officer worked for tribal police and, with his angular features and darker skin, he definitely had Native blood. Darrell didn't think the other patrons in the diner could've overheard his conversation with Edgar. But maybe this man knew something that could help.

"Did you investigate her disappearance? Do you know anything about what happened to her?" Darrell blurted out.

The gray eyes narrowed behind the black frames. "You tell me. What do *you* know about her? Why are you coming around here asking questions about Sheila Birdsong?"

Darrell shook his head. "Not much. I know she worked for my aunt and quit to take another job. Not much more than that." He thought, I know she's not a mermaid.

The cop looked Darrell up and down. "We've heard of your supposed *gift*." He shook his head. "We don't need your help." He barked a derisive chuckle. "The last thing the Potawatomi need is for some white man to come in and rescue us." He spit on the ground, narrowly missing Darrell's shoes. "We can take care of our own. That's my job."

"Have you made any progress finding out what happened to her?" Darrell asked, surprised at himself.

Firestone didn't answer. He handed Darrell back the license and registration. "I suggest you finish your business with the Embrys," he spit on the ground again, "then take your wife and son and head back to Maryland." Firestone's tone made it clear it was no mere suggestion.

The man turned and walked back to his cruiser, his posture stiff. Pointing to the sky, he said, "And stay within the speed limit. If you don't know these back roads, they can be treacherous, especially in the rain."

Chapter 36

The cop got in his car and pulled out, extinguishing the flashing lights and driving down 128[th.] As the cruiser passed, Darrell read the "Gun Lake Tribe" logo on the side. Once again, he scanned the road both ways and saw only a few cars. About a quarter mile down the road, the cruiser turned around in a driveway and, a few seconds later, barreled past, the draft hitting Darrell. As he stood there, the only other cars which passed were a small red SUV and some compact he didn't recognize. He also checked the side streets. No dark SUV.

Climbing in, he slammed the door. Checking both ways again, he eased the car off the shoulder and onto the asphalt. When he covered the same quarter mile the cruiser had, he saw it. On his right, he read "Leaving Gun Lake Tribe Land." No wonder the cop pulled him over where he did. A little farther and Darrell would've been out of his jurisdiction.

What was that all about? Why wouldn't the tribal police want Darrell asking questions about Sheila's disappearance? Wouldn't they want any help, even from a *white guy*? He realized the Natives were territorial and naturally suspicious of others' motives—and given the history, they had every right to be. Still, his exchange with the cop seemed more strained than mere cultural distrust. Edgar, the elder, had been skeptical at first, but seemed satisfied when they finished their conversation.

He'd sent Darrell to Sheila's mother.

Darrell steered the car around one of the tight bends Officer Firestone had warned him about. What about Hannah Birdsong? She seemed perfectly normal *and* suspicious at first. She also seemed certain her daughter had died. Hearing that, Darrell had almost told her about seeing Sheila's ghost and confirming the mother's contention. But he feared that would only make her more skeptical. But a mermaid?

Taking the car through another sharp curve, Darrell glanced again in the rearview mirror. He couldn't be sure but a little ways back, he saw a car banking out of the bend, he thought a dark SUV. He had to maneuver through another curve and lost sight of the car behind. When the road straightened out, he stared again and watched as the SUV came out of the curve. A black SUV with dark tinted windows.

His stomach clinched. It had to be the same one. Out here, on this country road, there couldn't be two of those cars. He stared ahead and concentrated on his driving, went through another curve. When the asphalt straightened out, he checked the rearview again. It was still there and seemed to stay there, not dropping back or getting closer.

So, he was being followed. He glanced back again. Same black SUV, same dark tinted windows. What did that mean? Why would anyone want to shadow him as he came to Shelbyville to talk with the Natives? Someone must have been concerned about what he'd learn. But what did he learn? Not much.

He focused on the road ahead. Straight shot again. What should he do? What could he do? He glanced down at the flip phone lying on the shotgun seat. Keeping one hand on the steering wheel, he grabbed up the phone and flipped it open. Who could he call? The phone screen lit up. No signal. Of course. Just his luck. Out here with no signal. He threw it back down and suppressed a curse.

He breathed, in and out, in and out. Checked on the car trailing him. Still there. He tried to think. So, someone was following him. There wasn't much he could do about it. He guessed he had maybe seven more miles on 128th before he got to Hamilton. Once there, he could pull into the gas station again. Maybe his phone would work there. Still, who would he take a chance on calling? And what would he tell them? A shiny black SUV was following him? Besides, what would he do if the SUV simply pulled into a bay and waited for him again.

All he could do was concentrate on driving. *And* keep an eye on the black SUV. He heard his breath slide in and out, the sound loud in the silent car. He mashed the accelerator harder and watched the needle edge past seventy...seventy-five. The Cadillac SUV was still there, no closer, no farther back. He was matching Darrell's speed. He shot a quick glance out the side window. Long furrowed rows and then an old red barn flew by. Quickly, he brought his gaze back to the road and needed to slow down to make the next bend. Easing off the gas pedal, he cast another look at the rearview. No change. And he didn't see any other cars behind him. No witnesses.

Coming through another curve, his concentration diverted, he drifted into the oncoming lane. An angry horn screeched. Darrell jerked his car back into his lane. In two seconds, a blue sedan flew by, heading east.

Damn! First, no cars anywhere except this damn

SUV following him, then one almost hits him coming the other way. His breath erupted, two, three times. He peered at the road ahead, relieved to see no more cars coming at him. And 128th looked straight now, as far as he could see ahead. He kept both hands on the steering wheel and tried to force his breathing to settle down. In and out, in and out.

He chanced another look in the rearview and saw the SUV accelerating, closing the distance. Darrell stared, fixated on the wide silver grill growing larger in his mirror. Alternating glances from the road ahead to the car behind, he watched it move closer, now less than a car length. He stared at the shield, could make out its colors of silver, gold, black and red. He checked out the road ahead then shot another look at the Cadillac emblem. In the center of the shield, he saw a small nick, like a stone from the road had chipped it. His gaze returned to the asphalt ahead of him.

He punched the accelerator and felt his Taurus respond. When the distance between the cars opened up, he checked the speedometer. The needle moved past eighty. The scenery flew by. He didn't think he could keep this up for long. At least, the road was straight…for now.

He sensed more than saw movement behind him and yanked his gaze back to the rearview mirror. The SUV accelerated even more and drew still closer, the black frame and tinted windshield filling his mirror. Darrell's knuckles tightened on the steering wheel. The car came so close, the grill with the shield disappeared from his view. The darkened windshield was all Darrell could see through his mirror.

God, he must be within a foot. He's going to ram me.

He floored the gas pedal and the engine whined in protest. The needle passed eighty-five. He wanted to turn his head and look back through the rear window but couldn't chance it. Not at this speed. He had to stay focused on the road ahead. His Taurus raced along the blacktop.

Then it started. First, a few thunks on the roof and, within seconds, the sky opened up, the rain cascading in sheets. He flipped the wipers on high and stared through the windshield at the rain-slicked asphalt. Damn, what else can go wrong? Driving like this in the rain was major-league stupid.

He needed to slow down in the downpour but couldn't. He feared if he slowed, even a little, the larger SUV would slam into him and probably run him off the road. He chanced another glance in the rearview and saw...nothing. All he could see looking back was the torrential rain slicing down onto the blacktop.

Where had the Cadillac gone? Could he have turned off when the rain hit and Darrell hadn't noticed? He didn't think so but where was the car? He stared ahead and then shot another glance in the mirror. Nothing.

Then, he caught some movement in his peripheral vision. The Cadillac SUV had slid over into the oncoming lane. He was passing the Taurus on the left. He must've disappeared into Darrell's blind spot before pulling even with the Taurus. Darrell stared from the SUV beside him to the road ahead. As far as he could tell, both lanes seemed empty of traffic, but the rain reduced how far he could see.

He shot a glance to his side. The Cadillac had pulled up, almost even with his car. He peered across but could make out nothing but the damn dark tinted glass. He jerked his gaze back to the road. What was this idiot going to do? Pass him and make him skid on the wet road? He risked a glance in the rearview to see if there was a second car, to block him in. Nothing.

The SUV inched forward, both cars hurtling at almost ninety! This was crazy. No, this was suicide. He should brake and slow down, let the Cadillac whiz by him. But he feared what might happen in the rain. He could hydroplane, lose traction and skid.

He had no time to consider any options.

Right then, the SUV surged forward and steered hard to the right, angling in front of him, cutting off the Taurus. Darrell had no choice. He stepped on his brake so as not to hit the Cadillac. Out of the corner of his eye, he saw the SUV whiz into his lane right in front of him. He yanked the wheel to the right, swerving to avoid hitting the other car. His tires slipped on the rain-slicked asphalt. He tried to control the steering wheel but felt the car skid onto the narrow shoulder. He slammed on the brakes as hard as he could and watched the car go over the edge of the shoulder. His heart raced. He practically stood on the brake. The car bumped over the shoulder. It bounced down into a ditch and partway up. The Taurus jerked to a stop, slamming his head into the steering wheel.

Everything went dark.

Chapter 37

"Mom, where is the big sailboat?" Leo asked, his eyes wide.

Erin stopped on the edge of the trail, agape. She stared out into the water. No sailboat, make that, no yacht, sat in the quiet water. The small harbor was...empty.

Had the boat somehow come lose and drifted out into the lake? She stared out at the open water. Looked left and right. The only thing she spied was another sailboat, this one with a multi-colored sail. Only a tiny speck on the horizon. Not the *Fantasea.*

"Mom?" Leo asked, his voice edged in panic.

"It's okay, son. It'll be okay." She struggled to make her voice sound reassuring, but heard the strain in her words.

She tried to think. Maybe they'd taken a wrong fork on the path. Maybe they'd come out in a different harbor. And the *Fantasea* was sitting quietly around another bend of the island. She turned and looked back the way they came. She back tracked a few steps and stopped. She spotted it. A few feet away, a tall tree stood with its branches stretched out into the harbor. There it was. The same branch she had snapped trying to tie up the bow line. She shook her head. Stared at the trunk she'd tied the rope to. Only now, there was no rope. No bowline knot. No boat.

What were they going to do? When they'd taken off on their sail, she was hardly worried. True, she didn't know Lake Michigan. But she was confident in her ability to pilot the much larger sailboat. And, if they encountered any problem, she could always call for help. On the ship radio. Which was on the yacht.

Then, her thoughts jumped to something else. Who would do this? Thieves after a prize yacht? She hadn't seen any other boats around as they made their way to the island. But she wasn't looking for anyone else. She was focused on her son and navigating the new sailboat. The yacht would command a huge price. Still, knowing Gertrude Embry, Erin believed the *Fantasea* was probably well known and any details about an attempted sale of it would set off alarm bells up and down the coast. Surely, thieves would know that. Not a good choice for boat theft.

Okay, then who? And maybe why? Did someone want to isolate her and Leo? Her heart thumped with fear for her son. She peered again at the water, searching for any threat. She saw nothing. No one. But isolate for how long? Surely, another boat would come along and they could flag it down. Get a ride back to Wentworth. The seasoned sailor in her told her not to panic.

Still, who knew they had the yacht? Who knew where they were going? Gertrude, of course. But she seemed thrilled that Erin was going to take the *Fantasea* out. And Tom Salazar. He'd been so helpful in showing her the yacht's functions. Plus, he'd given her some ideas of a few short destinations. Including Pirate Isle. And Silvio probably knew, since he put together such a nice lunch for Leo and her. Most likely, everyone at Wentworth knew she was taking the *Fantasea* out and maybe where they were headed. But why would *they* do anything like this?

Setting down the basket and life vest, she stared out again across the water. Far away, a tiny patch on the water, she saw a red and white sail, way too far away to hail. Then, she recognized a different threat. From the west, ominous, dark clouds rolled over the open water. As she watched, she could see the line of showers in the distance heading toward Pirate Isle. Toward them. She'd seen this phenomenon many times on Chesapeake Bay. As a storm approached across the water, you could see the stretch of rain almost like a curtain line of showers. The first time she saw it on the Bay, she remembered thinking it looked precisely like the caricature they drew of showers on cartoons, puffy black clouds with a straight curtain of rain underneath. She glared at the downpour, measuring its progress. They had maybe fifteen minutes. Then, they were going to get drenched.

"Mom, what are we going to do?" Leo squeaked.

"It's going to be okay," she said, the first thing which came to her.

He looked up at her, deep green eyes wide. "How are we going to get to…Aunt Gertrude's?" He sniffled. "I wish we were home, on the Ches'peake."

She pulled Leo to her and hugged him. "So do I, son." She stared at the water. "So…do…I." She knew she needed to comfort her son, but what could she say? She'd tried never to lie to Leo. She scrunched down next to him. "Mr. Salazar knows where we were headed. When we don't come back in time, he'll send someone to go look for us. We simply need to wait."

"You think so?" Leo sniffed.

"I do," Erin answered, hoping she wasn't lying to

him. "But for now, since your dad's not here, I need you to be a big guy for me. You think you can do that?"

He gave a slow nod and stuck out his chest. "I'll try."

Erin hugged him again. "That's my big boy." Still low next to him, she pointed out over the water. "See that line?"

"You mean that dark row?"

"Yeah, that's a storm."

"It is?" The fear was back in his voice.

"Yeah, and it's coming this way." She patted him on the chest. "The good news is it doesn't look like there is any thunderstorm with it." She pointed again. "No lightning."

"O-kay." He swallowed the two syllables.

"It means we're going to get wet. But hey, didn't we just spend the last few hours getting wet?"

He nodded.

"I think we can stand a little rain. What do you think?"

He looked at the approaching curtain of rain and then at his mom. "I guess so." He sniffed again. "But mom, I'm scared."

She hugged him tight. "It'll be okay. You'll see." She hoped she wasn't lying. "Hey, I just thought of something. Remember the cave we passed on our way to the waterfall? The one you wanted to explore, but I wouldn't let you?" She glanced at the curtain of rain, then back at her son. "I think now would be a great time to check out the cave. What do you say?"

"Okay," he gulped.

"If we hurry, we might even be able to beat the rain." She grabbed the picnic basket and the preserver. "I'll race you."

As they trotted down the trail they'd left a few minutes ago, she cast one last glance over her shoulder. *But no one will be able to see us hiding in the cave...if they come looking for us.*

Chapter 38

The rain pounding on the roof of the car woke him. Darrell had no idea how long he'd been out. He shook his head and it all came back to him, like a slowly evolving video. The black SUV on his tail. Their hell-bent speed. Then the Cadillac pulled up alongside him. The car cut in front and Darrell had to jerk his car onto the shoulder. He lost control and swerved off the road.

He felt his forehead. It hurt, bad. He must've hit it on the steering wheel. At least the airbag hadn't deployed. The car was still drivable, he thought. The Taurus hadn't conked out, the engine idled quietly. Darrell decided he better get out to assess the damage. He put the car in park. When he was about to turn off the ignition, he hesitated. What if it didn't restart? He let it alone.

He pulled the handle to open his door, but it only moved about an inch and then stopped. He buzzed the window down and the rain sluiced inside. Darrell did his best to ignore it and looked out and down. He saw the edge of the ditch about a foot deep next to his car, his door.

Yanking his head in, he raised the window back up. No need to get any more wet than he had to. He climbed over the console and practically stumbled into the passenger's seat, Erin's seat. At least she hadn't been with him. The speed and the near collision would've infuriated her…and terrified her. Hell, it terrified him. He hoped she and Leo were having a great time out on the water. The rain pounded on the steel frame of the roof. He prayed they weren't dealing with this storm out over Lake Michigan.

Putting his shoulder against the passenger door, Darrell got it open partway and he could feel it pushing against the mud on the ground. He squeezed through the opening and out the door. His feet squelched in the mud. In seconds, the hard rain drenched him, his clothes soaked. At least it wasn't cold. The rain had cooled it, but the temperature still hovered in the high seventies, he guessed. Since he was out and soaked, he forced himself to struggle in the mud and check out the car. His feet getting sucked into the muck, he tromped his way around most of the frame. The Taurus appeared to be okay, though some parts of the body were so mud-splattered he couldn't be sure. He'd driven off the road and over the shoulder but the culvert must have caught the car, the sloppy mud cutting the speed before he could run into anything else.

He worked his way back to the passenger door, opened it, and threw himself inside, shutting the door behind. Getting out of the pounding rain felt good and he wiped his face, trying to brush off as much water as possible. Sitting on the leather seat, he looked down and saw the cellphone lying on the floor. He grabbed it up and flipped it open. No signal. He dropped it back on the seat.

Eyeing the center console, he took a deep breath and then contorted his body to get back in the driver's seat. By the time he finished, he was breathing heavy. He did a few breathing exercises, in and out, in and out, to try to get himself back under control. Now that his fear had largely dissipated, his frustration was fighting with his anger.

Who the hell was in the damn Cadillac SUV? Someone who didn't like him doing what he was doing. Maybe Erin and Leo were in danger too. He needed to get back, to warn them. He shoved the car in gear and pressed down on the accelerator slowly. The Taurus edged forward. He pressed harder. The wheels spun and the car rocked forward a foot or so. He depressed the pedal farther. The car moved forward, then stopped, the wheels spinning. He pressed again and the tires only spun in the muddy ooze. And he figured the rain cascading down would only make the soil more impassable.

Damn. He slammed his fist against the top of the dashboard. How did he get himself into these situations? Then he chortled at the question. Ghosts, er spirits as the Natives preferred, got him into this problem. Again. What the hell was he going to do?

He exhaled. He had no choice. He'd have to get out and hike in the rain to the next farmhouse. He had no idea how far that was. He braced the center console, readying himself to twist his body to climb over and around it, so he could get out of the car again. As he lifted his right foot, he heard it. A growling sound of an engine, not coming from the road, he thought. He tensed.

What now? With the rain pounding on the roof, it was difficult to pinpoint the direction of the sound. He strained to look out the windows, front and side. The pouring rain obscured his vision as well. He thought he saw something coming from the right, across the field. In the curtain of rain, the thing looked…green. He tensed.

He peered and watched it close in. Not much he could do. He was a sitting duck. If the car or truck rammed him from the side, Darrell could be trapped inside. He decided he better get out now. He climbed over the console and got back into the passenger seat. When he landed on the phone, he grabbed it and stuck it into the center console. He turned to see the green vehicle barreling toward him. Only it wasn't a car or truck. It was a tractor, a large green John Deere tractor. Darrell breathed a sigh of relief. He got the door open and stood outside in the rain, his arms hailing the driver of the tractor.

The John Deere stopped a few feet away, the monstrous tractor towering over Darrell. The driver's door open and a man in worn overhauls and a stained John Deere cap stepped out onto the step. "Could you use a lit'l help?"

Darrell held his hand above his forehead so he could look at the man and keep some of the rain off his face. "You got that right. Some guy ran—"

The farmer interrupted. "Saw the whole thing from the front of the barn." He pointed over his shoulder, and Darrell noticed for the first time a large red barn in the distance. "Looked like you guys were in some kinda race and he run ya off the road."

"No, it wasn't any race. The car was following me. Then it swerved into the oncoming lane. I thought he was going to force me off the road so I sped up." Darrell heard himself rambling but couldn't help it. "Then the rain started."

"Yep, that road can git pretty slick in the rain." The man nodded, indicating the 128th. "And yep, I saw that idiot driver cut you off and you try to avoid hitting him. I think you're lucky ya didn't flip your car."

Rain dripping down his face, Darrell said, "I don't feel very lucky." He glanced at his car, mud up to the axles. "If you give me a ride back to your house, I'll call a tow to come get me out." He pointed back to the car. "I have a new cellphone but can't get a signal."

The famer shook his head. "Naw. It could take Sal—he's got the only tow truck around here—it could take him a couple of hours to git to you."

"But," Darrell protested but the farmer stopped him.

"I got a better idear. I'll back up Betsy here," he patted the frame of the tractor, "and then I'll hook her up and pull you out. Won't take that long. I'll have ya out a whole lot faster than waiting for Sal to get here."

"Um, that would be great." Darrell didn't know what to say. "Thanks."

"Climb up here in the cab and dry out some while I get her in position." He indicated the steps on the other side of the tractor. "Then ya can get soaked again, hookin' up the chain." He chuckled as he climbed back inside the driver's seat of the green John Deere.

Darrell didn't think it was all that funny.

Chapter 39

"What do you mean you don't know what happened to Erin?" Darrell asked, his face only inches from Tom Salazar.

Even with the help of the farmer, it had taken almost an hour to free his car from the mud. The farmer, whose name he learned was Chuck, wanted Darrell to come inside and get dried off, but Darrell declined the offer. After what happened, worry about Erin and Leo consumed him. Once the car was free, he thanked the farmer and tried to pay him but Chuck would have none of it.

"The good Lord says help those who need it...er, something like that." He winked. "I'm just earnin' my way to heaven a litl' quicker."

Darrell thanked him again and jumped into his car. He tore down the rest of the 128[th,] made the corner in Hamilton, then covered the miles on 12th Street. He ignored the speedometer and went as fast as he thought he could in the driving rain. He didn't even care about any lurking troopers. They could come along to Aunt Gertrude's. He might need them if something happened to his wife and son. The possibility they could be in danger was all he could think about.

Salazar stared him up and down. "Where have you been? You look a mess."

Darrell inched his face closer to the caretaker.

"Never mind that for now. Where is Erin and Leo?" He shot a glance down at the white pier, sitting empty.

Darrell realized he must have looked crazed but didn't care. Clothes soaked, rain running through his hair and down his face, eyes wide, nostrils flaring. Normally all this would freak him out, but it all paled in comparison to his fears about his wife and son. He brushed some of the rain off his face and glared at Salazar.

Tom Salazar pointed back over his shoulder at the front door, several feet away. "Let's get you out of this rain." His old, wide-brimmed straw hat protected his face from the downpour, though his worn overalls and white T-shirt were getting soaked.

Darrell pointed at the empty dock. "*Where* are my wife and son?"

Salazar shrugged. "We're not exactly sure."

"What do ya mean, you're not sure?"

"Darrell, let's at least get under the portico, where we won't get pummeled by this rain." He turned and walked back toward the wide front doors, stopping under the eaves.

Darrell didn't have any choice but to join him...if he wanted some answers. And man, did he want answers. Those answers, those possible answers gripped his heart. He cast one more glance at the empty slip—as if staring at the space would make the sailboat appear—and then scanned the lake beyond. The storm stretched over the water, dark grey clouds hovering over Lake Michigan like foreboding thunderheads, though there'd been no thunder or lightning, yet. That was the one good thing. Still, angry waves churned up the lake surface as far as he could see. Rough going for anyone out there on the water. Erin was a great sailor but still.

He turned and retreated to the relative safety of the eaves, the cessation of the rain feeling strange at first. The two Native servants appeared, coming through the front doors and carrying bath towels. They handed each man one. Before Darrell could say thanks, the girls disappeared back inside without a word. Once he wiped enough water from his face and hair, he turned and challenged Salazar again. "Now, tell me what happened with Erin and Leo."

Tom Salazar looked at his feet before meeting Darrell's gaze. "Like I said, we're not sure." He took a deep breath. "This morning, around ten I think, I wasn't paying attention to the time, Erin asked if she could take the *Fantasea* for sail. Gertrude agreed and I showed her the cockpit. She asked for some suggestions for a short sail and I gave her a few." He glanced at his watch. "That was almost six hours ago."

Darrell tried to process it all. "These destinations, how long would it take? To sail there and back?"

"Two hours, maybe three at the outset." His gaze moved to the empty dock and the lake beyond. "Even with some time at any of these places, they should've been back a while ago. Then, this storm moved in, hours before it was predicted." He shook his head.

"Doesn't that fancy yacht have a radio? Get on the radio and call her." Darrell heard his voice climb and didn't care. He didn't care about anything other than getting Erin and Leo back safe.

"Of course, the *Fantasea* is equipped with a radio," announced a stern, high voice behind him. Darrell turned to see Gertrude in the open door, cane in hand. The woman wore a pair of worn blue jeans and a light summer blouse. On her, even these looked expensive. "The finest ship radio we could buy. We've been trying to raise the ship for more than two hours. Ever since this storm started." One crooked finger pointed at the sky. "We haven't been able to reach the ship. I've been frantic about the *Fantasea*...and Erin and Leo, of course."

Darrell glanced back at the water, then met his aunt's gaze. "Erin's a great sailor. She's handled a sailboat on waters far worse than this."

The door opened wider and his mother stood there, looking sharp in white stirrup pants and a dark blouse. He noticed her blonde hair looked perfect, as if she'd just been to a salon. "I'm sure Erin can handle herself," Susan Henshaw said. "She's probably simply waiting out the storm." She looked Darrell up and down. "Now, why don't you come in and get into some dry clothes. It won't help your wife and son if you catch pneumonia."

Normally, being soaked, mud-spattered and bedraggled would've really irked Darrell, would set off some of his worse OCD. But he found his anxiety about Erin and Leo overrode all other concerns. All he could focus on was making sure Leo and Erin were safe.

He ignored his mother and turned back to Salazar. "These destinations. Which ones did you suggest?"

The old caretaker tilted his head. "Um, I think I gave her two. She said she wanted to do something with your son, so I suggested heading to South Haven. There's a really great hiking trail there, the Van Buren Trail." He paused, then added. "I also mentioned Pirate Isle. It has a small waterfall I thought your son might like. Oh, and I also mentioned Holland."

Darrell knew about Holland, gorgeous gardens, especially in spring, and had visited once as a kid. Erin would love that. And she was a big hiker. They'd hiked trails all over the Eastern Shore. But he thought she'd be most tempted by the waterfall at Pirate Isle. If he had to bet, that would be his first wager.

But wherever they went, Erin would've taken no chances with Leo. He knew she would put Leo's safety above everything else. So, what happened to them? If she was waiting out the storm, why hadn't she called on the ship radio to let them know? After his near miss with the Cadillac SUV, he feared the worst.

He looked back at the caretaker, his expression changed. "Tom, you're a good sailor. I'm sure you or my aunt," he turned and looked at Gertrude Embry, "can get a hold of a speed boat. Let's go check each location. See if we can find them." His last few words came out anguished.

Gertrude huffed. "Absolutely not." The crooked finger jutted toward the angry lake. "The water is way too dangerous right now. Could capsize any small boat."

His father pulled open the other door and stood next to Gertrude and his mom, wearing his usual polo and a pair of tan khakis. He placed a hand on Darrell's shoulder. "We're all worried about Erin and my grandson but, like you said, Erin can take care of herself. I'm sure she's quite resourceful and won't let anything happen." His gaze took in the thrashing waves on the lake. "This storm is supposed to break in another hour or so. The lake will settle down and we can head out."

Scott Henshaw shot a glance around the waiting group and brought his eyes back to Darrell. He squeezed his son's shoulder. "Knowing Erin, I bet the ship radio isn't working for some reason and she's waiting until the water settles. Once the storm breaks, I bet we'll see her sail that big old yacht right into the dock. And she'll have a great tale to tell."

Darrell met his father's gaze. "Thanks for trying, Dad, but I'm almost certain the actual situation is far worse."

Susan Henshaw stepped forward and laid her hand on his other shoulder. "Son, I love you but you can be so melodramatic. I'm sure we'll all be laughing about this at breakfast tomorrow."

Darrell took a step to the side, moving out of both parents' grasp and shook his head. "When this is done, I doubt anyone will be laughing. We need to do something *now*."

Gertrude piped up, her voice sharp, "If you're so sure Erin can handle herself and the *Fantasea*, what's the urgency? An hour or so can't make that much difference." She spoke as if hers was the last word.

Darrell decided he had no choice. If he wanted to get help for Erin and Leo, he needed to tell them. He faced the four of them, each one staring at him. He took a deep breath. "The urgency is someone tried to kill me this afternoon. And I'm scared to death they might go after Erin and Leo."

Chapter 40

"Someone tried to kill you?" his mother screeched, her hands going to her face.

"Preposterous," Aunt Gertrude spouted. "What are you talking about?"

His dad said, "Oh my God. Let's all get out of the rain and you can tell us what happened." He stepped back, indicating for Darrell to follow.

Darrell shot another desperate glance at the empty dock and nodded.

As he stepped across the foyer, he noticed he left muddy prints on the hardwood floor. He caught his aunt's glare as he passed her. "What happened to you?" she asked, then yelled into the interior of the house, "Rachel and Anna, clean up this mess."

The group moved into the great room. Darrell heard the rain drumming on the skylights and looked up. He watched as both teens got on their hands and knees and wiped the wet mud from his shoes. As the others edged around him and took seats in the big room, he moved to one of the remaining chairs.

"Don't sit there. That's a *Desmond* armchair." Gertrude squealed. "Rachel!" As she lowered herself into her own chair, Gertrude pointed at the servant. "Put a towel on that chair so the mud doesn't ruin it."

The teen rose and did as directed, then handed Darrell another towel. He took the one from around his

249

shoulders, now drenched, and gave it back to her. When he accepted the fresh towel, he made sure he said, "Thanks, Rachel."

Her dark eyes met his, a warning in her brown pupils. After wiping up all the footprints, rather than leaving, both Natives retreated to the corner of the great room and waited. Probably expecting to be called again.

"Okay, Darrell, what's all this—" Gertrude started in her sharp tone but Scott Henshaw cut her off.

"That's enough, Gertrude." She looked wounded but his dad ignored her and asked, "Why don't you simply tell us what happened?"

The darkened skies cut the natural light coming through the tall windows and the skylights, giving the space a gloomy, foreboding sense. Darrell swallowed and looked from one person to the other in the room. Then he explained about the black SUV following him and eventually trying to run him off the road. He repeated the farmer's comment he was lucky not to flip over and die. He finished with, "I had to stand in mud foot-deep to get my car out of the culvert. Got mud all over me, my clothes, the car." He shot a glance at his aunt.

No one said anything for a few seconds, the silence heavy in the dim room.

Finally, his mother said, "That's terrible. Drivers today! This car followed you and tried to drive you off the road. Sounds to me like one of those cases of road rage I've read about. Did you do something to aggravate this driver?"

"No, Mother," Darrell said, his tone stern. "I'd never seen the car before until he started following me."

Tom Salazar asked, "Why would someone follow

you…and run you off the road? Where *were* you when all this happened?"

Darrell wondered if the caretaker's question was genuine. On his drive back to Wentworth, he figured Sheila's fate *had* to be connected to her work here somehow. She'd left Wentworth for a "great new job." At least, that's what she told her mom. And, not long after, she went missing. He thought the chances were good somebody here knew something. Something about the new job, something about Sheila going missing, something. He pondered if someone here was connected to her disappearance. Was Salazar connected somehow?

He decided to plunge ahead. "Today, after visiting the historical center—which was really interesting, by the way—I drove to Shelbyville."

His mother said, "Shelbyville? Why Shelbyville? A small town in the middle of nowhere? I've heard they're talking about putting a casino there…on Indian land in a few years. You know, they can do that. What's in Shelbyville?"

"Not what, who," Darrell said, trying to read the expressions of his aunt and Salazar. "You remember I mentioned we learned about a few missing Native girls on our way here? When I explained to Leo about the girls going missing, he became very concerned." He turned to his parents. "Your grandson has a big heart."

His dad beamed. "He sure does."

Gertrude harrumphed. "What does this have to do with you being followed and run off the road?"

Darrell said, "Leo and I have been asking around, talking with a few people about Sheila going missing."

"Which people?" Gertrude asked, her voice rising. "These are my friends and neighbors. God, I hope you haven't been harassing them." She gave an exaggerated sigh. He expected her to put her palm up to her forehead next. "We only have a few days to celebrate together…as a family. I don't understand why you would squander your time looking for a teenager who probably got bored and ran away." She gathered up herself in her large chair. "You know these Indians are not like us. They don't have a home life like us." She glanced over at the two Native servants in the corner of the room but offered no apologies. "Which people?" she repeated, more demanding this time.

Darrell tried to think. They mostly had received a few clues from the ghost—at least, he thought he had—and hadn't spoken to that many people.

"We asked a waiter at Coral Gables, another Native, if he knew Sheila." Then he remembered, "Oh and Leo saw a girl on a boat at Saugatuck and asked the owner, Dwight Newsom about Sheila." He turned to his mom. "The Native steward on the boat, a teen named Sarah, did look a little like Sheila—especially to a little kid."

Gertrude complained, "I hope you didn't trouble the Newsoms. Dwight and Cynthia are some of our oldest friends."

Darrell wondered if her nasty tone came from her fear of embarrassment or something else. He didn't even bother to respond. "And Leo and I talked to a cop named Thatcher we met when we climbed Mt. Baldhead."

"Jim Thatcher? I know him, though I know his parents better. He's a good man. What did he say?"

Darrell sighed. "He said she probably ran away."

"See. Well, there you have it. That should've been enough," Gertrude announced with certainty.

Darrell ignored her. "Anyway, I received an

invitation from someone in Shelbyville who had information about Sheila."

"Who would that be?" asked Tom Salazar.

"An elder in the Gun Lake Tribe, a man named Edgar Ramshead," Darrell said. "He knew Sheila. She was…er, is his cousin's daughter."

His brother limped into the room from down the hall, Dianna a step behind. Craig came over and looked Darrell up and down. He chuckled. "What you'd do, lose a game of tug of war?" Both looked like they hastily dressed, shirts untucked, wearing shorts and standing in bare feet. Craig grinned. "Sorry, we were…indisposed. What did we miss?"

Dianna came up beside Craig and placed a hand on his arm. "Craig, read the room." She turned to Darrell. "What's wrong? Are you okay?"

Darrell shot another quick glance at his muddied clothes. "It's not me. I'm okay. It's Erin and Leo. They're missing."

Gertrude harrumphed again. "We don't know they are missing. They borrowed my yacht for a little sail and haven't returned. Yet."

As Darrell watched his aunt's protestations, he saw Ilya, the worker who helped with the cars step into the room, wearing a dark hoodie and worn blue jeans. He stood behind Gertrude's chair, almost in the shadows. The huge room was getting crowded.

Darrell addressed Craig and Dianna, "Erin and Leo should've been back hours ago. And after someone tried to run me off the road, I'm worried about them both."

"Someone tried to run you off the road?" Craig's tone lost all its earlier mirth. "Who? Why?"

"I dunno. Some big SUV." Darrell said.

Susan Henshaw interrupted, "Like I said, it was probably one of the road rage incidents. People are such crazy drivers."

Darrell scowled at his mom but she merely said, "Well, they are. On our way here, some crazy driver in a Mustang cut in front of us on I-96 and almost caused a wreck."

His dad tried to sound a conciliatory tone. "What happened to Darrell didn't sound like road rage."

Darrell scanned the faces around him again, searching for the truth. Did somebody here know something? Something about what happened to Sheila? About who tried to kill him? About Erin and Leo? He was too exhausted to ferret out the truth but he couldn't do anything about getting help for Leo and Erin without them.

He addressed Salazar. "Tom, how soon is the storm supposed to break? How long before we can go out and look for Erin and Leo?"

Salazar glanced at his watch. "According to the weather service, the storm should pass in less than an hour. Your aunt has a weather radio and I checked it before you got here. The forecasters said the storm would pass over the lake by 4:40."

Darrell glanced at his own watch. Almost four o'clock. He gestured at his soiled clothes. "I think I'll get out of these and take a shower and change. While I change, could you work on getting us a boat to search?"

Salazar looked at Gertrude before answering. "Consider it done. I'll call around and borrow a speedboat. Should have it all lined up by the time you change."

Darrell nodded. "Thanks." Using the plush arms of

the chair, he pushed himself but kept the towel protecting the expensive fabric between the chair and his filthy body. He felt drained and realized the adrenalin which had fueled him earlier had faded. He simply wanted to lay down and sleep. His exhaustion threatened to swallow him but he had to push through it if he wanted to find Erin and Leo.

At that moment, he hated Michigan and was glad he'd left it behind ten years earlier. It no longer felt like his home. Just like after he'd been dumped at the altar, he felt like the state had conspired against him. He realized it was ridiculous but that was how he felt. He regretted having come back and bringing his family back. He regretted getting tangled up with another ghost victim. If anything happens to his little guy— He stopped in his tracks. What about the new little one Erin was carrying? What if something happened to the baby? As he trudged back the corridor, he pushed the thoughts out of his mind.

Instead, he willed, *Hold on Leo, Erin and the new Leo. I'm coming for you.*

Chapter 41

It stopped.

When he finally dragged himself out from under the shower and dried himself off, taking far longer than he would normally, Darrell hadn't noticed at first. The repetitive tattoo of the raindrops on the roof had been so constant, the change hadn't registered. Perhaps, it was the effect of his exhaustion but it took his mind a while to realize something was…different. Then it took a few minutes longer to recognize the rain had stopped. After he pulled on a fresh set of clothes and stuffed his feet into loafers, he hurried into the great room. It was empty. He stared up at the skylight and saw the water drops clinging to the glass and above, blue skies. They could go searching for Erin and Leo.

"Tom? Salazar? Got a hold of a speedboat?" he yelled, hearing his voice echo down the hall. "The rain stopped." He ran a hand through his wet hair, which he hadn't taken time to comb. "Tom?' he repeated at the top of his voice.

From somewhere inside the house, Salazar called, "One momento. Working on it."

Darrell noticed he'd forgotten his wallet and watch, still in the bundle of his dirty clothes on the floor. Not to mention his flip phone. He hustled back to their suite, glancing out the tall side windows. He watched the dark gray clouds marching inland, away from the water.

Snatching what he wanted from his pants, he set his keys on the armoire and stuffed the rest into the pockets of his jeans. Without glancing in the mirror, he brushed his unruly mop of wet hair. In thirty seconds, he made it back to the great room and headed for the front door.

Any speedboat would have to pull into Gertrude's dock so he decided he might as well start down that way. Hand on the door handle, he yelled, "Tom, I'll meet you down by the dock."

He opened the door, hurried through and closed it behind him. He bounded down the three stone steps, looking out toward the pier, and pulled up. It was *there*, sitting next to the dock. The *Fantasea* sat there, bobbing up and down in the small waves, the deep blue hull bright next to the red dock fenders. He couldn't believe his eyes. He was thrilled.

He ran back up the steps, opened the door and yelled at the top of his voice, "They're back! They're at the dock." Without waiting for a response, he sprinted down the steps and ran full out down the long sloping hill. His footing slid on the wet grass, landing him on his butt. He got right back up and ran the rest of the way down the long hill.

Maybe his dad was right. Maybe the radio wasn't working in the storm and Erin couldn't call. She must've waited until the storm passed and then worked her way back. Relief flooded him and he released a long breath. He was so glad to see that yacht rocking on the gentle waves.

When he was halfway there, he called, "Erin? Leo?" but got no answer. Even as he half ran, half stumbled down the slope, his gaze stayed fixed on the boat. He couldn't see them! Erin was not at the helm and she wasn't tying up the boat. He stared but couldn't find Leo sitting on any of the chairs or cushions along the side or running along the deck. Desperation erased his brief euphoria. "Erin? Leo?" he screamed.

No response.

In fact, he saw no one on or around the yacht. Its dock lines were secured to the pier and the sails were furled. Only the jib remained up, flopping in the easy breeze. It was as if someone had docked the yacht but hadn't finished the process.

He ran onto the pier, his footsteps on the painted white boards echoing across the water. His gaze went to the lake, its surface now tranquil and clear like glass. He scanned north and south and all he saw was one sailboat halfway across the open expanse of water, its red, white and blue sail, tiny in the distance.

His glance returning to the *Fantasea*, he saw no one. Still, he called, "Erin? Leo?" The only response he got was the creaking of the boat against the fenders. He climbed up the ladder and made his way to the cabin, hurrying inside. Maybe they were there, cleaning and finishing up some tasks and couldn't hear him, he told himself, even though he knew the idea was far-fetched. Inside the cabin, he even checked the head. Empty, the same as the rest of the ship. The words "ghost ship" floated through his brain and he immediately tried to shove them aside.

The boat rocked.

"Darrell?" Tom Salazar called.

"In here," Darrell called from inside the cabin.

Salazar stuck his head in. "Anything?"

"Well, there's no one here," Darrell said, hearing the bitterness in his voice. He walked through the cabin and came out to find Salazar over by the electronics.

"Calling the Coast Guard," Salazar announced as he held a mic out.

"Coast Guard Station 289 here. Do you have a problem?"

Salazar hesitated, then clicked the mic to life. "Not sure yet. This is Tom Salazar aboard the *Fantasea*. I'm checking things out. I'll get back to you if we need assistance."

"Roger that. We'll be here if needed." The mic clicked off.

Salazar turned to Darrell, who now stood next to him. "Well, that settles that. The ship's radio works fine." Walking around, he examined the vessel. "And everything on the ship appears to be okay."

Darrell barked, "Except no Erin and Leo."

"I don't know what to think." Salazar patted the steering wheel. "The last time I saw them was when Erin stood at this helm and waived to me as she eased the boat out of the slip."

"Then where are they?" Darrell heard his voice climb.

Salazar stood up to Darrell's anxious scowl. "You can't think this is my fault. Our fault. All we did was let your wife borrow our million dollar yacht."

Darrell straightened and stared down the caretaker. "I'm so glad you have your *property* back. Now, *where* is my wife and son?"

Salazar couldn't continue to meet Darrell's stare and looked down. "I have no idea."

Darrell glanced around the empty yacht. "Someone had to bring the yacht here and tie her up. Did you see this boat come in? Did you see who sailed it here?"

Salazar shook his head hard. "No. I was on the phone arranging for a powerboat we could use for searching. I found one we can borrow." He glanced at his watch. "It should be here in about thirty minutes."

Darrell cursed himself for lingering under the shower and taking so long to get dressed. If he'd been quicker, maybe he could've seen something, could have caught sight of who brought the yacht in.

"What about anyone else at the house? Maybe somebody else saw who brought this into the dock?" Darrell's glance went up to the mansion. "Gertrude? Or maybe the teens? Maybe we should go up and ask them."

Salazar shook his head again. "Not likely. Unless you're outside or at the front door or on the second story balcony, you don't really have any sightline to the dock. None of the other windows look out toward the dock." He walked over and put a hand on Darrell's shoulder. "But we can go up and ask them in a minute." His gaze took in the deck of the sailboat. "Let's do a thorough search first. Maybe we can learn something here."

Darrell nodded. "Okay, you take the cabin. I got the deck."

Both men went about their work searching, lifting cushions, looking in cupboards and opening hatches. Darrell heard Salazar opening and closing wooden doors as Darrell himself checked under seats and in storage, looking for something, anything. When he got to the last hold, the one right next to the helm, he saw it. His heart caught in his throat.

Erin's oversized mom purse sat there, nestled between a stack of life vests and a fire extinguisher. Its rope-like handles folded across the top, the abstract pattern of bright red, yellow and orange fabric stood out even in the darkened compartment. He pulled it out gently, almost reverently, and set it on the wooden bench. It felt normal, full with the items shifting around as he moved it. He laid it on the wood and it flopped open. He stared into it. Rather than the usual water bottles, granola bars and small box of tissues he expected, he saw a single sheet of white paper with a message, typed in large capital letters covering everything. Hands shaking, he brought it out.

His breath caught and angry tears welled up as he read.

IF YOU PAID MORE ATTENTION TO YOUR OWN KID RATHER THAN WORRYING ABOUT SOME DAMN REDSKIN SLUT, MAYBE LEO AND ERIN WOULD BE SITTING HERE.

Chapter 42

Darrell collapsed on the bench, the paper flopping in his hand.

Salazar came up beside him and gestured to the white sheet. "Can I see that?"

When Darrell handed it over, Salazar read the message aloud. "Is that it? There anything else in the bag?" He pointed to the large purse.

Darrell had to shake himself from the terror that was paralyzing him. "What?"

"Did you check the rest of the bag? Maybe there is something else there which might tell us something?"

Darrell pulled items out of the cavernous bag and set them on the wooden boards of the bench next to where he sat. A half-used box of tissues, two unopened granola bars, a brush with some red hair tangled in its tines, two tampons in bright pink wrappers, a ring of keys, a folded map of Michigan, a half pack of her favorite gum, a tube of bright red lipstick and two cheap pens.

That was it. Nothing else, no clue or indication of what happened. As he returned the things inside her mom bag, he realized everything looked undisturbed, as if Erin had left the purse there to go ashore, expecting to come back on board and pull out a tissue or hand their always-hungry son a granola bar. It looked completely normal—except for the damn note.

Oh my God, where were Erin and Leo? What's

happened to them?

Salazar pulled Darrell out of his stupor. "Let's take this up to the house and see if anyone has any ideas." When Darrell started to object, he continued, "That way we can see if anyone up there saw the *Fantasea* coming in. Maybe get some idea what's going on with this." He waved the paper in his hand.

Stunned, Darrell didn't know if he could trust Tom Salazar but he didn't see any better option.

He snatched the threatening note out of the caretaker's fingers, slipped Erin's mom purse on his shoulder and started for the boat ladder. Fear, dread, and desperation coursed through his body and he bounded across the pier and up the steep slope. Salazar used the stairs, his steps pounding behind him, the older man's breath coming in huffs. Darrell didn't turn around. Twice he slipped and went to his knees, the moist grass leaving green splotches on his skin, but he ignored them and powered past the circular driveway, up the stone steps and through the front door.

Somebody was going to give him some answers. Somebody had to.

A few seconds behind him, Salazar came through the front doors, grabbed a breath and faced Darrell. "You have no idea who could've left that note. Someone had to bring the *Fantasea* into the dock. Did you see anyone else? Any other boats?"

"What note? What are you talking about?" Gertrude demanded. She sat across the room on her velvet chair.

Darrell ignored her. "I didn't see anyone near or around the yacht. When I got down there, all I saw was one sailboat far across the lake. I could make out only a red, white and blue sail."

Gertrude said, "That sounds like the Herrold's sailboat. He could hardly be involved. They're some of our oldest friends." She addressed Salazar, "But it is the *Fantasea?* Is the yacht okay? Damaged in any way?"

Salazar's answer was quick. "She looks fine. Darrell and I did a thorough search and didn't find anything amiss. She looked perfectly ship-shape."

"Yeah, except my wife and son weren't on board!" Darrell nearly screamed.

Shifting in her chair, Gertrude announced, "I wasn't very worried. No one was likely to steal the *Fantasea.* I don't know how they do things on the Chesapeake but around here, yachts are like fingerprints. No two are alike. People up and down the shore of Lake Michigan know our yacht and word would get back to me if someone tried to sell it."

"I'm so glad you have your precious yacht back," Darrell snarled. "It's only the small fact that Erin and Leo are missing and someone left this note on the *Fantasea.*" He shoved the paper in the air.

"I heard," Darrell's dad said as he came into the great room, his mom right behind. "The *Fantasea* is back but Erin and Leo weren't on it?"

Darrell shook his head. "No, and we have no idea where they are or if they're okay." His voice caught as he finished. "You guys didn't see anything? Down by the dock?"

His dad shook his head. "No. We were in our room."

"May I see the note?" Susan Henshaw asked in a quiet voice. Darrell handed it to her.

She read it and her eyes came up to meet Darrell's. "What's it mean? Who is this redskin slut?" Her lips curled as if she tasted something nasty.

Darrell sighed. "I'd guess they're talking about Sheila Birdsong."

"Who?" his mom asked.

Darrell rolled his eyes. "The girl in the flyer." He reached into his pocket to pull it out, then realized he changed clothes. It lay on the floor in his bedroom. "The Native girl who went missing last month and we've been asking around about her."

Salazar raised, "Who would care that you were asking about what happened to a Native girl? Girls from the Gun Lake tribe go missing all the time. It seems like there's a new poster up every month. Why would they want to threaten your wife and son about that?"

Darrell said, "It doesn't look like they threatened them. It looks like they kidnapped them...or worse." His voice caught.

Gertrude shook her head at Darrell and harrumphed. "I told you but you didn't listen. You should've left it alone. Some runaway Indian girl is not your problem. You're not even from here. What do you care?"

Darrell felt white hot fury. He stomped across the room toward his aunt's chair but his dad stepped in front of him.

Scott barked, "That'll be enough, Gertrude." He turned to Darrell. "What can we do?"

Darrell shook his head. "I dunno." He gestured toward the caretaker. "Tom worked on getting a powerboat so we can search the places Erin might've taken the sailboat. Said it would be here in a few minutes."

Salazar, now in his usual place by the fireplace behind Gertrude, glanced at his watch. "No more than ten minutes, I think."

Darrell's mom pulled him aside "I don't understand it, son. What is the big deal about this Sheila? Do you know this girl? Why would you be wasting your time on an Indian girl who probably ran away?"

Darrell stared down at his mom. "I'm pretty sure she didn't run away. And she is hardly alone. A young woman is missing and likely murdered and you say I'm wasting my time asking questions about her."

His mom's brilliant blue eyes flared. "Who said anything about a girl getting murdered?"

Darrell scanned the room, trying to gauge responses, but came back to meet his mom's gaze. "This isn't only about Sheila Birdsong. Hundreds of Native women are disappearing, maybe thousands. And nothing is being done."

Susan Henshaw said, "Where did you hear that? That can't be true. I've never read about that. Hundreds?"

"Maybe thousands. No one is keeping track."

"I don't believe it." She turned to her husband. "Have you ever heard of this?"

Instead of answering, his dad asked, "If that's true—and I doubt it—but if it's true, why not let the cops handle it. It's their job."

"Because they write it off…just like everybody else." Darrell knew he sounded crazed but didn't care. "After all, these are just damn Indians—"

The doorbell interrupted him, its chime echoing through the house. Hurrying, Salazar strode across the floor. "That will be the powerboat." Darrell joined him at the door.

"Here, you go, Tom." A squat, middle-aged man with a dark tan and thinning blond hair held out a set of keys attached to a red rubber float. "*Riptide*'s all gassed up and ready for you to take her out." He looked from Salazar to Darrell, both standing shoulder to shoulder in the doorframe. "He's—"

Salazar said, "This is Darrell, Darrell Henshaw, Gertrude's nephew. It's his wife and son who've gone missing." He turned. "Darrell, this is George Blade."

Darrell shook the extended hand, feeling the puffy fingers and light grip. The man wore a light blue sleeveless tee, cutoff jeans shorts and navy flip flops.

"Thank you, George," called Gertrude from her chair.

Salazar stood aside so the guest could step inside. George tipped an imaginary cap to Gertrude. "You're looking fine as usual, Gertrude."

Darrell watched as Gertrude pretended to blush. He turned to Salazar and barked, "Let's get going."

Palming the keys, Salazar asked, "George, you going with or can we head out?"

George shook his head. "Mimi is on her way over to pick me up in the Porsche. *Riptide* is all yours."

Darrell said, "Thanks. I really appreciate it."

He nodded to the man and opened the front door again. He didn't turn but heard Salazar a few steps behind. Like before, he hurried down the steps and hustled down the hill, slipping once this time on the still damp grass. His gaze took in the large powerboat, at least thirty feet long he guessed, tied up to the dock, opposite the *Fantasea*. The hull and deck of the powerboat were both silver, which gleamed in the sun which had emerged from the cloud bank. As he came down the end of the slope, he caught sight of the three large motors attached to the rear of the silver craft.

Salazar had said the boat would be fast and it wouldn't take much time to check the destinations. Seeing those huge black motors, the boat looked like it could really move across the water. Maybe Salazar was on the level. Maybe.

Darrell turned to see how the caretaker was doing, taking the wooden stairs rather than sliding down the hill. The older man had made it about halfway down the long stairway. Darrell reached down and began untying the dock lines to the powerboat. When he got the first loose, he heard something and stopped.

Some guitar music, a few chords on the strings, floated across the water. Darrell frowned and stared out at the lake and thought he saw something. He raised his hand to shield his eyes and looked again. There, still a way across the expanse, he spotted another craft. It was small, looked to be even smaller than the *Second Wind,* the sailboat piloted by Erin's dad. The boat had one triangular sail and, when Darrell squinted, he saw figures on the boat, he couldn't tell how many. The little dingy looked crowded.

Another set of chords floated across the water and he saw one figure near the bow stand up and wave. He thought, not possible. His eyes were playing tricks on him.

"Erin?" he screamed at the top of his lungs.

The wind across the lake overfilled the sails and pushed the little craft quickly across the water. The music stopped and another figure, this one near the rear, stood up and waved a guitar over his head. "Ahoy!" yelled a high male voice.

Darrell turned to see Salazar making the last few wooden steps and called, "Tom, look." He pointed out to the water. He stared again and saw a smaller figure next to Erin, his little arms waving now.

His heart exploding, Darrell slipped off his shoes and ran into the harbor, soaking the clothes he'd just put on. He didn't care. It was shallow for a good way out, so Darrell could stand and push through the water. When it got deeper, he swam, slashing hard strokes against the surface.

He got to the end of the long pier about the same time as the little sailboat came alongside. Since the two huge boats filled both slips of the dock, the little craft would have to be satisfied with the pilings at the end. Treading water next to the dock, he grabbed the dock line a pimply teenage boy tossed him. Darrell dragged himself up onto the wooden slats, pulling the line tight, as Erin stepped off the boat and finished tying off the other line. She turned and grabbed Leo, lifting him off the dingy and setting him on the dock next to her.

Tears running down his face, Darrell wrapped his wife and son in a huge hug. He tried but couldn't get anything to come out of his mouth. He kept his eyes on his wife's slightly sunburned face and sobbed, as relief swept over him.

Erin started crying too but managed to get out, "You're not going to believe what happened to us."

Chapter 43

"Well, the waterfall was so much fun. We must have gone down it a zillion times," Leo exclaimed, his voice filled with excitement. "I mean we had to climb these rocks to get to the top each time but the slide down was crazy. You should've been there, Dad."

Darrell nodded and used his forearm to wipe the tears from his eyes. He still found it hard to talk. "I wish I'd been there," he choked out.

After Darrell had been able to tear himself away from the hug on the dock—it had felt *so good* to hold his wife and son—he turned to the teen piloting the small sailboat. "Thanks so much for bringing them back."

"Sure, man." The kid pointed to Erin. "We wanted to chill at the waterfall but she asked us if we could take her back. Said you'd pay us."

Darrell reached into his pocket to pull out his wallet but Salazar stepped in front of him. "Here." He handed each boy a hundred dollar bill.

The teens' eyes lit up. "Thanks, man. You're okay."

The boys untied and the boat floated out while the group made their way back up to the mansion and into the great room. After initial greetings, Leo held court, the room filling up. Even Gertrude seemed intrigued.

"Mom called it our great adventure and she was so right." Leo looked over at Erin who managed a tired smile. Darrell squeezed her shoulders.

"Then, when we got back to the shore, guess what?" He didn't wait for anyone to respond. "The sailboat wasn't there. I mean, Mom had tied it up when we sailed into Pirate Isle, but when we got ready to leave, it wasn't there. It wasn't. Mom said the *Fantasea* was playing hide and seek and we had to look around to see if we could find it. Only, we didn't. We checked everywhere but couldn't find it." He turned to Aunt Gertrude. "Your boat is sure good at hide and seek."

Gertrude let a small chuckle erupt from her stern lips.

"Well, it was," Leo continued. "Then, after the rain, these boys came by in that little sailboat. They were headed for the waterfall and saw us. Mom asked them if they would take us back to Aunt Gertrude. They didn't want to at first, but Mom said we'd pay them. Well, Dad was going to pay them. I don't have any money." He shrugged.

Scott said, "We'll have to make sure our grandson has a little cash. You know, for the next time."

"Well, the boys were nice and they played loud music the whole trip back. It was okay but they weren't very good." He leaned over to his grandpa. "And they smoked this little cigarette that smelled funny." Leo wrinkled his nose. More chuckles in the room.

Rachel stepped forward. "Leo, you look hungry. How about I take you back to the kitchen and let's see if Silvio can fix something for you?"

Leo took her hand, looking up at her. "I'm famished. Mom said that means really hungry. Do you think Silvio can make a peanut butter and jelly samwich?"

"Let's go ask."

Once Leo and Rachel were out of earshot, Erin

asked, "How did the *Fantasea* get back here? Is it okay?"

"We don't know. Someone sailed it here and no one saw anything." Darrell glanced around the room. "The boat's fine. I found this on board." He reached behind a chair and picked up the giant mom purse and handed it to her.

"Oh, good. I thought I'd lost it. This was still on the yacht? In the compartment by the helm?"

Darrell gulped. He looked around and saw the note sitting on the end table. Picking it up, he showed it to her. "This was sitting on top of your things inside your bag." He pointed to the purse.

When Erin read it, her eyes went wide.

Tears fighting their way out, Darrell hugged Erin again. "I was terrified I lost you and Leo."

Erin's voice faltered. "Well, you didn't. We're…okay. A little sunburned and hungry but fine."

Dianna came up beside her and handed her some crackers and a glass of iced tea. "I thought you might need these." She raised one eyebrow.

Erin took the crackers and started crunching. "Thanks," she managed between munches.

"Are you…really okay?" Dianna patted her baby belly.

"Just a little queasy."

Between bites, Erin looked into Darrell's face. "Are you okay?"

Craig, who had limped up next to his wife, said, "Someone ran Darrell off the road today. Tried to kill him."

"What! What happened? Are *you* okay?" she repeated.

"I'm fine. Now that you're here." He looked into her

face.

Erin looked like she was holding it in for him, maybe for everyone. This only ramped up his anxiety. She was his rock. If she crumbled, he feared his world would fall apart. He took her hands in his. "I think we need to leave. Head for home."

Chapter 44

Darrell's words drew responses from almost everyone in the room.

His mom said, "Aw, we get to see you so seldom. Can't you stay at least a few more days?"

Coming up alongside his wife, Scott laid a hand on his son's shoulder. "You're upset right now." Then he hurried on, "You have every right to be, after what you two have been through today." He placed his other hand on Erin's shoulder. "But maybe you should wait to give time for the two of you to think this through before you decide." He dropped his arms.

Dianna stepped close and hugged her sister-in-law. "I've loved our times together and I'd miss you but I understand. This all had to be traumatic."

Erin was able to muster a tired smile and even that concerned Darrell. She said, "I've enjoyed it as well. Whatever happens, I want to make sure we stay connected."

Craig gave his brother a gentle slap on the arm. "I'm here for you, bro. Whatever you need. Dianna and I are in your corner."

Without leaving her chair, Gertrude announced, "You can't leave *now*. We have our big picnic here at the estate Friday afternoon. That's only two days." She turned to Salazar. "How many have confirmed, Tom?"

Salazar said, "Last I checked the number was fifty-three."

She slammed the tip of her cane onto the hardwood floor once. "Everyone will be there and we'll have drinks and games." She brightened. "You and Erin can defend your championship in that cornhole thing. I don't think it's too much to ask to have you here…as part of the Embry family. You and your family will certainly be safe here. Nothing will happen here, I can guarantee it." She raised her chin. "I won't turn eighty again."

Without moving from his spot, Darrell stared her down but said nothing.

After a brief silence, she added, "But you need to do what's right for your family." She turned her head to the side and mumbled, "I told you the thing about the Indian girls would only lead to trouble."

Darrell seethed but held his tongue. His insides in turmoil, he didn't trust what might come out of his mouth.

Darrell's dad said, "I don't get it. Why would anyone be concerned Darrell asked questions about some teenager who went missing?"

Darrell said, "I don't know. Someone must be worried about answers I might get."

Salazar spoke up in what sounded like a diplomatic tone, "I think people around here don't like others dredging up any Indian stuff. It's not about this one girl. I don't think it's even about Darrell. The whole thing makes people uncomfortable."

Ilya spoke for the first time, his voice coming from the back of the room. "Anyway, I don't know what all the fuss is about. That Sheila was such an uppity bitch."

Salazar barked, "Ilya, that's enough."

Ilya leaned against the fieldstone fireplace, dressed

275

in his usual worn jeans and slightly soiled T-shirt. His swarthy face broke out in a smirk, and he shook his head from side to side. "Well, she was, when she worked here. Always had an attitude and wanted to tell you what she was or wasn't going to do. Thought she was better than you."

Darrell shot a glance at Anna who flinched at Ilya's words but said nothing.

Salazar moved next to Ilya and muttered, "Don't you have something better to do?"

Ilya straightened, shrugged and mumbled, "I'm jus' tellin' it like it is, man." When he saw the look in Salazar's eyes, he raised both hands, as in surrender. "I'm jus' sayin' what everyone is thinking. I'm going." He sauntered down the rear hallway, his lazy footsteps echoing in the now silent space.

Darrell tried to read those in the room. Ilya was a snotty prick, but was there more to it than that? Gertrude sat through the whole exchange, her face expressionless. Her blue-gray eyes enlarged behind the bifocals, she merely watched, her stare fixed on her two male servants. It was impossible to tell what was going on in her head. Salazar seemed sincere enough…in cutting Ilya off. Was he embarrassed by Ilya's nasty words or was he worried the lad would let something else slip?

Again, was Sheila's exit from her job here connected in any way to her going missing and probably dead? His head hurt trying to parse it all out. He couldn't handle it. Right now, all he wanted was his family and home. Which was not here.

Darrell walked over to Gertrude's chair where she sat, her back stiff, one hand gripping the chair arm. "Aunt Gertrude, we're very grateful for your hospitality.

You have an incredible estate here and your staff have been wonderful."

He shifted his gaze to Anna and nodded. He received the smallest smile in return from the teen.

Turning his attention back to his aunt, he continued, "I do realize what a great occasion this is and I appreciate you letting us be a part of it. But I have to do what's right for my little family. We need to talk this through…as a family and decide."

For once, Gertrude didn't offer a retort. She simply stared back, her eyes large behind the lenses. Even Salazar dropped his gaze to the floor. His dad came behind him, placed a hand on Darrell's shoulder again and said in his quiet, calm voice, "We all realize you guys have had quite a day. Why don't you and Erin head back to your suite and discuss it. You both look exhausted. I'll send Leo back as soon as he finishes his peanut butter and jelly samwich." He mimicked his grandson.

Darrell smiled. "Thanks, Dad."

Erin squeezed Scott's arm. "Ditto, for me."

Darrell took Erin's hand in his. He turned and once more searched the faces of everyone in the great room, then headed back. Side by side, he and Erin walked down the hallway, each step feeling heavy. Every part of his body ached, not from pain but from the bent-up tension. He could sense it was all weighing Erin down as well. But Leo and Erin were here with him now, safe, he told himself and tried to breathe.

Out the tall windows facing west, he saw the sun starting its slow descent, the orange streak painting a stripe across the blue-gray water. The vision out the glass was stunning but only served to remind him how much he missed the breathtaking sunsets over the Chesapeake.

Wouldn't it be great to simply leave all this behind, pack up and head home?

Chapter 45

As soon as they were safely inside their bedroom and Darrell shut the door quietly, Erin began bawling. Huge sobs erupted from her and she collapsed on the edge of the bed. Darrell sat beside her. As she wept, Darrell held her in his arms, her head against his. For her sake, he tried to hold it back but couldn't help himself. He started crying too. It felt like each one's sobs fueled the others'.

Feeling her tears wet his face and mix with his own scared him. And hurt. He'd never seen Erin like this, so vulnerable and weak. Not even in Florida when someone shot at her, almost killing her. She was the rock he'd tied his life to for the past ten years. Feeling her body racked with sobs made Darrell feel helpless…and like a total failure.

It took several minutes for either to get their emotions under control, though Erin seemed to recover first. "I was so afraid, with Leo beside me. I've never been that afraid before." She sniffed more tears back. "When we returned to the shore and the *Fantasea* was gone, I was terrified but couldn't show it. I tried to brave it out for Leo." She started crying again, more weakly this time. Using the back of her hand, she wiped the tears from her eyes. "I'm sorry. I'm not usually like this." Her hand went to her belly. "I'm going to blame her."

Darrell sucked in a tear and placed his hand atop

hers there. "Or him."

She took a deep breath and said, "Tell me about your *grand adventure*." She copied Leo's tone. "What happened in Shelbyville? Did you learn anything?"

So Darrell recounted the details of his trip from meeting Edgar and Hannah Birdsong to the SUV following him, the harrowing car race in the rain and the Cadillac running him off the road. He even told her about the farmer who pulled him out of the ditch.

When he finished, she asked, "And you weren't able to see who was driving the SUV?"

Darrell shook his head. "No, all the windows were tinted dark. And when he pulled up alongside, I was too worried about crashing. I was concentrating on staying on the road."

"You were lucky. The car okay?" When she saw the look on his face, she added, "Will we be able to drive it home?"

Darrell nodded. "I think so. It drove okay after, on my way back to the mansion. I'm sure it has some dents beneath all the mud but it should be okay. Before we do any big driving, I need to go through a car wash so I can make sure there's no major damage."

Erin said, "And then you come back here to find out we're missing." Her face came up, her tears shimmering in the slants of dying sunlight through the window. "Did you call the police?"

"I tried but, out on the country road, I couldn't get a signal on my cellphone." He stared around, trying to remember where he'd laid it. He spotted the pile of wet, dirty clothes on the floor and saw the flip phone next to them.

He returned his gaze to her. "Then when I got back

and found out you two were missing, I went crazy. I told them we needed to call the cops but Salazar stopped me. Well, he said Gertrude said she didn't want to involve the authorities. At least, not yet. Said they could handle it themselves. She had Salazar borrow a speedboat from some friend to go searching the places they thought you'd sailed to." He shrugged. "I think she was more worried about getting her precious yacht back. The speedboat was the silver boat sitting in the other slip when the teens brought you back. We were getting ready to power it up and head out when I saw you."

Tears crept back into his eyes again. "I was so worried when I found this message." He pulled the sheet with the ominous typed warning out of his pocket and laid it on the bed next to them. "I thought I lost you. I couldn't bear the thought."

This time Erin held him, his shoulders shaking. Mouth close to his ear, she whispered, "But I'm okay. We're okay. We're safe."

He lifted his head so their eyes met. "Yeah, but for how long? I think maybe we need to go home. Home, home. We need to leave the mystery of Sheila's disappearance for someone else to solve. I can't worry about Sheila Birdsong anymore."

At that moment, Leo wandered into the room, his mouth wearing a purple jelly moustache. At the sight of their son, both parents straightened up, wiping off their faces.

Erin forced some brightness in her voice. "Well, it looks like Silvio was able to rustle up your peanut butter and jelly samwich. Was it good?"

Rather than answering, Leo looked from mom to dad, his small eyes going wide. "We're not going to try to help Sheila? I thought you said we needed to find her—" he scowled trying to remember. "To find her justice. Now we're simply going to forget about her?"

Chapter 46

It took them close to thirty minutes to get Leo settled down.

He couldn't understand why their "grand adventure" meant they had to go home and forget about Sheila. They said little about Darrell's harrowing experience on the road and downplayed what happened with the *Fantasea.* When Leo came into their bedroom, Darrell had snatched up the threatening note, not wanting to frighten their son. They intended to shield him from the danger and it looked like they had largely succeeded. From his questions as he undressed and got on his pj's, it was clear he couldn't understand why they were so upset and wanted to go home.

As Darrell pulled the covers up over the boy's small body, Leo looked up at his dad and said, "But we have this special ability." He lowered his voice to a whisper, even though they were alone in the room. "We can see ghosts. Doesn't that mean we can find out things no one else can? If we just go home, who is going to find out what happened to Sheila?"

Darrell didn't have any answers, so he simply said, "I don't know." He shook his head. "It's complicated, adult stuff. Your mom and I are going to try to talk it out. Don't worry, I know how you feel. I want to help Sheila if I can, too."

Leo gave a big yawn, then said, "Would you ask

Mom if she could read me a story?"

Darrell kissed his son's head, struggling to hold back tears. "I'll send her right in."

While Darrell watched from the doorframe, it took Erin reading two stories and more than a little cajoling before Leo closed his eyes. When he did, he was asleep in less than a minute.

After standing there together in the doorway watching their son slumbering, Darrell and Erin made their way to their room, stripped and climbed into bed together. Darrell's relief was so great, his euphoria at having Erin and Leo safe after everything, Darell felt tears trying to squeeze out again. "I was terrified I had lost you," Darrell said, as they held each other.

"We're here, together," Erin said and pressed her lips to his. He tightened his embrace of her smooth body, feeling her skin contact his, the sensation both comforting and electric at the same time. After the fear, the terror, he drank it in and reminded himself how lucky he was to have this woman—no, the three of them—in his life.

As they lay wrapped together, he said, "I think it's time for us to head home. Today was too close, for all of us." Erin didn't respond at first and he tilted his head so he was looking into her face. "When it was only me or even you and me in trouble, that was one thing. But now we have Leo to worry about." He moved a hand to her abdomen and kept it there. "And now we have a little Leo—"

"Or Lisa."

"Or Lisa," he continued, "we can't take the chances we took before."

After another silence, Erin said, "I know, but there

is something bad going on here, really bad. Didn't you say there are hundreds of missing girls like Sheila?"

"Edgar said more like thousands, but that's all over the country." He paused, then added, "Not something we could do much about."

"Still, thousands of girls and women gone." She gave her head a small shake.

"I feel terrible about it but it's a problem we can't solve." Darrell pleaded. "I can't take the chance *you* could become one of those missing."

She said, "Look, I appreciate your instinct to protect our family but I know you. Giving up on this Indian teen will haunt you…and I don't just mean the ghost. You don't like giving up on kids. It's one of the many things I love about you."

When Erin didn't say anything more, he added, "Look, I know Sheila wants us to find her justice *and* I know something terrible happened to her. Someone stole her dream of becoming a nurse. When I visited Hannah Birdsong, I felt her mother's pain. But even she knows Sheila is dead and she's come to terms with it."

Erin shifted her body and looked up at him. "What do you mean she knows her daughter is dead? How? Did you tell her something?"

"No, it wasn't anything I said. I don't know. It's an Indian thing maybe. Hannah said something about Sheila being in the water. She said she dreamt her daughter was now a mermaid."

"A mermaid?" Erin narrowed her eyes. "Is that some belief of the Potawatomi tribe?"

Darrell shook his head again. "Hannah was not very lucid…and I don't blame her. She said in their tribe women are responsible for water. And she dreamt Sheila has strong water powers now. She said her daughter is a mermaid. I didn't understand it when she told me."

"Maybe that isn't merely a grieving mother's wild dream."

Darrell leaned on an elbow. "What do you mean?"

"Well, you saw Sheila's ghost near the water twice, once at the chain ferry dock, then Leo saw her on the yacht. The one with the blue hull?"

Darrell supplied the name. "The *Wanderlust,* the sailboat owned by the Newsoms. Yeah, but I don't know what I do with that."

"I don't either. I'm simply thinking out loud." She squirmed closer and kissed him again. "How about a compromise? Maybe we could stay through Saturday morning like we planned—it would make your mom and aunt happy—but we stay together and watch each other's backs. We don't need to take any more chances."

"I don't know."

"Before all this happened, Dianna asked me to go shopping with her for the baby—hers, not ours. I was planning to do that tomorrow before all this. And they're going to take a ride on the Star of Saugatuck, you know, the paddlewheel which takes tourists down the Kalamazoo River and out into Lake Michigan. She asked us to join them. It'll be relaxing and you'll enjoy spending time with your brother."

"I don't know."

"We don't need to take any chances. Then, Friday we hang around for your aunt's last blowout and Saturday we pack up and head for Maryland."

"Maryland. The Eastern Shore. Home. That sounds great right about now." He heaved. "I guess we can manage two more days, if we stay close together. But I'm not going to let you and Leo out of my sight."

She whispered in his ear and he felt her hot breath on his skin, "I especially like the part about close together."

He felt her sinewy body press against his, then she moved atop him. He stared at her stunning figure outlined in the dim moonlight that sliced into their room. *How did I get this lucky?* As she leaned down and kissed him again, he surrendered his fears, anxieties and worries and gave in to the moment as they came together, Erin taking the lead this time. When both finished, they lay side by side, both out of breath, her naked body curled inside his embrace. He drifted off to sleep.

His blissful slumber did not last.

Chapter 47

He awoke to…something. Or rather some…thing woke him. One moment he was asleep, adrift in a captivating dream of he, Erin and Leo on her dad's *Second Wind*, the breeze off the Chesapeake tossing her beautiful red hair. Leo laughing. Then something dragged him from his slumber. For a few minutes, he lay there, eyes shut, willing himself to sleep again, to return to that beautiful dream.

But that didn't happen.

Exasperated, he slid quietly from the bed, went to the bathroom to relieve himself and then slipped on his PJ bottoms, still lying on the floor next to the bed, where he and Erin had shoved them in their lovemaking. Standing next to the bed, for a minute he watched his wife sleep, the outline of her body beneath the cover sheet, her face a picture of contentment and the long red hair falling across the side of her face. He searched the room for some sign of what drew him from blissful slumber but found nothing amiss. And no ghost lurking in the shadows.

His stomach growled, the sound surprisingly loud in the silent room and, without really thinking, he mumbled "Sorry" to no one. It dawned on him he hadn't eaten since the eggs at the diner and he was "famished," echoing his son's earlier claim. With his adrenalin drained, his body now demanded food. He padded out of the room, heading for the kitchen. He'd no doubt find something in the fridge.

He started down the long hall, keeping his footsteps light. At Leo's room, he cracked the door open and checked on his son. The boy lay curled up on the bed, the cover sheet twisted around his small body. Darrell tiptoed in and gently eased the sheet loose and re-tucked it around him. He stood there for a minute, simply watching his son sleep.

Thinking of the danger Leo and Erin had survived, Darrell's heart ached. What if no one had come to Pirate Isle to find them and sail them back? Probably he and Salazar would've come upon them, but how much longer might that have taken? He wondered how long Erin could've kept up the charade of the "great adventure" with their son. Remembering her collapse into tears hours earlier, he pondered how much more could his beautiful wife take? And who the hell did this to Erin and his little boy? When the answer came, shards of fear sliced through Darrell. The same heartless person who would murder a Native teen.

He wouldn't let anything happen to Leo…or Erin. He couldn't.

He backed out of the room, closing the door quietly, and made his way down the rest of the hall and into the great room. He found the cavernous room empty, no ghosts lingering and only the moon streaming in through the skylights. He crossed the room to the other hallway following the wooden path, making sure his steps made little noise. He didn't want to wake anyone, didn't want to argue again with his mom or aunt.

When he reached the kitchen, he opened the door and shut it behind him. Alone in the darkened room, it took a bit for his eyes to adjust. Then, his vision adapted to the dark and the digital time readouts from the appliances shed enough light for him to make his way around the large island and to the refrigerator. When he opened the fridge doors, a slice of bright light cut across the kitchen, reflecting off the silver pots hanging over the island and revealing more of the room. Keeping the door open and using the light, he glanced around the kitchen. He'd stepped in here before but never really paid any attention. The appliances, lined up against one wall, were massive, the stovetop with six burners next to a large double oven. Next sat a commercial dishwasher beneath two microwave ovens. At the end stood a full-sized commercial freezer. Atop the island sat a block of blond wood housing a dozen black-handled knives. His aunt's galley was equipped to feed an army.

Returning his attention to the fridge, he tested a few containers until he found one holding cooked chicken. He grabbed a leg and thigh, reclosed the plastic lid and shut the door. Needing something to put the chicken on, he glanced around but couldn't make out enough in the dark to do any searching. So he opened the door again and held it wide as he rummaged through some cupboards. He got lucky with the third door. He pulled out a small China plate and closed the cupboard again. When he stepped back to the fridge to close the door, he sensed someone behind him. He whirled, almost dropping the expensive China piece. He stared but saw no one in the shadows of the kitchen. He shut the fridge door again.

He knew his aunt or Silvio wouldn't mind, but he felt embarrassed to be caught poaching cold chicken at three o'clock in the morning. Relieved he was indeed alone, he walked over to the long island and sat down on one of the stools, setting the plate on the polished wood tabletop. Sitting there doing some late-night snacking reminded him of nights during practice. Two-a-days were only two weeks away and, even though they meant long grueling days and sometimes raiding the fridge late into the night, he found he missed them. He longed to return home, to take care of his student athletes. He missed balancing Erin's hectic schedule in the OB department with his crazy teaching and coaching demands, all the while taking care of Leo. And soon, they'd have another little one to add to the mix.

Besides, he couldn't wait to be back in the classroom in front of not-so-enthusiastic teens. He reveled in the challenge of getting them to see the world differently, of showing them maybe they didn't know everything, maybe the past had something to teach them. He could picture those young faces.

"I would've graduated this year," a quiet female voice whispered.

Darrell stopped, half-eaten chicken leg in the air. He felt the prickle down his neck and tried to scan the room. He saw nothing, no one, only the shadows of pots and pans hanging from the ceiling rack and the bulky silhouettes of the appliances. The dark outline of the knife block loomed next to him. Just when he thought— hoped—he'd imagined it, the prickle intensified, like an electric shock spreading from his neck down his back.

"Sheila?" he called, his voice a hoarse whisper. No response came but the prickle didn't ease up. He knew she was here, in the room, and stared harder. There, in the doorway back to the hall, he saw her figure, the high forehead, the silhouette of long black hair down the back.

"I'm sorry," he gulped. "I'd like to help but I have my family to think about."

The shadowy figure stared back and he could make out the large almond-shaped eyes.

"I was nearly killed today." Then he added, "And I thought someone had taken Erin and Leo. I didn't know what happened to them and it terrified me."

Darrell heard his words whispered in the spacious kitchen and recognized the hypocrisy of what he was saying. "I'm really afraid for my son. He's only five," he finished, his voice pleading.

The figure before him didn't move. Sheila stood straight, large eyes glaring back at Darrell. The ghost's features didn't move, her lips pulled tight in an almost straight line. Still, inside his head, Darrell heard, "Ask Sarah. Help Sarah."

Ask Sarah what?

Chapter 48

"Hey, bro, aren't you glad you stayed and we did this together?" Craig called across the aisle, his bad leg propped on the seat next to him.

They sat on the upper deck of the "Star of Saugatuck," a few feet from the bright red paddlewheel of the tourist boat, which churned through the placid water. Across the way, Dianna leaned comfortably against her husband, her palm resting on her small baby bump, her gaze scanning the shoreline. On Darrell's side of the aisle, his son and wife half-sat and half-leaned on the railing, peering into the water below and checking out the other shore.

"Hey, look at that!" Leo pointed down at the river, a small, narrow sailboat puttering past them powered by a quiet engine, its sails furled. The polished teak deck and bright yellow hull gleamed in the sunlight. "Cool," Leo called and looked over at Erin, who grinned at him.

Craig got up and hobbled over next to Leo, glancing down. He patted the boy on the shoulder and echoed, "Cool." Casting another look at the sailboat, he turned back to Darrell. "That reminds me, did you hear about the girl who thought she was a sailboat?"

Darrell rolled his eyes and snuck a glance at Erin, who tried to smother a smile.

Without prompting, Craig finished, "She was a little dinghy." He chuckled. "Get it, a little dinghy."

Leo turned from the rail, laughing. "A little dinghy. I get it. Good one, Uncle Craig."

Darrell said, "Don't encourage him."

Craig didn't let up. "See. if you guys left for the Eastern Shore already, you would've missed my jokes."

Darrell shook his head. "Oh, yeah. I don't know how we could've ever survived without your puns." He tried to keep a straight face but couldn't stop the corners of his mouth from turning up.

These past few days with his brother and Dianna had been a real gift, one he'd not expected. He'd forgotten how much he enjoyed Craig's company. Years ago, when they were young, he and Craig had been "best buds." Even back then, Craig had tried to be a jokester. In those days, Darrell had confided everything to his older brother. It was he and Craig against the world, or at least against their parents.

But, after Darrell's first haunting and Craig's "accident," all that ended. In the twenty years since, every time he looked at his brother's damaged leg, the guilt simply ate at Darrell. And, after that afternoon so long ago, the connections between two brothers had frayed over time.

Darrell had missed those connections. After this week, he decided they needed to find a way to get together with Craig and Dianna, especially with two little ones on the way. Besides, there were only six hundred miles between Michigan and Maryland.

"Leo, what did the lake say to the sailboat?" Craig asked, pointing to the small sailboat that had passed them.

The boy scrunched his eyes, trying hard to come up with an answer. He shrugged. "I don't know."

"Nothing. It just waved." Craig laughed at his own joke.

Leo nodded his head in earnest. "Sure. It waved. Another good one, Uncle Craig."

Dianna patted her husband's arm. "Everyone knows you're the great pun-ster."

"Okay, okay, one more. Why did the sailboat do drugs?" Craig's gaze went from one to the other. "Anyone?"

Dianna sighed, her blue-gray eyes leveling at him. "I'm probably going to regret this but I'll bite. Why?"

Craig grinned and pointed down to a long dock that stretched out into the water. "I think it was the pier pressure."

Leo looked from Craig to his dad, his green eyes narrowing. "I don't get it."

Darrell explained, "It's the spelling. There are two peers, p-e-e-r, which means your friends and p-i-e-r, which means a boat dock." He pointed to another dock they passed.

Leo frowned at his uncle. "Uncle Craig, that's not very funny."

"Okay, I give," Craig said, his hands up in surrender.

Dianna said, "I'll forgive you, especially since you let me buy such nice things for the baby."

From one of the three shopping bags next to her, she pulled out a cute onesie, a bright teal color with a fish splashing into the water on the front, the word "Saugatuck" above it. After they'd finished shopping for the baby, Darrell had offered to run the bags back to the car, but they didn't have time and needed to board the riverboat. Anyway, Dianna was more than content to alternate her attention between the beautiful houses along the shore with the pretty items they'd found for the baby.

Craig, out of puns for the moment, joined the others gazing at the beautiful properties which lined the shore. Their perch on the upper deck gave them a great vantage to the river below and to the spectacular houses. Another hot July day, the summer sun overhead warmed them but the breeze from the water was enough to keep them comfortable.

Darrell stared at his brother and Dianna. He was glad he agreed to stay the extra day and come along. He shot a glance at Leo, whose face beamed. His son certainly seemed to be having fun. He had an urge to reach out and gather Leo close but he fought it. When he thought something had happened to him and Erin yesterday, Darrell could hardly breathe. He damn near cussed out the ghosts aloud. Only he couldn't tell anyone else about the ghosts. They wouldn't understand. He felt relieved—somewhat—they were heading home after the barbeque tomorrow. And, until then, he wouldn't let Leo or Erin out of his sight.

Though he still felt guilty about abandoning Sheila—if he were honest. Once again, he recalled the anguish in Hannah Birdsong's eyes when she talked about losing her daughter. Darrell got a glimpse of that yesterday, in the mirror. God. He shivered again, remembering. But what was he going to do? Besides, he had no idea what Sheila meant, ask Sarah? Ask her what? And when? When would he even see the young woman again? Darrell shook his head.

He had to take care of his own family first. He watched Erin and Leo staring at the shoreline, pointing and laughing. He was doing the right thing.

As they cruised the river, they passed the homes that lined the shore, each one more extravagant than the previous. Most sat two or three stories tall with lines of tall windows facing the river and a long dock stretching out into the water. Some magnificent structures had sculptured shrubs and a perfectly manicured lawn, sloping down to the river, while other displayed a tiered garden ablaze with golds, reds, pinks and whites. It was obvious some structures had been there a while, with towering trees flanking the house, itself covered with carved limestone or weathered siding. Other homes looked to be more recent, with the grounds still untamed and the new windows winking in the sunlight. A few owners had even built two matching structures. As they passed one of these, all four adults stared at the full-size house in black siding with white windows complete with a wooden deck and railing, then below it, a matching but smaller boathouse in the same colors and design.

Erin pointed to the matching home and boathouse. "Some of these are over the top but that is really cute."

Craig said, "I think that one belongs to a successful lawyer from Chicago. A woman lawyer."

Dianna said, "Good for her. She has taste."

Craig turned to Darrell. "Talking successful, most of these properties belong to investment bankers and money managers from Chicago. And they only use them during the summer. They'll close all these properties around Labor Day."

Erin stared at the large houses, mansions almost, as they floated by. "Seems like a huge expense for only a few weeks."

Dianna chuckled. "Chump change for these guys."

Every property had its own dock which stretched a

good thirty feet into the water. Tied to the docks, tall sailboats, sleek powerboats and fancy yachts bobbed on the gentle waves caused by the riverboat. On a few piers, they could see men and women untying the rigging and readying to take the crafts out onto the lake.

The riverboat made its way past the wealthy properties and the river opened up. They floated past a large marina with scores more boats docked and beyond them, a squat red lighthouse rose out of the water. When they got to the mouth of the Kalamazoo River that opened up to Lake Michigan, Craig pointed south down the shore. "You can't see it from here but Aunt Gertrude's place is about a half mile down the coast."

Ahead of them, they saw a yacht coming toward the mouth, its red, white and blue sails full with the wind. Erin stared at the sailboat as it neared and Darrell saw something in her face.

"What is it?" he asked.

"Probably nothing." She continued staring, watching the sailboat close the gap. She shook her head. "When Leo and I came down the trail at Pirate Isle and saw the *Fantasea* was gone, I looked out across the lake and saw a sailboat that looked like…that." She pointed to the red, white and blue sails. "At least, the sails. It was far away and I couldn't make out much more. Maybe I dreamt it."

Something clicked for Darrell. He shook his head. "I don't think so. I may have seen the same boat across the water when I saw the *Fantasea* in the dock. When I came down looking for you and Leo. I remember those distinctive sails."

Leo looked up at his dad. "You mean when Mom and I had our great adventure?"

Darrell patted his son's head. "Yeah, exactly." He turned back to Erin. "Could be a coincidence."

Erin shook her head. "You don't believe in coincidence." Her gaze studied the yacht as it approached the bow of the riverboat, getting ready to pass on the port side. "I'd like to know whose boat that is."

Dianna watched as the boat came closer, almost alongside. "That's easy. I'm pretty sure that's the *Nauti-Boy*, the Herrold's yacht. You know, Roger and Jane Herrold. Roger was one of the roasters at Gertrude's party, Short guy, bald with a big—" she indicated her belly.

"How do you know that?" Darrell asked.

Craig answered for her. "We saw their boat docked at Aunt Gertrude's place when we were in town for that romantic getaway a few years ago. We stopped in and said hi to Gertrude—not like we had a choice." He shot a look at his wife.

Dianna finished the explanation. "The Herrolds were leaving as we pulled into the driveway. They introduced themselves to us and headed down the hill to Gertrude's dock. Then, while we sat on the veranda having a drink, we watched the Herrolds get into that boat." She pointed at the craft approaching. "Once they were out a little, they raised those red, white and blue sails. From what Gertrude told us, they sail this part of the lake often. Not surprised you saw them. Oh, I'm sure they'll be at the party. They're good friends with Gertrude."

"You think they are the only ones with sails like that?" Darrell asked, without taking his eyes off the yacht.

Craig said, "Don't know. Gertrude or Salazar might."

As the main sail filled with air and the yacht floated alongside the riverboat, all five stared down at the deck of the sailboat. Two couples sat around a table, tumblers with brown liquid in front of each. The two men leaned close to each other and appeared to be discussing something, while the pair of women looked on. As the two boats cut through the water next to each other, the four around the table turned to look up. The angle down was significant but Darrell thought he recognized a few faces.

Leo called out, "Hey, it the Newsoms, the nice people who let me use the bathroom on their boat." He reached over the rail and waved one arm back and forth. "Hey, it's me, Leo."

Darrell watched as the four people on the boat shielded their eyes and looked up to the riverboat.

Leo waved harder. "Hi, we're up here."

The four on the deck of the yacht continued to stare but didn't even acknowledge Leo's shouted greeting. Darrell stared at the faces and, for just a moment, he thought he read something in their features. He studied Dwight Newsom, white captain's hat tilted on his head, tufts of black and gray hair escaping around the rim. The man's eyes narrowed and an ugly scowl crossed his face as he met Darrell's gaze.

Why would Dwight Newsom harbor any resentment toward him? He and his wife had been polite and even kind to Leo. And he had asked if they were making any progress on finding Sheila. He glanced over at his son, who was still waving as the sailboat passed out of view, broad smile held on his face.

Leo turned to his dad. "I guess they couldn't see us." He looked up into the sky. "Maybe because of the sun."

"Maybe," Darrell said. He let his son have the simpler explanation, but Darrell was considering other possibilities. Still, he couldn't be sure. From the top floor of the riverboat, he was pretty far away from the yacht's deck and his angle was oblique.

Then, as the sailboat passed them but was not completely out of his sight, Darrell continued to stare. He watched a figure emerge from under the white umbrella, off to the side and beyond the table. This one he definitely recognized. Tall, dark skin, brown hair. Ilya.

What would Ilya be doing with the Newsoms...and the Herrolds? And why was he hiding, if that's what he was doing?

Still, the Herrolds were quite rich—he could tell from the man's bragging at his aunt's roast at the Butler—and they have a magnificent sailing yacht. Dianna said they like to sail this part of Lake Michigan. Heck, they probably own one of those huge houses along the shore. They're probably merely sailing the yacht back into their dock. Maybe Dwight Newsom's look and scowl were because he was simply looking into the sun.

Perhaps, it was nothing. Or maybe it was all a coincidence?

A voice inside his head argued, you don't believe in coincidences...not when it comes to the ghosts.

Chapter 49

The next day, Darrell resolved to put the haunting aside, once and for all. He told himself he'd probably not encounter Sarah again. If she was still working on the *Wanderlust*, the yacht could be anywhere. He expected to see the Newsoms at his aunt's barbeque but he could hardly ask where their servant was, could he?

Ask her.

And even if he happened to see Sarah, what would he ask? What would he say? Sheila Birdsong's ghost told him to ask...something? It sounded crazy, even in his head.

To keep busy, he focused his attention on getting ready to head home.

Home. That sounded *so good.*

As part of the compromise he and Erin had worked out, once they returned from their riverboat cruise and shopping, they spent the rest of the day relaxing and playing games with the family but they also took time out to organize everything for their trip home. Darrell's plan was, between board games and rounds of cornhole, to pack most of their stuff in the car ahead of time, so when the final celebration ended Friday night and they awoke Saturday, they could simply dress, eat and leave. It was a solid plan and it kept his mind off abandoning the missing Indian...mostly.

He again experienced the sense of luxury. While he

and Erin faced off against Craig and Dianna in successive rounds of the bean toss game and his mom and dad sat at a table playing UNO and laughing, the entire staff at Wentworth worked silently around them. Rachel and Anna were busy cleaning every surface in the mansion, sometimes climbing tall step ladders. The two teen Indians even apologized when they had to work around the card game to wash the skylights, making sure the glass sparkled. Darrell felt embarrassed and even lazy watching the girls hustle around the house, mop and cloth in hand, while he relaxed with his family. He wanted to offer to help or at least hold the ladder, but he'd been scolded before and he feared any assistance by him might cause problems for the teens. On three different occasions, Silvio came out of the kitchen to ask if he could fix them something special or refresh their drinks.

While the family played rounds of the card game, his mom winning most often, several delivery vans arrived with booze, local beers, vegetables, ribs, steaks and brats. They all sat and watched Silvio come through the hall next to the great room on the way to the kitchen, arms full of food ingredients and loudly chastising drivers for coming to the front door rather than the kitchen entrance. Even Salazar appeared from time to time, carrying chairs and tables out to the veranda and yard. The frantic activity and preparations went on Thursday into Friday morning. The only staff member Darrell didn't notice was Ilya. Maybe, the young man was likely taking care of the garage and vehicles.

Darrell, Erin and Leo had enjoyed their time with the family so much, he and Erin didn't get as much done Thursday as they intended. They did consolidate everything into the suitcases and totes but he hadn't taken time to carry them out to the car. With all the staff was doing for the cookout—they seemed to be even busier Friday morning—he didn't want to bother any of them, so he rolled the first two pieces of luggage himself around the house to the garage, tucked behind the mansion. He'd only seen the side of the building when they passed it on the long driveway, so he had little idea what to expect. But he found his aunt's extravagance was still able to astound him. Coming through a side door, he flicked the switch and the interior exploded with dazzling light. The garage ahead of him looked huge. It must've had at least ten bays, most of them full. Cars sat in each one, washed, cleaned, and polished, their shiny finishes gleaming under the fluorescent lights.

Dragging the suitcases across the floor, he noticed the polished surface at his feet looked to be Terrazzo, or something like it. He'd heard discussion of the cost of such a floor when he attended a meeting about school construction. In his head, he did some quick calculations. The price tag for this huge floor alone was staggering, costing more than he'd make in a year. He shook his head as he passed his dad's white Volvo, looking like it just rolled off the showroom floor. Next sat Craig and Dianna's Bug, its fire engine red finish gleaming like it had a new wax job. In the next bay sat the black Lincoln Navigator they had taken down to Oval Beach. If possible, its black finish was even shinier than the other cars.

He passed a silver Mercedes convertible and a deep blue Lexus SUV Darrell had seen a commercial for but couldn't remember the name of the vehicle. The exteriors of both luxury models shone even more than the others.

He found his Taurus in the next stall and stood there studying it. It too had been cleaned, washed and waxed, as good as his eight-year-old car had looked in a long while. He walked around it, inspecting the fender, grille and side panels, looking for damage. Just as he expected, he found a few dents which bore witness to his harrowing road experience, but overall, the old car came through it fine. He was still surprised—and relieved—the driver airbag had not deployed. It should have. He'd need to have it checked when he got home.

Using the fob, he opened the spacious trunk and slid in the first two suitcases. Thankfully, there was plenty of room for more. Traveling with Leo had about doubled their belongings. He shut the trunk lid and stood back, letting his gaze roam up and down the bays. Every car had been tended to. He didn't see Ilya but perhaps his earlier impression of the young man had been mistaken. The guy had done an amazing job with each of the automobiles, especially his mud-splattered Taurus. He needed to say a special thanks to him.

Darrell glanced down at the end and saw two pickup trucks, one obviously old, its finish showing a few rust spots and a second one much newer, its black finish shining as brightly as the other cars. In the last bay, he spied another car under a large green tarp. It was none of his business but his curiosity nagged at him. The amount of wealth his uncle and aunt had amassed in the construction and shipping business continued to amaze Darrell. As a young boy, he'd had no idea. He couldn't recall his parents ever mentioning his uncle and aunt's wealth. Darrell realized his mom and dad did quite well. His dad had a very successful dental practice and his mom was a library director. They had never struggled.

But, from the mansion to the yacht to these luxury cars, it was clear Aunt Gertrude had money to burn. He stared at the outline under the green tarp, his interest rising. Maybe, she had purchased a Ferrari or a Lamborghini. He examined the covered vehicle in the last space. The shape hidden beneath the covering looked higher but Darrell had no idea how high off the ground those cars sat. He'd never seen either in person.

He strolled down the rest of the way, past the trucks and two empty bays. He looked around, somehow feeling guilty for his snooping, but saw no one else around. When he got to the last stall, he stood at the foot of the hidden car. He scrutinized the shape, trying to guess what was under the tarp. Shooting another quick glance around and seeing no prying eyes, he tugged up the front edge of the cover. A large, shiny silver grill faced him with an emblem in the center. The colors of red, green, black and gold had been polished to a high sheen.

"What the hell!"

Chapter 50

"Tom, I need you to see something. Right now," Darrell almost barked. He couldn't help himself.

Standing on the veranda, Salazar stretched up on his tip toes, his hands fumbling with the mechanism inside one of the umbrellas. "This doesn't want to open," he said through gritted teeth. Glancing at Darrell, he rolled his eyes. "I'm a little busy here."

Darrell stepped up next to him on the wooden slats and used both hands to pull the steel ribs of the umbrella apart. As he did, the gear clicked and the little motor purred, spreading open the red fabric.

Salazar watched it open fully and looked from the spread umbrella to Darrell. "Thanks," he grumbled, before moving to the next table. "Can't it wait? I have a lot to do before the guests arrive." He pressed the button on the second. The motor started, and the second umbrella opened easily to its twelve-foot diameter.

"No, it can't wait. And it's a hell of a lot more important than these." Darrell gestured at the fancy crimson canopies. "Besides it won't take that long. I just need you to come to the garage."

Salazar stepped off the veranda to follow, then stopped. "The garage. What for?"

"I found something in the garage and I need to ask you about it."

Darrell turned to go but Salazar didn't budge. "If it's

about the cars, check with Ilya. They're his responsibility."

Darrell shook his head. "I know. I couldn't find Ilya so I came to you."

The old caretaker gave a quick point toward the garage building. "Okay, let's get on with it. I've got several jobs to get done before the guests start arriving in," he glanced at his watch, "about thirty minutes."

Together, they strode around the house and came to the garage, Darrell keeping a quick pace and Salazar hurrying to stay up. Darrell opened the access door, stepped through and stomped past the other cars, their white, red and gold colors still shining under the bright fluorescent lights. He halted in the last bay and, without a word, yanked off the tarp of the covered car. The Cadillac's finish gleamed like the others, the black taking on an evil aura.

Darrell demanded, "Whose car is this?"

"W-w-what do ya mean?" Salazar pointed to the trucks in the next stalls. "These all belongs to Gertrude." When Darrell stared him down but said nothing new, he continued, "Gertrude owns all these but she lets us drive them when we need to."

Darrell stabbed at the SUV. "This…this is the car that followed me and ran me off the road."

Salazar raised his eyebrows and spoke like he was talking to a child. "Don't be ridiculous. It must've been a different car." He turned to head back to the house. "I got things I have to take care of."

Before he took a half step, Darrell grabbed his arm, stopping him mid-stride. Releasing his grip, he met the older man's gaze and held it. "Look, Tom, I know this was the car that tried to kill me. I memorized every detail about that car. Those dark tinted windows and…"

Salazar was shaking his head before Darrell could finish. "Gertrude had those put in because she said the sun hurts her eyes."

Darrell glanced at the caretaker sideways. "I don't know my aunt that well but I've seen her out basking in the sun a few times just this week."

"Okay, I think she simply didn't want anyone looking in. She values her privacy."

This time Darrell shook his head. "Yeah, and that's why she's invited *fifty* of her closest friends to her birthday barbecue."

Salazar placed both hands on his hips. "It can't be this car. You have any idea how many black SUV's there are on the shore?"

Darrell grabbed the caretaker's arm. "No I don't. But like I said, I memorized every detail about that car." He gestured toward the grill. "I stared at the damn emblem when it was only a few feet behind my rear window. I got to see it up real close, nice and menacing. I watched it through my rearview mirror, thinking any minute it would ram me." He leaned down and placed a finger over the slight chip in the shield. "I noticed that little nick in the middle, between the bottom red and gold. See?"

Salazar lowered his face and studied the logo in the center of the silver grill. His rough fingers brushed the surface. "I've never noticed that."

When Salazar straightened up, Darrell jabbed at the SUV. "*This* is the car that tried to kill me."

The caretaker's eyes got wide. "You don't think *I* had anything to do with that?"

"Well, somebody sure did. And the car sits right

here in this garage."

Salazar shook his head hard. "I was here. All day."
He sputtered. "And-and-and remember, I did everything
I could to help you locate Erin and Leo." His gaze went
from the car to Darrell. "You're Gertrude's nephew.
Why would I want to hurt you, much less kill you."

"Well, somebody sure as hell did. Who else has
access to the cars?"

Salazar shrugged. "I don't know. Anyone."

"Anyone?" Walking around the side of the car,
Darrell lifted the handle to the driver's door. It didn't
open. "It's locked. I tried earlier."

Salazar took four quick strides to a board attached
to the rear wall of the garage and pointed. "The keys are
kept right here."

Darrell examined the board and saw a row of hooks
with numbers above. Keys hung from most of the hooks
and he noticed his duplicate dangling from slot five. The
last hook held another set of keys and a fob attached to a
key chain with the Cadillac logo.

He asked, "Who has access to this garage?"

Salazar brushed his straw hat back on his head, the
filmy eye clouding. "We don't usually keep the garage
locked. This is the Michigan shore not Chicago." He
glanced around the garage. "Ilya takes care of the cars,
we can ask him." When he looked back at Darrell, his
features bore a look of desperation. "I promise I'll help
you get to the bottom of this but right now I have to get
back to the party preparations." He looked at his watch
again. "I only have twenty minutes now."

Without another word, he turned and left, striding
quickly through the opening. As Darrell watched him
disappear, he asked himself, did he believe the man? He

glanced at the SUV, the ceiling light reflected in the shiny black finish. Darrell ran his fingers over the smooth paint job. Once more, his index finger explored the tiny nick in the emblem, as if to prove to himself it was real.

Someone used this car to run him off the road and here it sat. He shook his head. There were no coincidences…not as far as the ghosts are concerned. He needed to tell Erin. Maybe she'd have some idea.

Chapter 51

"You're not going to believe what I just discovered in the garage," Darrell whispered to Erin as they sat atop their bed. She'd finally gotten Leo to lie down for a short nap before the party—or at least, pretend to nap—and Darrell didn't want his son in the next room to overhear. He needn't have worried. Salazar's thunderous voice could be heard all through the house and drowned out everything else.

"Rachel, bring two more chairs!" he screamed. "Anna, get the red-checked tablecloths from the linen closet!" Footsteps pounding through the house. "Ilya? Has anyone seen Ilya?"

Darrell realized, with all the activity, Leo would be up in a few minutes so he gave a quick rundown of what happened in the garage.

"He claimed it wasn't the car?" she asked.

"He tried but gave in when I showed him the nick in the shield on the grill. He didn't know what to say."

"You think he was on the level?"

Darrell shrugged. "I don't know. He looked genuinely shocked when I laid it out for him."

"And he said you needed to talk with Ilya?"

"Who is conveniently absent," he said with a smirk.

The door opened a crack and Leo stuck his head in. "I tried but I couldn't sleep. I promise I'll be good for the party." His gaze went to the bags and luggage on the floor next to the bed. "Can I help you take more things to the car?" His large emerald eyes pleaded.

Darrell couldn't be mad at his son. "Sure. I can always use help from my big guy." He pointed to the two shopping bags. "Can you carry those two bags? They're a little heavy."

Leo went over, grabbed one in each hand, and lifted. He said, "Sure," but his voice had a bit of strain in it.

Darrell and Erin had spent the morning and early afternoon organizing everything. They had held back one case for pj's, toiletries and clothes for tomorrow. After they stored the last cases in the car, their exit tomorrow morning would be easy and, hopefully, uneventful.

Darrell grabbed the two remaining pieces of luggage and half-carried and half-rolled them down the hallway, Leo following a step behind. Neither spoke as they made their way out the door, down the driveway and into the garage. Shooting a glance around the structure, Darrell set the two suitcases down behind the Taurus and Leo did the same. They were alone. Studying the trunk space, Darrell decided he had to move some pieces around to fit in the remaining cases and bags from the stores.

While he was bending over, stretching to slide a piece onto the rear shelf, Leo asked, "Which car tried to run you off the road?"

"What?" Darrell jerked his head around and bumped it on the upper frame. Rubbing the spot he hit, he finished pushing the case onto the shelf, pulled his head out of the trunk area and straightened up. "What'd you say?" he asked a little too sharply.

Leo's eyes got wide and a guilty look crossed his face. "I-I-I just asked which car?" he mumbled.

Darrell squatted down so he was eye level with his

son. He made his voice gentle. "How do you know about that?" He had taken pains not to say anything about his near wreck when Leo was around. At least, he thought he had.

Leo looked embarrassed. "I heard people talk. Grandma and Aunt Gertrude were talking about it and I heard. Then I heard you and mom talking about the car you found." He looked at his dad. "Am I in trouble?"

Darrell pulled his son into a hug. "No, of course not. I just didn't want to worry you." He stood up and pointed to the bags Leo had carried. "Let's get the rest of these in here so we can have fun at the party." Together, they fitted the remaining pieces into the hold and Darrell made sure the trunk would close. The lid shut with a satisfying thud.

Darrell raised a palm. "High five. We did it."

Leo smacked his hand onto his dad's and Darrell turned to head back to the mansion. Leo didn't budge and instead asked, "Will our car be okay? Will it be able to take us back home?"

Darrell ran his hand over the blue paint on the trunk. "This girl has a few bruises but she'll be fine. And nothing I can't get fixed when we get back home. Okay?"

Leo nodded. "Okay." His gaze traveled across the cars parked in their bays. "One of these cars ran you off the road?"

"Oh, okay, come on." Darrell strode down to the final space and indicated the car under the dull green tarp.

Leo walked up to the covered car and lifted the tarp, staring at the black and silver of the front before dropping it. He looked up at his dad. "Do you think it's because this place is haunted?"

Eyebrows raised, Darrell said, "I told you the house isn't haunted and..." He stopped, recalling Sheila's latest visit. "Why did you say that?"

Leo put both hands on his hips and faced his dad. "Look, I know Aunt Gertrude's house is haunted. I saw Sheila's ghost the other night and I saw you follow her. I'm a big guy, remember."

"Yeah, I remember. You did, huh? I thought you were sleeping. Did Sheila's ghost say anything to you?"

Leo shook his head. "No. I woke up and felt something. So I got out of bed and went to the door. She was there and just looked at me. I saw you coming so I got back into bed."

Okay. So, it looked like his son had seen Sheila only the one time. They would need to talk about this more...but they could do that on the drive home. Then, Darrell remembered something.

"When I told you about the car, you asked if it was because the house was haunted. Why?"

Leo looked like he was doing some deep thinking. "Well, you and Mom said you don't believe in coincidences when it comes to the ghosts." He shrugged his small shoulders.

Darrell glanced from the tarp-covered car to Leo and grabbed his son on the shoulder. "You are not only a big guy. You're also one smart guy. I need to check it out." He looked over at the mansion. "I think they have some homemade lemonade ready. I don't know about you but I could sure use some. What do you think?"

"Me, too." Leo grabbed his dad's hand and they half ran back to the mansion. As they hurried down the driveway, two cars navigated the asphalt, heading for the garage, a sleek white Porche followed by a silver Corvette convertible. Darrell's gaze followed their route and took one more glance back at the covered Cadillac SUV.

Chapter 52

They heard the music before they rounded the mansion.

"Cool," Leo shouted. "Let's go see." They ran the rest of the way.

A five-piece band had set up at the far end of the veranda and two guitars, a keyboard, a trumpet and drums were pounding out an all-American tune. Darrell caught some rendition of "God Bless the USA," which then morphed into "Battle Hymn of the Republic," or so he thought. The musicians were dressed in patriotic outfits of red, white and blue, each one wearing a white captain's hat with blue trim. He and Leo stood, watching and listening and, before the second song ended, Erin came down the three entry steps, her smile wide and her figure slim as always. Like Darrell, she wore white shorts with a patriotic tee. Both outfits were similar, though it definitely looked better on her. She'd even managed to find a smaller version of the combination for her son. Erin squeezed Leo's hand and the three stood together, listening as the band frolicked on.

The guests began arriving, pair after pair, as quickly as Salazar could take their keys and drive the BMW's, Mercedes, Lexis and Lincoln SUVs around the house over to the garage driveway. The guests, decked out in beach dresses and sailing outfits, ambled across the manicured lawn to the party area with the view of the

317

lake below. Plenty of white pants for the men and flowered patterns for the women, red, white and blue colors dominant. In between his valet duties, Salazar came over and introduced Darrell to the guests as they sauntered by. Most were older couples, mainly in their 60's and up, but there were a few younger couples, even a couple of children. When Leo saw a young girl about his age skipping across the lawn, his eyes lit up.

After both families were introduced, Leo asked in a quiet voice, "Can I show her my *atlatl*?"

Erin said, "Sure. I knew you'd want to play with it so I brought it out." She pointed to the veranda. "I laid it on the first table there."

She and Darrell watched the two kids run over to the table, Leo pulling off the spear and leading the young girl to the side, away from the others. The little girl looked as excited as their son. No doubt, she was probably glad to find a playmate and not be stuck with the adults.

Staring out at the lake and beyond, Darrell thought Gertrude must've ordered up another gorgeous day as the sun hung above the horizon, creating a perfect mirror image on the lake below. Only a few white, wispy clouds floated by, just enough to give contrast to the stunning azure sky. Three long sailboats, their white sails full with the breeze, glided across the blue-green surface, as if filling in the last few perfect details of the picture. Although it was another warm July day, the breeze from the water blew in from the lake, cooling the grounds like a built-in air conditioner.

Another couple ambled by and Salazar did the introductions. "Beverly and Bob Heinman, Erin and Darrell Henshaw. Darrell is Gertrude's nephew."

Bob extended a hand and he and Darrell shook. The

older man said, "We're great friends with your aunt," and the pair walked away, headed for the bar.

Salazar watched the couple leave and, when they were far enough away, he mumbled, "I'm going to kill Ilya when I find him. Our biggest event this season!"

"You still haven't seen him?" Darrell asked.

"No, but if I do, I might shoot him myself." Salazar waved to another couple exiting their car. "I'll be right there." He hurried in that direction.

All the hubbub of the party distracted Darrell, at least for a while. For a few brief moments, with the festivities, the music, and the laughter, he hadn't thought about getting run off the road or visiting ghosts at night. It was almost...nice. Oh, he still hadn't changed his mind. He needed to get his family, his Erin and Leo, out of harm's way. He was unmoved on that point.

But the discovery of the tarp-covered car had re-ignited his fury against those who were so bent on stopping him asking questions. The same person or persons who tried to kill him and the same responsible for Sheila's disappearance and, no doubt, murder. He hated letting them get away with all of it. That black Cadillac sitting under a dull green cover in the garage seemed to mock him as if to say, *I'm right here and there is nothing you can do about it.*

For days, he'd sensed there was some connection between Sheila's death and someone here. Now, it looked like that someone was Ilya. Maybe there was a chance he'd be able to confront him, right here.

But where was Ilya? Darrell's gaze swept the gathering crowd, looking for the swarthy face of the young man. He didn't see Ilya anywhere. Still, there was much party to go. He'd keep searching the crowd.

He and Erin met couple after couple, each pair dressed smartly in summer outfits. Introductions were made, often by Salazar, other times by the couples themselves. When they learned Darrell was Gertrude's nephew, each reaction was an echo of the one before.

"Oh, you're her nephew from Maryland, the teacher and football coach. She is so glad you made the trip. We're such good friends with your aunt." Then they would move on, almost always toward the bar.

Darrell pondered, all these people were such *good friends* with his aunt. He let his eyes wander through the crowd, studying the individuals. As he watched, he felt that familiar prickle slide down his neck and back. He stared again at the partiers, thinking he might *see* Sheila floating among them. He turned in his place and, when he circled around, he had to use his arm to block the glare from the sun. He felt another pang of guilt about his failure to help find justice for a missing Native teen. But Sheila never materialized among the people laughing, drinking and dancing. Still, the slight prickle persisted, causing Darrell to arch his neck to try to get it to subside.

Why the sensation? Could any of these people have been involved with Sheila's disappearance?

Erin watched him, her eyebrows rising. "Are you okay?"

Darrell whispered, "I...um, sense something."

"Here?"

"Yeah." Darrell's gaze kept roaming the crowd.

"Do you see Sheila?" Erin searched the throng.

He shook his head. "No, that's the problem. It's like she's here and wants to communicate something but won't show herself to me."

"Why?"

"Very good question."

Erin grabbed his hand. "I thought we were going home tomorrow?"

"We are."

"Well—" she started but was cut off.

"Oh, there you are," Susan Henshaw said, the slightest pout in her voice.

Even with the one whiff, Darrell could tell his mother had already consumed a few. Her one hand gripped a tall tumbler of brown liquid and she laid the other on his arm. She was dressed in a fashionable top—with a vee cut a little low in Darrell's opinion—covered in red, white and blue sequins which sparkled in the dying sunlight. Below, she wore a pair of white shorts and low heels decked with matching sequins.

"It's been wonderful to have us all together for the week." She patted his arm. "And I'm so glad you decided to stay for the barbecue. I know she doesn't always act like it but your aunt really appreciates it."

"She has a funny way of showing it."

Susan Henshaw drew her lips into a smirk. "Well, that's your aunt." When Darrell started to respond, she patted his arm to shush him. "And I'm glad you've given up this crazy obsession about the Indian girl who ran away. I'd hate for you to ruin our last night together as a family."

Darrell managed between gritted teeth, "It's not crazy. And the Native girl didn't run away."

His mom gave him a face he'd seen many times before. *Really, come on.*

Her expression did it. Darrell couldn't help it. He said, more forcefully, "Do you have any idea how many Indian women and girls *disappear?*" He strained to make sure the sarcasm came through. "Thousands! Maybe tens of thousands!"

"Oh, that can't be true. We would've heard about that many girls going missing." Susan Henshaw gave a giggle, one part drunk, one part dismissive.

Darrell wanted to give a retort but the band played a loud, dramatic crescendo, drowning him out. The lead announced, "Ladies and gentlemen, I give you our hostess, the star of this show and the most lovely octogenarian I know. Gertrude Elisabeth Embry!"

Chapter 53

Anna and Rachel opened the double doors and Aunt Gertrude paraded through, halting on the top step. While the band played a tune which sounded like "Hail to the Chief," she surveyed the crowd, one hand on her ornate cane. With shouts of "Our hero!" and "Bravo!" the guests broke out in enthusiastic applause.

Gertrude was decked out in a flaming patriotic top, vertical stripes of red, white and blue running down her torso, bejeweled with thousands of colored sequins. Below, she wore a long white skirt with three matching stripes running around the hem. She sported a faux cowboy hat and white cowboy boots, both also covered with sequins. When she acknowledged the guests' admiration with a perfunctory nod, the cowboy hat shifted slightly, a few gray hairs escaping.

Gertrude marched down the three stone steps, her cane making cracking sounds. Once down on the driveway level, she steadied herself, broadened her smile and the guests swarmed her.

Darrell watched the whole pretentious ceremony, head shaking, and turned to say something to Erin, most likely not kind. Before he got a word out, he heard his name shouted.

"Darrell and Erin, I'm not sure you've met Roger and Jane Herrold yet," Tom Salazar announced, bringing an older couple over. Instead of his battered straw hat, he now wore an oversized Stetson, though without the sequins. It looked as silly on him as Aunt Gertrude's did on her. "They were anxious to talk with you." Then back to the couple, "Darrell is Gertrude's nephew." He backed away.

Darrell extended his hand and shook, finding the man's grip both sweaty and loose. He remembered the pair from the luncheon at Coral Gables when he and his wife had come up to their table. The older man nodded, his polished bald head reflecting the sunlight. His two bushy black eyebrows arched over bloodshot eyes.

"So glad t' see ya again," Roger Herrold said, slurring the words slightly. "We're very good friends with your aunt, ya know." He glanced over to his wife, who smirked.

Unlike her husband, Jane Herrold still had most of her hair but it had been dyed black. She had a round face, rosy cheeks—Darrell couldn't tell from alcohol or make up—small brown eyes set close together, and bright red lips. The couple were dressed in patriotic colors from hats to boots, every piece covered with gaudy sequins.

Erin stepped up and took Jane Herrold's hands in hers. "Very nice to see you again."

Jane glanced around. "And where is that cute little boy of yours? We heard a lot about him and were hoping to meet him." She exchanged a smile with her husband.

Erin said, "Oh, he's playing with some of the other kids here. I'm afraid he prefers their company to ours." She pointed a finger at the couple. "Aren't you the ones who own that stunning sailboat, the one with the hull *and* sails in red, white and blue?"

Roger Herrold smirked. "Had it specially made. Can never be too patriotic, I always say."

Erin said, "My dad has a sailboat...back in Maryland. *Second Wind* is a nice little sloop but nowhere as large as yours."

Darrell said, "Erin and I both spotted your beautiful yacht on Lake Michigan." He nodded and Erin nodded along with him.

Erin said, "Yeah, we sure did. Couldn't miss it."

Roger and Jane Herrold narrowed their eyes and stared back. Jane managed, "W-w-when did you see our *Nauti-Boy*?"

Erin said, "Is that the name of your boat? How appropriate." After a bit, she glanced at Darrell and posed, "Which day was that? Do you remember?"

Darrell cast a glance upward. "The days have been so hectic, they all run together." In the brief pause, Darrell looked out of the corner of his eye at the older couple. Roger and Jane exchanged surreptitious glances.

Reaching out, Erin laid a hand on Darrell's arm. "Was it the day of—?"

He thought, she's really going to mention Pirate Isle?

Erin lifted one finger to her lips. "Oh, I remember. It was yesterday on the *Star of Saugatuck*. The riverboat." She looked at both Herrolds. "We were on the top deck of the riverboat and your sailboat passed us in the mouth of the river."

Roger and Jane breathed a slow sigh, one of immense relief, Darrell thought. He picked up the story. "Yeah, we were up there and saw you on the deck of your yacht and we waved to you. Our son, Leo, waved like crazy."

Roger gave an embarrassed chuckle. "Oh, that was you. We heard someone calling out from the riverboat but couldn't see who it was. 'Cause of the sun."

"Yeah, you were sitting with the Newsoms," Darrell continued. "And we noticed Ilya was with you."

"You did?" Jane Herrold asked, the worried look returning to her eyes.

Darrell said, "I didn't realize Ilya worked for you guys. I thought he was employed by Aunt Gertrude."

"Oh, he is," Roger explained, his fleshy hand swishing the air in front of him. "He was simply doing a few odd jobs on the boat for us. Ilya's very good with his hands."

Darrell glanced at Erin, then back at the older couple. "He's taken great care of the cars. He made our little Taurus shine, a minor miracle after the...um, incident on the road." He watched to see if his words about the car drew any reaction. He saw none.

Erin asked, "Have you seen Ilya? We heard Tom Salazar was looking for him."

The Herrolds glanced at each other and shrugged. Roger said, "Haven't seen him around here." He took a step and stumbled.

Darrell caught him. "You're not driving home, are you?"

Roger Herrold sneered. "Of course not." He glanced at his wife. "We sailed here in the *Nauti-Boy*. She's docked at Gertrude's pier. We got the other sloop." He pointed down the slope. Both husband and wife must've thought that hilarious as they couldn't stop laughing, though the laughter sounded forced.

After the couple ambled away, their steps unsteady, Erin turned to Darrell. "Did you see what I saw?"

Darrell nodded again. "From the look on their faces, they looked awfully guilty." He studied the couple, now gesturing to the bartender. "I'm not sure if it was the booze, or if they'll even remember in the morning, but those scared looks when we said we recognized their boat on the lake were as good as a confession."

Erin gave a brief chuckle. "I thought Jane might've wet her pants when we mentioned seeing their boat on the lake."

"They're sure as hell involved in this whole mess. I have no idea how…but I'm not sure how much good it'll do us."

Erin added, "And we're out of here in the morning."

"Yeah, there's that."

She laced her arm through Darrell's and pulled him in close. "I know we have to do what's best for our family but…"

"But what?"

"But I hate abandoning Sheila. And I feel like we're abandoning all the other Native women who have disappeared." She studied his face, eyes narrowing. "Any more prickles?"

Darrell held on but shook his head. "And no sign of Sheila. Looks like my mom took care of that. Selfish Susan strikes again."

She gave him a playful slap on the other arm. "Quiet, you're talking about Leo's grandmother."

"Well, Mister Darrell and the Mrs.," another drunken male voice called. "The parents of the cutest five-year-old we know." Dwight Newson guffawed and his wife Cynthia leered. The two also dressed up in cowboy chic, complete with rhinestones and blue sequins. Dwight had swapped the captain's hat for another Stetson which sat funny on his head, the thinning gray hair splayed out beneath the rim.

Cynthia perched her lips. "Did you bring little Leo to the party?" She shot a glance to where Aunt Gertrude stood, still surrounded by admiring guests. "Of course, Gertrude might be envious. Those sympathetic green eyes of Leo would probably steal the show." She giggled like she just told an inside joke.

Erin smiled along, though looked uncomfortable. "Leo's playing with a few of the young kids in the side yard." She pointed to the left of where most of the guests gathered.

Cynthia Newsom smirked. "Children are such a precious gift, especially when they're as darling as your Leo. If he were mine, I wouldn't want anything to happen to him. Ever. You know children wander off. I'd do whatever I could to keep him safe." She tilted her head. "Nothing is more important than family, don't you agree?"

Erin said, "Yes, of course."

Dwight took a step toward the bar and stumbled. Darrell reached out an arm and caught him, holding the older man up.

"Thanks. You're not such a bad guy." Red veins pulsed in his blue-gray eyes and, when he tried to straighten, he stumbled again.

When he regained his footing, Dwight Newsom said, "It's been good talking with you. I'm sure you're anxious to get back home to the Chesapeake Bay. Safe trip back to Maryland." His eyes went to Darrell, then Erin. "Take care of each other. You're all you got...and Leo." His smirk grew and he nodded to his wife. "Come, let's go share some birthday wishes with the octogenarian."

When the pair were out of earshot, Erin said, "Did

you get what just happened?"

"I did. If we look past the drunkenness, I think the Newsoms threatened our family. A sideways threat, but still a threat."

Erin stared at the man and woman barely able to hold each other up. "Both couples seemed awfully interested in Leo."

"Yeah, they did." His gaze went to the side yard where they'd last seen Leo playing. He was not in sight now. "Maybe you should go check on Leo."

"You don't think anyone would try anything here? At your aunt's party?"

Chapter 54

Erin's heart beat hard. She tried to hurry, to push her way through the partiers. They were busy drinking, laughing and talking. The guests crowded in together, blocking the whole lawn area. Try as she might, she couldn't find a way around them.

"Excuse me," she said, again and again as she bumped one person after another. People stared at her, chuckling and gesturing, often with a drink or plate of food in hand. Erin had to duck a swinging arm more than once.

Two guests tried to ask how she liked Saugatuck and Michigan. Both women also asked about her cute son they'd heard about. She gave curt answers and hurried on. Their questions, no doubt innocent, only amped her anxiety.

The second woman, older and closer to Gertrude's age with a full head of silver hair, said, "Heard about you losing the *Fantasea* while on Pirate Isle."

"I didn't lose—" Erin started and then blurted, "We're fine. I need to check on my son."

She *had* to check on Leo. After everything, she couldn't believe they—whoever they were—would try anything right *here* at Wentworth. Gertrude wouldn't have it unless... She shook her head. Darrell was overreacting. They were both overacting.

Still, she hurried.

When she managed to navigate her way through the throng, she came around the side of the huge mansion. Even here, the music of the band and the chattering of the crowd persisted. Ignoring the crowd noise, she scanned the narrow patch of perfectly manicured green shaded by the side of the house on one side and tall leafy trees on the other. The lawn area was littered with toys, the two slanted boards of the cornhole game and alongside, a pair of yellow pegs in the ground with large, colorful plastic flower petals around them. Leo's *atlatl*, the Indian toy, lay alone, discarded.

Leo would never have left it like that.

Two young boys and a girl, the one they'd met earlier, stood next to one of the pegs. The girl looked up and saw Erin looking. She ran over.

The young girl said, her blue eyes bright, "I remember you. You're Leo's mom."

Erin tried to call up a calm smile. "Good memory." She looked over at the abandoned *atlatl*. "I...uh...I just came to check on Leo." Her gaze swept the area and came back to the girl. "Did he go to the bathroom?" She fought to keep a smile on her face.

"No." The girl shook her head hard, blonde curls swinging in the motion. She pointed toward the back of the mansion. "Some guy came and got him. He said he was taking him to you."

"Some guy? Who?" She snapped, paranoia leaking through her words.

One of the boys stopped playing with the flower petals and joined the girl. He looked a few years older, maybe seven or eight, with brown hair and eyes. He said, "Some tall dude, with dark skin and a mean face."

Ilya. God.

331

Erin turned to go. The little girl said, "Leo didn't want to go. He asked the tall guy what the secret word was. The guy didn't know. Said you were in a car crash and couldn't talk. He grabbed Leo's arm and took him. That way."

Erin's gaze raked the area where the girl pointed. She saw no one, just more damn perfect green lawn. She took off in a run. "Thanks!" she yelled over her shoulder. Her feet barely touched the ground. She covered the length of the mansion in a few seconds.

When she came out the rear of the house, she stopped, staring. The lawn opened up, the deep green spread out in front of her. She looked left and right. No one. Across the open space, she spied the corner of the garage, a hundred yards away. The doors on two bays were up. She thought she saw movement just past the second opening.

"No, I won't!" Leo screamed.

His voice came from the garage area. She sprinted that way.

"I won't go. You can't make me!"

Her heart pounded in her chest. Adrenalin flooded her veins. She forced her legs to move faster, pistons chugging up and down. She streaked across the distance.

"You stupid kid. I'm taking you to your mom. You're going to come if I have to drag you!" Ilya demanded, his voice full of anger.

Oh, God.

As she ran full out, the two came into view. Ilya stood over Leo, one long arm hauling her son. Or trying to. Leo pulled back, his small body dragging along the lawn. He dug both feet into the ground and tried to grab some grass with his other hand.

"If you don't stop that, I'm going to hit you." Ilya raised his other arm and made a fist.

Erin saw all this and processed it in seconds. No thought, just reaction. She increased her pace. She ran so fast, her lungs hurt. She crossed the last hundred feet like a champion sprinter.

Right before she got to them, Ilya glanced up. Surprise flashed in his eyes. Erin kept charging. At the last second, she lowered her head and dove right at Ilya's chest.

Whump. Air escaped Ilya's lungs. She collapsed on top of the tall, lanky guy, arms and legs entangled. He released Leo, who fell to the ground. Her son scurried backwards. Winded, Erin couldn't move for a moment.

Ilya huffed and growled between breaths, "Get off me, bitch." A nasty, alcoholic stench flowed from his open mouth.

Erin fought to get her own wind back and pushed herself up. Her gaze went first to Leo. He was safe, off to the side, large eyes watching her. She turned back around toward Ilya. He still lay there, rubbing his chest. He maneuvered around, bracing one arm against the ground.

"Damn, that hurts," he snarled. He shot her a look filled with venom. "I'm going to beat your cute little ass."

Those two sentences were more words than Erin had heard him speak all week. She watched him try to push himself up, to get his balance. She didn't think, she just reacted. She ran to where Ilya lay and kicked him in the side. Hard.

Another whump and Ilya crumpled back onto the ground.

She leaned over him. While he grabbed his side and gasped for air, she stared darts at him. "Leave my family alone."

She walked over to her son and took his hand. "Let's go see your dad."

They turned together and strode across the expansive lawn. Erin glanced back once to see Ilya, struggling to his feet. His face a mask of rage, he screamed, "Bitch."

She asked Leo, "Can you run?"

He nodded and they sprinted back toward the crowds, the music and Darrell.

Chapter 55

Darrell kept scanning the crowd. He watched the Newsoms and the Herrolds amble around and noted whom they spoke with. Each time he spied either man lean in to talk to a guest, he imagined furtive exchanges about him…and his family. He stared and watched as either one glanced back his way and laughed. He forced a smile and gave a feeble wave but each time his paranoia conjured up new threats.

Even as he watched the party crowd, he checked out the side of the mansion, where he'd seen Erin disappear. She could take care of herself. And she'd find Leo, probably playing with the other kids. He tried willing Erin to appear, Leo in tow.

Not yet.

The music paused and the band leader announced, "This next is a request by Gertrude. I know I'm as surprised as you'll be. Who would have thought she was a fan of the Village People? You're welcome to join in."

As the band started in with the opening chords of the dance favorite, the guests turned as one to watch and listen. When the musicians got to the familiar refrain, arms all over the crowd shot up and people screeched out, "Y. M. C.A." Even Gertrude got in the act, still sitting in her chair.

Darrell liked the old song, and he and Erin had done the over-the-head dance routine several times at wedding receptions on the Bay. But now, he couldn't get into it. Some of the more inebriated guests had trouble keeping time with the music and their arms were often a beat or two behind. Two men stumbled trying to get through. It looked comical but Darrell wasn't laughing.

Nothing has happened, he told himself.

Maybe he and Erin had concocted threats out of innocent fun by the Newsoms. All this could be merely his imagination. But the relaxed, easy feeling he'd had earlier at the party, brought on by the music and laughter, had vanished. Now, he felt only anxiety and tension. He took three slow breaths, like Erin had taught him, and tried to steady his breathing. Still, he could feel his heart racing.

Darrell began to second guess himself. They should've left when he found the wretched SUV hidden underneath the tarp. Simply packed up and hightailed it out of town right then, never mind what his mom and aunt wanted. He'd vowed to keep Erin and Leo close and now, here he was, away from them. What if they were in trouble? He felt his body tense and coil, as if waiting for a blow.

What was taking Erin so long? Was she having trouble finding Leo? Where could Leo have gone? Did she need his help? Erin could handle it, he repeated. He breathed in and out.

His glance scoured the crowd and he found his mom and dad over by the band talking with Aunt Gertrude. His aunt blessed him with a beatific smile but even that didn't help. He couldn't tell if the smile was real—like she was actually glad to have him, Erin and Leo here— or merely plastered on for the guests. From her demeanor and his parents' relaxed posture, it was hard to believe anything could be wrong. Maybe, he *was* letting his paranoia go wild.

He caught sight again of both couples he was supposed to be watching. Both men looked plenty drunk, tripping and almost falling, only to be caught by other guests. Darrell shook his head. How could they be trouble?

He glanced at his watch, trying to calculate how long Erin had been gone. Five minutes? Ten minutes? He paced back and forth on the edge of the crowd, trying to keep the side of the mansion in sight even as he kept an eye on the two couples. With each passing moment, his apprehension ratcheted up, the tension so great, he didn't even notice it at first.

Then, some part of his brain seized on it. The prickle started on his neck, at the base of his skull, and streaked down his back. Then it ran up his back and careened into his skull. He slapped at the back of his head, as if that could ease the sizzle. If anything, this seemed to intensify the sensation. He must've looked like he was swatting at mosquitos.

Two older women nearby stared at him. Beneath their fake cowboy hats, they glanced at each other and frowned, then edged away. He ignored them.

He'd never felt the sensation this strongly, at least, he couldn't remember any time it had felt like this. It was as if some invisible hand rapped him on the back of his head to say, "Look!"

Very slowly, he turned in his position and let his glance rotate from the crowd and the side yard, to the lawn down the slope. When he turned, the bright sun, which hung low over the lake waters like a fiery orange ball, struck his eyes. Darrell raised his arm to block the glare so he could at least make out something.

From the strength of the sensation on his neck, he expected to find Sheila standing behind him. But, when his eyes were able to adjust, all he saw were a few couples straggling a little way down the slope. The prickle didn't let up so he edged his arm across and he glanced down the hill to the pier where the two yachts sat bobbing in the quiet water. One hull deep blue almost matching the color of the lake and the second with the red, white and blue stripes. He stared. No Sheila. In fact, no one at the bottom of the slope, only the two yachts, their empty masts rocking in the waves.

He whirled back around, remembering he was supposed to be keeping an eye on the Newsoms and Herrolds. And watching for Erin and Leo to return. The older couples hadn't moved and Leo and Erin hadn't appeared on the side of the mansion.

He felt another sizzle down his back, this one even more pronounced, and he spun around. Seeing nothing new—except one couple busy with a little PDA—he shook his head. As he got ready to turn back, he caught movement on the dock. A shadow seemed to float over the white planks toward the Herrold's boat, though the faint image was difficult to make out. Darrell stared harder, willing his eyes to form something out of the image as the sensation burned his neck. A shadowy figure appeared near the *Nauti-Boy*.

Unless Darrell had imagined the whole thing. He stared hard at the yacht rocking gently in the water and now saw no movement, no person, no image. Maybe, he felt so guilty about abandoning the missing Native teen, he'd simply conjured up the vision.

Still staring at the dock and the yacht, sun in his face,

Darrell felt someone collide into him, nearly knocking him to the ground.

Chapter 56

"Yeah, we found you," yelled Leo, huffing and puffing and still stumbling from running into his dad.

Darrell recovered and grabbed up his son, wrapping him in a bear hug. His relief was so great, he felt tears leak out of his eyes. "Yeah, you did," he said, trying to keep the anxiety out of his voice.

"Dad, you should've seen Mom," Leo yelled over the music, once Darrell set him back on the ground. "She plowed into Ilya and knocked him down." He grinned at his mother.

Darrell glanced at Erin. "Ilya?"

Erin nodded. "He was trying to grab Leo."

Between panted breaths, she leaned in close so he could hear over the music and explained what had happened. When she got to the part about kicking the guy, Darrell said, "Good." He searched the crowd, trying to see if Ilya had followed his wife and son. He was ready to kick the guy himself. And maybe get answers to a few questions about the tarp-covered car.

"Why'd he grab Leo?" he asked. "What'd he want?"

"He claimed he was taking Leo to me." Erin shook her head.

"Yeah, but he didn't know the secret word so I knew he wasn't." Leo stuck his chest out.

Darrell patted his son on the shoulder. "You did great." His gaze went back to the crowd, expecting Ilya to run into the throng and confer with the Herrolds or the Newsoms. Neither couple moved and he saw no sight of the dark-skinned young man.

None of this made sense. Erin and he had been right. There'd been a real threat to Leo, but why? From their drunken state, it didn't look like Dwight Newsom or Roger Herrold could do much of anything. Who was Ilya working with? Everyone seemed to know they were leaving in the morning, so why snatch Leo? Why kick the hornets' nest?

The prickle returned and, without thinking, his hand went to the back of his neck. He turned and stared again at the Herrolds' boat, his other arm shielding against the sun's glare. Nothing. He whirled back. Neither Herrold nor Newsom had moved...or looked like they could move much.

Erin leaned in close and whispered, "What? What is it?" When he didn't answer right away, she added, "Did you see her? Did you see Sheila?"

"I-uh, I don't know."

Even though she tried to keep her voice quiet, Leo must've heard. "Dad, did you see Sheila?" he asked, his young voice filled with excitement. "Here?" The boy turned, searching the crowd, then he focused on the yachts. "She's on that boat?" He looked up at his dad and back at the yacht. "Let's go see her." He started down the slope but Darrell grabbed him.

"Wait a minute." Darrell glanced at Erin. In a quiet voice, he explained about the sensation and the image he thought he saw next to the *Nauti-Boy.* "Because of the sun in my eyes, I couldn't be sure. I might've imagined it." Without thinking, his hand went to his neck again, which still buzzed.

Erin pointed to his neck. "You didn't imagine that."

Darrell shrugged, his eyes straying back to the crowd. The musicians played another song he recognized, "Locomotion." Once the band got into the song, the guests made a long line, half parading, half stumbling to the beat. Gertrude clapped loudly while the unwieldy line moved through the green lawn, guests jumping on, one after another.

Erin studied the crowd and said, "I don't think we're going to get a better diversion than that."

Darrell looked and saw the Herrolds and Newsoms stagger into the makeshift dance line. "Let's go...but let's be careful."

Darrell took his son's hand and, rather than take the stairs, the three of them half walked, half slid down the steep slope. When they reached the bottom, he glanced back up but no one in the crowd seemed to take any notice. Darrell leading, they stepped onto the narrow white dock. Down here, by the water, the music still carried but it was not nearly as loud and their steps on the wooden planks sounded like claps. Both sailboats rested on the quiet water, the hulls bumping against the dock fenders with each small passing wave. The *Fantasea* was tied up on the right with its long, deep blue hull and the *Nauti-Boy* on the left.

Darrell and Erin stared at the red, white and blue stripes running along the hull of Herrolds' boat, then at the furled sail on the main mast showing the same colors. She shook her head and glanced back at Darrell. "This sure looks like the boat I saw across the lake."

"Me too." He studied the colorful stripes running the length of the boat. As they approached the yacht's ladder, Darrell felt something, though he couldn't identify what. Up this close, he picked up some kind of aura, some sinister atmosphere which emanated from the boat, in spite of the bright, patriotic colors of its hull.

Without hesitating, Erin took the lead and climbed onto the first rung of the ladder on the side of the *Nauti-Boy*. In a bright voice, she announced, "Ahoy, there. Anyone on board?"

The three listened but the only sound was the muted guitar and drums and the laughing of the guests up the hill. She shot another glance back at Darrell, who shrugged.

She called, "Erin Henshaw here. Permission to come aboard?"

No response came from inside the yacht. Darrell didn't expect Sheila's ghost to say come on in but he expected something...if he'd really seen her. Only silence greeted them.

"Coming on board," Erin announced, her voice upbeat.

She climbed up the three rungs, stepped onto the deck and over, only her head becoming visible. She disappeared for a few seconds, then reappeared at the top of the ladder again.

"I don't see anyone." She shrugged. "But then I wouldn't, would I?" Her head swiveled around. "Come on up and take a look."

After checking out the throng of guests—they were still doing a drunken Locomotion—Darrell helped Leo get his short legs up the rungs of the ladder. When the boy reached the top, Erin helped him climb onto the deck. His son was so short, Darrell could only see a few loose auburn hairs of the boy's head but heard him announce, "Made it, Dad."

The prickle returned, this time a light buzz along his neck. Darrell followed and, in a few seconds, stood next to his wife and son. He glanced around, the gleaming brass work and perfectly polished teak deck reflecting the dying sunlight. The three of them walked the length of the boat and stood next to the helm. Like Newsoms' boat, a pilot's seat and the helm sat at the stern covered with a tight, white awning. Just forward of the helm, six-foot wooden benches lined both sides of the deck, covered with thick cushions in matching patriotic fabric. The pilot's seat and benches sat empty. No sign of Sheila, or anyone else.

Undaunted, Leo said, "Let's check the cabin," and started that way.

Darrell reached out and stopped him. The cabin ran half the length of the fifty-foot boat with the only entry door aft, a few feet ahead of them. He knew Sheila meant them no harm but, with everything else that had happened, he was taking no chances.

"I'll go in first, then you and your mom follow."

Erin took her son's hand. One palm on the frame, Darrell edged down the two steps into the interior. The setting sun shot brilliant rays through the long windows and the light made the interior surfaces shine. More gleaming wood edged the walls and floors and white leather cushions, obviously thick and comfy, covered a couch on one side and what Darrell took to be a pull-out bed on the other. A few strategic pillows with the matching red, white and blue pattern were scattered atop the white leather. The whole place looked spotless and deserted. There was no sign of anyone...or anything.

Behind him, he heard Erin and Leo step through the opening. They came over and stood next to him, staring at the fancy space. Leo said, "Cool."

Maybe he'd imagined the vision of Sheila, though the sensation persisted on his neck. And the malevolent aura seemed to intensify inside the cabin. *Something* was here. He found his throat dry and croaked out, "Sheila?"

No response. He glanced over at Erin, whose eyes roamed the entire interior space as if she were looking for a hidden compartment. She shrugged.

He didn't know what else to do. He turned to his son. "Sorry, Leo. I thought we'd find something here but it looks like I imagined seeing Sheila." He shot another glance around. "I guess we better get back to Aunt—"

A door opened at the other end of the compartment, cutting him off. All three stared as an umber-skinned teen stepped out, pop can in hand and bulky headphones on her ears.

Leo blurted out, "Sarah?"

The girl dropped the can, the liquid gurgling onto the polished wood. Her brown eyes went wide.

Chapter 57

Ask Sarah.

Sheila's words came back to him. The ghost's appearance here, the prickle and the boat's eerie aura—there was a reason he was here. To ask Sarah, at least.

When they'd met her earlier, on Newsom's boat, Darrell hadn't taken that much notice of her. Seeing her here, he thought she was probably sixteen or seventeen. She looked and acted like the juniors in his classes. But he hadn't noticed before, she was strikingly beautiful, with a long, thin face with large almond-shaped eyes, a petite nose and plump, full lips, which bore a bright red lipstick. Her long hair, black and silky, hung straight down her back to her waist.

But, right now, the Native teen looked terrified, her brown eyes huge, her features pulled tight and her mouth a near perfect O. The abject fear in her face looked even more strange given her outfit. The girl wore a bikini, two small triangles of fabric stretched over budding breasts and a slightly larger triangle hanging beneath her waist and between her legs. The bright bikini contrasted with her darker skin, which pebbled with goose bumps. What made the sight more ludicrous was the colored pattern of the bikini perfectly matched the red, white, and blue pattern of the pillows sitting atop the cushions in the cabin. She looked like some guy's wet dream of a patriotic bimbo. Taking in the interior of the ship and her appearance, things fell into place for Darrell. And it made his skin crawl.

His first reaction was to give her something to cover up so he pulled off the button-down shirt he wore. He took one step and draped it over Sarah.

The teen shook her head hard and shrugged it off rather than accept it. She sniffed and said, "I can't. He won't let me." She glanced at her own bikini with loathing. "When he returns, he needs to see me like this." She extended the shirt back to Darrell.

Darrell took it and asked, "He?"

"Mr. Herrold. Roger. He said I'm to call him *Roger*," the teen said, disgust in the single word.

Darrell glanced back at Leo, who stood staring, his face etched with concern. "Well, he's not here. Please take it. You look like you're freezing."

She let him drape it around the swimsuit but her body still quivered. She stared at the dark brown liquid running along the slats in the wooden floor. "I-I-I'm sorry," she stuttered and tears ran down her face. With a swift motion, she slipped into the head and returned with a towel. She dropped to the floor, using it to mop up the mess. She rubbed at the wooden surface hard as if she were polishing it for inspection.

She spoke as she worked, "He'll kill me if he comes back and sees this mess. He *loves* this boat."

Erin knelt and took the towel. "Here, let me help."

The Native teen relinquished the cloth but stayed on the floor, on all fours. Darrell noticed this position made her more revealing, her breasts practically falling out of the tiny pieces of fabric, even inside his much-too-large shirt. He asked, "You've done this before? Had to clean the floor like this?"

Sarah slid back on her haunches and looked up through a tear-streaked face and nodded. Darrell reached down and gently pulled her to her feet.

Erin made a few more wipes with the towel. "There. Good as new." She stood up, bringing the cloth and pop can with her. "Where can I toss this?"

Sarah pointed to the door of the head and Erin disappeared inside and returned with a smaller towel, wiping her hands. She handed the towel to Sarah. "Let's sit down." She pointed to the white leather couch.

Sarah moved to the sofa, her movements stiff and robot-like, and sat. Erin sat next to her but Darrell and Leo stayed where they were. He didn't want to do anything to further upset the teen.

Erin said, "Sarah, I know you don't know us. I mean we only met you on Newsom's boat a few days ago. We'd like to help."

Sarah didn't look at her, staring across the space. "No one can help me." The tears flowed again.

Still standing, Darrell leaned his head down so he was eye level with the teen. "When we met, you were working for the Newsoms. You were a steward on their yacht."

"Steward!" Sarah barked a dry laugh. "That's a great word for it, though that's what they tell everyone."

Erin interrupted, "But you're on the Herrold's boat. You're working for them now, not the Newsoms?"

Sarah said, "I go back and forth. Whoever needs me. Whoever wants me." She rolled her eyes and the last words caught in her throat.

Darrell felt certain where this was headed and wanted to give Sarah a breather so he jumped in. "I'm guessing you heard we've been trying to find out what happened to Sheila Birdsong. We've been asking around…and it's made some people quite nervous. We know she used to work for my aunt, Gertrude Embry, but quit to take another job. We haven't been able to find out what."

He stopped and held the teen's frightened gaze. "Did you know Sheila?"

Sarah's bottom lip quivered and she nodded.

"Do you know what happened to her?" When she didn't answer right away, he added, "Do you know what job she took after she quit working at Wentworth?"

"I-I-I-I can't say," Sarah mumbled. "I don't know what they'll do to me if—" She broke off crying.

Erin edged closer to the teen and took her hands in hers. She waited until the girl's big brown eyes met hers. "We can help. We want to help."

Sarah shook her head and tears dropped from both cheeks in the motion. "No one can help."

Erin kept her gaze on the teen's face. "You don't know that. Maybe after you tell us, we can figure a way to help."

Sarah looked at Erin then at Darrell and Leo. She took a deep breath and glanced down at her skimpy swimsuit. "I can't. I'm too ashamed." She shot another glance at Leo.

Erin turned toward Darrell and Leo. "Why don't you two go up top and check on the guests, especially Roger Herrold?"

Darrell looked from Erin and Sarah, huddled close together on the couch, to his son next to him. He didn't want Leo's young ears to hear what he feared was going to come pouring out. "That's a good idea. You girls do your girl talk and the big guys will keep watch up top."

He turned and headed through the opening, letting Leo go up first. He looked back at his wife. She shot him a quick glance which he took to mean, I got this. He nodded.

Chapter 58

Erin swallowed. Sheila's ghost had told Darrell, ask Sarah. Now, she was going to have to do that. She looked across at the young Native girl, who seemed to shrink before her, looking younger and smaller. Erin had the nearly irresistible urge to wrap her arms around her. Tell her everything would be okay. But she didn't know that it would, so she held back. Some maternal instinct told her to stay at arm's length. So, she simply held the girl's hand.

Taking in what little the teen wore and this cabin, Erin had a pretty good idea what was going on. A thought hit her. She remembered when she met Sarah on the *Wanderlust.* Then, she wore some kind of steward uniform but it had been adapted so it looked more seductive. She hadn't noticed at the time because she'd been consumed with worry about Leo. But looking now at the tiny bikini, the image of the teen standing there in the skimpy steward outfit popped into her head.

Where could she begin? What should she ask first? Erin glanced at the hand she was holding, the skin amber, the fingers small and soft. She noticed a hand-woven bracelet in the colors of blue, purple and white on her wrist. A near perfect match to the one they'd discovered on the dune buggy ride.

"That's an unusual bracelet." Erin pointed to the teen's wrist. "Where'd you get it?"

Sarah yanked her hand and hid it behind her back. "I hate it but I have to wear it."

"You have to wear it?"

"They gave it to me and said I have to wear it." The teen dropped her head.

"They?" When the Native didn't answer, Erin said, "The Newsoms or the Herrolds?"

"Both." Sarah said no more and refused to meet her gaze.

"Shelia Birdsong had a bracelet like that, didn't she?"

Sarah's eyes went wide. "How do you know that?"

When Erin didn't respond, the girl's tears came flooding. She nodded but said nothing.

Erin waited. She knew Sarah was fragile. The muted sound of a guitar solo filtered into the cabin. Finally, Erin asked, "Sheila Birdsong worked for the Newsoms before you, didn't she?"

Sarah shook her head. "No, she worked for the Herrolds. I worked for the Newsoms. If you could call it that."

Erin thought asking about Sheila might be easier. "Why did Sheila start working for the Herrolds?"

"They paid really good. They offered more than three times what we'd been making at Wentworth."

"You worked at Wentworth before?" Erin asked, confused. She never heard Sarah's name mentioned there. They heard footsteps on the deck and Erin wondered what Darrell was doing topside. Both women glanced up, then Sarah answered.

"Only for a little while. Then Ilya told us about these jobs."

"Ilya recruited you for these…jobs?" Erin asked,

realizing how he fit in.

"Yeah. And he told us how much they paid. Sheila was saving to go to college and I was trying to buy a car. It was only going to be for a few weeks for the summer."

"What'd he tell you about the jobs?"

Sarah snorted. "He said we'd serve as stewards on the yachts. He said the families were wealthy and simply wanted some pretty girls to give the sailboats some class. *Stewards*!" She practically spit out the last word.

Erin hesitated. She wasn't sure how to ask the next question. "You weren't hired as stewards, were you?"

Sarah's eyes got big again. "Oh, we were stewards all right. For the first week, that's what we did. Fetch drinks, fix some food, do the dishes, clean up after a party. I remember talking to Sheila after that first week saying how lucky we were. The work was way easier than the chores at Wentworth and we were getting paid so much more." She shook her head, the tears falling to the floor. "Boy, was I wrong."

The Native teen stopped and dropped her face. Erin knew the girl didn't want to say more. Still, she and Darrell would need more before they could do something. Exactly what, she had no idea. She placed a finger under the girl's chin. She gently raised it until Sarah's eyes met hers.

"I promise we'll protect you. I'm a nurse. You can talk to me." Erin's voice was gentle. "What happened the second week?"

Sarah gestured to her revealing bikini. "Look at me. Do I have to spell it out?"

"They took advantage of you...sexually?" Erin whispered.

The girl wept and managed, "You wouldn't believe

what they made me do."

Unfortunately, Erin could believe. In the OB ward, the new mothers would talk. With the agony of labor and the terror of what they were facing, young mothers sometimes blurted out their story. She'd heard more tales than she could count of how sexual aggression or assault had led to a pregnancy. The thought of her own condition hit her and she stared at the girl's abdomen. Nothing yet, she hoped.

"What happened to Sheila? Do you know?"

"I don't." Sarah shook her head violently. "I really don't."

Erin knew there was more. "What *do* you know about Sheila going missing?"

The teen trembled. "They said I'd end up the same way if I told anyone."

Erin kept her voice quiet. "No one is here but you and me." She stopped and let the muted music of the party filter into the cabin. "Everyone else is at Aunt Gertrude's party." When this produced no response, she added, "Darrell and I are here for you. Besides, Sheila was your friend. She deserves better."

Sarah let out a long breath. "I only know what they told me."

"What did they tell you?"

The teen swallowed. "They took both boats out deep onto the lake."

"Lake Michigan?"

"Yeah. They sailed miles out into the middle of the lake. When we got there, they drew the two yachts alongside each other. There were no boats or freighters around. They brought us both out on deck in those stupid steward costumes. They said we weren't 'fulfilling our contract' and they wouldn't put up with it.'"

She looked over at Erin, who simply nodded.

"I was so scared, but not Sheila. She looked strong…and tough. Then one of them, Newsom, I think, hollered there would be consequences for *non-performance*. That's the word he used." She started crying again.

Erin prompted, "What happened then?"

Sarah shook her head. "The two boats separated. The *Wanderlust* with Sheila went out farther onto the lake and the *Nauti-Boy* headed back with me huddled inside the cabin, shaking and crying." She sobbed more. "I never saw Sheila again."

"Did you ask about Sheila, about what happened to her?"

Sarah said, "I didn't have to. They said if I didn't *perform* or if I told anyone, I'd join her out in the lake." Her eyes bulged wide and she shook her head hard. "They can't know I told you."

"I'm not going to tell them you told me anything." Erin pulled the girl to her. She felt the thin body shake. "It'll be okay. Darrel and I will—"

The sound of quick footsteps on the deck above them stopped Erin. Then, a hard thud, something or someone hit the deck. Both women froze and stared at each other. Sarah shrunk, eyes wide in terror.

Chapter 59

Sarah let out a squeak and Erin put a hand on her arm, cutting her off. The teen's face darkened and tears leaked out of her eyes. She brought a hand to her mouth. Erin raised a finger to her own lips. She stood up and pulled the teen with her. Together, they edged toward the opening, Erin in front, Sarah right behind. Erin stuck her head around the doorway. She saw two boots covered with sequins walk past. She recognized those boots and yanked her head back in.

"Get on up here, Mrs. Henshaw," a gruff voice called from the deck. "I think your husband can use a little…um, professional attention." A loud guffaw. "And Sarah, come on up here too."

Sarah's whole body quivered. Erin tried to think but couldn't come up with any idea of what to do. She worked to conjure up a light tone. "Hey, we'll be right up." Then she turned to Sarah and whispered, "Don't lose it. Darrell will figure a way out of this. Come." *She hoped.* She gently tugged the girl's arm.

When she came up the steps, what she saw made her lose all composure. A few feet to the right of the opening, Darrell lay splayed on the deck. Not moving. A slash on his forehead oozed blood onto the teak wood. *Oh, God!* Leo knelt over his dad, crying.

Forgetting everything else, she ran over and hugged Leo. Then she gingerly took Darrell's head in her hands.

She felt herself revert to nurse mode and examined the wound. Dark red had pooled down his scalp and matted his hair. Despite the blood, the cut wasn't that bad. Thank God.

Darrell responded to her touch and opened his eyes, his gaze unfocused. He'd probably suffered a concussion but at least the cut didn't look deep. "There you are," she said with a brave smile. She heard the rush of breath from her mouth. Darrell nodded, managed a small smile and winced, his fingers going to his head.

Before she could ask Darrell, Leo said, "That man and woman came aboard." His eyes darted to the couple standing in their red, white and blue outfits. "Dad started to say hi and the man hit him with his gun. For no reason." Leo's voice broke when he said the last, tears falling onto Darrell's shoulder.

For the first time, Erin saw the gray pistol Roger Herrold held at the side of his leg. She inhaled.

Leo's gaze went to the bleeding gash in his dad's head. "Is he going to die?"

Seeing the alarm on her son's face, she realized she had to fake it. "No, it's only a cut. I'll fix it up and he'll be as good as new." She struggled to sound convincing but heard her voice crack around the last words.

Erin turned to see Sarah press herself against the wall of the cabin as if she could make herself smaller. Her eyes looked like they'd jump out of her head. Erin tried to catch the girl's attention but the teen's gaze stayed fixed on Herrold. Erin needed to watch out for her.

Roger Herrold waved the gun at Sarah. "Don't just stand there. Go get the first aid kit. I think Erin here is goin' to need it." When the teen didn't move at first, he barked, "Get moving. You know where it is. You've had to use it enough."

Sarah slid along the wall of the cabin and disappeared inside. Herrold rolled his eyes. "You have to explain everything to those people."

The sun was setting, barely above the opposite shoreline, its glare near blinding. Erin had to hold her arm up to look that direction. She turned and glanced back up the hill. The band played on, the tunes rolling down the slope to the water. Up on the flat expanse of lawn, she could see figures moving and dancing. But they were too far away for her to call for help, and the band's loud music would simply drown out any cries.

She pressed her finger lightly to the wound and Darrell let out a quiet gasp. Within a minute, Sarah returned with the kit and Erin went to work, blocking out her fears. She cleaned the cut and, after fumbling through the contents, came up with a bandage she thought would work. She placed it against the wound and gently pressed the adhesive wings onto Darrell's scalp. He grimaced, then shook his head slowly, his blue eyes focusing on her. He struggled to push himself to a sitting position.

Seeing he was okay—at least for the moment—Erin stood up next to him and faced the couple. She now saw Roger and Jane had gotten quite sober...or they'd been acting the whole time. She looked from Leo and Darrell to the Herrolds. She took in Sarah, trembling again and flattened against the wall of the cabin. She asked Roger, "What now?"

Roger sidled over to his wife who stood at the helm controls. "Well, you two have put us in a difficult spot." He glanced down the length of the sailboat. "Ilya, cast off the lines." He turned to his wife. "Jane, when he's done, let her rip."

Erin watched the lanky figure of the young man ease himself off the front of the cabin, where he'd hid, and step onto the dock to untie the lines. She had no idea he was there, didn't know anyone else was aboard. That made three of them. When he finished and hopped back on, Ilya turned and faced her, a triumphant smirk on his face. He strolled over to the cockpit next to the Herrolds, like he had not a care in the world.

Erin's insides went cold and she pulled Leo to her.

Her son said, "Mom?" the one word full of fear.

The electric motor engaged and the sailboat eased away from the dock at a deliberate pace. Erin shot another desperate glance up the hill, hoping, praying someone would notice. And maybe sound some kind of alarm. But the guests continued partying in the dying sunlight. As the sailboat moved out of the channel, she feared the worst.

Roger Herrold looked over at Erin and Darrell, then glanced at his own wife. He shot a quick look back up the lawn and shrugged. "You guys have been a giant pain in the ass."

Jane Herrold said, "Oh, not your son. We meant what we said. He's the cutest little thing." She reached out to rub the top of the boy's head but Leo ducked back. "Anyway, it's a shame he's here. That's why Ilya was trying to get him away." She sighed. "I guess it's too late now." She flashed a smirk at her husband.

Roger grinned back. "No, not little Leo. But the two of you are too *dull* to take a hint. A couple of hints, actually." He looked at Darrell. "I don't get it. You're not from here. Why'd you even get involved? Why do you care about—" his hand gestured to where Sarah stood, shaking. "What's it to you what happens to these girls?"

Darrell started to answer but Herrold wasn't finished. "You know they're not like you and me. They don't feel things the way we do." He smirked. "Though they feel some things really well, don't you Sarah?" He grabbed his crotch.

The teen cringed and tried to shrink back into the wood.

Erin looked at Leo, then stared at Herrold. She snapped, "I have a five-year-old here. Keep it in your pants."

Darrell got to his feet, though still unsteady. He put a hand on Leo's shoulder and Erin grabbed the other. He spoke, his voice hoarse, "What's your big plan, Roger?"

Roger didn't answer right away. Jane worked a few icons on the screen and the sails unfurled, one after the other. Within seconds, the wind filled the sails, propelling the boat and lifting the fore section out of the water. The broad stripes of red, white and blue looked even more impressive up close. Everyone grabbed and held on while the sailboat cut through the waves.

Her black hair flying around her head, Jane called out, "It's a great evening for a sail," her grin broad.

Erin stared west and watched as the last of the sun's rays were extinguished in the darkening water. It would be full dark soon. What could she do? She glanced around, hoping to see a boat she could signal, call out or even jump and swim to. But she saw only two, far away, little more than specs on the horizon.

Then she remembered the gun and thought her plan to jump would probably only get her shot—or get someone else killed. She looked across the deck. Roger,

Jane, and Ilya stood next to each other on the port side of the cockpit, while the rest of them huddled on the starboard side.

Roger handed the pistol to Ilya, butt first. "Keep this on them. I'm going to take the helm. I know exactly where I want to go." He took his wife's place and she moved next to the young man.

Ilya said, "Gladly," and flashed his ugly leer at Erin.

Rather than keep the gun at his side, he raised the pistol and pointed it at Leo's head, his finger on the trigger. Leo's eyes went wide. Erin stepped in front of her son, one assuring hand on his shoulder. Ilya lowered his aim so the barrel pointed straight at her crotch, between her legs.

Rather than cower, she stood straight, her chest out. Instead of looking at Ilya, Erin turned her face toward Roger Herrold. "What is your big plan? You're going to have us join Sheila?"

Chapter 60

Darrell fingered his cut. He felt his head clear some and heard Erin's question. She had hutzpah and it made him proud. He used the railing to drag himself up and stood alongside his wife, keeping Leo behind them.

Roger's eyes darkened at Erin's words. "You know about that, huh?" He scowled at Sarah and the teen cringed. He returned his gaze to Darrell and Erin, then shrugged. "No harm in telling a dead man...or woman. Oh, and kid. Well, nearly dead." One hand rubbed his bare head and he flashed an ugly grin. "Dwight and I have this nice little arrangement. These *Indian girls* work for us and we give them what they really want." He smirked and looked at Sarah. "Right, girlie?"

The Native teen winced again.

He guffawed. "Except the bitch Sheila Birdsong wouldn't cooperate. We paid her big time but she wouldn't do what we hired her to do."

Erin asked, "To be your sex slave, right?"

Roger Herrold looked at Erin like she was questioning the earth being round. He said, "Duh. It's what they're good at. All those Indian girls are sluts and whores, you know. The only thing they know how to do is have sex, make babies and live on welfare."

Sarah sobbed at his words—Darrell thought maybe because it was close to what the Herrolds had turned the young girl into.

Roger shot the Native a look. "I'll take care of you later." Then he returned his gaze to Darrell and Erin. "Only *Miss Birdsong* thought she was too good for us." He said her name with undisguised contempt. "So, she had to be dealt with. Dwight took care of that. And we told everyone she'd taken off and run away."

Jane Herrold placed a hand on her husband's arm, the fingernails also colored in red, white and blue. "You see we *had* to make a lesson of her. So all the other little Indians would do what we wanted." She glanced at Sarah. "Right, dearie?"

The teen couldn't stop shaking and sobbing. Through tears, she muttered, "I'm sorry."

Erin asked, "Jane, you're okay with Roger treating women like that?"

Jane Herrold laughed. "Oh, honey. Roger's right, these girls aren't like you and me. They love this stuff." Then she flashed a look like they were gal pals. "At least, Sarah takes care of his, um…needs. He can be a bit much sometimes." She rolled her eyes at Erin. "Besides, I get to watch."

Darrell listened to the exchange and the woman's words made him want to throw up. These two were real psychopaths. They might do *anything.*

He squeezed his wife's shoulder. Darrell was impressed with Erin's steely composure. Before, when he'd tried to get justice for the ghosts, Erin had been there for him, his rock. She didn't have the gift like he and his son. But that never stopped her…or even slowed her down. Everyone else might've thought he was seeing things or worse, crazy. But she stood by him and loved him. He was lucky to have her. If—no, when—they got out of this, he needed to tell her all this, again. But he still felt fuzzy and his head hurt like hell. He doubted he could've sparred with the Herrolds nearly as well as Erin was doing. Although he wasn't sure what she might be planning, he trusted her. They'd had no chance to confer.

The sailboat bucked across some waves and Roger kept his hands on the helm, steering the yacht farther out into the center of the lake. Darrell had to steady himself more than usual, figuring the concussion probably messed with his equilibrium. He glanced around, searching for another boat or ship they could call to. He saw two white sails in the distance but doubted anyone on the sloops would hear them, no matter how loud they yelled. The farther the yacht pushed onto the lake, the darker and lonelier it became. Minute by minute, daylight leaked out across the lake, turning the water dark gray and the farther they got from the other sailboats.

Roger said, "So you see, it's not really our fault. You're the ones who kept asking questions."

Leo's eyes widened. "We were leaving in the morning. I helped Dad and we were all packed and everything. We're heading back to the Ches'peake."

Roger nodded. "Yeah, we know. That's how you discovered the SUV Ilya used to run your dad off the road. I talked to Tom Salazar and he told me the whole thing." He took one hand off the wheel and waved it in the air. "Besides, we couldn't take the chance you'd ask the wrong questions on your way out of town." The older man looked at Leo and his features softened, "Still, we're sorry about you, Leo. You didn't do anything. You can blame your parents."

Leo straightened and said, "I wanted to find Sheila, just like Dad. And I saw her ghost too, like Dad."

"Sheila's *ghost!*" Roger and Jane called in unison and laughed. "Sheila's ghost. That's a hoot. Sounds like an old Indian wives' tale."

In a few seconds, Ilya joined them, the three of them pointing at Darrell and Leo as if they were crazy. Ilya laughed so hard, the gun shook and Darrell feared it might go off. Roger kept laughing, twisting the steering wheel and Darrell felt the boat pitch. He had to grip the rail even tighter.

Seeing their response to his son's words, Darrell thought he might have an opening. Maybe he could rush them, while they were laughing and off balance. But, before he could do anything, they stopped almost as quickly as they started, stifling a few final chortles. Roger steadied the helm and the sailboat leveled. Ilya straightened and raised the pistol again so it pointed directly at his chest. Darrell realized any attempt would be fatal right now. They'd have to bide their time.

Pretending to ignore the ugly gray barrel of the gun, he struck what he hoped looked like a pensive pose and addressed Roger Herrold. "Have you thought this through? What are you planning to tell everyone about what happened to us? Certainly, you're not going to try the 'run away' ploy again."

When neither answered at first, Darrell came up with a bluff. "We told my Aunt Gertrude we were going to check out the boats on the dock," he lied. "She'll wonder what happened to us and send someone to check on us."

The ploy didn't work.

The couple exchanged glances and Roger said, "We've already covered that. When you were at the barbeque, and after your wife kicked Ilya's butt—" he glanced at the young man, whose dark complexion turned red. Ilya turned the handgun toward Erin.

Roger addressed Ilya. "Easy, kid. Keep your eye on the prize." Herrold used one finger to push the barrel of the pistol so it was again pointing at Darrell, center mass. Roger turned back to Darrell. "Anyway, our guy here had the last laugh. He took your car and drove it someplace no one will find."

Ilya smirked at Darrell and Erin. Keeping the gun trained on Darrell, he said, "You promised I could take her and do what I want with her." He nodded toward Erin. "Jane can hold the gun on him and let me have some time with her in the cabin."

Roger Herrold looked away from the waters and met Ilya's gaze. "Later, son. You need to practice a little patience. You'll get your turn. The night is young." He turned back to Darrell. "Where was I?" he asked, like some grand old storyteller. "Oh, yeah. If anyone asks, we'll simply say you wanted a tour of our beautiful yacht and you told us you decided to get an early jump on your cross-country trip. So you went straight to the garage and left while the party was still in full swing."

"You think everyone will believe that, even Gertrude?" Darrell challenged.

The old man stuck out his fat belly and huffed. "Oh, little teacher man. I'm a titan of the shipping industry and an old friend of your aunt. The old biddy has become quite forgetful in her advanced years and she'll believe whatever I tell her. I'll tell her you gave her a goodbye hug and thanked her."

He raised his eyebrows. "Remember, you're a southerner now and no one here really cares what happens to you." He grinned and then added, "Pretty much like the Indians. By the time anyone gets around to asking questions about you, we'll be long gone to our island in the Caribbean till it all blows over. Well, us and our little Indian squaw. Right, dear?" He smiled at his wife and she stepped over and kissed him on the cheek.

Darrell wondered if Roger were right. Would Aunt Gertrude simply think he, Erin and Leo had taken off? Would his mom and dad? Or his brother and Dianna? He felt certain someone in his family would ask some hard questions. Not that any questions later would help them now. His gaze met Erin's and Leo's. They were running out of options and he didn't know what else he could do.

Darrell tried hard to think, though he found he had to fight through his fogginess. He felt sure there was something he could try, some ploy to leverage, but he had trouble focusing. Maybe, he could pit one of them against the others? He doubted the Herrolds were planning on taking Ilya with them to the Caribbean. Maybe he could work with that. He started to say something and stopped.

Then he felt it. The prickle ran down his neck and streaked down his back, like someone had hit him with an electric charge. He cringed, curling his body to withstand the sensation.

Erin asked, voice thick with worry, "Are you okay? Is it your head?"

Darrell raised one hand and straightened up. "I'm okay. It's not that." He looked down the length of the boat. He saw...something there. In the fading light, he stared as a shadow moved down their side of the boat, little more than a dark mist crossing the deck toward them. The image, not yet a figure, stopped a few feet from them, beside the cabin. As he watched, the image filled in, misty detail by detail. In the dying light, the gray became black and the black became a form. When it finished, the figure looked substantial, not a ghostly appearance, as if Sheila was standing there in the flesh. Her long black hair ran down her back, smooth and sleek. Her round face came into focus, stern and resolute. Her deep brown eyes stared back. The full lips pressed together. Strong shoulders of a winning high school basketball player stood hunched as if set to get a rebound.

Darrell tapped Leo's head. His son had buried his face in his mom's legs.

"Huh?" Leo said and looked up at his dad. Darrell didn't say anything. Instead, he nodded toward the ghost figure behind them. Leo followed his nod and, when he recognized Sheila, his eyes went wide again. He mouthed, "Sheila."

Darrell nodded.

Erin stared at Ilya, watching the handgun. When Leo pulled away and turned, she did the same. Darrell watched her stare at the space at the end of the cabin and then her eyes went wider than Leo's. She jerked her gaze from the figure to Darrell. "Is that...Sheila?" she whispered.

Darrell asked, "You can see her?"

Erin nodded, her mouth agape, her gaze fixed.

Somehow, Sheila had materialized enough so others could see her, not only Darrell and Leo. Darrell looked from the figure to the rear and checked out Roger, Jane and Ilya standing together on the port side. The three were still having fun, laughing and congratulating themselves, though Ilya kept the gun pointed at his family. Glancing from the ghost to their captors on the other side of the boat, Darrell realized, because the height of the cabin blocked their view, they couldn't see Sheila, or Sheila's ghost. Not yet.

If Erin could see the ghost, then so would the others. A plan began to form in his head.

Chapter 61

Darrell hollered over to Roger Herrold, "Did you tell me Dwight agreed to take care of the little problem of Sheila Birdsong?" He used a sing-song tone, hoping to taunt the man. "What'd he say he did to her?"

Roger exchanged a glance with his wife and smirked again, prominent age lines extending from his mouth and his bushy black eyebrows rising. "Oh, why not?" He chuckled and the wind swallowed his laugh. "We know a spot out in the middle of the lake, nice and deep." He took one hand off the helm and pointed west, then returned it to the steering wheel. "He took her out there and made her jump. It's miles from the shipping lanes and away from everything, so way too far to swim anywhere."

Without thinking, Darrell muttered, "A mermaid," remembering what Hannah Birdsong had said about her daughter.

"What was that?" Roger asked, his tone sharp. Then his eyes brightened and he glanced at his wife, then back at Darrell. "Hey, I just thought of something. In a little while, you three will be joining little Sheila. Maybe, you'll see her bones on the way to the bottom. I'm sure the fish would've taken care of everything else." He laughed again and Jane and Ilya joined him.

Behind him, Darrell heard Leo whimper at the old man's threat. He said, "Dad?"

Darrell met Leo's gaze and patted him on the arm. He whispered, "It'll be all right." Then he turned and yelled at the Herrolds. "Are you sure of that? I mean, you weren't there, were you? You either, Ilya? You're certain it went down that way?"

Roger Herrold's face darkened. "Of course I'm sure. Dwight told me he took care of our *problem*." He shot a glance at his wife. "I saw him take the little bitch in the *Wanderlust.*"

Darrell turned and met the gaze of the ghost. He nodded. Then he whispered to Erin and Leo, "When I tell you, hit the deck." Erin and Leo nodded, their eyes wide.

"So, you only have Dwight's word on that," said Darrell.

Roger guffawed. "What are you getting at, little teacher man?"

Darrell rocked his head back and forth. "What if I were to tell you, I found Sheila?"

Herrold laughed but it was weaker this time. He shot a quick glance at Jane whose eyebrows shot up. He said, "You're crazy. Dwight sent that little bitch to Davy Jones' locker weeks ago."

Darrell shook his head back and forth. "I wouldn't be so sure." He glanced back at the ghost who appeared to nod. He looked at his wife and son and breathed, "Now." They dove to the deck. He fell on top of Leo, pushing the three of them against the side of the ship and using his body to cover them.

"What 'ya doing? Get up," Roger Herrold yelled.

Darrell didn't move. He had his face buried against Erin. He felt more than saw the ghostly figure move out from behind the cabin. From the port side of the deck, the shouts came rapid fire, one on top of the other.

"What the hell? You're d-d-dead!" Roger yelled.

"Is that? No, it can't be!" screeched Jane.

"What do you want me to do?" Ilya asked.

"Shoot her, you idiot!" Roger screamed.

"Now? The other boats might hear." Ilya's voice quavered.

"I don't care. Here, give me the gun."

Then the shots came, deafening, loud. Boom, boom, boom. Boom, boom, boom, boom, boom.

They came so fast Darrell lost count. Beneath him, Erin and Leo cringed at each crack. He pulled them closer to him. His adrenalin pumped so furiously through his body, he couldn't tell if he was hit. His ears rang from the explosions. He strained to hear and caught a sound that made him smile.

Click. They had a chance now.

The gun's cylinder clicked empty. Roger had fired at Sheila's ghost but the bullets passed straight through and fell harmlessly into the water.

Straining to hear himself, he hollered at Erin and Leo, "You okay?"

Both redheads nodded. Erin's green eyes met Darrell's. "I think so." She ran her hand down Leo's small body. "Yeah."

"Shit!" Roger screamed. Darrell looked back toward the helm when the dull gray pistol clattered across the teak deck and slid over next to him.

Darrell started to get up and grab the gun. The boat pitched. Oh, hell. It hit a wave hard and rolled, water sloshing over the deck. He heard the fast shuffling of feet from the other side of the deck.

He yelled, "Hold on!"

Roger must've let go of the helm when he took the

gun. The sailboat leaned hard to port, the large wave making it heel heavily. Another wave broke over the deck, soaking them. He was no sailor but he'd sailed enough with Erin to know if they didn't do something, the yacht could lean so much, they'd all be tossed into the waves.

Darrell looked at Erin, red hair plastered to her face. She met his gaze, then shot a glance at the helm and turned back to her husband and son. "You guys, take care of each other and hold on," she yelled over the wind and water. His son nodded hard. Darrell nodded once, then held onto the railing with one hand and wrapped his other arm around his shivering son.

When he glanced at the other side of the boat, he saw their captors were trying to grasp onto something. Roger grabbed the railing immediately behind the helm. His eyes darted from the tilting boat to the image of Sheila. The ghost stood in the center of the deck, unmoved, as if the motion of the ship had no effect on her. Not even her hair ruffled in the wind. The sailboat heeled farther, the tops of the masts getting perilously close to the surface, but the ghost stood, unmoved in the center of the deck.

Hand over hand, Erin grabbed the railing, pulling herself along to get herself aft, until she was behind the cockpit. She let go and lunged for the helm. She grabbed the wheel and wrenched it back, trying to force the yacht to starboard. Two more large waves, one after the other, hit the boat, making it lurch again and again. Water drenched everyone on board.

Jane Herrold lost her grip. She yelled, "Roger, help!"

Her husband's eyes got large but he stood frozen, still staring at the ghost. Ilya gripped the rear railing with both hands. Neither risked helping Jane. She slid toward the port side and the water. She hit the side of the boat and started going over the rail.

Erin let go of the helm. She took three quick steps sideways to where the woman flailed, half out of the boat. Erin grabbed hold of her arm. She yanked the smaller woman back down onto the deck. Jane rolled over and crawled back to the starboard side. She grabbed that railing.

Erin scooted back and regained the helm. Behind her, Roger stumbled and tried to regain his footing, still grabbing the railing. Erin shot a quick glance back, then her fingers moved over the console. The winch on the sails whined, furling them in. Her other hand held the helm steady.

Darrell held on to both the rail and his son, but checked the others. Roger straightened and next to him, Ilya got to his feet. Ten feet aft, Jane still curled herself against the starboard side of the boat, white-knuckled hands gripping the railing. It took a few more minutes but Erin's maneuvers worked. The sailboat bucked twice then righted itself.

Roger released the rail and glared at the center of the deck where Sheila still stood. Darrell's gaze went from the older man to the ghost. Sheila stood straight, shoulders back, head held high. She released a small smile.

Roger's eyes filled with rage and he spit out, "You stubborn little bitch!"

He charged at the figure, hands outstretched as if he was going to shove Sheila overboard. Instead, he simply ran right through the apparition. Once past the ghost image, he couldn't stop. His motion took him straight to the railing, arms flailing. At the last second, he reached for the metal rail but missed. His momentum propelled him over the side.

Darrell grabbed for him, but too late. The patriotic-colored clothing went by in a blur and disappeared over the side. Darrell heard the splash, straightened up and looked down into the waves. He didn't see the man.

Jane stared over the rail into the water. "Roger!" she screamed.

Chapter 62

The older woman turned to Darrell, her hair dripping, some of the black dye running onto her face. A lot of the sequins had broken and fallen off her vest, making the top look even more ridiculous. "You have to help him."

"Can he swim?"

Jane didn't take her eyes off the water. "He used to be a good swimmer but that was a long time ago. He's not in that great of shape anymore."

Remembering the man's figure, Darrell had a hard time picturing Roger Herrold in great shape ever. He scanned the water for any sight of the bright red, white and blue outfit among the black waves. Nothing. Night was closing in and seeing a person in the dark water was nearly impossible. He turned and stared, looking for any disturbance in the small white-capped waves. The lake was in motion but the waves were not that large. How long could a guy last out there? Especially an old, out-of-shape man.

Then, he thought about what the Herrolds and the Newsoms had done to the Native girls. They'd sexually abused them and treated them like they were less than human. Did Darrell really want to save such a psycho? Perhaps, he could simply let the waters take Roger, like they'd done to Sheila?

He turned and glanced around the rear of the boat.

First, he saw Sheila's ghost still standing there in the middle of the deck. In the dim light emanating from the cabin below, the only details he could make out clearly were her dark brown eyes, stern and unflinching. Roger Herrold certainly deserved to die. But then, all the details might die with him.

The light from the cabin filtered to the helm, where Erin worked to keep the boat on an even keel and behind her, at the rail, Ilya stood. She glanced across at Darrell at the starboard rail, next to Leo. Those two emerald eyes stared back...and he knew. He and Erin were not like that. They couldn't simply leave a man to die, no matter what he'd done. Maybe the man would survive in the water or maybe he wouldn't, but they were going to try to rescue him.

He turned to Sarah, who stood frozen by the cabin opening, wide-eyed, staring at where Sheila's ghost still stood. "Sarah, are you okay?"

She pulled her gaze away from the apparition. "Yeah...I-I think so." Her eyes flitted to the spirit and back to Darrell. She raised her hand and pointed. "That's Sheila."

Darrell watched as the ghost nodded and smiled.

Sarah repeated, "That's really Sheila, er her ghost."

Darrell said, "Yeah, it is." He glanced from the shimmering image to the teen. "Sarah?" he repeated her name to get her attention. When she looked his way again, he added, "Could you go down and get us some towels so everyone can dry off? And see if you can find me a dry shirt to wear."

The teen nodded and disappeared into the cabin, keeping her gaze on the ghostly figure as she moved.

Once she left, Darrell remembered what he had to

do. He shot a glance back to Jane, who still clung to the railing. "Where are the life preservers?"

"Uh, I don't know. We've never had to use them." She released one hand and pointed toward the helm, then returned it quickly to the rail. "Under the benches, I think." She looked back over the side. "Hurry, I don't know how long he can last out there."

Darrell said to his son, "You wait here and don't let go." Leo gave a brave nod.

Darrell got his sea legs, as Erin called them, under him. Taking wide steps, he worked his way to the wooden benches. He took a path that avoided where Sheila still stood as her image seemed to shimmer even more. Once he made it to the bench, he had trouble with the latch but, after a few seconds, managed to get it open. A life ring attached to a long rope sat right on top. Next to it, he found a smaller life vest. He slid the vest across the deck to Leo. "Can you get into that?"

Leo released his right hand and snatched up the vest. As Darrell watched, his son threaded the free hand though the opening, switched hands and did the same with the left. Then both hands grasped the railing again. He stared back at his dad, his own green eyes wide and watery. "I can't tie it. I need to hold on."

Darrell said, "That will have to do. Just keep holding on. You're doing great."

Sarah came up the steps from the cabin, arms full of towels, their red, white and blue stripes barely visible in the dim light. Atop the pile was a Hawaiian shirt, with crazy colors and images. She gave the shirt to Darrell.

Then, without being directed, she handed out towels, one at a time, starting with Erin and ending with Ilya who, rather than thank her, leered at her. Each person did their best to dry off using one hand, the other on a railing or the helm. Then Darrell handed out life vests to Sarah and Jane, who strapped them on. He did the same and tossed one to Ilya.

Darrell duckwalked back to the railing where Roger had gone over. He stared behind the boat, knowing they had moved well past where the man went in. Glancing around, he didn't see any color in the dark water anywhere.

It wasn't full dark yet but would soon be. As Erin worked to turn the yacht around to try to get back to where Roger had gone over, Darrell made his way back to the bench. Opening it, he fumbled around and came up with a long-handled flashlight. He clicked it on and a brilliant beam shot out. He shone the light on the water. He stood, his feet apart to keep his balance on the still rocking sailboat. One hand ready with the life preserver, the other focused the bright wide beam, searching for a splash of color. He saw none and looked back at Erin at the wheel.

"I say, leave the asshole in the water," Ilya muttered, one hand still on the rear rail. As the boat leveled out, he stepped up behind Erin and tried to push her aside. "I'll take over now."

Erin stood her ground and held onto the helm. He watched the fury ignite in her eyes.

Darrell said, "She's a much better sailor than you'll ever be. She'll get us back safe."

Ilya laughed. "We're not going back. I'm commandeering this boat for myself. Payment for services rendered." He shot a glance over at Jane still huddled by the starboard railing. "They only paid me a few hundred and they have *millions*. Maybe, head for the

Caribbean myself." He smirked. "I'll drop you guys along the way…if I feel like it ."

Eyes flitting from the dark water to Ilya, Jane called, "No. We have to save Roger."

Ilya laughed at her and grabbed Erin's shoulders. He tried to shove her aside but she didn't budge, her fingers tightening around the steering wheel and her feet planted on the deck.

Darrell's gaze went from the dark water—still no sign of Roger—to where Erin stood at the wheel, Ilya right behind her. He dropped the life ring and took a few steps over to the young man. "Ilya, I'm only going to say this once. Get your hands off my wife."

"What ya gonna do, little teacher man?" Ilya let go of Erin's shoulders and flexed his upper arms.

Darrell looked him over, sizing him up. The guy was about his height and a few years younger. Darrell guessed Ilya was a gym rat, working on his muscles with machines and reps. He was no push over. But Darrell had spent the last decade going head to head with teenagers, some much bigger and stronger than this guy.

Ilya smirked. "First, I'm going to *school* you." Then he slapped Erin on the butt. "Then I'll have this piece of ass."

Erin raised an elbow and Ilya moved away quickly, head ducking.

Sarah took a loud intake of breath and Leo mumbled, "Dad?"

Darrell looked at Leo and Sarah and said, in a firm voice, "It'll be all right." He turned his attention back to Ilya.

The young man strode toward Darrell and brought both fists up. As soon as the guy was clear of Erin and the helm, Darrell didn't hesitate. He flipped the heavy flashlight to his right hand and, in the same motion, brought it down hard across Ilya's arm just above the fist.

Something cracked and Ilya screamed. The guy's left hand went to the injured right arm and he squealed. Darrell took advantage of Ilya's hesitation. He dropped the flashlight. In the near dark, Ilya's gaze followed the light as it hit the deck, the beam illuminating the teak. Darrell swung his right fist into Ilya's face and connected. He heard something break and hoped it wasn't his fingers. His left followed with a hard punch to the stomach, right where the guy had left the life vest open and untied. Ilya collapsed to the deck, left hand holding the right, moaning.

Satisfied the guy wasn't going anywhere for now, Darrell hustled over to the wooden bench and grabbed some maritime rope he'd seen inside. It took him a few contortions—and several loud squeals of protest from Ilya—but in two minutes, he had the young man securely tied up. Darrell flexed his fingers, grabbed up the flashlight and the life ring again.

He turned to the young man, hogtied and sprawled on the deck. "By the way, you couldn't get to the Caribbean from Lake Michigan. Some sailor."

By now, Erin had moved the boat around, tacking so the sailboat could cover the water and get back to where Roger went in. She had leveled the boat and the yacht pitched very little. Darrell didn't know this lake, didn't know how deep it was or what the current was like or if Roger could even stay afloat in the time it had taken them to come back around. But he had every confidence in Erin and her navigation abilities. If anyone could get the yacht close to where Roger fell in, it was she. He didn't know if they'd find him or find him alive but this would at least give them a chance.

Darrell walked to the bow since now Roger should be somewhere ahead of them. He shone the strong beam of the flashlight, made for exactly this purpose, across the water, looking for some splash of color among the waves. All remnants of sunlight had disappeared and both sky and water were near black. The sprinkling of stars completed the nighttime stage but provided little help.

He heard small steps come up behind him and he turned the light on his son, life jacket still untied. He handed the flashlight to him. "Hold this a second while I tighten your vest." Darrell did and Leo handed him back the flashlight. "Hold onto the rail and you can help me look." Darrell spotlighted the gold metal railing and swung the beam across the water in slow arcs.

Another set of footsteps echoed on the deck and Darrell turned the flashlight and shone it into the eyes of Jane Herrold. Her face was ashen, her hair soaked, and eyes narrowed. "Any sign of Roger?" She grabbed the railing next to Leo and stared into the water. "You have to find him!"

Darrell said nothing and turned the light back over the water, sweeping it left and right. For several long minutes, Darrell swung the beam back and forth across the small waves and three sets of eyes scanned for any sign of the man. At least they weren't in the middle of a storm and the waves weren't too high. He guessed three to four feet.

He kept the light on the water but tried to steal a glance at Erin behind him at the helm and Ilya lying on the deck at her feet. But it was too dark and all he could make out some forty feet away was her figure behind the wheel and the shape of Ilya's body on the deck. He returned to searching the water.

Leo saw him first. "I see something, Dad. There, ahead and a little starboard, I think."

Shining the light, Darrell stared where his son pointed but didn't see anything. Then a wave rose and fell and he saw some color in the crest. He focused the beam on the spot.

"Roger!" Jane pointed too.

In the brilliant light of the beam, Darrell could see the red and white. Both arms waved back and forth. He yelled back, "I think we found him. Ahead and a little starboard."

He kept the light on the spot and felt Erin adjust the ship so they would come up alongside the man. As they neared, Darrell focused on the spot of color in a lake of black. He couldn't tell if the man was alive or if the arms moving was simply from the wave action. He figured if Roger had drowned, his body would've sunk to the bottom. The man had to have some life still in him.

As the boat came closer, Darrell handed the flashlight to Leo. "You keep it shining on him." He pointed to the red and white color of the shirt. "I'm going to toss him the ring so I can pull him in."

He son nodded and grabbed the flashlight, having to hold it with both hands. Darrell went to the starboard side of the boat. Ahead of them, Roger Herrold bobbed in the center of the bright beam, now waving like a madman, some thirty feet from the boat.

He called over the water, "You found me!" He tried to say more and coughed, swallowing water.

Darrell held up the preserver in the light so Roger

could see it. He yelled, "I'm going to toss you this ring. You need to grab it and hold on. Then I can pull you in."

Roger nodded up and down like a marionette. Darrell wound up and tossed the ring across the water, the rope uncurling behind it. Leo, Jane and he watched in the beam of the flashlight as the life ring landed a few feet away from Roger. To be safe, Darrell had tied off the other end of the rope to the railing. He untied it now and grabbed it. Aft, he heard the chain on the anchor as it descended and hit. Above them, the sails were furled in by machine. Erin was making sure the yacht wouldn't drift much.

They'd found him. A fat little red, white and blue dot in the blue-black waters and they found it. Rather, Erin's navigation sense got them to the right place and they found him. Darrell wasn't sure if he was happy or disappointed.

With slapping, clumsy strokes, the older man made his way to the preserver. "Got it," he yelled, immense relief in his voice. In the spotlight, they watched as he slipped it over his body. Then he yelled, "Pull me in," his words more demand than plea.

Darrell yanked in a few lengths of rope, then stopped.

Still pointing the flashlight, Leo asked, "Is something wrong?"

Jane screeched, "Come on. Pull him into the boat." Her eyes went to her husband, whose hands gripped the life ring. In the bright beam, the ring and Roger bobbed in the water about twenty feet from the yacht.

Out on the water, Roger screamed, "Pull me in the rest of the way. I'm exhausted from trying to stay afloat out here." His tone became more insistent, the sound of someone used to being heeded and obeyed.

Darrell leaned over the railing and stared at the man floating in the waves. He knew Roger Herrold couldn't see him in the dark but didn't doubt he could identify his voice. He yelled, "Roger?"

"Yeah?"

Darrell said, his tone non-plussed, "Before I pull you in, I think we need to talk first."

"What!" the single word exploded from the man. "What do you want, Darrell? Money? How much?"

Darell pulled another length of rope and stopped. "No, not money. Though Lord knows we could use the extra cash. I'm not interested in your money."

"What—" Roger started then stopped. He coughed and spit out another mouthful of water. "What is it? Pull me in and we can talk about it!"

Darrell shook his head, even though he knew the man in the water couldn't see. "I think, maybe we're going to talk *first*, then I'll pull you in. *If* I think you're telling the truth."

"What are you talking about?" Roger called from the water, desperation in his voice. "Henshaw, I'm a very rich man. I can pay you whatever you ask. Just pull me in and I'll make *you* a rich man. You'll never have to work another day at that silly teaching job!"

"You really don't get it, do you?" Darrell's head still hurt from when Roger had coldcocked him with the gun. He touched the bandage, then let out two lengths of the rope. The motion of the waves moved Roger, ring and all, a little farther away from the boat.

The voice on the water got frantic. "Okay, okay. I'll tell you whatever you want. It's better than dying out here."

"It certainly is." Darrell drew in the two lengths of rope he'd let out. He turned to Leo. "Give the flashlight to Jane and go get Sarah. Tell her it's okay." Leo started down the deck but Darrell stopped him. "Oh, and have her bring some paper and something to write with. She's going to take some dictation."

Chapter 63

While Roger bobbed in the water, Darrell had walked back to the cockpit and shared his plan with Erin. She grumbled, "That sounds like a plan but we could simply leave him in the water and tow him back to shore. It's what he deserves." Hands on the wheel, she shrugged. "I guess your plan is more humane." Still, she concurred in the end.

It had taken the better part of an hour to extract the full story from a very wet and angry Roger Herrold. At first, Roger had been stubborn and refused to give in. Instead, he tried to use his clumsy, untutored strokes to swim to the yacht. When he started in, Darrell whistled to Erin, who pressed a button on the console. The engine caught and the sailboat drifted farther from the man. The more he splashed, the farther she steered the boat away. Roger Herrold yelled, screamed, and slammed his fist on the water.

When none of that worked, he shouted for Ilya. "Ilya, get off your ass and help me. Take care of this little teacher man. What am I paying you for?"

From the stern, Ilya only cussed loudly. Darrell explained, "Hey, Rog. Ilya wanted to commandeer your boat and leave you. He and I had a little disagreement and he, well, let's say, he's indisposed."

Throughout these exchanges, one thing became obvious. Roger Herrold was a man accustomed to getting his way. He wore his arrogance like some invisible shield even though he looked ridiculous when the strong beam reflected off his bald head and his silly sequined shirt flopped open in the water revealing the skin of his huge belly. No matter how he threatened, bribed, cajoled or demanded, Darrell wouldn't budge.

When Darrell had once again released two lengths of rope causing the man to drift farther from the boat, Roger finally caved. He asked, in a voice that was still more demand than surrender, "Okay, okay, what do you want to know?"

Pondering the question, Darrell said, "Let's start with what you did to these poor Native girls." He turned to Sarah, who stood with a small tablet and pen. "When he gives specifics, I want you to write them down. I'll turn the flashlight so you can see. You think you can do that?"

The teen had settled herself on a seat in the bow. She glanced up at Darrell and nodded. He noticed she'd buttoned his shirt over the skimpy bikini and looked less self-conscious. Her pinched features bore out her determination. For the next sixty minutes, Darrell asked questions about their "operation" and Roger answered, often begrudgingly. Twice, he refused to respond and when Darrell let out more lengths of rope, Jane screamed at her husband, "Roger, tell them. I want you safe in this boat."

And talk he did, sometimes haltingly, sometimes as if he were bragging about his conquests. The details turned Darrell's stomach. More than once, when he flashed the beam on Sarah's paper, he watched her wince at recording how she'd been degraded. But she got it all down.

Darrell knew the man's "confession" would not hold up for the legal system, not to mention the Herrolds could afford the best lawyers money could buy. *This* was the definition of a coerced confession. But in Herrold's ramblings, Darrell was able to extract enough details which he thought would corroborate the confession. Darrell learned the names of the three other boats involved in the sex ring as well as their captains. Top of the list was Dwight Newsom.

Darrell got Roger to admit, so far this summer, the ring had "employed" six Native girls—though Herrold couldn't be bothered to learn their names, except Sarah and Sheila, of course.

Then, he went off in a tirade. "Listen, we took good care of these girls," he yelled over the wind. "You know we paid them really well for their, uh…time. I gave Sarah new clothes and the best food. She got to live on this beautiful boat, which is a whole lot nicer than that hovel her family calls home." After a brief pause, he added, "I cared for Sarah and treated her like a lover. The way she responded, I know she felt something for me."

In the dark of the boat, Darrell heard the teen spit onto the deck.

Darrell decided to ignore Roger's self-justification. Instead, he asked, "I don't understand. You said there were six Indian teens but only four boats. Did some yachts have two girls?"

"No, nothing like that. We hadn't planned on six. Two of the red bitches refused to perform the duties they'd been hired for. So they had to be dealt with…as an example to the rest."

Darrell gritted his teeth and asked, "One of those was Sheila Birdsong?"

"Yeah. These sluts needed to be taught a lesson about who was in charge."

When Darrell heard this, he almost let go of the rope. When he swung the light back so Sarah could record all this, he noticed she was crying but still writing it all down.

What clinched it was when Roger tried to brag about his sexual prowess. He divulged all the captains recorded their sexual conquests and dominations on board, so they could exchange the videos like trading cards. It made Darrell sick but he forced himself to listen. Herrold explained each of the yachts had been especially outfitted with a set of cameras and recorders, hidden in the fancy woodwork. It took a bit and another threat to let Roger go floating out into the darkness before the guy revealed how to get into the secret panel hiding the equipment.

Once Sarah wrote this down, she got up and stomped down the length of ship, disappearing into the cabin. A minute later, she came out with a DVD case marked simply "Sarah 6-1-07."

She yelled, "You dirty bastard!" and started to throw the plastic case into the water, but Darrell grabbed her hand. His gaze met hers in the dim light. "I know it's embarrassing but it's how we'll get him convicted. Get all of them convicted."

She dropped her shoulders and handed him the DVD. "There are maybe two dozen more of these," she mumbled, "half with my name on them."

When Darrell was satisfied he'd extracted enough details about the whole operation, he pulled Roger Herrold the rest of the way and helped get him into the boat. When the man came over the rail, he flopped on his back and Darrell shone the beam over him, checking him out. The light lit up his bald head and Roger raised his arm to block the glare. He'd busted two buttons on his shirt and his pale belly was sticking through the opening in the red, white and blue fabric. His skin was wrinkled and his eyes red but, other than that, he looked unharmed.

Jane knelt next to the man and cried, "Oh, you're okay. I was afraid I'd never see you again."

Roger growled, "Get off me, old woman. You didn't do anything to stop them. I wish I'd died out there."

Darrell called his bluff, extending his arm toward the railing. "I'll be glad to help you over and I promise we won't rescue you this time."

Roger just shoved his wife aside and struggled to get to his feet. "I need to get out of these wet clothes." He stood, headed toward the cabin as if he were still in charge. Darrell let him go and they all followed.

As the party crossed the deck, heading aft, Darrell glanced toward the stern where Erin stood at the helm. Closer to the cabin, he saw Sheila, or rather her ghost. As he approached, her image began to fade, her figure becoming translucent. He met her gaze and she smiled, her face looking again like the beaming face of the happy teenager on the missing poster. As he stared, her figure became but a shadow in the darkness. Then, she was gone.

Erin piloted the sailboat back to Aunt Gertrude's dock and Darrell was surprised to find a party waiting for them. Tom Salazar, his brother Craig and Dianna and his mom and dad stood at the foot of the dock.

When Erin puttered the yacht into the slip like an

expert and turned off the engine, Craig called, "We've been looking everywhere for you. Why didn't you tell us you were going for an evening sail?"

When Darrell led Ilya, Roger and Jane, their hands tied, out of the cabin, across the deck and down the ladder, Craig said, "I bet there's a real story here."

Darrell grinned at his brother. "Oh, it's a whopper." Then he turned to Salazar. "Tom, I need you to call the police. These three want to turn themselves in."

Salazar's eyes went to the three individuals with their hands bound in front of them and back to Darrell. "For what?"

Sarah came down the ladder and stood next to Darrell who put one arm around her. "Well, we'll start with sexual assault and rape and go from there."

Salazar's eyes went wide but he turned and headed up the stairs, pulling a flip phone out of his pocket, talking as he walked.

Chapter 64

By Monday morning, Darrell, Erin and Leo were glad to repack everything in the car and head for home. It took that long to talk with the police and give their statements. After some discussion, they'd decided to make the thirteen-hour drive all in one day. Darrell and Erin would alternate driving, resting and entertaining Leo and they figured they could probably pull into Wilshire near midnight. They'd brought games for Leo and plenty of books to share—Erin's favorite chore—and felt sure their son could make it. Besides, he'd been through a lot as well and the hours in the car would give them all time to rest and talk it out. Not to mention, Erin was already due back in the OB department and had to get someone to cover her Monday shift. They couldn't afford to lose another day's earnings.

When they were making their decision and mentioned the loss of money, Erin had mused, "Maybe we should have taken Roger Herrold's offer to give us more money than we've ever seen." Darrell shot her a look and she said, "Okay, I'm only kidding."

They were all anxious to get on their way home but Darrell prevailed on Erin to make one stop on the way out of town. On the way to Shelbyville, Erin asked, "How much do you think your aunt knew? Or Tom Salazar?"

Darrell waited a bit before answering. "They

393

claimed they knew nothing about the whole operation. Aunt Gertrude didn't want to talk about it. And Tom repeated they thought the girls had quit on their own. He said they thought Sheila had probably run away."

"But?" Erin left the question hanging.

Darrell released a breath. He shot a look back at his son, then brought his gaze back to the road. He wanted to be straight but didn't want Leo to have to deal with too much more. "I think my aunt and Tom simply wanted to believe the lie. Like most everyone else up here, they grew up with prejudice against Natives."

Erin started to object. "I've never seen any indication you're prejudiced."

Darrell nodded. "I still have a bias, maybe unconscious bias, but it's there. It makes it easier to accept the stereotypes. Because of everything, I may be more aware of it."

When they pulled into the rutted parking lot at Carlos' Diner—still with the letters missing in the marquis—Darrell said, "I don't even know if Edgar will be here but I'd like to say goodbye if I can."

"You want us to go with you?" Erin asked.

"I think you might as well stay in the car. Like I said, he may not even be there and, if he is, I don't think I'll be very long."

Erin nodded. "Then Leo and I will get started on *James and the Giant Peach.*"

When Darrell climbed up the crumbling steps and pushed through the door, the little bell announced his arrival. He was not surprised to see the same five men sitting at tables around the small room. At least, they looked like the same five men he'd seen, what, less than a week ago. The cop, in the dark blue uniform, sat at a table on the right and, when he glanced up, Darrell realized it was the tribal officer who had pulled him over when he left the diner. Darrell nodded at him and received, if not a positive look, at least not the scowl he'd gotten earlier.

There, at the table on the left sat Chief Edgar, in the same seat Darrell had seen him on his last visit. Without being invited, Darrell took the chair opposite the ancient Indian. The Chief did not object and stared across the table. He said, "Darrell Henshaw."

Despite steeling himself for this moment, Darrell felt his palms sweat and his lips turn dry. He cleared his throat. "Chief," he acknowledged. "I know you have a great telegraph system on the res but I thought I'd come by and give you what info I could."

"So, you are leaving?" his deep voice asked.

"Yes. My wife and son are in the car. We're driving all the way home to Maryland today."

Edgar turned his head and glanced out the glass which had replaced the plywood, then brought his gaze back on Darrell. He did not say anything else, which only made Darrell more uncomfortable.

Darrell dried his hands on a napkin and blurted out, "I found out what happened to Sheila." Then he corrected himself. "What they did to her."

The old Chief gave a slow nod. "She is one with the water now." He looked up at Darrell. "You could not save her but perhaps you have given Hannah some comfort."

Darrell nodded and muttered, "A mermaid."

"What?"

Darrell looked up. "When I visited her mom last week, she told me she dreamt her daughter was a mermaid now."

Edgar said, "Often, mothers know."

"You probably know but there were four men, four couples really, involved in the ring, trapping the girls."

His black eyebrows raised, the Chief said, "Four, very rich white men."

Darrell sighed. "Yeah, there's that. But the police found the secret recording devices on each of the yachts. And they uncovered more than a hundred DVD's with video of—." Darrell found it hard to say the rest. "The cops tell me it should be enough."

"We can hope."

Darrell said, "We were able to free all four girls and send them back to their homes."

Then he remembered, "And Ilya, the young man they hired to recruit the Native girls, he's turned on the others. He's agreed to testify against them."

Edgar narrowed his eyes, the lined crows' feet standing out. "And each rich white man will hire a rich white lawyer."

"The best money can buy," Darrell agreed.

"These wealthy men will try to bend the system to their will but perhaps our girls might see some justice." He paused and added, "Thanks to you, Darrell Henshaw."

Neither spoke for a while, then Edgar said, "Sheila Birdsong can now walk the path of souls. Thank you."

The old chief's phrase brought it back. Darrell remembered the words of the ancient Monongahela Indian who asked him to find justice for the lost girls. The missing girls.

"One more thing," Darrell said, meeting the old Indian's gaze. "I've talked to a friend from college, a

Kim Aldrich. She's a reporter now for the *Ann Arbor Gazette* and Channel 8 News. I gave her all the details of the ring—names, yachts, dates, everything and talked with her about the missing Native girls. She said they agreed to do a series of stories about the missing girls, starting with the Potawatomi teens. Whatever fancy tricks the lawyers play, they won't be able to sweep this under the rug." He shrugged. "It's not thousands of missing girls but at least it's something."

The expression on the chief's face didn't change but he nodded. "It is a start." After another pause, he asked, "How is your son?"

"Leo?" Darrell blurted out.

The old man's eyes softened. "Your son has the gift as well. He can see spirits like you."

"That's right," Darrell said, remembering he had told the old chief about Leo on his earlier visit.

"It is a wonderful gift he shares with you but it had to be hard for him." When Darrell didn't respond, Edgar added, "It has forced him to confront such ugliness far too early."

The chief's concern for his son warmed Darrell's heart. He said, "He was in the middle of it but I'm not sure how much he understood. He hasn't said much about it yet. Erin and I are going to try to talk with him on the ride home."

"Do not press the boy. He will talk and ask when he is ready."

Darrell nodded, not knowing what else to say. He slid out his chair and stood. "Erin and Leo are waiting for me. I better get going."

The ancient Indian stood across from him, his old legs struggling to stand. Darrell extended his hand and

Edgar took it in his calloused hands. He held it and stared at Darrell. The old man spoke, his voice gravelly, "There will always be evil and ugliness in this world. It is your job to show young Leo that this life has beauty and wonder as well."

Darrell watched the ghost of a smile cross the leathered face. "May the Great Spirit ease your path home, Darrell Henshaw."

MISSING AND MURDERED INDIGENOUS WOMEN

This work is fiction but the murder mystery portrayed in these pages reflects an all too real horror.

Our country has a long history of injustice, discrimination and persecution against Native Americans. Over the past two centuries, tribals lands were stolen via treaties that were never honored, their children were torn from their families and sent away to boarding schools and attempts were made to destroy the culture and heritage of Native peoples. But these injustices are not merely a history lesson. Indigenous people continue to suffer injustice and discrimination today.

My story highlights only one example of this persistent injustice. In 2007 and today, Indigenous girls and women are victims of sexual assault, rape, kidnapping and murder at far higher rates than other populations. In fact, studies have revealed that Native women and girls go missing and "disappear" at a rate **ten times** that of white women. Sadly, Chief Edgar's admonition to Darrell that thousands of Native girls and women disappear is conservative and, by now, out of date. I have merely attempted to use this novel to shine a light upon this horrible scourge on our society.

If you are interested in learning more about this very real problem, here are a few resources you might find helpful.

- https://www.nativehope.org/missing-and-murdered-indigenous-women-mmiw
- https://www.bia.gov/service/mmu/missing-and-murdered-indigenous-people-crisis

- https://www.niwrc.org/policy-center/mmiwr
- *Searching for Savanna: The Murder of One Native American Woman and the Violence Against the Many* by Mona Gable

Red River Girl: the Life and Death of Tina Fontaine by Joanna Jolley

AUTHOR'S NOTE

Like the other books in the Haunted Shores Mysteries, this entry is set in a very real resort town. Saugatuck, Michigan is a charming, small town on the eastern shore of Lake Michigan and is located at the junction of the Kalamazoo River and Lake Michigan. Most of the places included in this narrative are real, actual places. Visitors can have a wonderful dinner at The Butler or enjoy a delicious lunch on the water at Coral Gables, both staples of the town. Like Darrell and his family, they can ride the Saugatuck Chain Ferry, the Star of Saugatuck and the Saugatuck Dune Ride, each a different, fun experience. They can even spend the day at the shore at Oval Beach or test their endurance with a climb up the 300+ steps up to Mt. Baldhead like Darrell and his son Leo managed.

However, this is still a work of fiction and I have taken some liberties with the setting. Pirate Isle is purely a product of my imagination—so don't go sailing Lake Michigan looking for it. And although Shelbyville is a real town, don't drive there looking for Carlos' Diner, as it too is wholly made up. Also, Gertrude Embry's mansion, Wentworth, was inspired by several of the beautiful houses along the shores of Kalamazoo River and Lake Michigan, but it is, of course my creation.

Being fiction, all the characters of this story are fictional, merely products of my imagination and are not intended to depict any real persons, living or dead and any similarities to actual people is purely coincidental.

I hope you enjoyed your visit to this quaint town on the southwestern edge of Michigan as much as I did writing about it. Here's to great journeys for you both inside these pages and perhaps one day in person to this beautiful town.

A word about the author...

Dr. Randy Overbeck is an award-winning educator, author, speaker and podcaster. As an educator, he served children for more than three decades and has mined that experience to create captivating fiction, authoring two series, the bestselling series, "The Haunted Shores Mysteries," and the award-winning series, "Lessons in Peril." His novels have won critical acclaim and garnered national awards including Mystery of the Year (ReaderViews.com) Best Book Award (Chanticleer Books and Reviews) and the Gold Award (Literary Titan) and amassed hundreds of 5-star reviews on Amazon and Goodreads. Dr. Overbeck also hosts the popular podcast, "Great Stories about Great Storytellers," which reveals the unusual and sometimes strange backstories of famous authors, directors and poets and can be heard wherever listeners get their podcasts. He is a speaker in considerable demand, sharing his popular presentations about ghosts and the world of book publishing with hundreds of audiences all over the U.S.

As a member of the Mystery Writers of America, Dr. Overbeck is an active member of the literary community, contributing to a writers' critique group, serving as a mentor to emerging writers and participating in writing conferences such as Killer Nashville and the Midwest Writers Workshop.

When he's not researching, writing, speaking or podcasting, Randy enjoys traveling with his wife Cathy and visiting both his far-flung family and the scenic locations around this country, often in search of inspiration for his next story.

More info about his novels, programs and podcast can be found at his website
www.authorrandyoverbeck.com
randyoverbeck@authorrandyoverbeck.com

SOCIAL MEDIA CONTACTS
Facebook
https://www.facebook.com/authorrandyoverbeck
Twitter: https://twitter.com/OverbeckRandy/media
Instagram
https://www.instagram.com/authorrandyoverbeck/
BookBub
https://www.bookbub.com/authors/randy-overbeck
Amazon
https://www.amazon.com/Randy-Overbeck/e/B07QQHW7DM
Goodreads
https://www.goodreads.com/author/show/4825632.Randy_Overbeck